The M[illegible] Man

The Short Fiction of Stephen Laws

Stephen Laws

The Short Fiction of Stephen Laws

Stephen Laws

Seattle, 1999

Publishing history:

"He Who Laughs" was published in *Dark Voices 3: The Pan Book of Horror Stories*.

"Black Cab" was published in *Dark Asylum* Issue Number 1.

"Man Beast" was published in *Peeping Tom* Issue Number 17.

"The Song My Sister Sang" was published in *Scaremongers 2: Redbrick Eden*.

"Gordy's A-Okay" was published in *Heaven Sent* and *Dark Horizons* Number 32.

"The Fractured Man" was published in *Cold Cuts 3*.

"The Crawl" was published in *Dark of the Night* edited by Stephen Jones. Subsequently published in *The Year's Best Fantasy & Horror: Eleventh Edition 1998*, edited by Ellen Datlow and Terri Windling and *The Mammoth Book of Best New Horror 1998*, edited by Stephen Jones.

"Deep Blue" was published in *Kimota*: Winter 1994/5 Issue and also in *Scaremongers*.

"Junk" Originally published in *Scare Care*, Edited by Graham Masterson. Subsequently republished in *The Giant Book of Horror* & *The Mammoth Book of Terror*, both edited by Stephen Jones.

"Bleeding Dry" Published in *Narrow Houses*, edited by Peter Crowther

"Guilty Party" (First appeared in *Fear* magazine Number 2, subsequently in *Voyages into Darkness* (published by 'Bump in the Night Books' of Philadelphia). Also appeared in *The Mammoth Book of Werewolves and Northern Chills*)

"Yesterday I Flew With The Birds" (Winner of the 'Rediffusion Award'. Originally broadcast on BBC Radio Newcastle. Subsequently published in *Beyond Magazine* Issue No 1.

"The Secret" (Originally published in *Peeping Tom* #9. Subsequently in *Voyages into Darkness* published by 'Bump in the Night Books' of Philadelphia.

"Pot Luck" Published in *Voyages into Darkness* published by 'Bump in the Night Books' of Philadelphia.

Limited Edition ISBN 0-9675157-0-X

Trade Edition ISBN 0-9675157-1-8

Cover Illustration: Fredrik King

Author Photo: Terry White

Book Design: Brian Metz/Green Rhino Graphics

Manufactured in the United States of America.

Edited by John Pelan

Silver Salamander Press
4128 Woodland Park Ave. N.
Seattle, WA
98103

table of contents:

introduction: the midnight man

Many years ago, I remember reading an article on the classic ghost story/horror writer J. Sheridan Le Fanu - creator of *Carmilla*, *Green Tea* and the landmark collection *In a Glass Darkly* (which merely skims the surface of the gentleman's output). In his later years, it was said that he seldom emerged from his rooms, working through the midnight hour on his stories of the strange and bizarre. It created in my boyhood mind a belief that all the best writers in the genre must adopt this creepy lifestyle to be successful, with a quill pen scratching tales by candlelight as the clock struck twelve; tales of haunted castles and cobwebbed dungeons. In later years, the writers who inspired me most - Richard Matheson being top of the list - brought their terrors out into the sunlight. The horror was more likely to occur at a local supermarket than in a Transylvanian castle, or in the middle of a highway rather than in a dungeon or a cave. Which brings me in a roundabout way to the title of this collection, *The Midnight Man*.

When John Pelan approached me about publishing a collection, it was at a particularly apposite time. I'd just realised that there was finally enough material to warrant it. (I've gone into the reasons why this has been a long time coming in the 'Notes' section at the end of the book.) So I was delighted to agree. But what to call the volume? There's an equal balance of out-and-out horror tales here with other stories that are not so easily categorised. A 'straight' horror title wouldn't really be fair. I racked my brains - and John kindly helped me out by supplying a list of suggested titles. But I still couldn't hit on the right one. Then a couple of things happened. Firstly, I noticed that the editor of a magazine had used the title of one of my books - *Somewhere South of Midnight* - as a 'sign-off' to his editorial. Within twenty four hours of reading it, I saw in another periodical that someone else had done the same. I'd always wanted the title to have a 'Twilight Zone' resonance - and it seemed that it really was being adopted that way. As the novel's blurb puts it: " The place where terror and insanity lie in wait for the unwary traveller. The place on a long dark road, where our reality ends and the unknown beckons, Where our world ceases, and Darkness begins. Where some can find the answers to their darkest questions. Where others find their worst nightmares come true." The word 'Midnight' stuck in my mind and wouldn't go away. And then it came to me.

Before I became a full time writer, I worked nine-to-five in local government. My first novels and stories were written in the evening and well into the early hours. Over the years, my body-clock got used to that routine. And when did I find myself at the peak of my creative energy? You guessed it. Midnight. Even now, working full-time as a writer, I still find it hard to readjust the body clock - and more often than not, I'll be at the word processor when the clock strikes twelve. No quill pen, then. No guttering candlelight. No creeping shadows. Instead, a wonderfully comfortable study filled wall-to-wall with the books I love, overlooking the Willow Dene. Even on the wildest storm-driven nights when I'm working on a new story, this Midnight Man couldn't be further from that boyhood image of Le Fanu.

And what have I learned about the land I've created 'South of Midnight? Well, sometimes it's a place that J. Sheridan Le Fanu might recognise. But as well as fear and outright horror - there are other wonders to be discovered. Make no mistake, there are terrors out there in the darkness. But sometimes a lone candle burns brightest against a deep-black background, as I hope my novels have always suggested. And the beauty of the genre is simply this - until you take that step through Midnight's Doorway, you're never quite sure what you're going to get.

he who laughs

Don't make me laugh.

Please.

It's not that I don't have a sense of humour, don't get me wrong. I have. Or at least, I *think* I still have. It's just that... well... They found another one yesterday, didn't they? You saw the news items in the papers or on the television, I expect. This one was found in the back lane behind a dockyard pub, and although they don't go into the details of how he died, I know that the body is going to be in the same condition as all the others they've been finding recently... with the same look on their faces.

Look, perhaps it would be best if I tell you the whole thing from the beginning; then maybe you'll understand. Just... don't laugh. All right?

My name's Peter Marsh. Actually, it's not. But I suppose it's best that I give you a name, any kind of name, to help with the story.

It starts and ends with Martin Rogers. Good old Marty. Mr. Popularity himself. The whole world loved him because he was always good for a laugh. Hah. If only they knew.

I first met Martin at college. We were both taking the same Humanities degree. At first, we were just nodding acquaintances. Individually, we couldn't have been more opposite. He was fiercely gregarious, outgoing, extremely popular. I was shy, introverted and insular. He was popular with males and females alike. I was a loner by nature, not very successful with women at all. We were as different as chalk and cheese. You might think that it's strange then, that we should have become such close friends towards the end of the second term. In retrospect, of course, I now know Martin's motives in developing our friendship. But at that time, in my naivety, I was quite astounded by Martin's interest in me; blinded by the prospect of joining his sparkling social life and glad to be able to follow in his wake. In a sense, he was my social tutor. He surged ahead, forging acquaintances, courting popularity. I followed close behind. It was Martin's sense of humour that attracted people; his readiness with a quip to suit all occasions, his perfect comedy timing, his delivery of a comic line. People just couldn't help liking him. His pale face and red hair invited attention and I basked in his aura, allowing his sense of humour to rub off on me. I came out of my shell. Using Martin as an idol—and I don't think that's too strong a word to use—I imitated his style, gradually developing my own. I emerged from a chrysalis of solitude and loneliness, enjoying it tremendously when I found that I too had developed the ability to make people laugh. In my own way, I also became a popular guy. My loneliness, shyness, and awkwardness in company became a thing of the past. My mentor sailed through life; loving, laughing, living it to the full. I aspired to imitate him. For a while I was happy.

But then the revelation came about a year ago; that is, during the last quarter of the final term.

It was late. Martin and I had bought a couple of six-packs and taken them back to his flat in the College Halls of Residence. Martin also had some Moroccan Oil and we had smoked and drunk our way into a really good mood. Martin had just cracked a joke. I've forgotten what it was now, but I remember how hard I laughed at it. When the giggles had died down, there was a pause while we both swigged more beer. Martin sighed, gave me a strange kind of sideways look and ran a hand through his unruly ginger hair.

"We're good friends, aren't we?" he asked. And the way that he asked it took me by surprise. There was a seriousness to his voice which was rather puzzling.

"'Course not," I replied, smiling. "We can't stand the sight of each other." I took another mouthful of beer.

"Seriously."

"Of course we are."

Martin gave a half-laugh and lounged back in his chair, draining his can. He stared at the ceiling for a while and then looked back at me. It was a look that made me feel very uncomfortable; a serious expression that I had never seen before. Later, I realised what it was about his expression that had disturbed me so much. In retrospect, it seemed that Martin's normal face had been a mask and that this look, this other face which he now revealed was his *real* face; a face that had been previously hidden from me. It was an extraordinary feeling, not fully comprehended then. Martin smiled at me, but that look was not changed by the smile, and he continued: "How long have we known each other?"

"You're in a bloody funny mood..." I began.

"Two years." Martin answered his own question, giving a curious half-laugh. "Two years. And you still haven't realised."

"Realised what?"

"What makes people laugh?"

I smiled. "Well, you do, that's for sure."

"Yeah, I seem to be popular, don't I?"

"Modest, too."

"Open another can. Sit back. I've got a story I want to tell."

In mock sobriety, I lolled back in the chair, grabbed another can from the floor and cracked the tab with a flourish. "I'm all ears."

"There are lots of ways to be successful in life." Martin took a deep drag from his weed, watching me carefully as if for a response. As yet, I had nothing to respond to, so I stayed quiet. After a pause, he went on: "The first way is to be born rich."

"That rules me out."

"Me, too. But people respect money. No doubt about it. If you're born with money, you don't really need to achieve success; just make sure that you don't lose it all by stupidity. On the other hand..." Martin grinned, but even through that grin I could see the shadow of that other unsettling face. "On the other hand, a person might possess extraordinary skills: mechanical, intellectual, artistic. Those are other ways to be successful..."

"What the bloody hell are you going on about, Martin?"

"Let's not fool ourselves. This is a hard, cruel world where the little fish are eaten by bigger fish, who are eaten in turn by bigger fish. Right? And you become a little fish by joining the school and subscribing to the traditional rules that determine success. And when you're a failure, you're just bait for the big fishes."

"I still don't..."

"Look... the only way to really succeed is on a more personal level. The relationship level." I made a further move to interrupt. Martin impatiently waved me aside. "I'll tell you a story to illustrate what I'm on about." He took a deep snort on the weed, paused, and let the blue smoke curl out of the corners of his mouth. The smoke crawled over his face, but didn't recognise it and drifted off into nothingness. "One of my great heroes lived during the fourteenth century. His name was Tom Fool. Just that. Not his real name, of course. Originally, he was the son of a peasant farmer, but his real name's lost to antiquity now. He was head of a travelling comic troupe in Olde England; earning their crusts by travelling from village to village, staging their performances. Hard times. And some really nasty bastards about in those days. One particular nasty bastard, a baron, took a shine to Tom Fool. Very much against the poor bloke's wishes, the baron made him an offer he couldn't refuse and took him on as Official Court Jester. The rest of the troupe got out of it as quickly as they could. Virtually imprisoned in the baron's castle, Tom Fool entertained him for many years. Always under the firm declaration, apparently, that he would be put to death on the instant that the baron tired of his humour. Real Arabian Nights stuff, eh? Scheherazard had nothing on it. Tom Fool managed to keep the old sod happy for God knows how many years, taking his cue from the baron's multi-changeable moods and creating new material. Eventually, as you might expect, tales began to spread among the servants that Tom Fool's luck was too good to be true."

Martin gave a mock, evil laugh. "A dark figure had been seen one night talking to the Jester in his quarters beneath the dungeons; a dark figure which seemed to melt into the dripping stone walls when approached by one of the baron's guards. Naturally, tales of a pact with the devil arose." Martin laughed again, and then gave a rattling belch.

"Alas, poor Tom Fool. His luck did run out, eventually. But not because of his failure to make the baron laugh. The tale goes that he was so popular, so witty, so funny—he won the heart of the baron's mistress. Baaaad shit! Of course, there was hell to pay when the baron found out. Tom Fool was taken and walled up alive somewhere. The fate of the baron's mistress is not recorded."

Martin paused and looked hard at me as if expecting some kind of response.

I shrugged at him. "So being born in the fourteenth century was no laughing matter."

Martin leaned forward, stabbing a finger at his chest to emphasise the confidentiality. "I identify very strongly with Tom Fool. *There* was a man who had everyone eating out of his hand. Because he was so good, he stayed alive. Don't you see? He stayed alive by *making* people like him. And that's how *I* succeed. I make people like me. Even you, Peter."

"A natural talent ..."

"No!" The force of Martin's exclamation startled me. "You're missing the point. It's not a natural talent. It's an acquired talent. Look at this..." Martin rose from his chair and crossed quickly to his cheap MFI bookcase. Among the dog-eared textbooks and battered paperbacks was a large, rather expensive-looking leather volume. He pulled it from the shelf, returning to his seat and thumbing through its pages. Without looking up, he continued: "This book consists of notes written by me. Notes on everyone I've ever known. On their characters. What makes them tick. How I can turn that to my advantage by working on them. How I can make them like me by working on their own perception of what is and isn't funny. How I can use them..."

"What do you mean by...?"

"There are notes here about you, too," continued Martin. There was a kind of *cruel* look in those eyes. "Peter Marsh. Social and sexual inadequacy. How to bolster your ego by allowing you to bask in my glow. That gave you confidence, didn't it? Made you look up to me. Gave me control over you. I'm not being personal, Peter. You can see that, can't you? I *made* you like me. Just like I make all the others like me. Like I said, people can be used. Every time I make someone laugh,

I've scored another little victory. It's like... feeding... yes, that's exactly it... it's like feeding on their laughter. Each laugh's a little death."

Martin leaned back again and laughed. To me, it seemed as if the laugh was loaded with derision. It made me feel sick. I felt humiliated and betrayed.

I got up and left.

The last thing I heard before I slammed the door shut was another mocking laugh from Martin: "Come back, you idiot. Don't be stupid. Let me explain a bit more..."

I avoided Martin for the rest of the term after that. I'd found sufficient self-confidence by then to make my own way, finding new friends and generally keeping out of his way. He didn't seem to be bothered by my ignoring him; he kept right on as if nothing had happened—still the life and soul of everybody's party. Except that now, I could see his subtle manipulation of those around him. I could see his vast ego and power-play at work. It occurred to me to let everyone else know just what Martin was doing, but I couldn't bring myself to do it. It would have seemed cheap and shabby; the best and cleanest way was to have nothing to do with him.

Not that it has anything to do with the story, but we both passed our Humanities degree with distinction; although the thought did occur to me when I found out about Martin's success that humanity with a small "h" rather than a capital "H" was something which Martin knew nothing about. Anyway... we left college. And I never heard anything from or about him.

Until last October.

The letter arrived by Datapost, with a date stamp showing that it had been posted in Ebchester: a village about forty miles away. Intrigued, since I knew no one from the village, I opened it and recognised the handwriting immediately.

I'm staying at the Mockingbird Inn at Ebchester. Come immediately. Urgent. No laughing matter. Bring a suitcase for an overnight stay. Martin.

I crumpled up the letter and threw it into the wastebin. After all that time, the bastard thought all he had to do was send a three-line letter and I'd come running. What the hell did he take me for, anyway?

The next day, I bought a second-class return ticket to Ebchester.

Weak-willed. Idiot. Puppet. A fall guy. Easily led. I called myself all these things and more during the train ride to Ebchester. I'd made my mind up that as far as I was concerned, Martin could bloody well rot. But I still found myself buying the train ticket. I told myself that for all I cared, he could drop dead. But I was still sitting on the train as it pulled out of Newcastle station. And Martin Rogers could take a running jump off the end of the world if he thought he could make me run around after him like a lackey. But I still arrived, suitcase in hand, at the Mockingbird Inn after a short walk from the station.

The pub was set back from the main road, shrouded in vines and creepers. A dull red sun throbbed above the roof, its face crawling with skeletal branches from the surrounding leafless trees. The road leading to it was little more than a mud track; tractor ruts in the mud making for difficult progress on foot. A large black crow sat on a stile at my left as I approached, watching my progress with great interest. Its inquisitive eye seemed to catch the sun as it hopped into the sky like a tattered rag and flapped towards the pub, vanishing into the overhanging branches.

In a different mood, I might have been able to enjoy the bucolic atmosphere. But trudging through the mud with a suitcase, driven even after all these years by another man's domination of my own will, all I could feel was an inner-directed anger. I looked up at the inn. The bloody place was *laughing* at me. The windows were eyes. The door was a leering mouth. The leer widened as the door opened and, even from that distance, I couldn't mistake the gangling, ginger-haired, white-faced figure who emerged. It was Martin. He turned back and said something to someone inside the pub. There was an inevitable answering chorus of laughter from those within.

Bastard!

Martin strolled casually to meet me, a smile on his face.

"You really look the part, Peter."

"What part is that, then?" The suitcase had grown heavier. Martin's smile made it seem heavier still.

"Young-man-rushes-to-out-of-the-way-country-pub-in-answer-to-mysterious-summons."

He grabbed the suitcase from me. More maddeningly, he began to heft it towards the pub as if it weighed nothing at all. I hurried on behind to match his long stride.

"I don't really know why I've come, Martin. Not after such a long time. Not after what you said about me..."

Martin smiled, head down. He turned to me. "You're here because I asked you," he said. "Nothing else." His domination seemed complete. I believe that I've never hated myself as much as I did at that instant. We entered the pub.

"You'll want some grub inside," said Martin as I looked around. "A few drinks, maybe. And then I'll tell you what it's all about. But listen... I've booked us both in under false names. I'll explain everything later."

Martin moved to the bar, dumping my suitcase on the floor and waving a five-pound note. The landlord brought two pints of bitter. Caked in mud, breathing heavily, I watched as the other customers in the small lounge centred their attention on Martin. He continued a conversation with two locals standing by a log fire. The story that Martin completed was meaningless to me and the guffaws from the spectators, when they came, were sickeningly inevitable. As usual, Martin had succeeded in capturing the crowd. They loved him.

God, how I hated him.

After I'd been shown the room which Martin had booked for me (just the sort of cosy, olde world place I'd imagined it would be) I had something to eat and Martin took me down to the bar again. Everyone seemed to have a smile, a wave or a word to exchange with him, and we found a small corner niche with a battered table. Sipping his pint, eyes sparkling, he finally told me why he'd dragged me here to Ebchester.

"I've found him."

"Who?"

"He's out there in the woods. In the ruins."

"Who, Martin? What the hell are you talking about?"

"Tom Fool. The Jester."

I remembered our conversation. The betrayal and the humiliation were still fresh, even after all this time. Tom Fool, Martin's idol—the doomed jester.

"It's the most incredible bit of luck, Peter. It's like fate or something.

He's been lost—dead and buried for nearly seven-hundred years. Nobody knew where the baron had entombed him. I'm the only one who knows."

"And what makes you think I'm interested?" I asked. Although feigning indifference, despite my resolve not to be dominated, I *was* interested. Intensely interested.

Martin smiled again. "You're still smarting after all these years?"

"It was pretty shitty, Martin."

"I did it for your own good. It made you strong, didn't it? It made you able to stand on your own two feet and not be reliant any more." He was right. But I wasn't prepared to concede the point. "Remember what I told you about humour? Each laugh a little victory, a little death. I've never told anyone those things before or since. You're the only person who knows my philosophy. I knew you could be trusted; knew you wouldn't blab. You were hurt, I know. Maybe I misjudged your sensitivity. But you can't deny that knowing me did you good in the long term."

I couldn't.

"And you're the only one I've ever told about Tom Fool. That's why I asked you here, Peter. To share in my discovery. I knew that you would come. I've found him, Peter! I know where he's buried!"

"All right... how did you find him?"

He told me. And I've no intention of telling you how, why or where he obtained his information. I think it's for the best. Let's just say that Tom Fool was an obsession with Martin. He had studied and examined all the available historical information. He had uncovered some information of his own, analysed every text that he could lay his hands on, and using his own deductive reasoning (based mainly on a manuscript considered lost), pinpointed the exact location of the jester's secret burial place.

"So now what do we do?" I asked when he'd finished telling me everything.

"We go and get him."

"You're joking, of course. You mean we check the place over and then report our find. Tell the professionals, let the archaeologists have a..."

"Afterwards, Peter. First we dig him up."

"Martin, talk sense!"

"I've already checked the place out. I'm sure I know where he is. All I want ..."

"It's ridiculous."

"All I want to do is uncover him. I want to be the first. Afterwards, we'll do what you say."

I told him that I'd have nothing to do with his stupid scheme.

Later that afternoon, we left the pub and began walking along the dirt track inland. Martin was carrying a holdall and I could hear something metallic clunking inside it. It was over an hour's walk through fairly rough country and the ruins, when we arrived there, were densely overgrown in a copse. It's really no good trying to find them. Not only is the Mockingbird Inn not the pub's proper name, but Ebchester doesn't exist either.

Martin seemed feverish with excitement when we reached the bank overlooking the copse.

"I suppose we should have waited until midnight, Peter. The Dead of Night, and all that. Much better atmosphere. Just like a Hammer film. Bodysnatchers Incorporated."

I didn't answer. I was filled with loathing for myself. A loathing for Martin, but an even greater loathing for myself. What the hell was I doing here? Martin moved forward, bounding down the bank in a series of sideways hops. I stumbled after him. A kind of rusty, dappled light was seeping through the trees as we made our way inwards... and downwards.

Martin reached the bottom of the slope, bounding into the middle of what I could now see was a kind of small glade, shrouded on all sides by trees. He turned back to face me as my foot caught in a root and I fell the rest of the way down the incline, grazing my elbows. In anger, I pulled myself to my feet to see Martin standing with his hands on his hips, grinning at me, and obviously not in the least out of breath. It did nothing to ease my mood.

"We're here," he said.

I looked around and could see nothing but overgrown bushes and deepening shadows as the sun started to go down. He laughed at my puzzlement and strode further back into the undergrowth. I watched as he grabbed a handful of hanging ivy and other ravelled vegetation from the inderminate mass surrounding us.

"Ta-da!" With a mock music-hall fanfare, Martin pulled the vegetation back like some huge curtain. Behind that curtain, I could see what seemed to be a roughly hewn stone arch. Grey moss was growing on the dripping stones like an ancient cancer. I moved forward as Martin switched on his torchbeam and aimed it into the blackness beyond, seeing as I drew closer that there were wet and overgrown steps leading down in a spiral below ground.

"Down there?" I asked.

"Down there," replied Martin, giving one of those corny, evil chuckles that were his trademark. The laughter echoed away down those stairs, dissolving into dozens of different giggling echoes in the depths of whatever lay below.

"But you've already been down there, haven't you?"

"No. I found the entrance, just the way it was described. As soon as I did, I sent you that letter."

Leaning forward, I squinted into that darkness, trying to see a little further down, to no avail. "It could be dangerous. Those steps..." I didn't want to go down there.

"Never took you for a coward," said Martin, stepping briskly forward and starting down the steps. The curtain of vegetation fell back across me. I wrestled with it, throwing it angrily to one side. *Bastard!*

I hurried down after the circle of light thrown by Martin's torch. The air was freezing, as if we'd stepped into a deep-freeze meat store. The spongy moss underfoot *was* bloody dangerous. Four steps down, I skidded and grabbed at the stone wall to steady myself, taking a handful of that hideous grey stuff in the process. It felt like shit. Gagging, I threw it to one side, wiping my hand reluctantly on my thigh. Martin waited for me to catch up, holding the torch under his chin so that his face looked like something out of a cheap horror film. "Watch your step, Peter," he said in his pathetic Vincent Price voice. "There are probably *ratsss* down here."

We continued our spiral descent, a sewer-like stench growing worse as we went. It occurred to me now that I was totally dependant on Martin and his torch. He could play all kinds of stupid practical jokes if he wanted to, and as we continued downwards the thought also came to me that if he switched that torch off and left me in total darkness I would probably piss myself or worse...

We reached the bottom of the spiral steps. God knows how deep we were. Martin flashed the torch around, and I could see that we had reached an underground chamber of sorts about fifty or sixty feet in circumference. The walls, the floor and the ceiling were all hewn from stone and covered with that disgusting grey moss. Somewhere, we could hear water slowly dripping with a musical echo.

"This is it," said Martin, his voice echoing again. "I *knew* it would be here." His face was deadly serious, no clowning around now. He walked carefully into the middle of that chamber and I stayed close to him, close to the torch-beam. He placed the holdall on the ground and handed me the torch. "Here. Shine it down." I did as I was told, while Martin opened the holdall and took out a crowbar. He looked up at me again and said without any trace of humour: "Every grave-robber should have one."

"Come on, Martin. It's bloody *freezing* down here."

"Don't you know how important this is to me? I'm the first... we're the first... to find him. If I thought you were going to let me down..."

"Okay, Martin. I'm sorry. What now?"

"That's better." Martin stood up again and took the torch from me, swinging it around the chamber and back to the stone stairs. Striding briskly back to the foot of the stairs, he turned again to face me. Against my better judgement, not wanting to seem cowardly, I remained in the darkness while he did so.

"Thirty paces," said Martin. "But they were smaller guys in those days, weren't they? So... thirty medium paces, I think. " Martin began to walk forward again, counting the paces as he went. When he stopped at thirty, he was only about ten feet away from me. "You still there?"

"Yeah..." My throat was constricted. The word was half-strangled when it came out.

I started back in alarm as Martin threw himself down on the floor and began raking at the moss-covered stone with his crowbar. "Here... here..." He handed me back the torch and I stepped out of the darkness to take it, shining it down as he worked. There was a flagstone under all that grunge, about three feet square. Martin raked the end of the crowbar into the grooves around it. After two or three minutes, he had levered the crowbar under one of its edges and was heaving upwards. "God... it's bloody heavy... help me." I put the torch down and helped him lean on the bar as the flagstone began to lift with a grinding rasp that echoed back to us from the darkness. We both gripped the edge, letting the crowbar fall with a clang as we heaved upwards until the stone stood at forty-five degrees. It felt like ice. Heaving and straining, we dragged it to one side. Martin scrambled back to the bare patch of damp earth that was left. Small, many-legged things were scurrying from it, away from the torchbeam. He stabbed into the earth with the crowbar. It was soft and yielded easily. "Another one," breathed Martin, looking around him. "Help me lift another."

We had gone through the same procedure with three more of the flagstones when the crowbar broke in two, and we fell back into the darkness.

"Buggeration!" hissed Martin. He seemed feverish now with his task. "We need to lift another one at least."

"Listen, Martin. Are you sure he's buried under here?" My fingers were numb with cold and bleeding. "What if ...?"

"What if, nothing!" hissed Martin. "He's here. There's no doubt about it. I've spent too long researching and hunting for him. We're going to have the last laugh, Peter. Now... go back up and find something we can lift this last stone with. Even if we rake away the sides, we're still going to need something to lever it up..."

"There's only one torch. I can't leave you here in the dark..."

"Here, take the torch. Leave it at the foot of the stairs—that'll be light enough for both of us. You'll be able to find your way up and then back again easily enough."

"I'll break my bleeding neck, Martin!"

"Then *you* stay here, and I'll go and find something!"

Again, that look on Martin's face. A look that said: *So you're just a bloody coward, after all. Scared of the dark, Peter? Want your Mummy, Peter?*

"All right, all right!"

I grabbed the torch from Martin and stormed back to the staircase, the beam making shadows leap and dance in the chamber. The smell was awful. I looked back once to see that he was stabbing at the soil again with a broken half of the crowbar. He looked demented.

I jammed the torch at the foot of the stairs and started back up, step by careful step.

It was a nightmare. The steps seemed even more slimy than when I'd first descended. Every time I took a step in that total blackness, no matter how careful, my foot seemed to slip a few inches. I didn't want to touch the stone walls at either side as I climbed, for fear of touching that bloody awful moss-stuff again. So with every step, my arms waved about in empty air; like some kind of blindfolded tightrope walker. My breathing seemed louder in that pitch blackness, making me claustrophobic and panicky. Behind and below me, I could hear Martin digging with the broken crowbar at the bare patch we'd uncovered.

It seemed as if I'd been climbing for hours when I saw a sickly grey light up ahead. In the knowledge that I was nearly at the top again, I tried to hurry and only succeeded in skidding badly on a step, clawing at the air. In that instant, I knew that I was going to hurtle backwards down that rough stone flight, breaking my neck in the process. Somehow, my balance evened. Gasping for breath, I continued slowly and steadily upwards until I could see that waving curtain of vegetation ahead. I burst through it, running away from that stone arch and into the middle of the darkening glade, bent double, hands on my hips, coughing out spasms of that foetid air. My heart was hammering.

When I had steadied my nerves, I began to look around for something to lever that last flagstone. There were broken tree branches lying in the glade, but nothing which seemed strong enough. Coughing and wheezing, I climbed the bank that I had fallen down earlier and looked around again. There was a broken fence on the other side of the track, but when I reached it, none of that flimsy wood would seem to serve our purpose either. I was on the verge of turning back when I saw the rusted iron rod lying in the grass. I pulled it out of the undergrowth and weighed it in both hands. It was about three feet long, corroded... but strong enough. It looked like a piston rod or something from an old tractor. I hurried back down the slope into the glade. A strong wind was building on the wings of the night and the ragged trees and shrubbery around that forgotten and hidden gate were hissing and swaying when I pulled aside the curtain once more.

I didn't relish the descent again, but Martin was down there waiting alone. And I wasn't going to prove myself a coward in his eyes. Not bloody Martin.

I stepped through the arch again... and then paused, listening to the sounds that echoed and drifted up to me from below.

Martin was laughing.

Something must really be tickling his funnybone. It was laughter that he was struggling to contain, as if he'd thought of the funniest joke in the world. But even though he was trying to contain that laughter, it was still leaking out anyway in giggles and wheezes, the sounds accentuated by the acoustics of the underground chamber and the staircase. Puzzled, I started forward again into the darkness, using the rusted rod as a walking stick by jabbing it hard into the stone before taking a step. It worked much better.

And step by step downwards, I could hear Martin's laughter getting louder and louder. He wasn't able to contain himself now, giving vent to great peals of mirth that dissolved into gasping giggles. Sometimes he'd draw in a breath of air and be silent, just the way a crying child will do, before exploding again. The laughter was bouncing off the walls around me.

"Martin?" I was smiling too as I descended. "What is it? What's so funny?" Maybe he heard me, because his laughter became even more pronounced.

Had he found something? Was that why he sounded so overjoyed?

Martin broke into racking coughs, his laughter momentarily choking him. And then he whooped again before launching into more of that barking laughter. I paused on the steps for an instant in the darkness, holding on tight to the rod. For some reason, I didn't like that last *whooping* noise he'd made. Even though he was laughing his head off, there seemed to be an element of, well, distress in the sound. It sounded unhealthy, more like a scream. But Martin was still laughing, so everything must be all right as I continued on down.

"Martin? What's the joke? Have you found something...?"

I could see the torch beam down below, shining on the last few steps that led to the chamber. The light was flickering, so the battery must obviously be fading. We had to work fast if we didn't want to be lost in the dark down here.

Martin was screaming with laughter now as I reached the bottom of the stairs. Those sounds were much too loud, the echoes bouncing and crashing around me. The torch beam was directly in my face so that I couldn't see anything in the chamber. I leaned down, picked up the torch and shone it across to where I knew Martin would be.

Martin was on his knees at the spot where we'd levered up the flagstones. His face was ghastly white and streaked with mud. Even from where I stood, I could see the glassy look of terror in his eyes that reflected back from the torch beam. I could see the contorted look on his face. It was a contortion of horror and agony and mortal pain. And he was still screaming with laughter.

Something was standing over Martin.

I felt like screaming myself when I saw it properly.

It was horribly tall and ragged... and it was holding Martin's hand. Martin's right hand was stretched up towards it, and the tattered skeletal form was holding that hand as if he were some kind of mad child, grovelling at its feet. The abominable scarecrow shape was swathed in mud-caked rags. I'm sure that I saw a ribcage within its tattered folds.

And then I saw its face.

The thing had the remnants of a tattered, three-cornered hat on its head, and when the head turned away from Martin towards me, I could hear the jingle of bells. Within the hood, I saw a grinning, grey-white skull... the colour of that cancerous mould on the walls. But there were eyes in those sockets; glittering, feral eyes. And as Martin's hideous laughter pealed and echoed, I could see... without any doubt... that a *face* was reconstituting itself around that skull. I watched as a network of veins and arteries began to appear on that grey-white visage. I could see flesh and substance forming around those sharp, skeletal features. Muscle, fibre and tissue began to knot and coalesce there. The grinning teeth were fading from view as that flesh formed and moulded.

I dragged my eyes away in terror from that horrifying, ragged thing and looked back at Martin. He was forcing those shrieks of laughter through gritted teeth now. His lips were drawn back, his face contorted and his eyes staring wildly at me in pain and madness and distress. He was aging before my eyes, the flesh shrinking away from his bones, the colour fading from his ginger hair. His eyes were sunken hollows now, the rictus-grin of laughter on his face changing him into a Mr. Sardonicus. In the torchlight's beam, I watched him being drained.

And then the torchlight went out.

Martin's screams of laughter reached a new and horrible pitch as I turned and blundered back up those stone stairs, stabbing my way upwards with the iron rod.

"Peeeeter! Peeeeter! For God's sake, don't leave me!"

Those were the only words I could discern from that cacophony of insane and dying laughter, and I think that's when I began screaming as well. The laughter and the screams were like wild, shrieking, buffeting birds as I fought my way to the surface, feet skidding and slipping, desperately hanging onto the iron rod stabbed into the stone.

When I burst through the ragged stone arch, I threw the iron rod to one side and clapped my hands over my ears to drown out the sounds. I kept on running without looking back, until the laughter was far, far behind me.

I still don't remember my flight back to the Mockingbird Inn.

But I do remember a voice asking: "So where's your friend, then?"

That voice seemed to bring me back to real time again, and suddenly I found myself standing inside the inn, on the threshold of the bar room. Everyone inside was looking up at me from their drinks, and the shadows from the log fire were leaping and dancing on their faces. I couldn't be sure whether I had screamed or spoken. But the faces were, even now, losing interest in me and returning to their pints of bitter and their conversations. I looked down at myself, at the mud stains and grass streaks on my trousers. "Where is he, then?" asked the same voice again, and this time I could see that it was the landlord behind the counter, drying glasses.

"Gone for a walk," I heard myself say.

The landlord was clearly disappointed that the Life and Soul of the Party wasn't with me. Should I tell him, tell them all, just what had happened in that underground chamber? Should I start dragging at their sleeves, begging them to follow me out into the night, back to that terrible place to save Martin? I started to speak, but the words clogged in my throat.

"Drink?" asked the landlord.

"Whisky," I heard myself say again. "A large one."

I made my way on none too steady legs to the bar counter, hearing one of the farmhands at the bar sniggering to his mate: "City boys. One country walk and they're knackered."

The landlord gave me my drink. "On the slate?"

I nodded, knocking back the whisky quickly.

"He's a laugh, isn't he?" said the landlord. "Your mate, I mean. A joke-a-minute."

"Dead funny fellow," I said, and the words seemed to hang in the air.

"Another?"

I had just opened my mouth to speak, when the bar door slammed. The noise paralysed me, and for an instant I thought that I was going to give vent to the screams that were still inside me. I watched the landlord's face as he looked up in annoyance.

And then he began to smile.

"Thought you'd got lost," he said.

"Not me," said a familiar voice.

With ice in my veins, I turned from the bar to look at the door.

Martin was standing there, smiling.

"What... how...?" I croaked. The room seemed to tilt for an instant as Martin let the door swing shut behind him. He strode into the room, clapping his hands together as if warding off the night chill.

"Evening, landlord! How about drinks all round?" said Martin, and all the faces in the bar were turned towards him now as he joined me at the bar, all smiling and mumbling appreciatively. I couldn't believe my eyes. Martin hung over the bar as the landlord began to pull pints and place them on corroded, battered trays. He obviously knew what the regulars drank here, needing no prompting.

"Martin...?"

At last he turned to look at me, mirth all over his face. Then he did actually begin to laugh, slapping his hand down on the counter as he took delight in my bewilderment.

"Fooled you, didn't I? Really got you that time, Peter!"

A joke? Was that what had happened? Had I been the victim of Martin's deliberate, carefully planned and cruel joke? After all these years, had I again been lured by Martin? Is that what the bastard had done? I could see it now. I could see Martin's discovery of that underground catacomb, or whatever the hell it was. I could see the plan formulating in his head; a carefully planned revenge for having snubbed him and his philosophy all those years ago. I could see the elaborately contrived puppet in mud-clotted rags and death's head grin. And then the lure of the mysterious letter. How good he must have felt when I turned up at the Mockingbird Inn.

"You... bastard!" I grabbed at the refilled double whisky that the landlord had placed before me and downed it swiftly again. Martin was convulsed at the bar, taking a frothing pint from the landlord.

"What's the joke then?" asked the landlord.

"I'll tell you later," sputtered Martin, beginning to drink.

I slammed my empty glass down on the counter and stormed out of the bar. Behind me, I heard Martin saying something to the other bar customers. Naturally, everyone in the bar burst out laughing.

I had been *had.*

Upstairs, in my room, I lay on the bed and listened to the sounds of Martin's mumbled voice and the resultant howls of laughter from the customers below. Martin, Martin... always bloody Martin. No matter what he did, people liked him. No matter how much he used them. Martin, Martin. Goddamn Bloody Martin. Always good for a laugh. And now, downstairs... everyone was laughing at *me.* I couldn't hear anything that was being said, but I knew Martin all right. And I knew how well he could tell a good tale, how well he could tell a joke. They were lapping it up.

I flung myself from the bed and pulled open the curtains, looking out into the night. Rain was spattering against the window now; the ghostly spectres of trees writhing in the wind. And somewhere out there, in the night, was the scene of Martin's great practical joke. The chamber and its hideous puppet. I could see everything so clearly now. The way that Martin had sent me back up those slimy stairs for something to lift that flagstone, gambling (oh so rightly!) that I could be shamed by my cowardice into leaving, giving him time to rig up that skeletal monstrosity for my return.

A fresh burst of laughter from downstairs made me whirl from the window. I began to stalk the room. Now I was trapped in my room for the night. Forced to listen to that condemning laughter until the small hours, until Martin's free drinks had taken their toll and sent the pub customers staggering home to their beds. And what would happen come the morning? More humiliation? Or... worse... a patronising speech from Martin; a friendly pat on the shoulder and an admonition that I should learn how to take a joke, not take myself so seriously. Even worse still, perhaps I *would* just shrug it off and leave.

No! Not tonight. I had lived my life in Martin's shadow. He had made me a Fool before, and he had made me a worse Fool tonight to teach me a lesson. No more! I'd had enough of it. I would go downstairs, burst into that bar and take Martin by the scruff of the neck. He was no bigger than me, after all. I would pin him to that bar counter and I would tell him just what I thought of him and his tricks while the rest of the customers listened in awe. After I'd finished, I'd pour Martin's pint over his head, give two fingers to the rest of them and leave. First thing in the morning, I'd be on the train back to Newcastle. And if Martin tried to talk to me before then, if he tried to use his oily technique on me… well, I'd smash him in the face! And I'd like to see him laugh that one off.

I heard another muted chorus of laughter from downstairs. Enraged, I flung open the bedroom door and started down, mentally rehearsing just what would happen when I strode into that bar and Martin turned in puzzlement to look at me, just before I…

I flung open the bar door. It banged sharply against the wall, snapping shut as I entered. I already had my hand raised, finger pointing at the spot where I knew Martin would be standing. Sure enough, he was there, leaning on the bar with his back to me. Martin the Performer, on stage… with the pub audience glued to his every word.

"You!" I shouted, striding forward.

And then I stopped.

Something was wrong. Terribly, terribly wrong.

The pub customers seemed to be in the same seats and at the same tables as I'd left them. But they were *different*. I turned to see that some of them were slumped over the tables, heads up, attention still riveted on Martin. Others held empty pint glasses, their mouths open, spittle dripping. Others were slumped back in their seats in what seemed to be a state of semi-collapse. And now, just beyond the bar counter rim, I could see that the landlord was actually lying on the floor, looking up at Martin and grinning.

In the next instant, I saw their faces.

I saw their shrivelled and hollowed faces. I saw their grinning, skull teeth. I saw the leprous grey and shrivelling flesh as it withered and disintegrated on the bone. I saw the skeletal fingers which grasped those empty glasses. But most of all, I saw a familiar reflection of abominable distress in the dying gleam of those eyes.

Martin mumbled something at the bar.

And those horrible corpse-like things in the pub began to laugh. Braying, choking... *dying*... laughter. In the far corner of the pub, beside the window, one of the customers collapsed to the floor in a skittering bundle of bones. Even as that corpse disintegrated, it giggled and twitched.

I turned back to Martin.

He looked over his shoulder at me... and smiled.

And then I knew that I hadn't been the victim of a practical joke.

Because it wasn't Martin at all.

With the braying, choking sounds of laughter in my ears, I staggered backwards out of that bar. The Thing that was now Martin watched me all the way, with a hideous knowing glint in its eyes. I hit the bar door hard and tottered outside. It slapped shut when I was in the corridor, blocking out the sight of those eyes and muffling the sound of that terrible laughter.

I ran again.

Out into the night, into the storm and the rain and the howling wind. And I kept on running as the storm soaked me to the skin. The wind in the trees was mocking me. No matter how hard I ran, it seemed as if that wind carried the sound of laughter all around me. Laughter from the pub, laughter from that place underground. I thought that I must go mad and die.

When I woke at last from that nightmare, I was curled up on a bench in Ebchester Station's waiting room. Grateful, I rested my head on the scarred and pitted wood and slipped into a fevered sleep.

Morning came.

My suitcase and clothes were back at the Mockingbird Inn, but my wallet was safely in my overcoat pocket. I clambered aboard the first train that arrived at the platform, and even though I had to change twice, I finally arrived back in Newcastle hours later.

For two days, I stayed in my flat... getting drunk.

On the third day, I stumbled to the nearest store to buy a newspaper.

And there it was.

Twenty-three people had been found dead in an Ebchester pub.

The details were fairly sketchy, as I knew they must be. But it was clear that the police suspected foul play. They had been somehow poisoned. Regional breweries were up-in-arms, assuring the public that their beer was untainted. Meanwhile, beer consumption was slumping dramatically.

What a joke.

I waited.

I knew that it would start happening again.

And then I began to read those other reports in the newspapers. Reports of the mysterious deaths in the towns and villages around Ebchester, and then further afield. Details of cause-of-death were vague, and I suspect that's because the police may be afraid of causing some kind of panic. They know about the deaths in the Mockingbird Inn, after all. Then there was the report about the man who was found at the bottom of an embankment. A farmer, I think. His body was shrivelled and drained. And there was a look on his face. A wild, staring, rictus-grin of insane dead humour.

All the others are the same. And there're more of them every day as He grows more whole.

I feed on their laughter, Martin had said. *Each laugh is a little death.*

He who laughs last, laughs loudest. But I wonder what kind of joke He's telling?

So... now you know the story. And where it ends I've no way of knowing. It's up to you whether you believe any of it or not. But like I said at the beginning, please don't try to make me laugh. Don't try to cheer me up, don't try to tell me a joke.

Please don't make me laugh.

Because once I start, I don't think I'll ever be able to stop.

black cab

It prowls the streets at night.

Glistening black, its sleek bodywork shines like the rainwashed streets. Neon reflections from pubs and nightclubs strobe and curve over its black metallic surface. The windows seem darkly tinted, unusual for a taxi—making it almost impossible to see the hunched form of the taxi driver up front. The engine is well-tuned. It makes an ominous, deep-throated purring sound as it cruises the city-centre streets, or slides down black alleys. That sound is the sound that a panther might make, grumbling deep in its chest as it anticipates the prey ahead.

Soon, someone will hail that Black Cab from the pavement.

The Black Cab will slide up to its customer.

A back door will open.

A silhouette will climb inside—and the beast will slide away from the curb again.

Off into the night.

To a place where screams can't be heard.

To the place of the Kill.

-⊕⊕⊕-

We're standing in the taxi rank on Percy Street when she says the words that kill me inside. You know the rank I mean? That's the one next to the pre-fab shops, with the wonky iron railings that have been bashed a few times. Stacks of people there as usual at this time of night—half past midnight, when the late pubs have all kicked out and there's no buses from the Haymarket Station to be had just across the way. It's the usual Friday night. Everybody's either half or fully cut. I've counted three separate fights starting along this taxi queue, stretching all the way around the corner down towards the bus concourse. Must be a hundred, hundred and fifty people there. Some eating kebabs and fish and chips, some just necking up against the railings, some with full bladders having a you-know-what in the prefab shop doorways, some just... well never mind them. Others are starting to jostle and push in, because there hasn't been a taxi for a while. But we're okay, we're right at the head of the queue, pushing out and sort of declaring our territory as first in place.

Then this Black Cab swerves across Percy Street and heads across the tarmac towards us.

The whole thing is set in my mind, because it's really the time that my life ends, know what I mean?

In just one flash, in the words she says, I just take in everything that I've told you—like the whole scene is imprinted in my mind and I'll never forget it. Ever.

She says: "It's finished, Baz."

I say: "What?" And when I think about the way I say it, the word sounds awkward and bloody stupid. But it's like I should have seen this coming for a long time.

"Me and you," she says. "I'm sorry... but it's finished."

We've been necking against the railings, just like some of the others. You'd think I would have sensed something, picked something up. Surely you can't be as intimate as that with someone, and not know that they're going to ditch you ten minutes later? I suppose if I really think back over the last few months there were things I should have spotted... little clues. Little things that I should have noticed. Maybe I didn't want to give those little hints and clues headroom. Maybe I'm just stupid. Maybe the necking in the doorway was... I dunno... a ritual, I suppose. The thing you always do after a night out. Funny, I never felt her teeth before when we were kissing. But I did tonight.

"What the hell do you mean?" I blurt.

The Black Cab hits a dirty puddle on the tarmac, spraying some of the punters up against the railings. Someone swears. Someone else just laughs. Wish I could laugh.

"It hasn't been right. It's never been right."

"Wait a minute, you just can't..."

"I'm sorry, Baz. I should have told you before now. But it's over."

And she pulls open the rear door on the Black Cab and she slides in, really quickly. She pulls the door shut with this heavy chunking sound. And the way that door shuts, the noise it makes—sounds just like the word.

Ker—chunk! O—ver!

I can't say anything; can't find anything else to say. I just stand there like a gormless jerk, staring at her as she shrinks back in the seat and looks fiercely the other way. I look at the driver.

He's got a round face, with bad teeth. His hair is thinning, but what's left is a fiery ginger. There are freckles over the bridge of his nose. He looks like a forty year old kid. As I look at him, I suddenly see more of his bad teeth.

He's smiling.

A big, wide, rotten-toothed grin.

In just that one moment, this bastard has sussed out my situation. In that one shit-eating grin, he conveys his complete sense of superiority, of put-down, of knowing that I'm now totally screwed up by what Jesse has said to me. And I know, just know from the way that Jesse has said it, that we really are finished, and that there's no way to talk her over. And this ginger git knows it.

I throw myself at the front door, smashing my fist against the panel.

It gets a roar of drunken approval from the taxi rank. The roar is followed by demeaning laughter.

Come on, then! Stop the car, get out—and I'll take that grin off your face...

The taxi driver's smile doesn't change. With a smooth sweep of his hand, he engages first gear, and pulls the wheel over. The taxi, plus its dented panel, splashes through more dirty water... and speeds away from the rank, off up Percy Street and towards the North Road.

I stand there, like an idiot.

She's gone.

-⊕⊕⊕-

And I never see her again.

I ring her up at the flat, but her flatmates tell me that they don't know where she is. Three days later, and she's still missing. That's when everybody else starts to get worried. She hasn't turned up at the flat; all her clothes are still there. She hasn't turned up at college for her classes. There's been no message, no note to her friends or to me. Jesse doesn't have any family, no relations at all—so she hasn't "gone home". She was born in Retford, but since she moved up here to go to college, Newcastle has become her home, and she doesn't have any other really close friends she can go to.

That's when we get the police involved.

At first, they don't take it seriously.

They interview everyone—especially me, since it seems I'm the last one to have ever seen her. But it's as if they can't really be bothered. It's almost as if they're saying: Show us a body, and then we can really get moving. Don't you know how many people just go missing every week, every month, every year? Look, you've filled in the forms and answered the questions. Now, don't worry. We're sure she'll turn up again...

That's when I start to think.

There have been three murders in Newcastle over the past six months. Three girls, all about Jesse's age. No one has been caught, and the police are still making half-hearted noises about girls making sure that they have escorts home late at night, or that they shouldn't take shortcuts through badly lit places. The usual stuff. Anyway... one girl was found in St James Park, another up the North Road, and another down on Welbeck Road in Walker. For a while, I didn't put anything together. I mean—you read about these things in the paper, and it makes you depressed for a bit. Then you forget about it. But since Jesse went missing, these three other girls have been on my mind.

All three were found with their throats cut.

All three had been... well, you know.

And all three had been out with their friends night-clubbing.

Last seen... looking for a taxi?

-⊕⊕⊕-

Weeks go by.

Still no sign of Jesse, no word, no message.

Everyone fears the worst.

So I've got this theory.

Think about it.

Some guy out there in a Black Cab, cruising the streets, looking for a girl to pick up in the middle of the night. I mean, no girl in her right mind is going to accept a late night lift from a perfect stranger in his car. But who thinks twice about flagging down a Black Cab? You wouldn't get into a stranger's car in case he's a bloody maniac. But what makes you think that the guy behind the driver's wheel of a taxi isn't just that?

All I can see is the grinning face of that Black Cab Driver. The thinning, fiery red hair. The freckles. The smirking smile on his face. The glint in his eyes. The more I think about it, the more it makes me feel knotted and sick inside. That wasn't just a sarcastic one-upmanship laugh on his face. He knew that he'd found his victim for the night. He knew what was going to happen; knew that this would be the last time I'd ever see her. The thought of it makes me shake with rage and grief; makes me sweat until my shirt sticks to my back.

I go back to the police, and tell them my story.

It's worse than before.

Did I take the taxi number? The licence plate or the taxi driver's registration number. No, of course I didn't. And you think this guy's a serial killer, driving around and murdering girls? Okay, what's the description? Ginger hair, bad teeth. Fine. We've made a note of it, Sherlock Holmes. Just leave it to us.

The bloody idiots.

There's only one way.

I'll find that taxi driver again.

If it's the last thing I do.

-⊕⊕⊕-

The Black Cab Man smiles as he turns into the rank again. It's a smile which shows off those bad teeth to horrid effect. The eyes are blue—the blue of an innocent, which makes what he's doing even more ghastly. Seeing the queue up ahead, the thought comes to him that it's like a lottery. He can't dictate who he's going to pick up here. If it's a couple, or a bunch of friends, then his fun will be spoilt. But if it's a girl on her own…

Sometimes he just likes to cruise the streets, waiting to see if he can find someone alone. But on other occasions, when he's using the ranks like this—like a lottery—it adds extra excitement to his quest.

They'll never stop him.

Not him.

Not The Black Cab Man.

-⊕⊕⊕-

At first, I try to find him by enquiring at the Civic Centre. They give out the taxi driver's licences, so they must have a record of them all. But there's no register, and it's obvious from the office clerks I talk to, that they think I'm a nutcase. The local taxi firms are not much better. On one occasion, I narrowly escape being beaten to a pulp by two taxi drivers drinking tea in their Haymarket office.

So there's only one other way.

I walk the streets.

Day and night. Just watching the traffic, waiting for a Black Cab to pass by. Straining to look at the driver's compartment, trying to catch a glimpse of that hair and those teeth, and that insanely evil knowing glint. I stand at taxi ranks late at night. Not only the Haymarket rank, but the others on Northumberland Street and at the Central Station. I stand and watch and wait, letting everyone push in front of me in the queue as taxis come and go. I even keep my eye on the ordinary non-black taxis, just in case the bastard is using more than one car, or borrowing a friend's. They do that sometimes.

Days, weeks, months—I lose track. But, as I watch, I can feel that something is happening to me. Something inside. It's like the real me is dying as I walk these streets. I know what I must look like, but I don't care anymore. I look like one of those ragged people I've seen ferreting through dustbins looking for something to eat. I talk to myself a lot now. I can see people stepping out of my path as I walk. When I go home, I'm usually exhausted. I slump into my seat in front of the television. The images there don't make a lot of sense to me anymore. They just flicker and illuminate the darkened room. I can't sleep, because every time I do—I see that Black Cab prowling, looking for victims. I see images of what must have happened to Jesse. Images that are unbearable. When they find her body, what will the police do? Arrest me, probably. I was the last one to see her alive after all, by my own admission.

I've got to find that Black Cab.

I'm drinking too much. That, plus the lack of sleep are changing me. I don't know what I'm changing into, and perhaps I should be scared. But I'm not. I just walk, and watch.

And wait.

-⊕⊕⊕-

"Are you going far?" asks the girl when the Black Cab stops and she moves to the window.

"As far as you want, darling," smiles the man with the thinning red hair.

Maybe she should recognise what's in his words, maybe she should see the intent in his eyes, and just let this Black Cab slide off into the night. But it's late, and she's missed her last bus home. She's had a good night, but it's cold and wet now—and she needs the bathroom, quickly. The alcohol has softened her customary caution. Anyway, taxi drivers are alright, aren't they? I mean, they're screened by the council and everything.

She opens the door and climbs in.

"Hazlerigg," she says.

The Black Cab starts off in the opposite direction.

"Excuse me, I said Hazlerigg."

"Yeah, I know. But there's roadworks up at the main junction."

"I didn't see any when I came into town."

"They only started an hour ago."

"Oh..."

"It's alright. I'll just make a slight diversion. It won't cost you any extra, I promise."

"That's alright then," says the girl, settling back.

The Black Cab vanishes into the night.

-⊕⊕⊕-

What are the chances of me finding this guy again? A hundred to one? A thousand? A million? Yeah, maybe a million. And how many taxis have I seen since I started out? Seems like a million. Tonight is a million and one.

I'm standing at the front of the queue again at the Haymarket rank. It's eleven-forty, and I've been here since eight o'clock. I'm even starting to recognise some of those taxi drivers now. They recognise me, too. And I'm just about to stand aside and let this necking couple through when a Black Cab slides up to the rank.

And it's him.

The hair, the eyes, the teeth.

I shove the young guy away from me, and he lunges back as if he might want to start something.

"I'm first!" I yell at him, never taking my eyes off the driver. He's looking the other way, not wanting to get wrapped up in a big scene. "Leave it, Johnny! Leave it!" shouts his girlfriend, dragging him off towards the railings. "Must be mental, or on drugs. Just let him go!"

"Yeah, mental," I say... and this grin comes over my face when I see the dented panel in the taxi door where I bashed it. The taxi driver looks briefly at me and for a terrifying moment, I think that he might recognise me and pull quickly away, back onto Percy Street. But he scans my face with total disinterest, not recognising me at all—only checking to see that any potential aggravation has been cleared up.

Satisfied that everything is okay, he flips open the door.

I climb in.

"Where to?" he says, without looking back at me.

"The Quayside," I say.

"Whereabouts on the Quayside? That's a long stretch of water."

"Down by St Michael's. The warehouses."

He looks at me quizzically in the rear-view mirror. My heart jumps. Does he recognise me?

"I work down there," I say. "Bailey's Import. I've got to get back."

He looks at me a moment longer. Then he says: "Okay…"

We head down to the Bigg Market. There are still late night stragglers staggering homeward. Some couples, wrapped around each other. Crowds of kids staggering and singing. Every thirty seconds or so, someone lurches out into the road and tries to flag us down.

"Stupid gits," says the taxi driver. I stare at the back of his head, catching sight of his green eyes in the rearview mirror. My heart should be hammering, racing in apprehension and anticipation. But it's not. It feels dead and leaden in my chest. There's a coldness inside me that makes me feel as if I've turned into stone or ice.

"Busy night?" I hear myself ask.

"Not bad. Trade's picking up again now the factory fortnight's over. Tell you though, it's hard making a living these days."

"Thought a fella in your line of business could make a killing."

"No way. Not worth the aggro sometimes. I've known punters do a runner when there's less than two quid on the clock. Can you believe it? You could walk that far no bother. Reckon some just do it for a laugh. Women are the worst."

"Really?"

"Yeah, no kidding. You wouldn't believe some of the experiences I've had."

"I think I would."

"Eh…?"

"I said, like what?"

"Hen parties are the worst. Some birds work their ticket, just cause I'm a bloke—know what I mean? Others, well… I've known some tarts get a ride home with no cash in their purse. And then when we get where they're going, they want to pay me in kind. " The ginger haired man laughs.

"Ever take them up?"

"With a wife and two kids? Last thing I need is a dose of the clap—or worse. Nah, real tarts some of them. Deserve everything they get."

It's that last statement that does it. I don't speak anymore as we head on down City Road. We drive in silence past the Tyne Tees Television studios, then on down Glass House Bridge and along Walker Road.

We pass St. Lawrence Square, and finally make that right hand turn down towards the Quayside. There are warehouses on either side of this back lane, but the only street lamps are at the top of the lane where it joins Walker Road. Everything else down here is in deep shadow. Bailey's Import is about half way down.

I've never worked there.

"So where about do you want...?" he begins.

I lean forward to the little window, just behind his head.

"Just here."

"You sure?"

"Yeah."

The taxi bumps up onto a fractured pavement, and he stops it just under the "Bailey Import" sign. He begins to turn towards me.

In all the time I've been riding in these Black Cabs, I've been planning and picturing in my head just how I'm going to do it. The small window between the driver and passenger has been designed for security, but I've found a way. Every ride in a cab, I've been working it out.

I shuffle forward until I'm right up against that window, reaching into my jacket pocket for what he thinks will be the fare. I'm holding the flick-knife under my jacket, in my right hand—and he doesn't have a chance to see me.

I lunge my left arm through that aperture, grabbing a handful of that ginger hair. I snap his head back towards me. He slams awkwardly backwards out of the driving seat against the partition, and I keep on dragging as he begins to yell. The back of his neck is exposed.

I'm holding the flick-knife the way you're supposed to hold it. Like a screwdriver. I stab it in hard, between the tendons at the back of his neck, using underarm force. It shears through his windpipe and his throat easier than I expected. The handle jams against the back of his neck, the tip stabbing out just below his chin. He jerks forward hard across the driving wheel, making a gargling sound. That sudden jerk wrenches the knife from my hand, but it stays deeply imbedded. I slump back in my seat, breathing hard, as the Black Cab Man claws at his throat. His feet are drumming on the floor. He twists, and tries to turn towards me, eyes starting and wild. It's the last time he'll ever have that knowing glint. Strangely, there's no blood yet.

Then it comes.

And comes.

He collapses over the wheel now, the eyes fixed and staring back at me. The impact of his death throes has started the windscreen wipers working. They whisper back and forth, back and forth, as if trying to wipe away that immense red splash on the inside of the windscreen. It's over.

But now, it seems as if I can't move. I know that the central locking mechanism on these Black Cabs is only operating when the driver's foot is on the brake. Now that his foot's off, I can easily get out of the Cab. But I can't. So what happens next? I sit here, frozen in the back seat until the police show up. Then I get done for murder, and for the murder of those three girls. And Jesse.

I close my eyes... and now, somehow, I'm standing outside the Black Cab on the steep, cobbled lane. I suck in deep breaths of the cold night air. Now I can move again. Quickly, I look back to the main road. There's little traffic at this time of night, and what there is will pass by quickly without seeing us down here by the warehouses. I move to the front of the Cab. He hasn't locked his own door. I lean in, and switch off the windscreen wipers. He still stares at the back seat, as if I was still there.

Then I take the hand brake off, and guide the steering wheel as the Black Cab begins to gather speed down the lane. I begin to trot alongside, still holding that wheel. Then, at the last moment—I let it go. The cab rolls on down.

Towards the quayside frontage between the warehouses.

The cab has gathered sufficient speed—it hits the lip of the frontage hard, mounts it and then tips over quickly. I see a flash of the car's suspension and its wheels. Then it's gone from sight over the edge. The sound of the splash seems strangely hushed. I was expecting something grand, something dramatic. But all I hear is a slithering sound as the cab hits the dark water. It's deep here. That's why I chose it. I turn and walk back up the lane.

It's like I'm really standing at the top of the lane, looking down at this figure who is walking up towards me. The figure looks strange. Like a tramp. And there's something about the eyes that doesn't seem right.

But the figure's nodding as it walks. Nodding and with this fixed expression on the face that surely couldn't be a smile. The figure says only two words when it reaches the top of the lane and turns down the main street away from the warehouses, without once looking back.

"It's over."

-⊕⊕⊕-

This funny thought comes to me as reach my flat in Heaton and push the key into the front door lock.

Imagine if I walk into the front passage and smell that perfume that Jesse always wore. What if I hear that the television's on? What if I see a chink of light under the living room door? And what if I open that door… and see Jesse sitting there on the sofa with a glass of vodka in her hand, and a smile on her face?

What then? But the flat is dark when I push open the door. And there's a stale smell in the air which must be the six week old corn beef I took out of the fridge and threw in the kitchen bin. I walk straight in, down the passage and into the living room, slumping onto the sofa in the darkness. I sit like that for a long while. I never thought it was possible to think about absolutely nothing. But I do now. Everything is just a huge, total blankness. After a while, I see the small green light winking in the darkness just ahead of me. I reach over for the lamp on the nearby table. The light that it gives is dingy orange. Bloody depressing sort of light, really. It throws huge shadows all around me. The green light ahead continues to wink. It's the AnsaFone—the one I bought for a tenner in the pub. Off the back of a lorry, know what I mean? I push myself up, cross to the telephone and press: "Play."

Why don't I react, when Jesse says: "Baz, it's me."

Why don't I fall back on the sofa when she says: "Look, I'm sorry I haven't been in touch, but there was so much going on inside my head, I had to get away."

Why don't I throw up when she says: "I've been on holiday—with Brian. I love him, Baz. And that's the truth. It was his idea—for us to just go away to Majorca. To his flat. So we could talk it through, find out if what we've got between us is… well, real. I know I've been selfish, I know I've had everyone worried and all that. But I had to do it, Baz. Had to sort out what I really am, where I'm really coming from. Now I know. We're in love, Baz. It's as simple as that. Now we've had this time together, I know that we are. I'm sorry. Really, but…"

And then the line goes dead.

-⊕⊕⊕-

Dead.

I'm walking the streets again. Just walking. It's just before midnight and it's raining again. As I walk I catch sight of myself in a shop window. I'm wearing my black leathers—my "biker" gear, Jesse used to call it with a laugh. Never had a motorbike in my life. The rain makes the leather gleam black, just the way that the black bodywork of those taxis gleam when it's raining. My hair's short, but it's plastered to my head. That hair's brown, but it looks black. The face is white, and looks like it's the face of a ghost.

I'm not sure whether I'm dreaming or not when a car pulls up at the kerb beside me.

It's a Black Cab.

That's why I think it must be a dream, when the driver leans over and pulls down the window. I turn slowly to look at him.

"You don't want to be out walking in this rain, do you?"

I just look.

There's something about this guy's eyes. The way that they reflect the light. While he's waiting for my answer, he licks his lips. Then he says: "Come on, you'll catch your death."

Not aware that I've made the decision, I walk to the Black Cab and open the passenger door. I climb inside, water running in rivulets from my leather jacket. I slam the door and slump down heavily in the seat. There is already water on the floor of the cab from previous customers. In the darkness, it looks like blood. The windscreen wipers are hissing slowly and hypnotically up front as they try to wipe away the (blood) rain.

"Heaton," I say.

The Black Cab pulls away.

"Thought I'd made a mistake," the driver says after a little while.

"Mistake?" The voice that comes out of my mouth doesn't sound like mine at all.

"I thought you were a man, what with the black leathers and everything. Didn't realise you were a woman until I got right up close."

I look at the Black Cab Driver in the rearview mirror. He's looking at me, and licking his lips again.

"Yeah..." I say, and the Black Cab Driver smiles.

We're heading in the opposite direction to Heaton, but I don't say anything. I just look out of the windows at the empty streets and the blurred neon signs of the night clubs and the shop windows.

The Black Cab Driver isn't looking at me in the rearview mirror anymore, but he's still smiling. Concentrating ahead, on our ultimate destination.

My hand tightens on the flick knife in my pocket.

Then I think of Jesse, and that last message on the AnsaFone. She's got herself a new life now, found what she really wanted after all.

My hand relaxes on the knife. Then I clench it again. I keep on doing that; clenching and relaxing, clenching and relaxing. Yes or no? Is it him, or not? Either way, I'll not know for sure until we get where we're going. Will I do it again, make my move before he makes his?

What if it's not him?

But if there is a Black Cab Man—why don't I just let him do it? Maybe it won't be so bad. After all, there's more than one way to be dead.

Yes or no? So many questions.

I clench and unclench the handle of the knife.

And the Black Cab cruises on through the night.

man beast

He could not hide from the moon.

At first, he thought that he could avoid it happening again just by the sheer force of his will. He was known for his strength of character; felt sure as he stood on the cliffs looking out to sea that he could gradually force the evil out of him if only he tried hard enough. Surely that which was within him, that which separated him from being just a beast, was enough. Slowly and inexorably, a violet tinge had stained the cloud fleeced skies above the sea, as the sun had begun its descent past the horizon. He had remained there, looking out to sea. Arms outstretched, teeth gritted.

For a short while, a thin and mysterious ridge of orange-black cloud had passed the Earth Mother's brow; a flock of night birds skimmed the tree line on the cliffs, richly silhouetted against the sundown. The smooth surface of the ocean reflected a huge, wavering bronze image. But Garrick could not be awed by the beauty of the scene from his vantage point.

Because now he was screaming.

Even before the Earth Mother had gone to her resting place, even before the Night Watcher could rise in the full glory of its white, cold, and bloodless beauty, Garrick could feel the changes begin. He could feel it in his blood, in the changed tempo of his heartbeat. He hugged his body, and screamed defiant rage out to sea again. It was there in the sky now, at first pale and ghostly, but now filling with dreadful white luminescence as the Earth Mother sank into the sea. Now the sun was only a strobing orange light on the horizon of the ocean. The water was dark copper.

And with the night, came the final destruction of the strength and defiance which had drawn Garrick to the cliffs in a hopeless confrontation with forces that had consumed and destroyed so many others in the centuries past. A great fear enveloped him, and Garrick sank to his knees.

The changes within were accelerating. His face was changing.

He cried out again, hands like claws flying to his face—seizing the very flesh and trying to prevent it from moulding into that other, horrifying visage. But the inner forces brought about by the Night Watching Moon were contorting and stretching the muscles and the sinew beneath his claw-hands.

He had whirled from the cliffs then, flinging himself away from the hideous moonlight reflection in the sea—and had hurtled back the way he had come, through the woods. Branches lashed at his face as he ran sobbing through the night. In panic, he was trying to run from the changes that were taking place within him, the fear of what was happening almost matched by the self-disgust and loathing at what he knew he must become. The grass beneath seemed to be alive, tangling in his legs, trying to bring him down. He tried to scream again as he fled, but the sound that came out of his mouth was a hideous and fearful travesty of his own voice.

He was lost in the thickets now, smothered in foliage and branches. He clawed to get through, feeling the changes in his spine and legs. He prayed that he would suffocate in this bristling, slashing nightmare before the change was completed. But now he had exploded from the vines and the branches and the underbrush, out onto the rough path which bordered the cliffside. He fell to his knees, and saw with horror in the moonlight the changes that had already been effected.

The real agony began.

He could no longer run as his body twisted and spasmed. He rolled over onto his back, feeling the pain like fire all over his body. That fire was also inside—in his veins, twisting and contorting and reforming. The noise that issued from his throat was a guttural, keening, moaning series of curses towards the shaman whose wrath he had aroused. He cursed the Night Watcher, knowing that in seconds he would love Her. But most of all, he cursed himself for the coward he had become—and his inability to end the suffering by hurling himself from the cliffs into the hissing foam beneath.

Hissing foam.

Hissing breath.

Now, the change was complete. The strange and familiar elation which always preceded the transformation consumed him. He no longer loathed what he had become. The thing that had once been Garrick raised itself from the cliffside path and looked back to the village from which it had come.

When it ran again, it ran as a Beast—not a Paralander. And this time, there was no running away. This was a wild and abandoned race through the night, becoming at one with the Night Watcher. In exaltation, Garrick threw back his head and called homage with his new voice to that Great Enchantress in the sky.

-⊕⊕⊕-

The night air was vibrant with the excited hubbub of voices in the town square.

Two hundred Paralanders had gathered there, their attention focussed on the second floor building of the Civic Building. The townspeople were not armed, but many of them carried torches. They guttered and billowed in the wind which had risen in the night; casting bizarre, shifting shadows against the walls of the surrounding buildings.

Eight year old Jivio, son of Caron, sat on his father's shoulders—giving him a better view over the heads of the crowd. His eyes wide in excitement, Jivio suddenly caught sight of a movement on the balcony.

"The Prefect!"

Caron patted the boy's leg and told him to hush, but his call had been taken up by the crowd as the Prefect finally emerged. Their leader held his arms wide, and the excited murmuring of the crowd died away as the tall, dignified figure stepped forward and braced himself on the balcony rail.

"The Beast has been seen again."

Now there was only silence in the town square. A new feeling had become manifest in the crowd, a feeling that had so far been kept at bay by the safety of numbers. Young though he was, Jivio could sense it himself: Fear.

"On the cliffs overlooking the sea," continued The Prefect. "No one has been attacked yet, but it is in the nature of the Beast to kill. As you all know, an animal such as this has not been seen since the Dark Days. But the Elders and I have discovered that a shaman has cast a curse on one of our number. On nights of the full moon—as tonight—the victim will transform into a Werebeast. The shaman has been interrogated and punished according to our custom. And he has revealed the identity of the cursed one."

The Prefect paused for effect. No such pause was necessary. The crowd remained silent and tense. Somewhere, a night bird called.

"It is Garrick, son of the Ironsmith."

Now the murmuring began again. Garrick was a young man, much respected in the village.

"The creature which Garrick has become is the vilest, most savage thing ever to walk upon this Earth. All of its kind were considered long since dead. Only the magic of the shaman and his curse could revisit such a horror upon us. But... I have consulted with the parents of Garrick. And they have given their consent to what must be done."

In the sky to the east, the full moon gloated over the village—silver-white and promising death.

"We must find and destroy the abominable creature which Garrick has become!"

There was no wild outcry from the crowd. Only a sad and grim resolve. From the main entrance, the marshalls began to emerge. They were carrying weapons. The crowd awaited their instructions. Soon, the Hunt would begin.

-⊕⊕⊕-

Garrick crouched in the bushes on the summit of the hill which overlooked the town. Moonlight gleamed on his flanks. From this vantage point, he could see the flickering lights of the villagers' torches as they approached from below. An alien sound issued from his throat, as he slouched back into the darkness. Then he turned and crashed through the thick undergrowth towards the other side of the knoll.

Another semi-circle of torches were moving up the hill towards him.

He was trapped.

Enraptured by the velvet darkness of night and the new sensations of his altered form, Garrick had been careless and had given away his hiding place. He threw back his head and looked to the Great Enchantress in the sky. But her face was blank, white and unyielding. He could expect no help.

Plunging back through the undergrowth to his former position, he could see that the torches from the town were much nearer. In minutes, they would be upon him. A raw, uncontrollable emotion began to boil in his breast. Something which he had never experienced before in such intensity, something which was more savage even than the need to kill for food. It was a primal emotion which seemed to be so natural for his new, mutated body. He welcomed it—and embraced it. It was a feeling of savage, destructive rage.

He would kill the first creature that came over the rim of the hill.

-⊕⊕⊕-

Jivio was filled with excitement.

He tugged urgently at his father's hand as the line of villagers ascended the hill. Caron kept a firm grip on the small figure, and began to question whether he should have allowed him to come on The Hunt. This was surely no place for a boy. He could see that Jivio's eyes were filled with an urge for bloodlust. In one so young, it saddened him deeply.

Suddenly, they had reached the bushes which fringed the top of the hill. Torches thrust out before them, the villagers advanced over the rim and through the undergrowth in the moonlight until they had reached a small clearing. They could see the wavering torches of the other villagers who were, even now, advancing through the bushes on the other side of the hill towards them. But of the Beast, there was no sign.

"Father! Look!" cried Jivio, "the others!" In a sudden surge of excitement, the boy broke free from his father and dashed across the clearing.

"Jivio! No!"

But his father's warning was too late.

A dark, hunched figure which had been crouching behind a gnarled, uprooted tree trunk suddenly reared out with arms held high above the terrified boy. Jivio swerved in alarm, twisted and fell heavily to the ground. The Man Beast, silhouetted against the full, harsh light of the moon, lunged downwards to take him.

The first silver-tipped arrow hissed through the air, thunking into the Beast's left side. The impact of the arrow sent the creature whirling away from Jivio. Enraged, the Man Beast twisted and writhed, trying to regain its balance. It tore in pain at the feathered shaft—exposing its unprotected back to the second and third arrows. They sank deep, shafts quivering.

Garrick spun, clutching at the air, screaming his rage and pain to the Night Watcher above. But the Enchantress had deserted him. Dark ribbons of blood laced his body and sprayed into the undergrowth. A further volley of arrows hissed through the night and found their mark. Garrick fell to his knees.

A darkness that was deeper than Night was falling behind his eyes. But he would take the child with him. The Werebeast groped for the small form lying on the grass.

But Caron leaped forward, grabbed his son by the arm and yanked him to safety as the Man Beast clutched at empty air. In a last and furious burst of hate, the thing suddenly stood erect again. It remained frozen in that act of hate and defiance, its body pierced in a dozen places. It tried to raise its arms to the sky—but could not. With a final, defiant cry, the Man Beast keeled over and tumbled to the ground, snapping the shafts of several arrows in its death throes.

The gathered crowd stood silently and watched as the final breath of life left its body. Garrick—the Paralander—was at peace.

Cautiously now, the villagers drew closer, their torches forming a blazing circle around the fallen creature. Caron pulled his son forward until they were standing directly above it. The Beast's eyes were staring, but sightless. Jivio clung to his father's waist as if fearing that it would suddenly leap to its feet once again. But the memory of his son's bloodlust—an urge which every Paralander learned to quell before adulthood—was still burned graphically into Caron's mind. He pushed the boy closer to the ruined thing which lay before them.

"Look well, Jivio. Creatures such as these walked our Earth in the Dark Days. Abominable monsters which would destroy everything. They only lived to kill."

"It's... horrible, father."

"Horrible, yes. A creature which lived and breathed hatred. And revelled in the Bloodlust—in The Hunt. Just as you did tonight."

The other villagers remained silent, sensing that here was a valuable lesson for the young one to learn. Many fathers wished that their own sons were here tonight.

"Do you wish to be one with such as this?"

"I'm sorry, father." Jivio pulled back to his father, his eyes still filled with a fascinated dread of the thing on the ground. A dread not only of its horrifying physical appearance—but of what the the thing represented. But Caron could also see the look of repentance in his son's eyes. He pulled him close again, smoothing the rumpled fur at the base of Jivio's two delicately pointed ears. He was lucky to have such a fine boy. Jivio looked up at his father's face. It was a strong, dignified face with elegant whiskers and pointed snout. The guttering torch in his father's claw cast a reddish hue on his tousled mane as it ruffled in the wind.

"I can't look at it anymore, father," said Jivio. "What kind of creature is it?"

"It was called a Man," replied his father.

the song my sister sang

FOR MOST PEOPLE LIVING ALONG THE NORTH-EAST COAST, THE BIG EVENT THAT SUMMER WAS WHAT HAPPENED TO THE COAST-LINE AND ITS WILD-LIFE.

Just say the words *Edda Dell'Orso,* and see what kind of reaction you get from the local fishermen who ply their trade out of North Shields Quay. The captain and crew of that ill-fated tanker never made it out of the wreck alive, so the inquiry could only reach an open verdict; even though they'd had the specialists and the engineers and the aquamarine people from Blyth out there to try and find out why the tanker had drifted so close to shore. Close enough to become grounded; close enough to gash one of its main tanks on seabed rocks, close enough to cover the entire length of beach for ten miles on either side with a smothering sea-blanket of crude oil.

That, they'll tell you, was the horror that marred last summer.

They're wrong. The real horror wasn't the fouled-up beaches and the near-death of the local fishing industry. It might have all begun with the *Edda Dell'Orso,* but the real horror was... how do I put it?... much more personal than that.

It happened in the abandoned swimming pool on Tynemouth beach. Derelict and boarded up. Rotting under the salt-spray and the sun and the cruel sea winters. That's where the real horror began.

And where I might have lost my sanity.

Very soon now, I'll know for sure.

The open-air swimming pool had been a real crowd-puller, from its opening at the turn of the century right up until its closure in the 1960s. Built in an oval-shape, below the cliffs on Tynemouth beach, its sluices were open to the sea. One side faced the cliffs, the other out to the sea; the rounded end of that oval looking down on clustering rocks where children climbed and hunted for crabs and winkles. Back then, the pool itself had been tiled in blue and white; the surface of the water glittering under the summer sun like molten silver. I played there as a kid, with my sister, just before the place was closed. And every time I try to get a picture of it as it was then, I always seem to get *sounds* instead. The sound of the sea, beyond the walls and in the sluices. The cries of children splashing and diving matched by the wheeling cries of seagulls overhead. The cliff side of the pool was bordered by the pumping station and its chlorine tanks. There was a side-gate there, with a steep and tightly winding set of stairs that took you straight up to the promenade above. The main building housed the changing area. Inside was a maze of mini-corridors with individual tiled cubicles. Plastic curtains hung from the overhead rails. Again, the sounds come back to me. It seemed that the place was always filled with laughter; echoing screeches as kids ran and played; the slap of bare feet on tiled floors as they dashed in and out of those cubicles, consumed by holiday excitement. Lots of Scottish accents, I remember.

Bloody funny, that. The accents, I mean.

Every "factory-fortnight", all the shipyard workers from the River Tyne would pack the family up to Scotland for the traditional family holiday in cheap digs on the sea front. At the same time, all the shipyard workers from the Clyde would do the same thing, and head down here to Tynemouth and Whitley Bay. Staying in the same cheap bed and breakfasts, and doing pretty much everything their Geordie compatriots would be doing north of the border. I often wondered why everyone didn't just stay where they were. Anyway, I seemed to make a lot of Scottish holiday friends back then. Close as blood-brothers for two weeks, then gone forever after. Even though Amy and I were local kids, that swimming pool was an exotic visit for us; maybe two or three times a year, in a good summer.

And then that terrible, terrible thing happened.

No one ever told me this, but I reckon it was Amy's death that led to the closure of the pool. Two weeks after the funeral, the gates were chained. Thirty-odd years later, and the place still haunted me.

First, let me tell you what happened on that Thursday morning when the *Edda Dell'Orso* ran aground.

I guess you must have seen the television news reports about the oil slick that washed ashore, and what it was doing to the seagulls and the guillemots. I've heard it said that more people were enraged about what was happening to the seabirds than what had happened to the crew. Right or wrong, I guess people felt that it was the mens' fault at root, and that the "dumb" animals were suffering the consequences. I'm an animal lover; that's why I spend so much of my spare time working with the RSPCA and the RSPB; but I would never put animals before people, the way that some animal lovers do. Anyway, there was one hell of an outcry.

And I was down there on Tynemouth beach with the other volunteers, doing my bit. Trying my best not to scare to death the oiled-up gulls and the other seabirds which were bobbing on that tide of black filth; carefully trudging waist-deep through all that foamed-up crude oil in my waders and trying to get the poor buggers passed back to shore without getting my eyes pecked out. A difficult job in more ways than one; mess around too much trying to get your hands on a seabird and the chances are that it'll die of fright before you're able to get it back to where it can be cleaned. Same thing with the cleaning operation. The washing and cleaning is a gruelling, painstaking operation. No matter how careful you are, it's an arduous and distressing experience for them, and it wouldn't be the first time I've had a bird suddenly just die in my hands while I was trying to get the oil and the shit out of its plumage, no matter how gentle I was trying to be.

It was a particularly distressing experience on that Thursday morning. The oil was so thick close to shore that the waves just weren't "breaking" anymore. Undulating black ripples flowed around me as I worked. A lot of the birds had been early-morning feeders, and we hadn't got there until just after ten. Consequently, there were a lot of dead gulls as we made our slow way south down the beach. A lot had drowned in that oily morass, others had struggled to be free, their wings hopelessly gummed until they'd died of exhaustion.

And all the time we worked our way down the beach, I was aware that we were getting nearer and nearer to the abandoned swimming pool. I tried to keep its presence out of my mind, tried not to let those memories overwhelm me. To a great extent, it worked. The needs of those birds were so immediate that they outweighed the bitter memories. But even though the waves weren't breaking because of the heavy overlay of oil, I could still hear the sussurant rush of the sea further out, and, every once in a while, it brought it all back to me with a vividity that made me want to turn around and wade back to the beach. Luckily, there were twelve of us out there that morning, all relying on each other; so the thought of letting them all down, in what was a painstaking team effort, kept me going.

Then someone cried: "Over there!"

I turned to look back. It was Lorna Jackson. At first I thought she'd hurt herself, when I saw that there was a dark smudge right across her brow. Then I realised that it was oil, wiped there accidentally by her own hand. She was pointing urgently down the beach and when I turned to look I could see what had so alarmed her. A seabird had become trapped in one of the swimming pool's sluices; a three foot-round aperture set into the base of the pool's sea-wall. The rocks and the wall were stained by years of green and yellow sea-encrustment, but now the area around that sluice and the rim of the aperture were smeared with the *Edda Dell'Orso's* jettisoned filth. Right in the middle of that opening, wings flapping in distress as it bobbed up and down on a black mass, was a gull. Unlike most of the birds we'd come across, it still had a glimmer of white in its wings. Perhaps it had just come down on the rocks beside the sea-wall, too hungry for pickings to take any notice of its fellows' fate; but it didn't seem to be as badly oiled-up and that in itself made it a prime candidate for rescue.

"I'll get it!" I yelled, before anyone else could respond, and surged back to the beach. It was maybe fifty yards to the sea-wall.

I've thought about why I responded so quickly.

Sometimes I think it has to do with everything I've just told you. The bird not being so badly oiled-up and everything. Now I know it had to do with something altogether different. There were a million and one reasons why I should have kept away from that swimming pool after what happened to Amy. I've said it was a place that haunted me. More than that. On the grim grey days of my depressions, when nothing in the world seemed to make sense anymore, or when I was tottering on the edge of that pit of melancholy, almost ready to let myself fall... my thoughts always returned to that swimming pool, no matter how much I tried to prevent it.

Maybe that day I had a chance to grasp the nettle.

Perhaps I saw the opportunity to do something I'd thought about doing for a long time.

Not so much bearding the lion in its den, because there was no fucking lion in there. Just the echoes of those bygone days, keeping me awake at night. Now, I had a chance to go where I'd dreaded. Does that make sense? I didn't want to go in there, *couldn't* have gone in there just with the idea of laying my personal demons to rest. But hell, now there was a *reason*. That bird would die. And maybe... just maybe... setting foot in there might go some way to easing my pain. Even as I watched, the bird was being sucked in through the sluice, out of sight and into that hateful place. There was a collective moan behind me as it vanished, but I turned as I ran, oil splattering the sand from my waders, and I waved:

"Okay. It'll be okay. I've got it."

There was a concrete ramp on the beach, maybe a hundred feet long, leading right up to the rusted and padlocked front gate of the swimming pool. The fence was wire-mesh, so I knew that I could climb it if I had to. Not knowing whether my sense of urgency had to do with the plight of the bird, or my need to just get in and out of there as quickly as possible, I hopped the last few feet on either foot as I pulled off my oil-stained waders and dropped them on the ramp. I yanked at the padlock and a fine cloud of brown rust furled and blew away on the sea-breeze. The fence seemed to vibrate away on all sides; a strange noise, like the "singing" that sometimes comes from telegraph wires. That sound affected me badly and I didn't know why. Back on the beach, the others were continuing with their job, but were still watching me. Gritting my teeth, I hooked my fingers through the mesh and climbed.

The fence was about twenty feet high, and I had no problem with heights. But my heart was hammering as I swung my legs over the top and began the climb down to the other side. When I hit bottom, I still clung to that fence, sweat making my shirt stick to my back and running in itchy rivulets down my face. I screwed my eyes shut. Then, with an angry curse I pushed myself around, ran past the empty life-belt stand, and came face to face with the cracked and rusted fountain that I had played in as a kid.

Back then, it had been a wonderful conical pyramid of bright blue and white paint, standing by the shallow end of the open air pool. There had been steps there, so that the kids could climb up and stand beneath a glittering curtain of breath-catching, cold sea water. Now, it was just a cracked and stained mass. I barely had a chance to take it in. Or the graffiti-ridden walls and the yawning, empty doors and windows of the changing area block off to my right.

All I could see was the swimming pool itself.

No more glittering water. No more sparkling blue and white tiles.

The surface of the pool was a black mass, undulating and shifting as if there was something alive beneath it. Rubble, shattered spars of wood and tangled ironwork had been dumped into that pool, but it was impossible to make anything out clearly. Hundreds of gallons of the *Edda Dell'Orso's* crude oil had been sucked in through the sea-sluices and had coated the entire surface. But it was not this that made the sight so obscene. It was what the tanker's spilled load had brought with it. The tide and the clinging oil had sucked more than one sea bird in through that sluice. There were birds all over that undulating mass. Maybe a hundred, maybe more. It was impossible to tell. Most of them were dead, and the only flash of white feathers I could see was down by the sluice itself, where the bird had been sucked in. It flapped and struggled as it was carried further into that seabird's graveyard on the rippling ebony surface.

I ran forward, knowing that there was no way I could wade into that pool. I'd have to find something to pull the gull into the side. I glanced at the abandoned changing rooms as I ran alongside the pool to where the bird was struggling. The echoing sounds of kids laughing and of bare feet slapping on cold tile floors somehow seemed very real to me. Now, I didn't know whether I was doing the right thing by coming in here, or whether I was just going to make the dreams and the memories even worse than they already were. It was replaying in my head now, the day when Amy died. I didn't want it to, but just being in this place brought it back with a horrifying intensity.

It had been my birthday party the day before, and Amy had stolen all the attention as usual. It was supposed to be my day. A special day when Mam and Dad could show me that they loved me just as much as her. But sure enough, just when it seemed that everything was going well; when the kids were all playing and I was feeling really good—the party was brought to a halt when Amy told everyone that she wanted to sing her song and do her dance. And I remember looking at Mam and thinking: "They won't let her do it. They won't let her spoil the party. Any other time, any other day. But not now. Not at MY birthday party..."

And Mam had told everyone to be quiet and had picked Amy up and put her on the table, and even though the other kids had seen it all before, they were made to be quiet, and Amy was asked... was ASKED... to do her song and her dance. I could have cried and begged and ranted, in the way that a nine year old will, but I was just so hurt. So hurt, that I couldn't say a thing. My throat was constricted as I stood there and watched Amy be made the centre of attention as she sang...

I tried to push those memories out of my mind, but it was impossible. The seagull's movements had become weaker. It raised one oil-covered wing as if it was trying to wave at me. In another moment, it must succumb.

And Amy began to sing:

"Ain't she sweet? I ask you, ain't she neat? Now I ask you very con-fi-dentially: Ain't! She! Sweet!"

Her little feet began to pound out that tap-dance rhythm on the table and the kids shuffled and watched and God how I wanted that table to collapse beneath her, or for her to miss a step and fall and begin crying and...

There was a broken spar of wood lying by the side of the pool. I picked it up. The wood was so rotten that it was crumbling in my hands even as I hoisted it out over the surface of the oil.

The next day we had gone to the beach. The sun was shining and there were lots of families all encamped on the same stretch of sand that I'd just come from. But inside, I was feeling over-shadowed in a way that I'd often felt. I wanted to be alone, that's why I asked Mam and Dad if I could go on up to the swimming pool. Dad had insisted that I take Amy with me. After all, I was the older brother and it was my job to look after my little sister. That constricted feeling was in my throat again. Couldn't I do anything without having her along in tow? Didn't they realise that I wanted some time for myself? I sulked, but they made me take her. We were already in swimming costumes, so there was no need to use the changing facilities.

"Keep in the shallow end," Mam had said.

I was able to reach the seagull with the spar, but the bird began to panic, even though I was being as gentle as I possibly could. Its one free wing began to flap and splatter the oil, and I began to make shushing noises as if I was dealing with a small child.

"Easy... easy..."

I didn't want to take her. They shouldn't have made me take her. What the hell were they thinking about, Mam and Dad? I was only nine years old, Amy was seven. What did they think I was? Amy's nurse-maid?

Slowly and gradually, I drew the seagull in to the side. Its wing ceased to flap. It looked at me with one blank eye, giving in to its fate.

There were other kids there. Kids my own age. Amy wanted to play, began to cry when I said she had to stay there in the shallow end while I went to play with those others. I knew why she wanted to come. She just wanted to be the centre of attention, as usual; would probably sing that bloody song again and just embarrass me. So I left her there while I made new friends. And the first I knew that something had gone wrong was when that woman screamed...

Still making that shushing sound, I reached out and gently took the bird by its wing. It didn't resist. It just kept looking at me as if it knew that I was going to rend it apart and devour it. I let go of the spar and it slid soundlessly beneath the surface of the oil. I had the bird now and lifted it to the side; long tacky threads of oil spattered and flurried in the sea breeze.

...and when I looked back down to the shallow end, I could see three men ploughing through the water; could see one of them lunging down and dragging something from the bottom and the woman was just screaming and screaming, making the other kids down there begin crying too, as...

The seagull was dead. Its head lolled on its neck. Its one eye was still blank and staring. I could feel that constriction in my throat again; just as if I was nine years old once more. What had I done by coming into this place again? How could I have been so stupid as to believe that I could exorcise those memories? I lay the bird at the poolside and crouched down on my haunches, looking back to the shallow end.

And then, about six feet out from where I sat, something moved beneath the oil.

I saw it from the corner of my eye. At first, I thought it might be sunlight reflecting on that ebony surface. I stared at the place where I thought I'd seen movement. It came again. Something that flapped out of the oil, smaller than a seagull's wing, but with the same kind of movement. Another sea bird, trapped beneath the surface and trying to rise. I looked for the spar, then remembered that I'd let it drop into the pool. Frantically, I searched around for something else. Now, it seemed as if there was a chance to make good on my failure. If I could save even one bird from this morass, then somehow it seemed that my desperation need not be so intense. There was nothing at hand. Perhaps back there in the changing rooms…?

But then there was new movement, something so strange and graceful and eerie that I could only sit there and watch.

A swan was rising from the oil.

What I had at first assumed to be a wing was a swan's head breaking the surface. Because now that swan's head was rising and I could see its long and graceful black-coated neck as it emerged slow and dripping from the pool. But there was something wrong with that neck now. It had been broken in the middle. It was bending at an impossible angle as the neck emerged from the oil and…

This was no swan's head, no swan's neck.

It was a hand, and an arm; now bending at the elbow as something came up out of the pool.

A head crested from the oil. Long hair, black and dripping.

And all I could do was sit, frozen and terrified, as the woman finally stood up in the pool, so completely covered in black filth that she might have been a statue carved out of basalt. She was motionless now, facing me, as if waiting for me to do something. But all I could do was sit there and stare. The woman's eyes opened, two white orbs in that hideous black visage.

I opened my mouth, but I couldn't say a word.

And then the woman began to sing.

The voice was ragged and halting, as if she had been under that oil for a long, long time, and had perhaps forgotten how to use her voice properly. Her face remained blank, but her eyes never left me as she sang.

"Ain't... she... sweet? I ask you... ain't she neat...?"

That's when I must have fainted, because it seemed that the black oil was everywhere then, filling my eyes. The horror of what I was seeing and hearing was too unbearable. I remember hearing:

"...ask you very con-fi-dentially..."

And then there was nothing.

There were no dreams, no nightmares. Just this terrible buzzing in my ears and a dreadful taste in my mouth. I knew then, even in that dark place behind my eyes, that I was asleep at home and in bed. I had been drinking again. And when I finally surfaced from that sleep, I would have a king-sized hangover. I would wake up and realise that everything about the swimming pool and the thing that had emerged from it was an alcohol-induced nightmare. Something was wrong with the mattress on my bed. It felt too hard, too uncomfortable. I struggled to wake... and felt concrete. Dislocated and afraid, I jerked out of that sleep and struggled to rise.

I was still lying by the side of the swimming pool.

It was still daytime.

The oil lay thick and dark and heavy on the surface of the pool.

And not ten feet from where I lay, the young woman was still there.

She had pulled herself to the edge of the pool, had tried to crawl out of that black mass, but her strength had given out at the last. She had hauled her upper body out of the pool, her arms stretched before her and her fingers clawing at the concrete. Oil lay spattered around her; thick streamers of the damned stuff. But her lower body and legs were still in the pool, hidden beneath the oil.

Instinctively I recoiled, backing away until I sat heavily and groggily on the concrete steps which led up to the derelict changing rooms. The ringing was still in my ears and I struggled to contain my nausea. I looked at my watch and realised that I couldn't have been unconscious for more than a few minutes. Remembering the others back on the beach, I decided to run and get help.

But then the woman groaned and one hand groped feebly as she tried to haul herself the rest of the way out of the pool.

I hesitated, thinking: *This can't be happening.*

The woman groaned again, unable to pull herself any further.

But she's alive. The least you can do is get her out of that pool and then you can run for help.

Unsteadily, I moved back to the poolside.

"It's alright... you're all right... "

I didn't want to touch her, was still struggling to contain the feeling that I hadn't woken up yet and that this was an ongoing nightmare. I'd had a terrible shock when I'd seen her emerging like that, but I must have imagined that she was singing that song. I *must* have. The woman tried to lift her head to look at me, but was too exhausted. Fumbling at her face, she tried to brush the straggling long hair away.

"Please..." Her voice was so faint that I could hardly hear it. *"Help me."*

And without being aware that I'd made the decision to help, I was suddenly kneeling beside her. I took one arm. It felt terribly cold. I pulled, but the woman hadn't the strength to assist, and she remained half-in, half-out of the pool. Standing, I took her under the armpits and hauled her from the oil, leaving a great black trail on the concrete lip. For the first time, I realised that she was naked; her frame slender and slight. Perhaps it was the oil coating her from head to foot. When she was clear of the pool, I turned her over and helped her to sit.

"You wait here," I began. "I'm going to get help."

"No," she replied, gagging as oil flowed from her lips. My God, was she going to die?

"You're going to be all right, I promise. But I need to get a doctor and..."

And the woman opened her eyes to look at me.

"Dean," she said, calling me by my first name.

Everything is fractured after that. I've tried to put the pieces together in my mind, but a lot of it just doesn't make sense. I seem to remember crying and laughing at the same time, calling my sister's name. That might be wrong; that might just be all in my mind. But I do remember those eyes, because suddenly that was all I could see. The whites of those eyes were somehow shocking, set into that black-oil sculpted face. The irises were so green that they sparked, and looking at them somehow hurt my own eyes. They were growing larger as I looked. And then I seem to remember something to do with the side-gate to the swimming pool; the gate behind the changing block beyond which lay a steep flight of stone stairs, leading up the cliffs to the seafront parade and its rows of hotels.

Something to do with a length of corroded steel pipe that was lying around.

Something to do with enormous effort on my part.

I think, although I can't be sure, that I smashed the lock and chain on that side gate. And we must have climbed those stairs. We must have, because that's where I'd parked my car. I must have wrapped my own jacket around her, helped her into that car. Perhaps there were people up there; staring in astonishment at us. I seem to recall faces. Perhaps not.

I must have driven home to my flat.

Because the next thing I remember clearly is standing in my living room, just outside the bathroom. I was staring at that door, and when everything around me registered properly again, I realised that the shower was on. I could hear the water hissing. I raised my hand to shove the door open, but something made me stop. I looked around, trying to convince myself that I wasn't still dreaming. Yes, this was my living room; just as I'd left it earlier that day. When I tried to move, my legs were weak. I staggered, clutching at the sofa, and ended up at the window looking down to the street, six floors below. It was evening, and my car was in its usual place.

And there was a dark stain on the pavement, from the car to the communal entrance. As if someone had spilled something there. From this distance, it looked horribly like blood.

I squinted at my watch. I'd lost about nine hours.

I braced my hand on the window sill and shook my head. When I turned and looked around again, I expected somehow that everything would have changed; that this strange dream would take a different turn. But the living room was just as I'd left it that morning before heading off to the beach. I suddenly felt nauseous and took a step back towards the bathroom. Fear cramped my stomach with the sudden knowledge that Amy... she... whatever... was in there. It acted like an inner safety valve, preventing me from throwing up then and there.

What *was* in there?

"Amy…?"

When the telephone rang, it was like some kind of electric shock. My teeth clamped shut so hard that I nicked my tongue, and my mouth filled with blood. With the second ring, I realised that I wasn't going to have a heart attack. By the third, the fear had returned with a sickening intensity. It suddenly became important that whoever or whatever was in the bathroom not be disturbed by the sound. Staggering across the room, I snatched up the receiver.

"Dean?"

It was Lorna.

"Yes…"

"What the HELL are you playing at?"

"Sorry?"

"We've been worried sick about you. What happened to you? Where did you go?"

"Go? I'm not sure what… I mean…"

"You ran off to the pool to get that poor bird, and then you just vanished from the face of the Earth. Have you any idea what trouble you've caused? When you didn't come back we went to look for you and you were nowhere… nowhere… *to be seen. Christ, we've had the coastguard and the police out. We thought you'd gone into that fucking pool, or something. They've sent people down to drag the bloody thing. So what happened ...?"*

"I'm sorry, Lorna. Something… something happened… and I had to leave and…"

"You had to leave*? I mean, without saying anything to anyone? Without telling any of us? You… you* shit*! We've been worried sick. Well…"* Unmistakably, anger building out of control. *"look… look… you can telephone the fucking police and the coastguard and tell them to call off the search, and while you're at it you can tell them why you…"*

"Goodbye, Lorna."

I put down the receiver. My hand was shaking badly.

Beyond the bathroom door, the sound of the shower had suddenly ceased.

It had been turned off.

I stood there, looking at the door. A part of me knew that I should just turn and get out of that apartment as fast as I could. But I couldn't move. I tried, but I was rooted to the spot.

Something was going to happen.

And there was nothing I could do.

I tried to speak, but my voice choked in my throat.

My heart was hammering. I could feel the blood pulsing in my temples.

And that's when I heard the singing again. So low as to be almost inaudible. Sly, and hideously mischievous.

"Ain't... she... sweet?"

"Oh Christ, Amy. I didn't mean to leave you in the pool."

Somehow, my voice sounded like the voice of the nine-year old I'd once been.

"I... ask... you. Ain't... she... neat?"

"It can't be you. Is it you? Amy, I'm so *sorry...*"

The sorrow erupted from me. Thirty years of contained grief. The tears flowed down my cheeks to mingle with the blood in my mouth. It was the salt taste of the sea.

"Dean," said that voice, with a sibilant echo that must surely be impossible in there.

"Yes?"

"Come and open the door, Dean."

"Oh God, Amy. I can't ... "

"Come and open the door!"

"I'm afraid..."

There was laughter then. Girlish laughter; low but still somehow echoing, and with a terrifying sense of intent.

"Come let me taste your tears."

Suddenly, I was moving. There was no conscious effort on my part. The voice was drawing me to it, and there was nothing I could do.

Through the blurred vision of my grief and my terror, I saw my own hand reach forward for the bathroom door as I stumbled forward.

The telephone began to ring again. It sounded thin and distant, nothing to do with me at all.

I watched my hand turn the handle, saw the door swing open.

Beyond, I could see only steam from the shower. Some inner and distant part of me knew that there shouldn't be steam in here at all. There was never steam when I showered. But it was there, and all the details of the bathroom were shrouded in that swirling, undulating mass. Ragged whisps and rapidly dissolving tentacles swirled over the threshold into the living room, dissolving before they reached me.

"Come here, Dean," said something hidden from sight.

In terror and grief, I stepped into the bathroom and felt the warm embrace of the steam.

And that's when everything becomes fractured again.

Something happened in there, but it's as if my mind is either incapable of comprehending it, or that the horror was so great that it shuts off every time I try to understand what was being done to me. I'm trying to think of it now; trying to get impressions, but nothing will register. I know it's in there, locked in my head, but nothing will come.

When it ended, the nightmare had changed location again.

The first thing I became aware of was the wind. It smelled of salt and seaweed, and when my vision cleared I could see the sea. I was standing on a beach, and moonlight was shining on the water. When I looked down, I could see that I was standing on shale, not sand. I'd spent enough time on the north-east coast to know that I was a great deal further south than Tynemouth or Whitley Bay. There was no oil on the water.

I turned to look away from the sea and to the ragged cliffs behind me. The movement was too much for me, as if I'd been standing in the same position for hours and my limbs had frozen. I fell to my knees, retching. When I'd finished, something made me look back to the sea.

She was standing in the water, silently watching me.

I knew that she hadn't been there before, that there was no way she could have suddenly appeared like that. But there she was, the water troughing around her naked legs. The moonlight silhouetted her from behind. I could see no details of her face or, thank God, those eyes.

"Please..." I began.

I knew that if she began to sing that song again, I must surely go mad.

But she didn't say a word. She just stood motionless, watching me.

I lowered my head once more, feeling the nausea swelling within me.

When I looked up again, she had moved closer. But it was as if she hadn't moved at all. As if she had somehow *floated* closer to shore. The water foamed around her shins, but she was still in the same motionless position.

"Dean."

The voice echoed impossibly once more. I moaned and waited for the end.

"Stand up."

I staggered to my feet. I had no will to resist.

"Come closer."

I took three shambling steps to the water's edge. We were perhaps six feet apart, but I still could not see her face. I don't know how long we just stood like that, facing each other. A part of me wondered if we'd stay like that forever, frozen in that tableau; with the hushing of the sea, the smell of salt and weed, and the flickering of moonlight on the water.

"Stay away from Deep Water," she said at last.

"...why?..." I barely recognised my own small voice.

"My sisters and I feed there."

This time, she did move. Three languid steps towards me. For the first time, I realised that there was no trace of oil on her naked body. Her long hair moved around her shoulders in the wind, as if it had a life of its own. And now I could see that her eyes were closed. I knew then that she could still see; knew with utter certainty that she could see into my mind and read everything that was there.

She raised a graceful arm and placed her hand on my shoulder.

It's difficult to tell you what happened next.

I can't really tell you how, but I *felt* something then.

Something hideous.

She remained in that position, and there was no physical change in her. But that touch of her hand brought images in my mind; images that still haunt my nightmares.

I seemed to see something that looked like a sea anemone; something with tentacle-like clusters surrounding barbed and voracious mouth-parts, moving greedily like the mandibles of a crab or a sea spider. I felt the cold touch of scales, the foetid breath of something that fed on the corpses of the drowned. I don't know if I screamed or not, but I felt that I must have.

My senses still swimming, I watched her turn from me and walk back into the sea. She moved with that same languid grace, the hair swirling around her head. She didn't dive into the water, didn't swim away. She just kept on walking until the water had reached her shoulders. When it reached her neck, she half-turned her head to look back at me as if she was going to say something else.

But she said nothing.

And in the next moment, the water covered her head and she was gone.

I wasn't aware that I'd fallen to my knees.

For a long, long time I just knelt there, staring out across the moonlit water, listening to the wind.

When dawn began to creep up behind me, I staggered to my feet and headed for the rough path that wound up the cliffs. My car was parked up there, crude oil smeared on the back seat.

I didn't look back at the sea when I climbed into the car and headed home.

So there you have it.

End of story.

And all I have are the bad dreams and the unanswered questions. Was it Amy? Or was it something that only looked human when it wanted to, and could pretend to be anyone it wanted to be by reading minds? Was it my sister, a grown woman thirty years later? Or one of those whom Ulysses had heard, when he was lashed to the mast of his ship while his companions' ears were filled with wax? In the darkest moments, I wonder if those who drown become what I saw and experienced that day.

Come let me taste your tears, she had said.

What did she find there that prevented her from doing what she was created to do?

Stay away from Deep Water. My sisters and I feed there.

Why did she spare me and warn me?

The beaches are clean again. I spend a lot of time down at Tynemouth, on the beach and looking out to sea. Usually at night. The water has a strange attraction for me. I know that one day soon, I'll have to go out there, no matter what she said.

Tonight, I heard sounds across the dark water. That's why I've written all of this down.

It sounded like whales, calling to each other.

But perhaps it was just another siren-song as the sisters moved through the deep.

They've demolished the swimming pool now. It was sealed and drained before the work could commence. No one expected what they found in there. It was the Captain of the *Edda Dell'Orso* and one of the crew. Sucked in through the sluices with the oil slick. They say their faces were eaten away by fish. Except that there were no living fish in that black morass.

So many unanswered questions.

And as much as I used to hate the song my sister sang, there are times when I stand on that beach in the moonlight and with the sea-wind coming in cold and harsh from the east, I pray with all my heart that I might hear it again. Sung in that strange, echoing voice.

Some day soon, I'll find out whether it really did happen, or whether I've just lost my mind. I'll hire a skip, and head for Deep Water. Maybe then, if she's watching and she can still taste my tears, she'll have to do what she refrained from doing that day.

I won't be afraid, I won't resist.

Because perhaps... just perhaps... I'll have the answers to all those questions before the waters close over my head and I submit to her caress.

yesterday i flew with the birds

JESSICA HAD BEEN TEACHING HER NEW CLASS OF SEVEN-YEAR-OLDS FOR THREE WEEKS BEFORE SHE FIRST NOTICED THAT THERE WAS SOMETHING DIFFERENT ABOUT FRANKIE.

It began in the schoolyard. Jessica was on yard duty, strolling amidst a throng of children as shrill screams and laughter danced and echoed in the warm summer air.

Frankie was standing beside the railings, looking up at the deep blue, cloudless sky. A flock of pigeons circled overhead, the sun glinting silver on their wings. None of the other children appeared to notice Frankie as he stared silently upwards, and the sight conjured up a strange emotion in Jessica; a sad feeling which dissipated before she could grasp and analyse it. Fascinated by the small boy who seemed so distanced from the other children, Jessica walked over to him, noticing the look of intense concentration on his face as he scanned the sky; saw his expression turn to annoyance when she approached—as if she was interrupting something important. Before she could speak, Frankie had run away.

In the weeks to follow, Frankie remained a mystery. A small, isolated and generally unresponsive boy from an apparently happy family background who preferred to be left alone and whose wishes appeared to be respected by his classmates. Frankie seemed disinterested with school life and all it had to offer. School work was a chore which had to be endured. And when playtime came around Jessica knew that, as always, he would be found standing beside the railings searching the sky.

Jessica's attempts to make him respond failed consistently and she began to find herself becoming very preoccupied with Frankie; wondering at her own interest and feeling that a concentration on one individual must have an adverse effect on all the others in the class. But Jessica was unable to analyse or dismiss her obsession.

The breakthrough was an essay. Jessica had told the children that they could write on any subject and, as her class streamed into the schoolyard at playtime, she sat alone in the silent classroom, submitting to a strange impulse to read Frankie's essay first.

"Yesterday," it said, "I flew with the birds. I was down at Grandad's pigeon cree. I like it there because he lets me feed the pigeons while he goes down to the pub and Grandma never finds out. I like it there because I can understand what the pigeons are saying to each other and no one else can. And I can talk to them too—except I don't use my voice. All I have to do is *think* really hard and they can hear me. They were frightened at first. For ages they just ignored me. They don't like people much because people are crool. They only stay with Grandad because he feeds them. But the birds know that I'm their friend now and wouldn't do them no harm. And they promised that one day I could fly with them because there was something speshul about my mind. So they started teaching me how to think myself into being a bird and every time I went to the cree I would practiss.

"Last Sunday I got it rite. I turned my thinking inside-out and went behind my eyes and done it. There was a loud fluttering noise like millyins of wings flapping in my mind. And the birds took off and I was flying with them. We went up and up and up and I could see all the houses and the school and the wind was on my face and although it was high up I wasn't even scared. We could feel the wind like it was alive and holding us up on the sky and we could use it, even the tiniest bit, to go swooping and diving just anywhere we wanted. And it was funny because it felt like all of us, all of the birds, were *one* bird really. All riding the wind together and turning together and going really fast together. After a while, the pigeons took me back to the cree and I turned my mind outside-in before Grandad got back."

Jessica was stunned by the essay. It showed an imagination and expression she could never have believed possible in seven-year-old Frankie. But it also showed why he was so distanced. He was living in a world of daydreams. If only she could develop the talent which Frankie showed in his imaginative writing but at the same time bring him down to Earth. And so began Jessica's intensive programme to draw Frankie out of his shell and integrate him into the class.

Months passed and Jessica's unrelenting grip on Frankie's development began to bear fruit. He began to respond in class; to show an interest; to join in games in the schoolyard. And gradually, the lonely vigils by the railings began to hold less and less importance for him. Frankie's imaginative writing, Jessica noticed with satisfaction, began to show signs of a response to the real world.

One morning in October, Jessica found Frankie crying in a corner of the schoolyard. She knelt down beside him; felt surprise as the pulled roughly away from her.

"It's all your fault!" he cried in a small, choked voice, "I went down to the cree yesterday and the birds told me that the time was coming soon when I wouldn't be able to fly with them anymore. They told me you were going to teach me things I needed to know before I could grow up properly. Things that would make me think differently. And then I wouldn't be able to fly with them or speak to them. But I won't let it happen! I won't!"

That afternoon the incident seemed to have been forgotten. Frankie was still as responsive in class and Jessica dismissed it from her mind—until that November afternoon which was to remain with her for the rest of her life.

The children had long since gone and Jessica was leaving the main building for home when she saw a small, familiar figure standing beside the railings. Jessica started to call his name, but some unknown instinct prevented her as she moved slowly and quietly towards him, noticing how Frankie's head was cocked to one side as if listening, his gaze directed beyond the railings. No... not beyond... but *at* the railings.

Twenty feet from Frankie, Jessica froze in her tracks. A sparrow was sitting on one of the railings. And it was upon this that Frankie's intense scrutiny was concentrated; his small, white face set in a deep frown. The bird's chirping sound seemed unnaturally loud in the late afternoon air and Jessica watched entranced as, with a slow, mysterious grace, Frankie raised one hand out before him. Jessica could not move, could make no sound of surprise, as the small bird fluttered through the air to perch on Frankie's hand. Frankie's expression remained unchanged as the bird's song continued. And then the sparrow was gone, fluttering upwards and away into the darkening sky.

"Was... was it speaking to you?" Jessica heard herself ask.

"Yes," said Frankie, without turning his eyes from the small speck on the horizon. "He had a message. He was sent to tell me 'Goodbye'..."

Frankie looked up at her. There was no anger or recrimination on his face. Only a very adult expression of sadness; a remorseful farewell to something very special. Frankie was running away now, and Jessica could see that two boys and a girl from her class were waiting for him at the gates.

And that was when Jessica felt again the same barely discernible emotion which she had experienced on the day she had first seen Frankie by the railings. She grasped for it, feeling it slip away like a handful of smoke. It was a sadness that made the breath catch at the back of her throat. It was a taste of gingerbread; the smell of Mother's fresh clean washing on a Monday morning; the sound of a newly born kitten mewing in the long grass; the knowledge that each and every new day should be treasured like gold. Even now, the feeling was vanishing like a ghost.

Jessica stood for a long time as the late afternoon sun cast slanting orange light across the schoolyard. As a flock of pigeons wheeled lazily overhead, Jessica realised that she had almost grasped the key to an important truth that all adult minds have discarded and forgotten many years ago. But as the pigeons disappeared over the silhouette of the city skyline, they bore the secret with them on whispering wings. Tears were brimming in her eyes with the final, heartbreaking realisation that she had been a predestined but unwitting agent in taking something special from Frankie which could never be replaced. But it was more than that. It was the realisation that Frankie had not been unique and that her initial fascination with him had been born, not from concern, but from an unrecognised empathy.

For Jessica knew that, many yesterdays ago, she too could have flown with the birds.

the fractured man

"GAS COMPANY" SAID THE MAN AT THE FRONT DOOR.

His regulation company jacket seemed at least a size too small, fading hair parted across a wrinkled pate. Those furrows spread down over his forehead to the eyebrows, giving a perpetual hangdog look, as if he expected a rebuff from anyone with whom he came into contact. He was holding a clipboard under one armpit and his gloved hands were making a "washing" motion. From the worried expression on his face it seemed as if he was expecting a physical attack from the man who had opened the door.

"Yes?" asked Campbell brusquely, waiting for the man to elaborate.

The man in the gas company jacket actually took a step back. Rheumy eyes glittered nervously as he gave a small cough.

"The gas meter?" said the man. "I've come to read the gas meter."

"Why didn't you say so straight away?" demanded Campbell.

The man opened his mouth to speak but couldn't find anything to say. It was an expression which Campbell seemed to remember from his cinema-going days as a youngster. The comedian Stan Laurel's attempt to answer a question, mouth opening and then brain suddenly realising that there was no answer there. Campbell closed his eyes in irritation. It had been a bad day today, with a bunch of lazy bastards masquerading as a sales' force and a lost contract.

"Identification?" snapped Campbell. "Can't trust any bastard these days."

The man's face lit up. This was something that he could provide. Fumbling in his jacket pocket, making the sleeve ride up almost to the elbow, he produced a plastic wallet with the Gas Company logo, an identification number and a photograph of himself bearing a cheesy smile.

Campbell grunted and turned away from the door. Without inviting the man in, he walked through into the lounge. The man nervously followed, carefully closing the door as if any noise on his part would invite further wrath.

"Through here," instructed Campbell.

The man wiped his feet on the "Welcome" mat and then tiptoed cautiously over the thick pile of the carpet, checking his shoes as he went to make sure that he hadn't left any mud. Campbell had already crossed the room and was in the kitchen beyond. There was a tennis match taking place on the television, and the crowd suddenly began to applaud as the man peered around the kitchen door. Campbell was standing at the pantry door, holding it open but looking impatiently at the ceiling.

"In here," he said. "The gas meter's on the floor there, behind the ironing board. Can you make it quick?"

Eager to please, the man hopped into the room and stooped at Campbell's feet. On his haunches now, he shuffled into the pantry, fumbling again in his jacket pocket to take out a torch. He shone it into the darkness, fumbling again with his clipboard and trying to get a reading. It seemed as if the pen, the clipboard and the torch were proving an impossible juggling act. Above him, Campbell exhaled; a long, hissing exclamation of impatience.

"Just be a moment, sir. Just a... oh dear. Oh dear, oh *dear*."

"What's the matter?"

"This meter reading, sir. Oh dear, I'm afraid this isn't very… oh *dear!*"

"What the hell are you on about?"

"Someone's been tampering with the meter, sir. It's obvious. I mean, look at it."

"Tampering with it? What the hell are you on about?"

"This really is very serious. I'm afraid I'll have to report back to central office."

Campbell pulled the door wide and crouched down, peering past the man into the darkness, trying to make sense of the dials set into the metal box behind the ironing board.

"Where?" demanded Campbell, anger rising. "What the *hell* do you mean?"

The man shuffled backwards out of the pantry. "See for yourself. I mean, it's obvious." He handed the torch to Campbell and hunkered out of the way to allow him a clear view. Campbell squatted down and shuffled forwards, face red and colour rising. He shone the torch onto the dials, as if he knew what he was looking for.

"You're talking a load of bollocks," continued Campbell. "And if you're suggesting that I've been tampering with the meter then I'm going…"

"You're not going to do anything," said the man.

And then he brought the ball-pane hammer down squarely on top of Campbell's head. The sound was somehow *wetter* than the man had anticipated. He'd tried out a few blows at home first on a football in a pillow case. Then, it had been a hollow *whap!* But this was nothing like it really; more like the sound you heard if you put your foot on a frozen puddle—that crunching, crackling wet sound as the ice cracked and crazed. Campbell pitched forward onto his face, hand groping feebly at the back of his head. His legs were twitching, feet making a scrabbling noise on the linoleum. More curious still, the man noted that there was no blood yet. Campbell tried to turn, eyes wide in shock and focussed not on the here-and-now, but on some inner point of hideous, all-consuming pain.

"You shouldn't have called me a Nancy Boy, Campbell," said the man calmly, stepping forward again until he was astride the man on the floor. "Shouldn't have made them all laugh at me." From the television in the lounge, the tennis crowd applauded again.

Campbell's mouth was working, spittle hanging from his lower lip. And the man hoped, how he sincerely *hoped,* that he had heard those words as he gripped him by the collar with one hand and then brought the hammer down again with a savage and carefully aimed blow. The rounded head of the hammer embedded in Campbell's eye socket, the eye itself squirting down over his cheek and onto his shirt front like egg-white. Campbell gargled and looked as if he was drawing breath for the scream which had so far been absent. The man yanked the hammer free and hit him between the eyes. Campbell's remaining eye shot up into its socket, showing white. His teeth champed. The man stood quickly back, keeping his shoes well away from the dark red pool that had begun to spread on the lino behind Campbell's head. He didn't want to leave any footprints.

The man stood back, nodding his head as Campbell squirmed and thrashed in his death throes. He had not over-exerted himself as he had feared, was still controlling his breathing. He looked around, checking the kitchen windows to make sure that there was no one in the garden beyond.

Campbell juddered and was still. At that moment his bowels and bladder opened. A dark stain at his crotch became a yellow puddle between his legs which crept over the linoleum towards the man with the hammer.

"Who's the Nancy Boy now, then?" asked the man, putting the hammer back into his pocket beside the pen and the fake identification card. "Peed yourself, didn't you, Campbell? Only Nancy Boys do that. Am I right?" Picking up his clipboard, he walked back into the lounge, adopting the same "wouldn't hurt a fly" pose that he had adopted when he had first entered.

At the front door, he called back.

"That's okay, Mr. Campbell. I can see myself out."

Just in case anyone was watching. But no one had seen him arrive.

And no one saw The Fractured Man leave.

•2•

Later, at home, standing in the kitchen and looking down at the bloodied hammer lying in the sink, The Fractured Man felt that sense of healing begin to evaporate. Instead, something like anguish was beginning to flood him. Had he been wrong all along? Was his strategy flawed, would the fractures remain unhealed? He looked at the blood in the sink, and then his mother had spoken to him.

You can't take a life like that, without giving something back.

"What do you mean?"

Flesh for flesh. If you want to heal yourself on the inside, you have to make a token sacrifice on the outside. Make your own reparation for what you've done. To show that you're serious. To show that you mean it. Only then will you be made whole.

The Fractured Man remembered how his mother would stick needles into her arms and thighs if he disagreed with what she wanted. He remembered how she would cut herself and then threaten to report him to the social services for maltreating her. He thought he knew what she was getting at now.

"Like this?" he asked.

The Fractured Man reached for the serrated bread knife on the draining board beside him. He drew the blade across the top of an exposed arm. The skin peeled from the blade and a glutinous tide of crimson spilled over his arm and into the sink. The blood from the wound followed the blood from the ball-pane hammer down the plughole.

That's exactly right. Flesh for flesh. Now you've made reparation. That first fracture will be healed.

The Fractured Man smiled as he watched the blood swirl in the sink. Mother was right. He could feel the warm glow of healing returning, could feel it flowing inside to fill and repair that first fracture. A neat thought came to mind as he embraced that feeling. He had not seen or talked to Campbell—or the others—in over thirty years. There was nothing to connect them. No one could possibly know the motive. The same principle applied to all of the others on his list. How could the police possibly tie them together? Perfect crimes, each and every one of them. The Fractured Man had only been in trouble with the police once in his lifetime. It was for a drunk-driving offense a year and a half ago. And there was nothing really unusual about that. Lots of people made minor misjudgements. The kid on the zebra crossing had recovered, hadn't she? It wasn't as if he had a record for violent crime or anything like that, was it?

The Fractured Man was filled with a burning clarity.

The healing process for The Fractured Man had begun two months earlier. He had been lying on his bed and staring at the ceiling, just as he was doing now. And it seemed as if the key events of his life were being played out on that rough, cracked plaster expanse. Everything had turned out bad, beginning age eleven—a crucial time in his life. Ever since then, everything he'd wanted had been beyond reach; everything he'd turned his hand to had turned out bad. At eleven years old, his father had walked out on them, never to be seen again. Round about then, his mother had gone crazy. And when he followed that downwards spiral of memory to the present day, the forty-year-old Fractured Man could see that he had suffered all of the really bad damage in his eleventh year. His inability to keep a job, the yoke around his neck which was his mad mother (now dead these two years past). His inability to sustain any kind of relationship.

Inside, he was a Fractured Man. It didn't show on the surface, because he would not *allow* it to show on the surface. The damage was underneath the skin, the fissures were in his heart and in his soul. Those first wounds had been done to him in that eleventh year of life, and the fractures had remained ever since. He'd never had a chance to become a whole person, never been allowed the chances to make a good life for himself. He'd spent a long, long time thinking about it since his mother's death.

There had been six blows to his soul, six damaging incidents which had marked him for life. And now, in this last two months, he had come to the profound realisation that the only real way to make himself whole at last—to heal the fractures inside—was to make restitution. To act now, to eradicate those who had wreaked the damage. Campbell was the first. They had been in the same class together back then. At Campbell's front door, posing as the gas man and dressed in his late uncle's uniform, The Fractured Man had wondered whether, after thirty years, he might recognise him. To a great extent, his nervous act had not been an act at all. But no, Campbell did not know him, had no memory of the pain he had inflicted.

The Fractured Man thought back to the day that they had been playing football in the schoolyard. He had never been any good at sports, was never picked by his peers to play. But perhaps someone had taken pity that morning and had dragged him into the game. He was clumsy, unused to competitive sport. And when he missed yet another pass, Campbell had shouted: "You're no bloody good! You're prancing around like a Nancy Boy!"

Everyone had laughed, then. Every single one of them.

The Fractured Man had walked away from the game, with that laughter ringing in his ears. And that had been another damaging blow, another fracture in his essence about which he had brooded and wept and felt shameful over the years. The mocking laughter still rang in his ears.

The Fractured Man had already located the other sources of his pain. He already knew where two lived, and had found another three (including Campbell) by looking through the telephone directory. Luckily, none of them had moved away since school days, and still lived locally. Simple, really—even though he'd had to secretly visit eleven Campbell households in the area to make sure that he'd found the right one. The last one had not been listed in the telephone directory, being ex-directory. However, The Fractured Man knew that he had his own business on the industrial estate, so he must also still live locally. A trip to the local council offices and an examination of the electoral register had provided the address. As with the others, he had spent time watching the house, observing the domestic routine and making his plans.

Campbell had proved easier than he had expected. He seemed to live alone; no wife, no girlfriend, no live-in relatives. After three days, The Fractured Man had made his move. He had discovered his uncle's old uniform in the wardrobe after his mother's death. God knew how it had got there, but the identification card was still in the inside pocket and it had been an easy task to stick a new Polaroid of himself under the see-through plastic cover of the wallet, covering his uncle's face. Then he had walked up and down the street for a further two hours, pretending to be on a "round" of visits but keeping an eye on Campbell's house to make sure that no one else was with him. He had seen Campbell let himself in only a few minutes after his arrival. Luck was with The Fractured Man, making a belated entry into his life after all these years. That first fracture was healing, he could feel it knitting and making him more whole.

One fracture healed, only five to go. Then everything would be well, and he would be complete. The Fractured Man sighed and hugged himself, as if hugging the child under his skin.

"Time for Number Two," he said.

And Number Two was Dennis Mulrooney.

•3•

Once upon a time, when they were both seven years old, Dennis had professed to be The Fractured Man's best friend. But when they had moved on, had got to the first-year of Senior School, Dennis had found other friends and had discarded him. The Fractured Man still remembered how Dennis had beaten him up in the street behind the school when he insisted on following him and his new friends.

The pain and the shame was still vivid now as The Fractured Man followed this stooped and somehow shrunken figure up the sidestreet and into the darkness. Was he ill? He didn't look anything like the chubby, strapping boy he remembered. The Fractured Man quickened his pace on this deserted street, overtook Dennis and walked on ahead. Thirty feet or so beyond, he stopped and held a hand to his head—as if thinking. He turned as Dennis came up from behind.

"Excuse me?" asked The Fractured Man. "Do you know where Hetherington Street is?"

Dennis looked nervous, the eyes of the boy still recognisable in that heavily lined and grey face. The red hair had become gingery-grey.

"Hetherington Street? No, I'm not sure..."

"Don't remember me, do you?"

And did those eyes flash with recognition? Was there even a hint of a smile on that face, a warm greeting ready to emerge with all memories of the hurt he'd done forgotten? The Fractured Man was not prepared to wait. Wounds needed to be healed.

The knife blade glinted like his own welcoming smile,

Perhaps, in the long run, he had done Dennis a real favour.

He looked so ill.

And there seemed to be hardly any blood.

At home, later that day, The Fractured Man had made the required reparation.

The tooth and the bloodied pliers lay in the kitchen sink.

But that agony was as nothing to the healing taking place inside. And he felt much, *much* better.

"Time for Number Three."

•4•

On 10th July of his eleventh year, The Fractured Man had finally summoned up the courage to ask Marlene Francis if she would go to the pictures with him. She often stood with her friends at the corner of the street where he lived. Under the streetlamp there, just carrying on and watching people go by. In the past, he had been too embarrassed to talk to her. And if she had been there with her friends when he'd had to run an errand to the corner shop just beyond, he had always gone around the block in the opposite direction, the long way around to avoid them. Tonight had been different because there had only been Marlene and one friend. Quickly, he had Brylcreemed his hair, put on his long coat and stepped out onto the front street. Taking a deep breath he forced himself to walk towards them. They watched him coming, and The Fractured Man went over his oft-rehearsed speech as he approached.

Marlene had been chewing gum, he remembered. She pulled a long strand out from her teeth as he stood before her and asked if she would go out with him. If they hurried, they could make first-house at the cinema in twenty minutes. Marlene's friend had sniggered, but her own face had remained blank as she pulled on that pink strand of gum. When he had finished talking, she had rolled it up and snapped it back into her mouth.

"Fuck off," she said in a blank voice that matched the blankness of her face.

The Fractured Man's blush became a furious crimson glow of shame that seemed to fill his eyes with tears. Turning quickly on his heels, he had walked away—back to his front door. Behind him, Marlene remained silent. But her girlfriend was howling with laughter.

For the remainder of his school career, The Fractured Man had been forced to avoid Marlene and her taunting friends.

And now, standing in Marlene's back garden tonight, the laughter seemed louder than ever. She and her husband were both in the front room, watching television. An hour and a half into his vigil, Marlene had finally come into the bathroom. The light from the window spilled out across the back garden, making The Fractured Man shrink back further into the bushes. Marlene was humming, and it seemed to him that even that tuneless melody was a taunt. There was a soft hiss of water as Marlene switched on the shower and The Fractured Man watched her silhouette begin to disrobe. Then he picked up the lemonade bottle at his feet. He had to act quickly. He had been waiting for her to come into the bathroom, but hadn't expected that she'd be wanting a shower. The water might spoil his plan if he didn't move fast. In the next instant, he struck the match and lit the oily rag in the neck of the bottle. It flared in the darkness.

"Fuck off," she had told him, her face blank.

Marlene was still humming, still disrobing, as The Fractured Man ran across the lawn with the petrol bomb held behind him as he came. Keeping the flame well away from him, he flung it wide-armed at the bathroom window.

A crashing of glass, an eruption of orange flame.

And now the silhouette in the bathroom was no longer humming that taunting melody. She was screaming and flapping and twisting in agony at the flaming shroud which engulfed her.

"No, *you* fuck off!" yelled The Fractured Man, vanishing into the night.

Behind him the screams faded.

•5•

And later, with three fractures healed, he stood once more in darkness at the kitchen sink. He listened to his mother's words again, about the need for reparation. The need for an outward sign, to reinforce that inner healing.

This time, he picked up the same knife from the draining board. Opening his shirt, he carved a cross on his chest. Lips tightly shut against the burning pain, refusing to let any sound come out as the warm blood ran over his skin and pooled in his belly button and around his flabby waist. But even as the blood ran, the healing quickened. When he did open his mouth, it was to sigh with satisfaction.

•6•

Gordon was Number Four.

Gordon McAlpine, the bastard. *He* was the one who had passed that note in class about Blakey the French Teacher being a French git. It had travelled down the line of desks until it had landed up thrown on The Fractured Man's desk. And Blakey had chosen that moment to turn from the blackboard.

"Bring it to me!"

Too scared to move, The Fractured Man had remained seated.

"I said bring it to *me!*"

The French Teacher's anger had only made things worse. There was no way in the world that The Fractured Man could ever rise from the chair.

Blakey had stormed to his desk, grabbed the note and turned a strange mauve colour when he read what it said about him. Seizing The Fractured Man by the jacket lapels, he had dragged him from the desk to the front of the class. And the next fracture had been made at the core of his soul when Blakey had given him six straps across the hand with the leather belt. Three for the note, and three for silent insolence.

By rights, Blakey was the one who should be making reparation. But Blakey had died ten years later, The Fractured Man had learned. On the ferry to Calais, he had over-imbibed on duty-free whisky and fallen overboard. His body had never been found. After careful thought, The Fractured Man realised that Gordon was the real instigator, and that he would take Blakey's share of the blame, too.

On this occasion, The Fractured Man realised that there was no need for a direct meeting or confrontation. Gordon, married with three kids, was obviously something of a "car" man. For a week, The Fractured Man watched him carefully from a safe distance as he worked on his Ford Capri; a car once scorned, now becoming regarded as trendy. The Fractured Man had started his own garage business once. Obviously, it had gone bust. But he knew his cars, and he knew just exactly what to do if you wanted the brake and accelerator to fall apart after the car got to fourth gear.

It wasn't hard to break into Gordon's garage, was no great task to slide under that car with his flashlight and tools to do the necessaries. Only once did he pause, wondering if anyone had heard the noise of the heavy-duty bolt-cutter. He had tried to wrap it in burlap, but the noise was still loud. After five minutes of lying in the darkness, and with no sounds of anyone rising from sleep, he had continued with his work.

Four hours later, he was standing on the pavement opposite Gordon's house.

He simply stood and watched as the Ford Capri pulled out of the garage, turned in the street and headed down into the heavy traffic on the main road.

Later that night, eating his evening meal, The Fractured Man watched the news report on the television of what had happened. Gordon had been travelling on the motorway at the time, had obviously realised that something was wrong and had tried to slow the car when it reached 80 miles per hour by driving it sideways on at the crash barrier. It hadn't worked. The car had rebounded out into the fast lane, clipped a lorry carrying frozen chickens and hurtled straight over the central reservation. A car and caravan trailer had smashed into his side—and the Ford Capri had hurtled straight over a concrete wall, dropping seventy feet onto the Southbound traffic below.

Gordon and three other drivers were dead, one of them killed by a ricocheting frozen chicken through the windscreen.

The Fractured Man watched and listened to the news report, finished his meal and daintily dabbed at his mouth with a napkin. In the kitchen, he moved to the bench and looked at the tools which lay there. He looked at them for a long time, feeling the dull pain in his chest and his mouth. Then he took the heavy-duty bolt-cutter which he had used on Gordon's car, and pulled up a seat. Balancing the tool across his lap, he took off the shoe and sock from his left foot. He paused to take a deep breath and listen to his mother's words about reciprocal reparation.

It was an awkward manoeuvre, but he managed it.

The little toe of his left foot, between the blades.

One quick snap of the handle and blade.

A wet crunch, which sounded like someone biting into a stalk of celery.

Was he imagining that the pain got worse the nearer he got to his goal? There seemed to be more blood than before, but the half bottle of Dettol seemed to stem the flow and coagulate the blood. Even so, with a six-inch wad of bandage the blood still seeped through. But the healing inside was even better than before. The Fractured Man stooped to pick up that small and shrivelled thing that had once been part of him. He looked at it for a long time, and then—like a talisman—put it in his pocket as a keepsake.

•7•

Four Down and Two to Go.

And now The Fractured Man was faced with a dilemma. Which of the remaining two had been responsible for the biggest fracture, the biggest hurt? He spent a great deal of time thinking about it, weighing up the pros and cons of each case. But he knew that he could not spend too much time. After all, the healing was well underway and he hungered to be whole.

At last, he chose.

After diligent and careful research, he had found out only three years ago that his father had moved to a different county after he had left them both. Not having the simple decency to grieve for the rest of his life over what he had done and the misery he had left in his wake, he had remarried. Worse, he had started a new family. He had changed his profession, too; becoming a sales representative for a heavy engineering firm, and then after sticking with the job for twenty years, he had become a director of the firm. He had not been able to glory in his position for long. A year ago, he had been felled by a heart attack.

But his father would have to make reparation, would have to heal the hurt he had inflicted. And a mere inconvenience like death was not going to deter The Fractured Man.

•8•

With great consideration, the new family of The Fractured Man's father had chosen a graveyard plot in the middle of Holywell Cemetery.

"Dead centre," The Fractured Man laughed when he eventually found it.

His quest had begun as soon as the sun had gone down, and it had taken him a careful two hours to locate the gravestone. There seemed little chance that he would be disturbed here. On three sides of the graveyard were open fields, with a motorway far beyond. On one side, a council housing estate; but it was far enough away to provide little threat of being observed.

"Much Beloved of wife Emily, sons Jon and Phillip, and daughter Hilary" read the gravestone.

The Fractured Man smiled grimly, resisting the urge to use one of his tools to hack those names out of the marble. He lowered the work bag carefully to the ground. Working methodically and carefully, always keeping a watchful eye on the darkness, he took out his tools and laid them neatly side by side. The grass over the graves here had been cut recently, so he would have to be especially careful. Using his fold-up spade, he carefully cut twelve diagonal lines across the breadth of the grave space with the edge of the blade. Then he centred the spade edge in the middle of the grave stone and cut another full length ridge from top to bottom. Carefully levering the blade under each of the sections, he lifted the turf, making sure that the grass and soil didn't fall apart as he carefully laid them at the graveside; taking careful note of the space from which he had removed each section.

When the grass had been removed, The Fractured Man found that he had worked up quite a sweat, despite the chilly night air. Taking off his coat, he looked for a place to put it—then hung it with a wry smile over the gravestone. Now the heavy work could start.

There was a gravel path at one side of the grave, about three feet away. As he shovelled out the soil, he tried to make sure that the mound gathered on that path. Too much soil on the grass at the side might be difficult to clear away, and he did not want any attention drawn to what he had been doing. As he worked, he realised that he had never felt better. The healing was good, the fractures filled in. Only two more fissures to fill—the biggest—and everything would be resolved. With each spade of soil, he felt that he was digging deep into one of those fractures; as if he had become a microscopic bug at the core of his soul, cleaning out the fissure so that it could be filled with healing balm. He could feel the throbbing of his heart, feel the echoes of its beat in his temples as he laboured.

Three hours later, his spade hit something solid.

The Fractured Man forced himself not to drop down on all fours, scrabbling at the lid. There was still more work to be done, still a lot of soil and clay to clear away before he could open the coffin.

The next hour was deeply frustrating. He had not cleared enough space around the coffin lid. As a result, it was impossible to open the damned thing because he was standing on it all the time. When he tried to cut a wedge at one side of the grave wall for him to stand in, soil began to cascade down from all around across the lid.

Eventually, when that frustration threatened to overwhelm him, The Fractured Man champed his teeth together to prevent the scream erupting from his throat. Raising the spade like an axe, he brought it down heavily at the top of he coffin lid. The wood was flimsy, dampened by the weight of six feet of soil above. The blade sliced straight through. The Fractured Man yanked it out, turning the blade sideways as he did so and tearing out a chunk of crumbling wood in the same movement. He swung the spade again, still unable to see what lay inside. Moonlight had provided the bare illumination necessary so far, but down here he needed to see more. Jumping up out of the grave, he took the torch from his jacket and returned to the edge, shining it down.

What had he expected to see? A scene from a horror movie? A clean white skull, or something hideously still resembling his father?

It was neither.

His father's head looked like nothing more or less than a rotted cabbage shrouded with something that looked like cobwebs. There was no vestige of humanity about that shape, no discernible features. Just a dark and matted mass that conjured no emotion at all in him. As he played the torch beam around that vague mass, he thought that he could see a collar and tie where the neck might be.

"Good."

He jumped down onto the lid.

And both feet went straight through into the coffin with a wet and shocking *crack!*

The Fractured Man clawed and clambered at the grave edge for support, dropping the torch. In that one moment, he felt convinced that the walls of the grave would suddenly cave in on top of him in an avalanche of damp clay and soil. Was that how it would all end? Reunited with his father at last, in his father's own grave? Sobs wracking his throat, he braced both hands on the crumbling walls and waited for it to happen.

But nothing did happen.

And far from being trapped in the grave, The Fractured Man realised that his drop onto the coffin lid had done the job for him. The wood had split and fractured from end to end. Still sobbing, but this time elated, he stooped and tore at the shards of the coffin lid. In seconds, he had torn the damp and rotted wood to one side and was able to look down on yet another source of his pain. Retrieving the torch, he shone it before him.

The suit was recognisable, the hands merely balls of cobwebbed moss.

The Fractured Man carefully placed the torch at his feet, noticing how his sudden descent had flattened the trouser legs of the corpse. It was as if those trouser legs had been empty, the fabric trodden flat. In the same movement, he picked up the spade and adjusted his position.

He drew breath and began.

"*That's* for the picnic at Plessey Woods!" The spade shattered the cabbage head. Now it was merely a tangle of cobweb and moss and writhing wet things that glinted in the torch beam.

"*That's* for the fishing trip at The Tweed!" The spade sliced through the chest, snagging in the torn fabric of the suit. When The Fractured Man yanked the spade free, part of a disintegrating rib cage came with it.

"And *that's* for the holiday at Cleethorpes!" The Fractured Man discarded the spade and launched himself at the corpse, kicking it to fragments in the grave. Kicking and kicking and kicking, until he had to stagger back against the grave wall, panting for breath.

Each of those blows had been for a good memory, not a bad memory.

Because the good memories of his father were the reasons for the hurt and the fractures. When he'd left them both, that was all that The Fractured Man had to remember him by. And over time, those memories had been agonising. The nights he had cried himself to sleep remembering them. Each act of kindness, each memory of laughter. All a reminder that it had been taken away forever.

When The Fractured Man had finished, he climbed from the grave and began the long, long process of filling it in again. It was an easier task than digging it out, but he still had to work quickly before the sun began to rise. He shovelled the soil from the gravel path directly back into the desecrated grave, on top of the scattered fragments. As he worked, the healing had already begun—and he completed the task with a big smile on his face. Using a fold-down rake from his work bag, he covered over the smattering of remaining soil on the path with gravel. Then, just as carefully as he had removed the turf, he placed it back—piece by piece, and in exactly the same places from which he had removed each section. When he had finished, it was still possible to see the ridges where he had cut the grass. But in a few days, with a little rain, the grass would have grown to cover those marks.

It had been a good night's work.

And the sun was just beginning to rise as he climbed over the graveyard wall with his workbag over his shoulder.

Luck was with him again. No one was about.

He whistled all the way home, feeling that fracture healing over inside.

•9•

At home, he slept for seven hours.

His dead mother's voice woke him. The healing was wonderful and he was ravenously hungry, but she reminded him that there was something more important to which he had to attend. Naked, he stood before the kitchen sink, splashing cold water from the tap over his body in preparation. Moving back to the table, he hefted the bloodstained bolt-cutter onto the draining board. Sucking in lungsful of air, he tried to get the cutter to lie lengthways, with the blades open. He lay one forearm across it, trying to steady the damn thing. But it kept wobbling, so he lay it flat and pushed the blades out over the sink, leaning heavily on the shaft. It still wouldn't work properly. Swinging it from the draining board and standing it in the corner, he decided on a more simple approach.

The serrated kitchen knife in the top drawer.

The same knife that he had used before.

Bracing his left hand on the draining board, he moved his little finger out as far as possible from the others. He remembered with a wistful smile that he'd seen Robert Mitchum do what he was about to do in a movie about the Japanese Mafia. What the hell was that movie called again? *The Yakuza.* Yeah, that was it. Those Japanese gangsters did it as an act of reparation. What a wonderful thing that he should have thought of it. How apt.

Grinning, The Fractured Man brought the knife blade down hard on his little finger, leaning his weight on the knife. *Crack* and *chop*, the finger came off as easily as he might cut a carrot. A thick red pool began to spread on the draining board. Quickly, The Fractured Man wrapped the tea towel around his wrist, tying it tight. The blood still flowed, but was no longer pumping. He reached for the bottle of Dettol and the bandages.

The pain was worse than the pain in his foot. With stained bandages around his hand bigger than a baseball catcher's mitt, he returned to the draining board and looked at the severed finger for a long time as the pain and the healing fought inside him.

At last, there was only the healing, and the prospect of becoming whole after his next task.

• 10 •

The final part of the Fractured Man's plan was put into operation two weeks later. It had been necessary to leave it that long, to allow his hand to heal. The stump was still a long way from healing completely, and needed a lot of attention. And although the act had been necessary to hasten the inner healing, he realised that undertaking his last visit with a damaged hand that might disadvantage him could be a mistake. Now, it merely throbbed and leaked, but he could use it if he had to. With his gloves on, no one would notice.

The gas company plan had been a good one. He decided that it would be good to finish with a ploy that had begun his healing process. Donning his uncle's uniform again and holding his clipboard in an official stance, he stood in front of the mirror for a long time, listening to mother. He could feel the hurt on the outside. On his chest, his foot, his hand, in his mouth. It meant nothing compared to the feeling in his soul, at his very core.

Only one more Fracture to heal.

Danny McGovern. The real bane of The Fractured Man's existence in that fateful eleventh year. He was the one who had made it his business to make the Man's life a misery. He was the one who had organised the concentrated bullying, the one who had burned The Fractured Man's schoolbooks in the field beyond the school playground. He was the one who had broken his wrist, and in his fear of reprisal The Fractured Man had been too afraid to tell anyone about it. He was the one who had made him eat dog shit, the one who had stuck his head down the lavatory bowl in the toilets.

And now The Fractured Man knew where McGovern lived.

Straightening his tie in the mirror, he moved back into the kitchen only long enough to retrieve the two lucky charms that he would need. The severed toe and finger.

Popping them into his inside pocket, he zipped that pocket emphatically closed and set off on his last visit, whistling again.

• 11 •

The Fractured Man rubbed his throbbing left hand after he had rung the doorbell. He tried to whistle again, but suddenly his mouth was too dry. Was it fear, or anticipation of the wholeness to come?

McGovern was alone. His wife and two kids had left half an hour earlier. That time of waiting had been the worst of all. What if he stayed all day and never caught McGovern by himself? It might take weeks or months to catch him alone. Could he bear the agony of having to wait? But no, Luck was with him again—making it as easy as possible for him. Only a three-hour wait, and there they went; McGovern waving his family off at the door with a can of lager in his hand. The Fractured Man still recognised him. Of them all, he seemed to have changed the least. As soon as he'd gone back inside and the family had vanished around the street corner, he made his move.

"Gas company," he said, when the front door opened again.

McGovern had the same sullen look from schooldays, the same hunched shoulders and burly demeanour, the same piggy eyes. Glittering and set close together.

"Eh?" McGovern took a swig from his can.

"I've come to read the gas meter."

"You what?"

"The meter. To read the meter..."

"I heard what you said. But they sent someone around yesterday to read it, didn't they? So what the hell are you on about?"

The Fractured Man's throat constricted, his heart began to pound. Instantly, there was sweat on his brow. The stump of his finger, his chest and foot had suddenly begun to hurt badly.

"Oh? Did they?"

"No, wait. Hang about. Maybe it was the Electricity. Yeah, maybe that was it. Come in."

"Identification?" The Fractured Man fumbled in his pocket.

"Nah," said McGovern, swigging from the lager can. "Just come in. Quick, will ya. I'm watching a game on the telly."

The Fractured Man stepped in as McGovern closed the door behind him, and waited while he led the way into the front room. No tennis crowds to watch him today, but there was a football video playing on screen. McGovern sauntered into the room, flopped extravagantly onto the sofa and continued to watch the game.

"Meter's in the room next door, second cupboard on the left, near the floor."

The Fractured Man cleared his throat and walked quickly past him into the kitchen. Second cupboard, near the floor. He opened the door and hunkered down, taking out his torch. The cupboard was full of vegetables, a rack of old potatoes growing stalks. It reminded The Fractured Man of the smell from his father's grave. He shone the torch into the darkened space, at the same time reaching into his inner pocket for the same hammer that had killed Campbell. It was in there, upside-down. Sticking out of the pocket, handle up and ready. The Fractured Man cleared his throat, ready to say: *"Oh dear, I think we've got a problem here."*

"Here, I think I *know* you don't I?" came a shockingly loud voice from the doorway. The Fractured Man whirled in alarm to see that McGovern had swung silently from the sofa again and followed him. He was leaning in the doorframe, still holding his can of lager. His eyes were glittering with growing amusement, the pupils so grey that they could hardly be seen.

"No, I don't think so. I'm sure... I mean, look. I think there's a problem with the..."

"Yeah!" laughed McGovern, swigging again. "We went to Manor Park School together didn't we? Same class. What's your name then?"

"Not sure you've got the right person," stuttered The Fractured Man, feeling suddenly weak and wanting to get away now as quickly as possible. "I never went to Manor..."

"Wait a minute. Don't tell me. I'll get it in a minute. I'm usually quite good with names. Been a long time, but I know you. That's for definite."

The Fractured Man saw the glittering amusement in those eyes and knew that McGovern was summoning up pleasurable images of the kid whom he had so mercilessly tortured in that hellish eleventh year. He was smiling while he thought, drinking again.

"Hang on now. Nearly got it... nearly..."

Someone scored a goal on the television and the crowd erupted in a joyful roar. Still thinking, can moving to his mouth, McGovern turned to look back into the living room. Watching for the action replay, but almost on the verge of remembering.

And that was when The Fractured Man knew that if he did not act now, his courage would desert him altogether. He stood quickly, reaching into his inner pocket for the handle of the hammer. His fingers fumbled, then it seemed that the hammer was jammed in the fabric of his coat as he took a step towards McGovern. The hammer was free at last, and The Fractured Man lunged at the doorway swinging it high.

The next three seconds were blurred.

When his eyes cleared, The Fractured Man was lying on the carpeted floor of the living room. He had double vision, did not know what had happened. Then McGovern loomed into sight from the doorway.

"You little *shit!*" the two-headed form hissed at him. "You tried to fucking brain me, you little *shit!*"

The Fractured Man's vision cleared. The hammer was still in his hand. He braced himself to rise, fear eating like a sick cancer in his stomach. In the next instant, McGovern had stamped on his chest, slamming him back to the floor. Seizing The Fractured Man's wrist, he tried to wrest the hammer free. The Fractured Man fought back weakly, but was still dazed from the blow to the jaw that had sent him reeling. McGovern delivered a back-hand slap to his face that jerked his head one side. And then he had the hammer.

"*Now* I remember!" shouted McGovern, standing back. "*Now* I remember who you are!"

The Fractured Man tried to rise again, and this time McGovern gave a tight little run at him and lashed out with his foot. The boot slammed his face to the other side, raising a weal across his forehead. The Fractured Man grunted and lay still.

McGovern moved back to the kitchen. There was a telephone extension there, attached to the wall. Still holding the hammer, he moved to it and grabbed the receiver. Face suffused with rage and still keeping an eye on The Fractured Man's prostrate form, he stabbed out 999 and asked for "Police..."

"McGovern," said The Fractured Man in a blurred voice from the floor.

McGovern looked up, still hefting the hammer and ready to use it again if his attacker tried to rise from the floor. What he saw made his eyes bulge in terror.

"I never wanted to use this," continued The Fractured Man. "Too easy. But in the circumstances..."

McGovern flung up a hand as if to ward it off.

The Fractured Man had pushed himself up from the carpet on one elbow. In his free hand he was holding the .38 Automatic pistol that he had taken from his other pocket, the gun hand held out hard and straight.

"Don't..." began McGovern, voice breaking.

And then McGovern's head snapped back as the flat bark of the gun filled the room. The bullet entered his right temple as he turned, exiting from left. His eyes exploded in their sockets, a dark fan of airbrushed crimson decorating the telephone and the wall to which it was attached. McGovern never made a sound as his bulky body curled to one side and hit the kitchen floor like a sack of potatoes. The Fractured Man felt the impact of the body even from where he lay, shivering the floorboards.

"Didn't want it that easy," he said, picking himself up from the floor.

He staggered to the kitchen. McGovern was still holding the hammer. The Fractured Man pried it from his grasp and shoved it in his pocket again, ramming the .38 into his other pocket at the same time. The gun was untraceable, the easiest tool available. Never mind. The job was done, and that was the important thing. The Fractured Man retrieved his clipboard and his torch, which had somehow whirled into the living room. The television crowd roared at a near miss.

Straightening his clothes, rubbing his bruised jaw, The Fractured Man checked the kitchen window. Just as he had done with Campbell. Had anyone heard the gun's retort? But there was no one there. He hurried to the front window in the living room and scanned the street. There was an elderly couple at the far end of that street, just turning the corner. But no one else. What about the neighbours? Maybe they had assumed it was a car backfiring.

Quickly, heart hammering once more, The Fractured Man let himself out of the house.

Luck again, you see.

No one saw him come. No one saw him go.

He tried to whistle on the way home, but he was still too dry.

•12•

Exhuasted, The Fractured Man collapsed onto his bed once more and slept as if dead. He could feel the immense changes taking place inside just before he slipped over that brink into the chasm of sleep. The fractures were filled, the fissures knitting together. The cracks in his soul had healed, and in that brief moment just before unconsciousness he knew that he was on the verge of great changes. Changes in his fortune, in his life, in everything to which he turned his hand.

As before, it seemed that his late mother's voice was calling him back. Back to carry out the final act of reparation that would set the seal on all the work he had so diligently undertaken. But there was a greater urgency to the voice in his dreams, a note of desperation which alarmed him and made him rise quickly from the darkness like a deep sea diver questing for the surface.

His mother's voice was alarmed, was hammering at him.

Hammering, hammering.

The Fractured Man emerged from that inner place, eyes blurred, the pain of reparation still burning on his body. He was still fully clothed, had fallen into bed in a state of nervous exhaustion.

Hammering...

Someone was hammering at his front door.

"Police! We know you're in there. Make it easy, or we'll force the door!"

In the next moment, The Fractured Man was on his feet; moving so quickly from the mattress that he came down heavily on his mutilated foot. He staggered, clutching at the counterpane, wide eyes fixed on the door. The hammering and the voices continued.

"What?" he almost yelled. "What do you want?"

Now they knew he was in there.

"Make it easy for us, son. Or we'll have to use the sledgehammer on the door. We've got a warrant, and you can't get out."

The Fractured Man hobbled into the kitchen, eyes still fixed on the shuddering front door. He turned to stare out of the window beyond the sink. Six floors straight down and with no drainpipe nearby. What the hell had happened? What the hell had *happened?*

"I didn't do it!" he yelled at the door. "It wasn't me!"

"Yeah?" came a faint voice. The hammering ceased. In his mind's eye, The Fractured Man saw those beyond standing to one side as the sledgehammer was carried forward and brought to bear. "Tell that to Danny McGovern."

McGovern!

And then, with sudden and blinding clarity, The Fractured Man knew what had happened. He began to laugh. Softly at first as he staggered from the kitchen and back into the living room, still staring at the door and waiting. That laughter began to build inside. He was almost completely healed, and that had brought with it such a blaze of crystal clarity. Giggling, he fumbled with his good hand in his jacket pocket. The .38 automatic was still there, the identification wallet was still there.

The severed toe was still there.

But, just as he had guessed, the severed finger was no longer there.

His fumbling fingers found a tear in the lining of the pocket.

That giggling laughter erupted out loud. He had been so careful.

In his mind's eye, he saw his struggle with McGovern, saw himself flying over the living room carpet, saw McGovern beating him. During that struggle, his severed finger had fallen unnoticed from a tear in his pocket lining.

Only once had he been in trouble with the police. A drink-driving offence, in which a small child had been injured. And as part of the normal proceedings, his fingerprints had been taken...

The Fractured Man's laughter could not be contained as he was consumed by this huge joke and the police outside in the corridor began to take the sledgehammer to the door. He raised the .38 automatic, pointing it at the door.

Quick, you fool, said his dead mother. *Quick. How can you be completely whole if you haven't made reparation?*

The Fractured Man's laughter choked in his throat. He bent double, shaking his head.

Quick! screamed his mother as the doorframe cracked and one of the hinges flew spinning into the room. *Quick!*

"No..." said The Fractured Man, straightening up and still shaking his head.

QUICK!

"No!" He threw the automatic underhand onto the bed.

Moments later, the door imploded with shocking force.

The Fractured Man was on his knees now. Tears of laughter were streaming down his face, but he was no longer laughing out loud and he did not flinch as that shattered door fell apart and they rushed in. He was still smiling that great big smile—and when they saw him, they halted in shock.

Somehow, the same serrated bread knife with which he had severed his finger was in that maimed and throbbing hand. He could not remember picking it up from the draining board. Luck again, just when he needed it. He dropped the knife to the floor, both hands moving to his chest. Those white hands became crimson in the flood which poured from the gaping red smile in his throat. He turned those hands back to the police, bloodied palms up in a gesture that told them all that they were too late. Then he pointed to the automatic on the bed.

Too easy, he mouthed, repeating what he had said to McGovern. *Much too easy.*

And although he could not laugh, he smiled and smiled and smiled as he slowly began to pitch forward.

The Fractured Man had carried out his final act of reparation.

At last—at long, long last—The Fractured Man was entirely Whole.

the crawl

THE DAYS ARE BAD, BUT THE NIGHTS ARE ALWAYS WORSE.

Since it all happened and I lost my job, it seems as if the front door is always the focus of my attention, no matter what I'm doing. I try to keep myself occupied, try to read, try to listen to music. But all of these things make it much worse. You see, if I really *do* become preoccupied in what I'm doing, then I might not hear it if...

If he... if it ... comes.

I've recently had all my mail redirected to a post office box where I can go and collect it, since the clatter of the letterbox in the morning and afternoon became just too much to bear. I had to nail it up against junk mail and free newspapers. The house has become a terrible, terrible place since I lost Gill. God, how I miss her.

And in the nights, I lie awake and listen.

The sound of a car passing on the sidestreet is probably the worst.

I hear it coming in my sleep. It wakes me instantly, and I'm never sure whether I've screamed or not, but I lie there praying first that the car will pass quickly and that the engine won't cough and falter. Then, in the first seconds after it's moved on I pray again that I won't hear those familiar, staggering footsteps on the gravel path outside; that I won't hear that hellish hammering on the front door. I listen for the sounds of that hideous, hoarse breathing. Most nights I'm soaked in sweat waiting for the sound of the door panels splintering apart. Sometimes I dream that I'm down there in the hall, with my hands braced against the wood of that front door, screaming for help as the pounding comes from the other side.

Sometimes I dream that I'm in bed, that he's got in and he's coming up the stairs.

That same slow, methodical tread.

I run to the door, trying to slam it shut as he reaches the landing. In slow motion, I turn and scream at Gill to get out quickly through the bedroom window as I heave the bedside cabinet across the floor to the door. But as I turn, Gill isn't there. She's in the bathroom at the top of the landing, so now I'm frantically tearing the cabinet away from the door as he ascends, but Gill doesn't hear him because the shower's running and I slowly pull open the door screaming her name just as the shadow reaches the landing and Gill turns from the wash basin and...

If I started by telling you that the whole thing began on the A1 just a half-mile from Boroughbridge, you might suppose that it has some kind of relevance for the horror that came afterwards. If it does, then that relevance has eluded me. Believe me, I've been over the whole thing many times in my mind, trying to make sense of it all. No, like all bad nightmares, it defied any logic. It seemed that we were just in the wrong place at the wrong time; like a traffic accident. Thirty seconds earlier or thirty seconds later, and maybe I'd be able to sleep at night a little better than I do these days. But since all stories start somewhere, the A1 turn-off half-a-mile from Boroughbridge was our somewhere.

The day had started badly.

We had spent Easter weekend with my wife's parents, and on the trip home Gill and I weren't speaking. There had been a party at her folks' house on the Sunday evening (we'd been there since Thursday), and that bloody personnel manager friend of theirs had been invited. I'd been made redundant from an engineering firm three years previously, and it was two years before I found another job. Not easy, but things were going fine again at last. Nevertheless, the use of my previous firm's psychometric testing to "reduce staffing levels" was a bug-bear of mine. ("What is the capital of Upper Twatland? You don't know? Then sorry, you're sacked.")

We were driving home on Easter Monday, and I had promised not to drink during the evening so that we could take turns behind the wheel. But this bastard personnel man (who I'd never met before, but whose profession didn't endear himself to me) was standing there all night, spouting off his in-house philosophy about big fish eating little fish, and only-the-strongest-will-prevail. My anger had begun as a slow-burn, and I'd had a drink to dampen the fuse. But then a second had begun to light it again. And by the third, I was just about ready for an intervention. By my fourth, I'd burned it out of my system, was having a chat with Stuart and Ann and their light-hearted banter was making everything okay again. Then, the personnel-man was left on his own and, having bored his companion to tears, decided to move over to us. If he'd kept off the subject, everything would have been okay. (But then again, if we hadn't been on the A1 half-a mile out of Boroughbridge, none of this would have happened either.)

Disregarding anything we were talking about, he started again where he'd left off.

And I'm afraid that was it. All bets off. Fuse not only rekindled, but powder-keg ignited. I could probably go on for three pages about our conversation, but since this tale is about the worst thing that ever happened to me, and not one of the best, it seems a little pointless if I do. Just let's say that without giving in to the urge for actual bodily harm, I kept a cold fury inside. I dispensed with any social airs and graces or the rules of polite party-conversation, and kept at his throat while he tried to impress us with his superior "if-they-can't-hack-it, out-they-go" credo. Like a terrier, I kept hanging at his wattles, shaking him down and finishing with a "who-lives-by-the-sword-dies-by-the-sword." Sounds obvious, but believe me; as a put-down it wasn't half bad. Maybe you had to be there to appreciate it. He left our company, and kept to other less-impolite partygoers. Stuart and Ann were pleased too, and that made me feel good.

However, I could tell by Gill's face that I wasn't going to get any good conduct medals. At first, I thought that maybe I'd overstepped the mark; been too loud, let the booze kid me that I was being subtle when in fact I was acting like Attila the Hun. But no, her tight-lips and cold demeanour were related to more practical matters than that. I'd seen off at least a half-bottle of scotch, and we had that long drive tomorrow. Remember? Well, no I hadn't. My anger had seen to that.

So by next morning we were in a non-speaking to each other situation.

I tried to hide the hang-over, but when you've been living with someone for ten years it's a little difficult to hide the signs. The two fizzing Solpadeine in the glass were the final insult. I stressed that I would take care of the second-half of the journey, but this didn't seem to hold water. Did I mention that she'd lost a baby, was still getting over it physically and psychologically, that she was feeling very tired all the time? No? Well, just give me the Bastard Club application form and I would willingly have signed.

Tight-lipped farewells to the In-laws.

And a wife's face that says she's just waiting for the open road before she lets rip.

Well, she let rip. But I probably don't have to draw you a map.

I let it go, knowing that I'd been a little selfish. But Gill always did have a habit of taking things a little too far. My temper snapped, and seconds later it had developed into the knock-down, drag-out verbal fight that I'd been trying to avoid.

"Boroughbridge," said the motorway sign. "Half mile."

"That's the last time we spend any time together down here at Easter," said Gill.

"Fine by me. I've got more important things I could be doing."

"Let's not stop at Easter. How about spending our Christmases and Bank Holidays apart, too?"

"Great. I might be able to enjoy myself for a change."

"Maybe we should make it more permanent? Why stop at holidays? Let's just..."

"...spend all of our time apart? That suits me fine."

There was a man up ahead, standing beside the barrier on the central reservation. Just a shadow, looking as if he was waiting for a break in the traffic so that he could make a dangerous run across the two lanes to the other side.

"God, you can be such a bastard!"

"You're forgetting an important point, Gill. It was people like that Personnel bastard who got me the sack. You should be sticking up for me, not..."

"So what makes you think we need *your* money? Are you trying to say that what I earn isn't enough to..."

"For Christ's sake, Gill!"

The shadow stepped out from the roadway barrier, directly in front of us.

Gill had turned to look at me, her face a mask of anger.

"For Christ's *sake!*" I yelled, and it must have seemed to her then that I'd lost my mind when I suddenly lunged for the steering wheel. She yelled in anger and shock, swatted at me but held fast.

And in the next minute, something exploded through the windscreen.

Gill's instincts were superb. Despite the fact that the car was suddenly filled with an exploding, hissing shrapnel of fine glass, she didn't lose control. She braked firmly, hanging onto the wheel while I threw my hands instinctively up to protect my face. The car slewed and hit the barrier, and I could feel the front of the car on Gill's side crumple. The impact was horrifying and shocking. In that split-second I expected the body of that idiot to come hurtling through into our laps, smashing us back against our seats. But nothing came through the windscreen as the car slid to a halt on the hard-shoulder, right next to the metal barrier, and with its nose pointed out into the nearside lane.

There were fine tracings of red-spiderweb blood all over my hands as I reached instinctively for Gill. Her hands were clenched tight to the wheel, her head was down and her long dark hair full of fine glass shards. I could see that her hands were also flayed by the glass and with a sickening roll in the stomach I thought she might be blinded.

"God, Gill! Are you alright?"

I pulled up her face with both hands so that she was staring directly ahead through the shattered windscreen. Her eyes were wide and glassy, she was breathing heavily. Obviously in shock, and hanging onto that wheel as if she was hanging onto her self-control.

"Are you alright?"

She nodded, a slight gesture which seemed to take great effort.

Twisting in my seat, making the imploded glass all around me crackle and grind, I looked back.

We hadn't hit the stupid bastard.

He was still standing, about thirty or forty feet behind us on the hard-shoulder. Standing there, unconcerned, watching us.

I kicked open the passenger door and climbed out. Slamming it, I leaned on the roof to get my breath and then looked back at him. He was a big man, but in the dusk it was impossible to see any real details other than he seemed to be shabbily dressed and unsteady on his feet. The sleeves of his jacket seemed torn, his hair awry. A tramp, perhaps. He was just standing there, with his hands hanging limply at his sides, staring in our direction.

"You *stupid* bastard!" I yelled back at him when my breath returned. "You could have killed my wife."

The man said nothing. He just stood and looked. His head was slightly down, as if he was looking at us from under his brows. There was something strange about his face, but I couldn't make it out.

"You stupid *fuck!*"

Then I saw that he was holding something in one hand, something long and curved in a half-moon shape. I squinted, rubbing my shredded hands over my face and seeing that there was also blood on the palms, too. The sight of more blood enraged me. Fists bunched at my side, I began striding back along the hard shoulder towards the silently waiting figure.

After ten or fifteen feet, I stopped.

There *was* something wrong with this character's face. The eyes were too dark, too large. The mouth was fixed in a permanent grin. I couldn't see a nose.

And then I realised what it was.

The man was wearing a mask.

A stupid, scarecrow mask.

It was made from sacking of some sort, tied around the neck with string. From where I was standing, I couldn't tell whether he'd drawn big, round black eyes with peep holes in the centre, or whether they were simply ragged holes in the sacking. I could see no eyes in there, only darkness. Ragged stitchwork from ear to ear gave the mask its permanent grin. Bunches of straw hair poked from under the brim of the ragged fishing hat which had been jammed down hard on the head. That same straw was also poking out between the buttons of the ragged jacket. More string served as a belt holding up equally ragged trousers. The sole had come away from the upper on each boot.

As I stood frozen, taking in this ridiculous sight and perhaps looking just as stupid, the figure raised the long curved thing in its hand.

It was a hand scythe.

This one was black and rusted, but when the scarecrow raised it before its mask-face it seemed as if the edge of that blade had been honed and sharpened. Then I realised that it was this that had smashed our car windscreen. The bastard had waited for us to pass, had stepped out and slammed the damned thing across the glass like an axe.

And then the man began to stride towards me.

There was nothing hurried in his approach. It was a steady methodical pace, holding that scythe casually down at his side. His idiot, grinning scarecrow's face was fixed on me as he moved. There was no doubt in my mind as he came on.

He meant to kill me.

He meant to knock me down and pin me to the ground with one foot, while he raised that hook, and brought it straight down through the top of my skull. Then he would kick me to one side, walk up to the car and drag Gill out of the driving seat...

I turned and ran back to the car. As I wrenched open the passenger door, I glanced back to see that the figure hadn't hurried his pace to catch up. He was coming at the same remorseless pace; a brisk, but unhurried walk. Inside the car, Gill was still hunched in the driving seat, clutching the wheel.

"Drive, Gill!" I yelled. "For God's sake, *drive!*"

"What...?"

I tried to shove her out of the driving seat then, away from the wheel and into the passenger seat. Still in shock, she couldn't understand what the hell was wrong with me. She clung tight to that wheel with one hand and started clawing at my face with the other. I looked back as we struggled. In seconds, that maniac would reach the car. He was already hefting that hook in his hand, ready to use it.

"Look!" I practically screamed in Gill's face, and dragged her head around to see.

At the same moment, the rear windscreen imploded with shocking impact.

Everything happened so fast after that, I can't really put it together in my head. I suppose that the scarecrow-man had shattered the glass with the hand scythe. There was a blurred jumble of movement in the ragged gap through the rear windscreen. And I suppose that Gill must have realised what was happening then, because the next thing I heard was the engine roaring into life.

"Go!" someone yelled, and I suppose it must have been me. Because the next thing I remember after that was me sitting in the back of the car, swatting powdered glass off the seat. Then I heard another impact, and looked up to see that the scarecrow was scrabbling on the boot of the car. The scythe was embedded in the metalwork, and the scarecrow was clinging on tight to it. I thrust out through the broken window and tore at the man's ragged gloves, pounding with my fists. The car bounced and jolted, something seemed to screech under the chassis, and I prayed to God that it was the madman's legs being crushed. We were moving again, but Gill was yelling and cursing, slamming her hands on the wheel. The engine sounded tortured; the car was juddering and shaking, as if Gill was missing the clutch bite-point and "donkeying" all the time.

The scythe came free from its ragged hole and the madman fell back from the boot. There was a scraping, rending sound as the hook screeched over the bodywork. To my horror, I saw that he had managed to snag the damned thing in the fender and now we were pulling him along the hard-shoulder as he clung to its handle. With his free hand, he clawed at the fender; trying to get a proper grip and pull himself upright again. His legs thrashed and raised dust clouds as we moved. Somehow, I couldn't move as I watched him being dragged along behind us. The car juddered again and I almost fell between the seats. Lunging up, I seemed to get a grip on myself.

The madman had lost his hold on the fender. We were pulling away from where he lay. I saw one arm flop through the air as he tried to turn over. Perhaps he was badly hurt? Good.

We were still on the hard shoulder, near to the barrier, as traffic flashed past us. But something had happened to the car when it hit that roadside barrier. Something had torn beneath the chassis, and Gill was yanking hard at the gear lever.

"It's stuck!" she shouted, nearly hysterically. "I can't get it out of first gear."

"Let me try..." I tried to climb over into the passenger seat, but in that moment I caught sight of what was happening in the rear view mirror. The scarecrow was rising to his knees, perhaps fifty feet behind us now. I lost sight of him in the bouncing mirror, twisted around to look out of the window again, just in time to see him stand. There was something slow and measured in that movement, as if he hadn't been hurt at all. He had retrieved the scythe.

And he was coming after us again.

Not running, just the same methodical stride. As if he had all the time in the world to catch up with us.

I faced front again. Gill was still struggling with the gears, and the speedometer was wavering at five miles an hour. As we juddered along on the hard shoulder, it seemed as if we were travelling at exactly the same pace as the man behind us.

"Hit the clutch!" I yelled, lunging forward again as Gill depressed the pedal. I yanked at the gearstick, trying to drag it back into second gear. The best I could do was get it into the neutral position, and that meant we were coasting to a halt. Behind us, the man started to gain. Gill could see him now, slapped my hand away and shoved the gearstick into first again.

"Who *is* he?" she sobbed. "What does he want?"

I thought about jumping out of the car and taking over from Gill in the driving seat. But by the time we did that, the madman would be on us again, and anyway, Gill was a damn sight better driver than me. There seemed only one thing we could do.

"Steer out onto the motorway," I hissed.

"We're travelling too slowly. There's too much traffic. We'll be hit."

"Maybe he'll get hit first."

"Oh *Christ*..."

Gill yanked hard on the wheel and the car slewed out across the motorway.

A traffic horn screamed at us and a car passed so close that we heard the screech of its tyres and felt the blast of air through the shattered windscreen as it swerved to avoid us. I looked at the speedometer again. We were still crawling.

I moved back to the rear window.

The radiator grille of a lorry filled my line of vision. The damned thing was less than six feet from us, just about to ram into our rear; crushing the boot right through the car. I yelled something, I don't know what; convinced that the lorry was going to smash into us, ram us both up into the engine block in a mangled, bloody mess. Perhaps it was the shock of my yell, but Gill suddenly yanked hard at the steering wheel again and we slewed to the left. I could feel the car rocking on its suspension as the lorry passed within inches, the blaring of its horn ringing in our ears. But we weren't out of danger yet. I reared towards the dash as another car swerved from behind us, around to the right, tyres screeching.

"You were travelling too *fast*, you bastard!" I yelled after it. "Too bloody *fast!*"

More horns were blaring and when I flashed a glance back at Gill I could see that she was hunched forward over the wheel. Her face was too white, like a dead person. There were beaded droplets of sweat on her forehead. In the next moment, she had swung the wheel hard over to the left again. Off balance, I fell across my seat, my head bouncing from her shoulder. I clawed at the seat rest, trying to sit up straight again. Suddenly, Gill began clawing at me with one hand. I realise now that my attempts to sit were hampering her ability to pull the wheel hard over. To my shame, I began clawing back at her; not understanding and in a total funk. She yelled that I was a stupid bastard. I yelled that she was a mad bitch. And then I was up in my seat again as Gill began spinning the wheel furiously back, hand over hand. Glancing out of the window, I could see that she had taken us right across the motorway and was taking a sliproad. The sign said: *Boroughbridge.*

She had done it. She had taken us right across those multiple lanes without hitting another vehicle. We were still crawling along, but at least we had got away from the madman behind us. I knew then that everything was okay. When we found the first emergency telephone, we would stop and ring for the police.

"Okay," I breathed. "It's okay... you've done it, Gill... we're okay now."

Until I turned in my seat and looked back to see that everything was far from okay.

The man in the fancy-dress costume was walking across the highway towards us, perhaps fifty yards back. His steps were measured, still as if he had all the time in the world, the scythe hanging from one hand. Grinning face fixed on us. Even as I looked, and felt the sickening nausea of fear again, a car swerved around him, tyres screeching. Its passage made his ragged clothes whip and ruffle. Straw flew from his shoulders and his ragged trousers. By rights, it should have rammed right into him, throwing him up and over its roof. But just as luck had been with us, crossing that busy motorway, it was also with him.

Our car began its ascent of the sliproad, engine coughing and straining. Gill fumbled with the gears, trying without success to wrench them into second. The engine began to race and complain.

"He's there…" I began.

"I *know* he's fucking *there*!" yelled Gill, eyes still fixed ahead. "But we *can't go any faster!*"

The speedometer was wobbling around fifteen miles an hour; even now as we ascended the sliproad, the gradual slope was having an affect on our progress. The needle began to drop… to fourteen… to thirteen.

When I looked back, I could see that nevertheless, we were putting a little distance between us and the madman. When a car flashed past, between the scarecrow and the entrance to the sliproad, I could see that fate wasn't completely on his side, after all. He wasn't invulnerable. He had waited while the car had crossed his path, and that slight wait had given us a little time. Not to mention a certain relief. The man might be mad, but he was human and not some supernatural creature out of a bad horror movie. As the car passed, he came on, the scythe swinging in his hand as he moved.

It came to me then.

There was a tool kit in the boot. If Gill pulled over, I could jump out and yank the boot open, grab a screwdriver or something. Threaten him, scare him away. Show him that I meant business.

"Pull over," I said.

"Are you joking, or what?" asked Gill.

When I looked at her again, something happened to me. It had to do with everything that had occurred over the last forty-eight hours. It had to do with the stupid fights, with my stupid behaviour. But more than anything, it had to do with the expression on Gill's face. This was the woman I loved. She was, quite literally, in shock. And I'd just lashed out at her when she'd been acting on my instruction and taken us across the motorway, away from the maniac and—against all the odds—avoided collision with another vehicle. I'd let her down badly. It was time to sort this thing out.

"Pull over!" I snapped again.

"He's still coming," she said. Her voice was too calm. Too matter of fact.

Then I realised. At this speed, I could open the door and just hop out.

Angrily, that's what I did.

I slammed the door hard as I turned to face our pursuer; just the way that people do when there's been a minor traffic "shunt" and both parties try to faze out the other by a show of aggression, using body language to establish guilt before any heated conversation begins. Inside the car, I heard Gill give a startled cry as the car shuddered to a halt.

The scarecrow was still approaching up the ramp.

I stood for a moment, praying that he might at least pause in his stride.

He didn't.

I lunged at the boot, slamming my hand on it and pointing hard at him; as if some zig-zag lightning bolt of pure anger would *zap* out of my finger and fry him on the spot.

"You're fucking *mad* and I'm fucking telling *you!* You want some aggro, *eh?* You want some fucking *aggro*? I'll show *you* what fucking *aggro* is all *about!*" If the "fuck" word could kill, he should be dead already.

But he was still coming.

I swept the remaining frosting of broken glass from the boot and snapped it open. There was a tyre-wrench in there. I leaned in for it, without taking my eyes off the scarecrow, and my hand bumped against the suitcase. In that moment, I knew that the wrench must be at the bottom of the boot and that all our weekend luggage was on top of it. I whirled around, clawing at the suitcase, trying to yank it aside. But I'd packed that boot as tight as it's possible to get. The only way

I was going to get that wrench was by yanking everything out of there onto the tarmac.

And the scarecrow was only fifty feet from us.

I looked back to see that he was smacking the scythe in the palm of one hand, eager to use it.

"Shit!" I slammed the boot again and hurried back around the car.

The scarecrow remained implacable. From this distance, I could see how tall he was. Perhaps six feet-seven. Broad-shouldered. Completely uncaring of my show of bravado. And, Good Christ, I could hear him now.

He was *giggling*.

It was a forced, manic sound. Without a trace of humour. It was an insane sound of anticipation. He was looking forward to what he was going to do when he reached us. As I dragged open the passenger door, I had no illusions then. If I engaged in a hand-to-hand physical confrontation with this lunatic, he would kill me. There was no doubt about it. Not only that, but he would tear me limb from limb, before he turned his attentions to Gill. I stooped to yell at her, but she was already yanking at the gear-stick and the car was moving again; the engine making grinding, gasping sounds.

The scarecrow's pace remained unaltered.

There was a car coming up the sliproad behind him.

Some mad and overwhelming darkness inside myself made me *will* that car to swerve as it came up behind the scarecrow. I wanted to see it ram him up on the hood and toss him over the fence into the high grass. But then I knew what I had to do. I skipped around the front of our own car and into the road as the car swerved around the scarecrow and came up the sliproad towards us. I ran in front of it, waving my arms, flagging it down. I can still hardly believe what happened next.

The driver—male, female, it was impossible to tell—jammed their hand on the horn as the car roared straight at me. I just managed to get out of the way, felt the front fender snag and tear my trouser leg as it passed. I whirled in the middle of the road, unbelieving. The car vanished over the rise and was gone from sight. I turned back.

The scarecrow was still coming.

"For Christ's sake!" snapped Gill. "Get in."

I stumbled back into the car and we began our juddering crawl again.

I wasn't in a sane world anymore. This couldn't possibly be happening to us. Where was everyone? Why wouldn't anyone help as we crawled on and on with that madman behind us? I turned to say something to Gill, studied her marble-white face, eyes staring dead ahead; but I couldn't find a thing to say. The scarecrow behind us was still coming at his even stride. If he wanted to, he could move faster, and then he'd overtake us. But he seemed content to match his speed with our own. At the moment, he was keeping an even distance between us. If our car failed or slowed, he would catch up. It was as simple as that.

We reached the rise. Down below, we could see that the road led deep into countryside. I'd lost all track of where the hell Boroughbridge might be, if it had ever existed at all. On either side of the road were fields of bright yellow wheat.

At last, God seemed to have remembered we were here and wasn't so pissed off with us, after all. As our car crested the ridge and began to move down towards the fields, it began to pick up speed.

"Oh thank God..." Gill began to weep then. The car's gearbox was still straining and grinding, but we *were* gathering speed. Leaning back over the seat I watched as the lip of the hill receded behind us. When the scarecrow suddenly re-appeared on the top of the rise, silhouetted against the skyline, he must surely see that we were picking up speed. But he didn't suddenly alter his pace, didn't begin to run down after us. He kept at his even march, right in the middle of the road, straight down in our direction. Following the Fucking Yellow Brick Road. Soon, we'd leave him far behind.

I swung around to the front again, to see that we were doing thirty, the engine straining and gasping. I gritted my teeth, praying that it wouldn't cut out altogether. But it was still keeping us moving. When I looked back again, the silhouette of our attacker was a small blur. Another vehicle was cresting the rise behind him. I heard its own horn blare at the strange figure in the middle of the road, watched the small truck swerve around him. It seemed to me that someone was leaning out of the truck window, and the driver was giving the idiot a piece of his mind. The vehicle came on towards us, picking up speed. Should I chance our luck again? Slow the car, jump out and try to flag down help?

"No you're not," said Gill, without taking her eyes from the road. She had been reading my mind. "I'm not slowing this car down again. I'm keeping my foot down and we're getting out of here..."

When I looked at the speedometer, I felt as if I was going to throw up; there-and-then.

"...and we're never, *ever* coming back to this fucking hellhole of a place," continued Gill, her voice cracking and tears streaming down her face, "As long as I ever live. Do you hear me, Paul? Not never, *ever!*"

"I've got to stop that truck before it passes us."

"You're not listening! I'm not stopping. Not for anything!"

"We are stopping, Gill! Look at the speedometer! We got extra speed on the incline, that's all. Now we're slowing down on the straight. Look."

Gill shook her head, refusing to look.

The needle had fallen from thirty to twenty and was still descending.

"Will you just *look!*"

"No!"

I lunged around. The truck was less than two hundred yards behind us, and soon to overtake.

"Gill, look! It's a *tow-truck!* From a breakdown service. It's stencilled on the side. Look!"

"NO!"

With the needle wavering at ten miles an hour, I did what I had to do. I kicked open the passenger door. Gill refused to take her eyes from the road, but clawed at my hair with one hand, screaming and trying to drag me back into the car. I batted her off and hopped out into the middle of the sun-baked dirt road. A cloud of dust enveloped me. I just made it in time. Five seconds later, and the tow truck would have overtaken us and been gone. But now the driver could see my intent. He slowed, and then as I walked back towards him, the truck trundled on up behind us, matching an even time at ten miles an hour as I hopped up onto the standing-board.

The man inside had a big grin. He was about sixty, maybe even ready for retirement. Something about my action seemed to amuse him.

"Don't tell me," he said, without me having to make any opening conversation. "You're in trouble?"

Something about his manner, his friendliness, made that fear begin to melt inside me. Now it seemed that the world wasn't such a hostile and alien place as I thought it had suddenly become. I was grinning now too, like a great big kid.

"How could you tell?"

"My line of business. Been doing this for thirty-five years. People always come to me. I never go looking for them. How can I help you?"

Suddenly, looking back at the scarecrow, now perhaps two or three hundred yards away and still coming down that dirt road towards us, I didn't know what to say.

"Well... the car. We had a bash and... and it's stuck in first gear. Can't get it any faster than five, six miles an hour. Got some speed on the incline there, but it won't last."

"Okay," said the old man with the lined face and the rolled up sleeves. "Just pull her over and I'll take a look."

If my smile faltered, the old man either didn't notice or failed to make anything of it. I hopped down from the board and, realising that I was trying to move too nonchalantly, moved quickly back to the car. Running around the front, I leaned on the window-edge, jogging alongside where Gill was still hunched over the driving wheel, still staring ahead with glassy eyes.

"We're in luck. It *is* a tow-truck. He says he'll help us."

Gill said nothing. The car trundled along at seven miles an hour.

"Gill, I said he'll help us."

Somewhere, a crow squawked, as it to remind us that the scarecrow was still there and was still coming.

"Come on, stop the car."

Gill wiped tears from her eyes, and returned her white-knuckled, two handed grip on the steering wheel.

"Stop the car!"

This time, I reached in and tried to take the keys.

Gill clawed at me, her fingernails raking my forehead. I recoiled in shock.

"I... am... not... stopping the car. Not for you. Not for anybody. He's still coming. If we stop, he'll come. And he'll kill us."

I thought about making another grab, then saw that the old man was leaning out of his window behind us, watching. He wasn't smiling that big smile anymore. I made a helpless, "'everything's fine" gesture and stood back to let our car pass and the tow truck catch up. Then I jumped up on the standing-board again as we trundled along. Behind us, I could see that the scarecrow had gained on us. The silhouette was bigger than before. Had he suddenly decided to change the rules of the game and put on a burst of speed to overtake us? The possibility made me break out into another sweat. The old man seemed to see the change in me.

"Got a problem?" His voice was much warier this time.

"Well, my wife. She... she won't... that is, she won't stop the car."

"Why not?"

"She's frightened."

"Of you?"

"Me? God, no!" I wiped a hand across my forehead, thinking I was wiping away sweat, only to see that it was covered in blood. Gill's nails had gouged me. The old man was only too aware of that blood.

"Well if she won't stop the car I can't inspect it, can I? What's she want me to do? Run alongside with the hood opened?"

"No, of course not. It's just that..."

"So what's she frightened of?"

"Look, there's a man. Can you see him? Back there, behind us?"

The old man leaned forward reluctantly, now suddenly wary of taking his eyes off me, and adjusted his rear view mirror so that he could see the ragged figure approaching fast from behind.

"Yeah, what about him?"

"He..." My throat was full of dust then. My heart was beating too fast. "He's trying to kill us."

"To *kill* you?"

"That's right. That's why the car's damaged. And he just keeps coming and won't stop and..." I was going to lose it, I knew. I was babbling. The old man's eyes had clouded; the sparkle and the welcoming smile were gone.

In a flat and measured voice, he said: "I don't want any trouble, mister."

"Trouble? No, no. Look, we need your help. If you just... well, just stop the truck here. And stand in the road with me. Maybe when he sees that there're two of us, he'll back off. Maybe we can scare him away. Then you can give us a tow. We'll pay. Double your usual rate. How's that sound?"

"Look, I just wanted to help out. I could see your car was in trouble from way off. Steam coming out from under the hood. Oil all the way back down the road. But I don't want to get involved in no domestic dispute."

"*Domestic* dispute?"

"Anything that's happening between you and the lady in the car and the fella behind has nothing to do with me. So why don't you hop down and sort your differences out like civilised people?"

"Please, you've got it all wrong. It's not like that, at all. Look, have you got a portable telephone?"

"Get off my truck."

"Please, the man's *mad!* He's going to kill us. At least telephone for the police, tell them what's happening here..."

"I said, get *off!*"

The flat of the old man's callused hand came down heavy where I was gripping the window-edge, breaking my grip. In the next moment, he lunged sideways and jabbed a skinny elbow into my chest. The pain was sharp, knocking the breath out of my lungs; the impact hurling me from the standing board and into the road. I lay there, engulfed in a cloud of choking dust, coughing my guts out and unable to see anything. All I could hear was the sound of the truck overtaking our car as it roared on ahead down the country road, leaving us far behind. When I tried to rise, pain stabbed in my hip where I had fallen. I staggered and flailed, yelling obscenities after the old man.

The dust cloud swirled and cleared.

The tow-truck was gone from sight.

Behind me, the scarecrow was alarmingly close; now perhaps only a hundred yards away and still coming with that measured tread. Despite my fears, he didn't seem to have put on that burst of speed. Relentless, he came on.

Gill hadn't stopped for me. The car had moved on ahead, itself about fifty yards further down the road. Perhaps she hadn't seen what had happened between the old man and myself, didn't realise my plight. So it was hardly fair of me to react the way that I did. But I reacted anyway. I screamed at her, just as I'd screamed at the departing old man. I screeched my rage and blundered after the car, the pain in my hip stabbing like fire. Even with my staggering gait, it didn't take long to catch up with the car, making the evil mockery of the scarecrow's relentless approach all the more horrifying. If he just put on that extra spurt of speed, he could catch up with us whenever he liked. I threw open the back door of the car and all but fell inside. I tried to yell my rage, but the dust and the exhaustion and the pain all took their toll on my throat and lungs. When I stopped hacking and spitting, I tried to keep my voice calm but it came out icy cold.

"You didn't stop, Gill. You didn't stop the car for me. You were going to leave me there."

Gill was a white-faced automaton behind the wheel. She neither looked at me or acknowledged my presence. In her shock I had no way now of knowing whether she could even hear what I was saying. I wiped more blood from my forehead, and struggled to contain the crazy feeling that I knew was an over-reaction to outright fear.

There was someone up ahead on our side of the road, walking away from us. He was a young man, his body stooped as if he had been walking a long while; with some kind of holdall over his shoulder. He didn't seem to hear us at first; his gaze concentrated downwards, putting one foot in front of the other. I moved towards Gill but before I could say anything, she said:

"Don't!"

"But we should..."

"No, Paul. We're not stopping."

I had no energy. Fear and that fall from the tow-truck had robbed me of strength. But as I leaned back, I saw the young man ahead suddenly turn and look at us. Quickly, he dropped his holdall to the ground and fumbled for something inside his jacket. We were close enough to see the hope in his eyes when he pulled out a battered cardboard sign and held it up for us to read: HEADING WEST.

I looked at the back of Gill's head. She never moved as the car drew level and began to pass the young man. The hope in his eyes began to fade as we trundled past. Did he think we were travelling at that speed just to taunt him? I looked back over my shoulder to see that the scarecrow was still closing the gap, still coming. The fact that I was looking back seemed to give the young man some encouragement. Grabbing his holdall, he sprinted after us. I wound down the side window as he drew level.

"Come on, man." His voice was thin and reedy. He jogged steadily at the side of the car as we moved. "Give me a lift. I've been walking for hours."

"That man... back there..."

The young man looked, but didn't see anything worth following up in conversation.

"I'm heading for Slaly, but if you're going anywhere West that's good enough for me. How about it?"

"That man... he's mad. Do you hear me? He tried to kill us."

Now, it seemed that he was seeing all the evidence that there was something wrong about this situation. The quiet woman with the white face and the staring eyes. The broken windows and the sugar-frosted glass all over the seats. The dents and scratches on the car as it lurched and trembled along the road, engine rumbling. And me, lying in the back as if I'd been beaten up and thrown in there, blood all over my forehead.

"You and me. If we square up to him, we can frighten him off. I'll pay you. Anything you want. And then we'll drive you where you want to go."

"I don't think so," said the young man. He stopped and let us pass him by. I struggled to the window and leaned out to look back at him. He waved his hand in a "not for me" gesture.

"Yeah?" I shouted. "Well, thanks for fucking nothing. But I'm not joking. That guy back there is a *psycho*. So before he catches up, I'd head off over those fields or something. Keep out of his way. When he gets to you, you're in big trouble."

The young man was looking away, hands on hips as if deciding on a new direction.

"I'm telling you, you stupid bastard! Get out of here before he catches up!"

I fell back into the car, needing a drink more than I've ever done in my life. Up in front, Gill might have been a shop mannequin, propped in the driving seat. She was utterly alien to me now, hardly human at all.

You've killed him," I said at last. Perhaps my voice was too low to be heard. "You know that, don't you? The guy back there is as good as dead."

When I turned to look back again, I could see that the young man was still walking in our direction. The scarecrow was close behind him. But still in the middle of the road. Perhaps something in the tone of my voice had registered with him, because he kept looking over his shoulder as he moved and the scarecrow got closer and closer. I couldn't take my eyes away from the rear window. There was a horrifying sense of inevitability. When it seemed that the scarecrow was almost level with him, I saw the young man pause. He seemed to speak to the scarecrow. Then he stopped, just staring. Perhaps he had seen its face properly for the first time.

I gritted my teeth.

The young man shrank back on the grass verge.

I could see it all in my mind's eye. The sudden lunge of the scarecrow, wielding that scythe high above his head. The young man would shriek, hold up his hands to ward off the blow. But then the scarecrow would knock him on his back, grab him by the throat and bring the scythe down into his chest. The young man would writhe and thrash and twist as the scarecrow ripped that scythe down, gutting him. Then it would begin ripping his insides out while he was still alive, the man's arms and legs twitching feebly, and then he would lie still forever as the scarecrow scattered what it found into the surrounding fields.

Except that it wasn't happening like that at all.

The man was shrinking back on the verge, but the scarecrow was still walking.

And now the scarecrow had walked straight past the young man without so much as a sideways glance. He was coming on, after *us*, at the same relentless pace. Now, the young man was hurrying back in the opposite direction; stumbling and fumbling at first, as if he didn't want to take his eyes off this figure in case it suddenly changed its mind and came lunging back at him. The man began to run, then was heading full pelt back in the opposite direction.

The scarecrow was coming on.

It only wanted *us.*

"You bastard!" I yelled through the shattered windscreen. "You fucking, fucking *bastard!* What was the matter with *him*, then? What do you want from us? What the hell do you *want* us for?" I think I began to weep then. Maybe I just went over the edge and became insane. But I seemed to lose some time. And I only came out of it when I realised that I could still hear weeping, and realised that it wasn't mine. When my vision focussed, it was on the back of Gill's head again. She was sobbing. I could see the rise and fall of her shoulders. Looking back through the rear window, I could see that the man had continued to gain on us. He was less than fifty yards behind, and the engine was making a different sound. I pulled myself forward, and it was as if the tow-truck driver was whispering in my ear at the same time that my gaze fell on the petrol gauge.

I could see you were in trouble. Oil all the way back down the road.

The gauge was at "empty." We'd been leaking petrol all the way back to the motorway. Soon we'd be empty and the car would roll to a stop.

Fear and rage again. Both erupting inside to overcome the inertia and engulfing me in an insane, animal outburst. I kicked open the door, snarling. My hip hurt like hell as I staggered into the middle of the road. I tried to find something else to yell back at the approaching figure. Something that could encompass all that rage and fear. But even though I raised my fists to the sky and shook like I was having a fit, I couldn't find any way of letting it out. I collapsed to my knees, shuddering and growling like an animal.

And then, crystal clear, something came to me.

I don't know how or where. It was as if the damned idea was planted by someone else, it felt so utterly *outside.* Maybe even in that moment of pure animal hate, a cold reasoning part of me was still able to reach inside and come up with a plan. Had I had time to think about it, I would have found dozens of reasons not to do what I did. But instead, I acted. I clambered to my feet again. The scarecrow was thirty yards away; close enough for me to see that idiot, grinning face and the black-hollowed eyes. I hobbled after the car, braced my hands on the metalwork as I felt my way along it to the driver's door. I knew what would happen if I spoke to Gill, knew what she would do if I tried to stop her.

So instead, I pulled open the door, lunged in and yanked both her hands off the steering wheel. She screamed. High-pitched and completely out of control. The violent act had broken her out of that rigid stance. She began to scream and twist and thrash like a wild animal as I dragged her bodily out of the car, hanging onto her wrists. When she hit the rough road, she tried to get purchase, tried to kick at me. She was yelling mindless obscenities when I threw her at the verge. She fell badly and cried out. Twisting around, she saw the scarecrow—and could no longer move. In that split-second as I dived into the car, already slewing towards the verge and a dead-stop, I didn't recognise her face. The eyes belonged to someone else. They were made of glass.

I jammed on the brakes, felt so weak that I was afraid I couldn't do what I was going to do. My hand trembled on the gearstick.

Yelling, I rammed the gear into reverse. It went in smooth. I revved up the engine and knew that if it coughed and died from lack of petrol I'd go quite mad.

Then I let up the clutch, and this time the car shot backwards. Maybe it was twenty, thirty miles an hour. Not so fast maybe, but three or four times faster than we'd been travelling on this Crawl. And it felt like the vehicle was moving like a fucking bullet. I was still yelling as I leaned back over the seat, twisting with the wheel to get my bearings right—and the scarecrow began to loom large in my sight-line, right smack centre in the rear window. Dust and gravel spurted and hissed around me.

The scarecrow just came on.

Filling the ragged frame of that rear window.

I just kept yelling and yelling as the scarecrow vanished in the dust cloud the car was making. It gushed into the car, making me choke and gag.

And then there was a heavy *crunching* thud, jarring the frame of the car. It snapped me back and then sharp-forward in the seat. The engine coughed and died. The car slewed to a stop.

I had hit the bastard—and I had hit him hard.

The car was filled with dust. I couldn't see a thing. I threw the door open and leapt out, feeling that stab of pain in my hip, but not giving one flying fart about it. I dodged and weaved in the cloud, crouching and peering to see where he had been thrown. I wanted to see blood in that dry dust. I wanted to see brains and shit. I wanted to see that he'd coughed up part of his intestine on impact and that he was lying there in utter agony. I wanted to see his legs crushed; his head split apart, his scythe shattered into hundreds of little bits.

The dust cloud settled.

I warily walked around the side of the car, looking for the first sign of a boot or an outstretched hand. I strained hard to listen in the silence for any kind of sound. I wanted to hear him moaning or weeping with pain.

But there was no sound.

Because there was no one lying behind the car.

I hobbled to the grass verge. The car was still in the centre of the road, so there was a chance that it had thrown him clear into one of the fields at either side. But there was no one in the grass at the left side, and when I skipped across the road to the other field, there was no sign of a body there either. I knew I had hit that bastard with killing force. But at that speed, surely he couldn't have been thrown the two hundred feet or so into the stalks of wheat out there. It couldn't be possible, unless... unless...

Unless he wasn't very heavy.

Unless he hardly weighed anything at all.

Like, maybe, he weighed no more than your average scarecrow.

The thought was more than unnerving. I cursed myself aloud. He'd had real hands, hadn't he? I'd seen them up close. But then a little voice inside was asking me: *Are you sure you saw them properly? Wasn't he wearing gloves?*

On a sudden impulse, I ducked down and looked under the car.

There was nothing there.

When I straightened up, I could see that Gill was staggering down the road towards me. She looked drunk as she weaved her way towards the car. I leaned against the dented framework, holding my arms wide, imploring.

"I know I hit him," I said. "I *know* I did. I felt the car hit him. He must be dead, Gill. I didn't want to do it, but it was the only way. Wasn't it? I'm sorry for what I did to you, just then. I shouldn't have. But I had to at least try and..."

She was almost at the car now; face blank, rubbing her eyes as if she might just have woken up. I felt the temptation to retreat into that safe fantasy. To pretend that none of this had happened. Lost for words, I shook my head.

I was just about to take Gill into my arms when she screamed, right into my face.

I don't know whether the shock made me react instinctively. But suddenly, I was facing in the opposite direction, looking back to the rear of the car.

And the scarecrow was right there.

Standing on the same side of the car, right in front of me, about six feet away. Grinning his stitched and ragged grin. Straw flying around his head. That head was cocked to one side again, in that half-bemused expression that was at the same time so horribly malevolent. Something moved in one of the ragged eye sockets of his "mask", but I don't think it was the winking of an eye. I think it was something alive in there; something that was using the warm straw for a nest.

The scythe jerked up alongside my face.

I felt no pain. But I heard the *crack!* when the handle connected with my jaw.

In the next moment, I was pinned back against the car. Instinctively, I'd seized the scarecrow's wrist as it bent me backwards. My shoulders and head were on the roof, my feet kicking in space as I tried to keep that scythe out of my face. He was incredibly strong, and I tried to scream when I saw that scythe turn in and down towards my right eye. But no sound would come, and I couldn't move. Somewhere behind, I could hear Gill screaming. Then I saw her behind the scarecrow, tearing at its jacket and yanking handfuls of straw away.

I slid, the impetus yanking me from the thing's grip as I fell to the road. Stunned, dazed, I saw one of the car wheels looming large; then turned awkwardly on one elbow as the scarecrow stepped into vision again. The sun was behind him, making him into a gigantic silhouette as he lifted the scythe just the way I'd envisaged he'd do it for the hitch-hiker. This wasn't real anymore. I couldn't react. I couldn't move. It wasn't happening. Somewhere, a long way away, Gill was screaming over and over again; as if someone was bearing her away across the fields.

Then the car horn rang, loud and shocking.

It snapped me out of that inertia, and everything was real again.

Somehow, the scarecrow's arm was stayed.

It just stood there, a black shape against the sun, the weapon raised high.

And then the horn rang again. This time, a gruff man's voice demanded: "You put that down, *now!*"

Someone had grabbed my arm and was tugging hard. I grabbed back, and allowed myself to be pulled out of the way and around the to rear of the car. Everything focussed again, out of the sun's brilliance.

Gill had pulled me to my feet, and clung tight to me as we both leaned against the battered bodywork. Neither of us seemed able to breathe now.

A car had pulled up on the other side of the road. Only fifteen or twenty feet separating the vehicles. A man was climbing out, maybe in his forties. Thick, curly grey hair. Good looking. Checked shirt and short sleeves. Perhaps he was a farmer. He looked as if he could handle himself. His attention remained fixed on what stood by the side of our own car as he slammed the door with careful force.

"I don't know what's happening here. But I know you're going to drop that."

The scarecrow had its back to us now. Its head was lowered, the scythe still raised; as if I was still lying down there on the ground, about to be impaled.

"You alright, back there?" asked the farmer.

All we could do was nod.

"Drop the scythe, or whatever it is," continued the farmer slowly. "And everything will be okay. Okay?" He moved towards our car, one hand held out gentle and soothing, the other balled into a fist just out of sight behind his back. "And you take off the fright mask, alright? Then we'll calm down and sort everything out."

The scarecrow looked up at him as he approached.

The man halted.

"Take it..." he began.

The scarecrow turned around to face him.

"...easy," finished the farmer. Suddenly, his expression didn't seem as confident as it had before. He strained forward, as if studying the "mask".

The scarecrow stepped towards him.

"Oh Christ Jesus," he said, and now he didn't sound at all like the commanding presence he'd been a moment before. He backed off to his own car, groping for the door handle without wanting to turn his back on what stood before him. He looked wildly at us. "Look, mister," the farmer said to me. "If we both rush him. Maybe we can take him. Come on, that's all it needs..."

I moved forward, but Gill held me tight and pinned me back against the car.

The scarecrow took another step towards the farmer.

"Come *on!*" implored the farmer, fumbling with the handle.

I tried to say something. But what would happen if I opened my mouth, and the scarecrow should turn away from him and look back at *me* again?

"Please," said the man. "Help... help... me..."

The scarecrow held out the scythe to the farmer, a hideous invitation.

I wasn't going to speak, but Gill put a hand over my mouth anyway.

The man yelped and dodged aside as the scarecrow lunged forward, sweeping the scythe in a wide circle. The tip shrieked across the bodywork of the car, where the farmer had been standing a moment before. Flakes of paint glittered in the air. The man edged to the rear of his car as the scarecrow jammed the scythe down hard onto the roof of the vehicle. With a slow and horrible malice, the scarecrow walked towards him. As it moved, it dragged the screeching scythe over the roof with it.

"Please help me!" shouted the man. *"Please!"*

The scarecrow walked steadily towards him.

We saw the man run around the back of his car.

We saw him look up and down the road, trying to decide which direction. He held both arms wide to us in a further appeal.

"For God's sake, please *help!*"

We clutched each other, trembling.

And then the man ran off into the nearest field of wheat. He was soon swallowed by the high stalks. We watched them wave and thrash as he ran.

The scarecrow followed at its steady pace.

It descended into the high stalks, but didn't pause. It did not, thank God, turn to look back at us. It just kept on walking, straight into where the farmer had vanished, cutting a swathe ahead with its scythe. Soon, it too was swallowed up in the wheat. We watched the grass weave and sway where it followed.

Soon, the wheat was still.

There were no more sounds.

After a while, we took his car. The keys were in the dash. I drove us back to the nearest town and we rang for the police. We told the voice on the other end that we'd been attacked, and that our attacker had subsequently gone after the man who had ultimately been our rescuer. We were both given hospital treatment, endured the rigorous police investigations and gave an identical description of the man who had pursued us in his Halloween costume. The police did not like the story. It didn't have, as one of the plain-clothes men had it, the "ring of truth". The fella in the tow truck was never traced, neither was the hitchhiker. They could have given the same description, if nothing else.

But the man who stopped to help us—Walter Scharf, a local farmer, well liked—was never seen again. And he's still missing, to this day. Despite every avenue of enquiry, the police still couldn't link us to anything.

That's what they began to think at the end, you see? That Scharf was somehow the attacker (maybe some sort of love-triangle gone wrong), that he was responsible for the damage to the car and/or us. And that we had killed him, and hidden him. I got a lot of hate mail from his wife. But they couldn't link us to anything.

So we got out of it alive, Gill and I.

But there was something neither of us told the police.

Something that neither of us discussed afterwards.

We never talked about the fact that when the first person to stop and volunteer to help, asked us... *begged* us... to help him: we kept quiet. We said nothing, and did nothing. And because of it, the thing went after him instead of us.

And we were *glad.*

But the darkness of that gladness brought something else into our lives.

Shame. Deep and utter shame. So deep, so profound and so soul-rotting that we couldn't live with ourselves anymore. Gill and I split up. We couldn't talk about it. We live in different cities, and neither of us drives a car anymore.

I know that she'll be having the same nights as me.

The days are bad, but the nights are always worse.

The front door is always the focus of attention, no matter what I'm doing. I'll try to keep myself occupied, try to read, try to listen to music. But all of these things make it much worse. You see, if I really *do* become preoccupied in what I'm doing, then I might not hear it if...

If he... it... comes.

And in the nights, I'll lie awake and listen.

The sound of a car passing on the sidestreet is probably the worst.

I'll hear it coming in my sleep. It wakes me instantly, and I'm never sure whether I've screamed or not, but I lie there praying first that the car will pass quickly and that the engine won't cough and falter. Then, in the first seconds after it's moved on I'll pray again that I won't hear those familiar, staggering footsteps on the gravel coming up the path; that I won't hear that hellish hammering on the front door. I listen for the sounds of that hideous, hoarse breathing.

Sometimes, I'll wonder if I can hear Walter Scharf distantly screaming as he runs through the dark fields of our dreams, the scarecrow close behind. Perhaps those screams aren't his, they're the screams of the next person who crossed its path. They'll fade and die... and the quiet of those dreams is sometimes more horrible than the noise.

And to this day, there are two things that terrify me even more than the sounds of a car, or someone walking up the drive, or the noise of that letterbox before I nailed it down.

The first is the sight and the sound of children playing "tag".

The second is a noise that keeps me out of the countryside, away from fields and wooded areas. A simple, everyday sound.

It's the sound of crows, cawing and squawking.

Perhaps frightened from their roosts by something down below and unseen, thrashing through the long grass.

Now, this crow stays home.

And waits.

And listens.

And crawls from one room to the next, making as little noise as possible.

The days are bad, but the nights are always worse…

deep blue

If I think back about it, the whole thing really began with Charlie Otis and his drunken talk about what music can do to you, depending on what kind of mood you're in.

He felt like talking that night, so I let him. That's the thing about The Portland. It's a kind of haven for people who feel the need to get seriously drunk or talk, or get seriously drunk and listen. It's a pub that's managed to survive the plague of brass and chrome that's infected so many of the city-centre drinking places since the late seventies. Just your old-fashioned, no-nonsense, peeling wallpaper kind of place; with a scarred bar top and fast service for the professional drinker. It's the kind of bar where a draughtsman, a Chief Executive, a shipyard welder and a lawyer can get drunk and talk about their problems with whoever's there, without resorting to talk of work, influence or profession. Anybody who breaks the unspoken rule gets the cold shoulder. Anyway, I digress, and you may as well know from the beginning... I'm no bloody good at telling stories. But bear with me.

So anyway, Charlie Otis worked at the Breweries, something in the Orders Section I think (not that it matters, like I say). I'd already got a couple under my belt when he walked in, but he was onto his fourth before I'd ordered my third, and he was pissed off. He didn't want to talk about his problem, whatever it was... just around it. There's a time for talking and a time for listening. In the Portland, you've got to be intuitive. So I in-tooted, and listened.

"That's the thing with some music," he said. "If you're in a good mood, you can listen to a real bluesy piece, about some fella who's lost everything, you know? And you can enjoy it, get into the feeling of it, without feeling too bad. Know what I mean? But if you're already blue... well, it can make you suicidal. You must know what I mean—you play that sort of stuff for a living."

Time for another digression. He's right, I'm a professional musician. I played Working Mens' Clubs for years with a group—if you can call our rag tag bunch that—by the name of "The Hellbenders". Yeah, I know it's a corny title. But we'd seen a Spaghetti western back in the sixties with that title, and it sort of stuck with us. We were what you might call "soft-rock", I suppose. My ambitions for super-stardom vanished a long time ago, and I don't play the clubs anymore. I'm a session man, but strictly small-time stuff. You ever listen to the music that backs those kids' commercials? You know the sort of thing—the heavy rock stuff behind *Super Auto Man* or *Lightning Raiders*. I'm proud of some of it, actually. Even cut a single of the *Raiders* theme, but it didn't go anywhere. Anyway, whereas the work pays the bills and the maintenance money for my Ex and two kids, it doesn't have any sort of street cred, so I don't talk about it too much.

So I said: "It's just a job to me, Otis."

"Come on, don't give me that," he says. "You're a musician. You've got to *feel* what you're playing."

"If I felt everything I played I'd be burned out."

"But that's the point, see?" He was on his fifth, and I was starting to tune out. "I mean, if you really felt some kinds of songs, I mean really *felt* them it would depress the hell out of you, wouldn't it? I mean... take 'Run for Home', that Alan Hull song. I can't bear to listen to it, 'cause that's the day Alice walked out on me..."

And so on and so forth.

Okay, so we're skipping ahead now. This is about a month later. I was in the same bar, and the same seat, getting on the outside of some happy hour Canadian Gold whiskey, when Gerry walked in.

Now I'd known Gerry for a long time. He had his faults, but he was basically okay. Actually, I owed him, because it was thanks to Gerry that I got started in the commercials work. He was involved with Implosion Studios in town, and that's where I recorded most of my stuff with the other session men that Gerry used to pull together for these kids' adverts. We were good and we were cheap, and the stuff we thrashed out for those London firms was bloody good, if I say so myself. But the thing with Gerry was... well, he was an entrepreneur. He thought he was Big Time, but he wasn't. And you had to ignore the way he went on sometimes about wanting to make the *Big* Big Time. For a while, I was dragged along in the enthusiasm of Gerry's dreams, but experience taught me that most of those dreams would stay that way. Gerry wasn't involved with commercials anymore at that time, he had moved off in search of his Big Dreams. Despite that, despite the fact that I've probably turned into some aged rock and roll cynic, we still had a beer occasionally in the Portland and I let him prattle on about the big deals he was always going to pull off.

Now, this was the second conversation, so I'll try and get it right.

Just how the hell we got around to talking about Buddy Holly, I don't know. But we did.

"Ask anybody," said Gerry. "Anybody..." (and he belched loud enough to draw the attention of the barman) "anybody who knows. And they'll tell you that Buddy Holly was the greatest, the most influential... the greatest..."

So I wasn't really going to argue with him. You know, it had been a really hard day and all I was really looking forward to was to wind down a bit, not wind up. So I took another mouthful of Canadian Gold and started picking idly at one of the rough scratches on the battered bar counter, remembering the time Stanley Usher had his teeth knocked out on it by some pissed-off long distance lorry driver.

"Who's arguing?" I said. "I think he was great, too."

And Gerry swigged down some more of his Newcastle Brown and said: "But... I mean... he was the *greatest*."

And round about then I started to think that he'd already been drinking tonight before he came into the pub. And maybe one too many snorts of the happy-baccy. I wasn't in the mood that night for meaningless, meaningful discussions, know what I mean?

"Know how he died?" asks Gerry.

"Plane crash," I replied. "Him and the Big Bopper."

"September 7th 1936 to February 3rd 1959," said Gerry. "And here's a quote: 'One day soon the reservoir of Holly's songs will be drained. I give the cult five years.' Adrian Mitchell, London Daily Mail 13th July 1962." Gerry ordered another Brown Ale and a whisky for me. So who was arguing?

"The Day The Music Died," I said in return. "Don McLean's 'American Pie'. And he was singing about the day that Buddy Holly died."

"But it's not dead," Gerry said. And there was something about the way he spoke that made me wonder if he was as stoned as I thought he was. "Not anymore." There was an eagerness about the way that he spoke; the keeness cutting momentarily through his drunken blur.

And then he fumbled in his inside pocket and took out a brown manila envelope, swatting it with dramatic emphasis on the bar. He sipped his drink again and sat back, leaving the envelope there, staring at me with that intense expression on his face—like I was supposed to say or do something. Instead I shrugged, inviting him to carry on.

"Know what's in there?" he asked.

"A contract for me to play with Bruce Springsteen on a world tour."

"You wish. But in fact, it's better than that. More than better. This is a bloody goldmine."

There was a pause then, and Gerry seemed to be savouring the moment. Then he nodded at the envelope, inviting me to open it. With a sour smile at his dramatics, I swept it from the bar and did just that. Inside were two sheets of yellowed paper. When I opened out the heavily creased and folded pages, I could see that it was old music paper with the two staves on it. It was a song. Handwritten, with the blue ink faded to grey. The scrawl at the top of the first sheet was hard to decipher, not helped by the Canadian Gold blur in my head.

"Deep... deep..."

"Deep Blue," finished Gerry, swigging back his drink and ordering another for both of us. "It's a blues number. Read the signature."

I squinted at the scrawl again, holding the page up to the light for a better view.

"Buddy..."

"Holly," finished Gerry.

I looked back at him for a long time.

"You're telling me that this is an original manuscript for a song by Buddy Holly?"

"Not only that. But it's the last song he ever wrote."

I finished my drink, still looking hard at Gerry. When our two refreshers came, I sipped at it for a little while, and then said: "Bullshit."

"I'm telling you. It's Buddy Holly's last song. Never been played, never been recorded. It's a goldmine."

"It's a forgery."

Gerry seemed impatient now. I'd obviously not reacted according to plan.

"No it's not. It's the real thing. I guarantee it."

"There's one big reason why it can't be a Buddy Holly song."

"Why?"

"Because Buddy couldn't read music, much less write it. He was self-taught."

"You think I don't know that."

"And you still say it's genuine?"

"I've had the handwriting for the lyrics tested by experts. Not only that, but every crotchet and quaver matches the handwriting style. They were written by the same hand, by the same man. Buddy Holly."

"I still say, bullshit."

"I've got the evidence. Look, you're not telling me anything I don't already know. But—maybe he'd started to learn. The simple fact is—it's his song. And it's his last."

"Where did you get it?"

"Indirectly—from the site where his plane crashed."

"You mean someone just picked it up off the ground, and it's never been heard of for more than thirty years."

"That's right."

"That bull is still straining in the ditch, Gerry."

"Some hillbilly farmer picked it out of a tree. Didn't know what he'd got, but his daughter did. Just like a lot of kids back then, she thought Buddy was Number One. Devastated by what had happened. She just kept those two pages locked in her trunk. A last personal reminder. Never let on about it. Just took it out of that trunk every once in a while and looked at it."

"And never thought about trying to sell it? Maybe make a fortune out of it a few years later?"

"She died. Suicide or something. Someone else found it in that trunk."

"So how come *you're* the first to get your hands on it?"

Gerry tapped his nose. "I'm not the first. I'm number ten, to be accurate."

"Nine people have had this song—and it's never been recorded?

"All nine owners died."

"They all died," I said, kind of flat, to get a reaction out of Gerry.

"They died. Tell you what, that song was *destined* for me."

"Sounds like you're spinning me a tale. What is this—a song with a curse?"

"A song that's never been recorded. This is the one that's going to make the big money."

"You sure this song wasn't composed by Tutankhamen?"

"What?"

"You know. A curse or something."

"Don't be bloody stupid."

"I still think it's bollocks."

"Yeah? Well, bollocks to you, an'all. I was going to cut you in on a piece of the action. I've got something really Big lined up. Special feature on a prime-time television special. And you could have been playing lead guitar on this one."

"Here, let me see."

"Hands off! You think it's all bollocks, remember? You may be able to sight read, and I might not know a crotchet from a jockstrap—but this is *mine*. And you just blew your chance to be part of Rock and Roll history."

Maybe it was the booze making him more touchy than normal, or maybe he was just so hyped up about the whole thing that he wouldn't take anything except wonder and amazement and envy from anyone hearing his crazy Buddy Holly story. But that was when Gerry stamped out of the bar, jamming that envelope back in his pocket. No one looked up as he made his angry way to the door—melodramatic exits were rather a feature of *The Portland*—and this only served to make him more angry. I could hear him cursing all the way out to the street. I remember laughing quietly then as I turned back to my drink, wondering just how much Big Money Gerry had coughed up for the rights to this forgery.

I haven't laughed since.

All the way home that night, in my blurred state of senses, I had this particular feeling. You know the sort of thing I mean? As if you've forgotten to do something, something important. And it nags away at the back of your mind. Even when I let myself through the front door of my rented apartment, I paused on the threshold and tried to remember just what it could be. Nothing would come. Inside, I decided against coffee and took the whisky bottle out of the cupboard. Had it got something to do with Angela, my ex-wife? Had I forgotten to send this month's maintenance money for the kids? Maybe it was the kids themselves, Jamie and Paula. No, their birthdays were four and eight months away. Pouring myself a house-measure of the old anaesthetic, I pulled my acoustic guitar out of the cupboard, flopped on the sofa and began to strum a few chords.

After a few minutes, I realised what had been chewing at the back of my mind.

It was the so-called Buddy Holly song.

Just as Gerry had said, I'm a pretty good sight reader from sheet music, and I also have a pretty good memory. I've only got to play a new number through once, and I can generally log it up in the old beanbox and remember it for the future. And although I'd only had a brief glance at the forgery, I could still see an image of it imprinted on my retina. It was a standard 4/4 signature, but there was something about the chord combination that seemed curious. I closed my eyes, and tried to strum out the brief snatch of what I'd seen. There was a chord change here from E major to A minor which was easy enough. Sorry, maybe you don't know what the hell I'm talking about. Now what can I liken that chord change to? Well, it's used a lot by that film composer, John Barry. It's the opening two chord-stabs from *Goldfinger*, and he uses it a lot in his other stuff. Unusual to start a Blues number with a dramatic "stab" like that. But, anyway, I kept on, swigging on the whisky bottle and trying to remember how it went on from there.

Yeah, A minor to A, then G—then…

Then I don't remember a lot after that.

What I do remember isn't very pleasant at all.

I remember the sounds of screaming, a feeling as if the whole world was tilting. When I try to think back about it, I only see "flashes": like I'm seeing some kind of psychedelic film that makes no sense. I remember something made of glass breaking. Later, they found that my front window was broken and there was blood on the panes, so I suppose it must have been that. They found the guitar out there too, on the street. I seem to remember running through rain (although it wasn't raining that night), and with the sounds of that hideous screaming all around me. I seem to see faces swimming out of mist, leering at me. But in retrospect those faces must have been passersby on the street shrinking back in fear as I hurtled past them in the night.

Then I remember the car, swerving around the corner with its headlights stabbing the night. I remember a shrieking of brakes that matched the terrifying shrieking all around me. Then the impact. A horrible black gulf of pain that killed the screaming dead. A feeling of flying, and the knowledge that the screaming was not coming from all around me, but was actually coming *from* me.

Then it was like I was a kid again, at the dentist's. Back then, when I had gas for an extraction, I would suffer the most terrible hallucinations. I reckon it must have been some reaction to the gas, because the experiences were always hideously painful. Jumbling black-white-and-red shapes. Magnified sounds, like the crashing echoes of someone dropping a tray of cutlery. And the twisting and turning of those shapes, and the sounds of that crashing cutlery were all, in themselves, causing the most hideous, gouging pain. Distorted voices moaning obscenities. Waves of nausea creeping and swelling through the pain...

And then I was awake again, fully expecting to be leaning forward to the unconvincing voice of a dentist telling me that everything was alright and would I please spit into the bowl. I tried to struggle up, but that hideous pain had transferred to my leg. I slumped back. I wasn't ten years old, I was forty.

I was in a hospital bed.

Sweat soaked my face, and I could feel it in the small of my back. And oh God, had I pissed myself as I lay there?

I lay there a while, breathing deep and trying to orientate myself.

There had been an accident. I remembered the car with its blaring horn and its shrieking tyres. My leg seemed to be in some sort of splint under the covers. Yes, that was it—I'd been hit by a car. But what about all that other stuff? The screaming and the breaking of glass and the running through the streets—and something to do with music? No, that must all be part of the shock of the accident. If I just lay still for a while and took it easy, everything would come back to me gradually. Maybe I'd just left Gerry in the pub, and walked outside, full of whisky—straight in front of a car. That made much more sense.

Gerry.

Somehow, I could hear his voice. I rubbed my face, screwed my fists into my eye sockets, shook my head. I could still hear his voice, then I could hear the shrill Liverpudlian voice of a famous TV star—and the sounds of an audience laughing.

I looked up.

There was a television set high up on a shelf, just off to my left.

And there was Gerry—on the screen. Chatting to the TV star.

My senses were still a little blurry. I tried to rise again and felt the pain, thought about ringing the bell at the side of the bed for assistance.

"So tonight's the night," said the woman in the bright red hair. "After all these years. You must be feeling very excited."

"More than excited," said Gerry's familiar voice. "I'm proud. Just proud that I'm part of such a big moment in Rock and Roll history."

"So no one's heard the song, none of the band back there have rehearsed it?"

"That's right. This is the first time that his last song will have been played to an audience. Just like the band back there, the viewers will be hearing *Deep Blue* just as Buddy composed it—for the very first time."

"I can't wait, chuck. Believe me. So viewers, tune in for tonight's Big Event—just after the regional news..."

And that's when I tore the IV wires out of my arm and shoved the stand aside. The wires sprayed liquid over the bedspread. I knew that the pain was going to be bad, but hadn't appreciated just *how* bad as I pulled myself out of bed and my strapped-up leg swung down to bang against the mattress. The pain almost made me throw up. I gritted my teeth, felt the enamel scraping—and hobbled to the cupboard. I was right, my clothes were in there. I dragged them out as the loud and brassy television theme music filled the room. My head was still swimming as I dragged the clothes on. There was a walking stick beside a chair in the corner. I grabbed it and hobbled to the door. So far, no one had noticed that I'd come around. I staggered, putting too much weight on my splinted broken leg. This time, I did throw up; reeling to one side as it came out of me.

In the next moment, I was out of the ward and hobbling down the corridor head down. I hoped to God that no one would stop me. Each step of the way, I gritted my teeth or chewed at my lips with the pain. By the time I'd reached the end of the corridor, there was a salt taste of blood in my mouth.

Outside, it had begun to rain. I stood aside as an ambulance pulled up at the entrance, kept my head down and tried to pretend that I was just a patient having a breath of fresh air as the back doors of the ambulance banged open and two of the crew loaded out some poor old guy on a stretcher with an oxygen mask on his face. As soon as they passed me, I hobbled out into the night.

How long had I been lying there in that hospital bed? Days, weeks, months?

Prime time television special, Gerry had said. How long would it have taken him to fix up a deal like that?

I stared out into the darkness. I'd never make it to the main road with this leg, and there was no guarantee that I would be able to flag down a taxi. I had to go back inside the hospital, find a telephone, hope that I wasn't spotted. How the hell could I convince anyone at the studio?

Then I saw the driver's keys, still in the ignition of the ambulance.

Now or never.

I yanked open the door, drew a deep breath, and began to clamber in. My leg bumped against the door as I climbed in—and I'm sure I passed out then. In a kind of dream I saw myself being hauled out of the ambulance, put onto a stretcher and taken back inside. But then the dream dissipated, and there I was, half-in-half-out, lying across the seat. My leg was on fire. I struggled up and pulled the door shut. The walking stick was going to have to serve the purpose of my damaged leg on the accelerator.

I gunned the engine into life—and the ambulance screeched off down the hospital ramp. I expected to see the two crew members galloping out after me, yelling and screaming. Expected to hear the sounds of police sirens at any minute. But there was no one to stop me as I came off that ramp into the hospital forecourt, and the ambulance screeched out on to the main road. If anything had been coming, there would have been no way I could have stopped. There would have been a pile-up, and that would have been the end of it. But, thank God, nothing came.

Where the hell was the siren on this thing? If I could find it, then I could get where I was headed with no problems of being snarled up by traffic. The other bastards would have to stop.

Nine previous owners of that song.

I found it—just before I went through that first set of red lights. A Volvo swerved up onto the pavement out of my way, juddering to a halt. Now I knew—I'd never get to that studio on time, would never get past the security guards in this condition. I rammed the gears into reverse and screeched down a side road. There was one other place I had to get to—and it was near.

Nine previous owners, all of them dead. Suicide, Gerry had said. That first girl who found it committed suicide. What about the other nine?

How long had I got? How long did the local news last for God's sake?

There were roadworks at the corner of the street I was headed for.

Buddy Holly composed it. Somehow. On that plane.

I swerved the ambulance in hard, tried to avoid the hole that the British Gas workmen had been working in. The left side wheel juddered on the edge as the ambulance slewed across the street, slamming into the red and white wooden barriers, splintering them and sending traffic cones whirling and clattering in the night.

He plays it for the first time. On that night, 3rd February 1959. He plays it on the plane.

Somehow, I didn't go sideways into the hole as I tugged at the wheel. The ambulance righted and roared down the street.

Those on board the plane hear the song. And something happens then. The plane pitches out of the sky, slams into the Earth killing everyone on board.

I jammed down hard on the brakes, pitching myself forward; the juddering agony in my leg making me yell out loud. But I couldn't stop now; not now, when I'd managed to get this far. I dragged open the door, leaving the siren wailing. Already, the curtains in the windows of this small side-street were twitching as those inside came to find out what the hell the noise was about. That was good. Let them come. Let them get away.

And out of that carnage, a sheet of writing paper flutters in the wind, coming to rest in the branches of a tree. There to be found, eventually, by a young girl. Taken away—and kept. A love song to her. From Buddy—or perhaps—from Something Else.

There was no way I could clamber down from this height, it was going to take too long. There was only one way. I gripped my leg hard, and rolled out of the seat, head down, hunching my shoulders to take the impact as I hit the ground. All the way down to the ground, I gripped hard on my leg trying to make sure it didn't bang against anything. The impact seemed to judder every bone in my body. Something ripped in my shoulder and now I couldn't see straight. Had I concussed myself?

And then the realisation. As I'd run screaming down the street, having played that song. That horrible realisation as the car swerved and its horn blared. The car was swerving to avoid me—but I'd heard, and now—I WANTED to die. I had thrown myself under that car deliberately.

No time to think, no time to lose. I dragged myself up, pulled the walking stick out of the cab and hobbled furiously towards that familiar front door.

It began to open as I approached.

It was Angela.

In her dressing gown, hair wet and looking as if she had just got out of the bath.

"Oh my God," she began. "It's *you*..." It was an automatic response of weary disgust, but her words shrivelled in her mouth when she saw my face, saw what kind of state I was in. Her mouth opened wide, and she had no time to react as I hit that half-opened door hard with my free hand. In shock, she staggered back against the wall and I blundered straight in past her.

"The kids!" I yelled. "Where are the kids?"

"They're watching the telly—what the *hell* do you think you're doing, busting into my house like that? There's a restraining order against you coming here. You know that? And what the *hell* is that ambulance doing...?"

I shouldered the living room door open. Jamey and Paula were already looking my way as I came in, eyes wide and fearful.

On the television, the red haired woman said: "And without further ado—not that there's been any ado going on anyway (laughter)—Gerry Cainton's band, *Surefire,* are here to play—for the very first time—Buddy Holly's *Deep Blue.*"

As the audience applause filled the room, I limped towards the television set, forcing myself not to care about the agony in my leg.

The band played those first two chords. Major to minor. The intro.

God in Heaven, I couldn't bend to switch the damn thing off, or even pull the plug out of its socket. The pain was too great. If I was to fall, I'd never get up again with this leg.

From the corner of my eye, I saw the kids shrinking back on the sofa, away from me.

The drums began, the bass started a riff. The lead guitarist strutted forward to his microphone.

And I seized the top of the television, yanking it from its table and screaming like a wild animal at the pain as the weight of it forced me to stand firm on both legs. Then I lunged forward as that first lead guitar phrase filled the room—and stumbled towards the windows.

The set's lead jerked free from the socket just as I hit the window. It shattered with a juddering crash, and the set went straight out into the street in a glittering wave like broken ice. I fell over the jagged edge, feeling the glass slice through my clothes and across my stomach and chest. I saw the television hit the gleaming pavement; saw the screen explode with a hollow cough, spitting out blue sparks, glass and shattered filaments in its last buzzing, spluttering death rattle.

I couldn't get my breath.

As I tried to suck in lungfuls of night air, as the rain spattered through that shattered window and the sounds of that ambulance siren wailed in the living room, I was racked by a keening, sobbing convulsion deep in my chest. It had something to do with the pain, the agony—but it was more to do with relief, with the fact that I never thought deep down that I was going to get there in time.

Now, there were hands on my shoulders. Small hands, gentle but strong.

That sobbing seemed to be convulsing my whole body as I was lifted out of the broken window. It was Jamey and Paula, their faces no longer terrified, their eyes no longer wide with fear.

"Here," said Jamey. "Here, Dad." And they were both trying to guide me to the sofa.

In the doorway, I could see Angela in her dressing gown. Face white and set in a mask of fury. She was on the telephone. I knew from that expression that she had just dialed 999.

"Police!" she snapped firmly at the phone, her eyes still fixed on me.

"Oh, God, Dad..." said Paula, her voice filled with a kind of soft horror. "What's that?"

I struggled to control that sobbing, and turned to see her looking past me, back out to the window.

"Listen," she said.

And I heard what she had heard, even above the sound of the ambulance siren.

Someone, somewhere out there in the night, was screaming.

And even as we listened, we heard the sounds of other voices joining in. The sounds of someone in mortal pain, or in an agony of distress.

Another voice, and another... and another. Then the sound of breaking glass, another clattering smash out there somewhere on the streets. A shriek of tyres, another juddering crash. More voices were joining that swelling chorus. Now it sounded like the caterwauling of night animals, a hideous and insane shrieking. Like the sounds of souls in Hell, souls in torment, filling the night air.

It was growing louder and nearer.

Now, people were screaming behind the doors of houses on this street.

An insane, heart-rending cacophony. The sounds of desolation and despair.

Those sounds had drowned the ambulance siren, as the kids clung close to me, staring out wild-eyed and frightened into the night.

When I turned back to Angela, she had dropped the telephone. It swung at the end of its flex from the table in the hall. Her face was still white, but this time not with fury as she stood silently watching and listening.

"What...?" she began.

And I could give her no more answers than I can give you now.

guilty party

"I've been a wild rover for
many a year
And I've spent all me money on
whisky and beer
But now I've returned with gold
in great store
I won't play the wild rover.
No never.
No more."

The last chorus of the old song reverberated from the swaying occupants of the battered bus as it sped down yet another country lane. As if on cue, a sudden turn in the road sent the chorus leader, who had been standing in the aisle, crashing across two of the seats.

There was a roar of drunken laughter.

It had been a good night. The usual office Christmas party with hired bus and a pub far out in the wilds. Stamfordham was usually a quiet little spot. Not really too remote, but "countryfied" enough to appeal to the most hardened of "city" types and to arouse the irritation of local residents when the "townies" arrived *en masse* to take over the only two pubs in the area.

Stuart heaved himself from the seat and struggled past Mark towards the back of the bus. Mark by this time had begun to lead the others in another typical "Oirish" folk song: "The Wild Colonial Boy"—and the strains of the boozy singers echoed in Stuart's whisky befuddled brain as he slumped next to Steve, who was near to falling asleep, partly because of the rocking of the bus but mainly because of the ten rum-and-Cokes which had passed through his system.

Moonlight occasionally flashed through the ragged trees which reared and loomed past the windows as the bus rattled on its way, city-bound.

"Hello, my good man," said Steve slurrily, "What brings you down here then?"

"Just had an idea," said Stuart, "An idea for a story."

Both men were fanatical dreamers and film buffs. Ideas for scripts and screenplays were often shouted across the office in between writing reports and drafting committee minutes.

"Just supposing," Stuart went on after a slight pause, "That there's been an office party just like this one, and we're on your way home. Just like this. Then, suddenly, one of the people on the bus sees something... *something*... outside in the trees, by the glare of the headlights."

Steve pursed his lips thoughtfully and screwed up his eyebrows. Then, after another pause he looked at Stuart.

"You mean... something vague. Something... not quite *right*."

"Yeah. That's right. Something pretty weird. So that he's not sure whether it's the booze or not."

"It would be a good starting point for..."

"...a horror film. Yeah."

They continued to bounce ideas off each other. Clichés abounded. Stock situations seemed to spring readily into mind. Completely absorbed, they'd forgotten everything else. Suddenly, a chorus of voices brought Stuart back to reality.

"Stuart! Hi, man! You don't want to sleep on the bus tonight, do you? It's your stop!"

"Is it?"

Stuart bundled to his feet and pulled his coat on.

"Don't forget, Steve! This one we can take up on Monday! See you!"

As he bustled to the front of the bus, a flurry of arms slapped him amiable across the shoulders.

"Get a move on, Stu! We've got to get home as well, you know!"

The hiss of the pneumatic bus door. The bite of the cold winter air. With his breath turning to steam, Stuart turned on the step and waved his arm in a mock dramatic gesture of farewell.

As he stepped down from the bus and into the night, the cries of farewell were snuffed out as the door snapped shut. With a coughing roar of the engine, a shifting of gears and a crunch of gravel, the bus sped off rattling into the blackness of the country lane.

Country lane?

"What the hell am I doing in a country lane?" thought Stuart, spinning none too steadily on one heel and surveying the bluc blackness of his surroundings. In the cold moonlight he could just make out the row of hedges bristling on each side of the road.

Clutches of trees like gnarled giants crouched along the roadway, their spiny fingers dancing in the freezing air as if conducting the weird melody which the wind was playing amongst them.

"The stupid idiots have dropped me off in a country-bloody road! Miles from anywhere!"

It was a little while before he realised that he was standing directly under a rusted signpost and when he squinted up at the weatherbeaten lettering, he realised what happened.

"Don't forget," he had said in the Bay Horse Pub, "I've got to be dropped off at Crawpost when we head back. My mate's picking me up there and taking me on home."

The signpost had only two placenames on it... Newcastle 13 miles: Crowfast Farm 2 miles. Maybe Crawpost *had* sounded like Crowfast after ten whiskies, but it didn't make Stuart feel any better disposed towards his fellow man as he started to walk down the lane. Turning up his collar he looked for a telephone box or the tell-tale flashing headlights of an approaching car. Nothing. Not even the distant glow from a farmhouse window.

Nothing.

He began to curse under his breath that the party had been organised so far away from Newcastle. Why couldn't it have been held in the town? Or at least near to a bus route. Here he was, miles from anywhere on a lonely country road. Anything could happen. He could fall into a ditch and break a leg or something. Unnoticed for weeks maybe. That was a good idea for a story...

Stories later. The first matter of priority was a phone box or a farmhouse with a telephone.

It seemed that only ten minutes had passed before a gradual feeling of unease began to creep over him. Continually, he found himself glancing over at the other side of the road as the hedges hissed and swayed with the wind. Stuart was not a nervous man. Admittedly, being stranded out in the wilds was an irritating experience to say the least, but no reason to suppose that someone was...

Damn it, someone *was* following him! Creeping along behind the hedge on the other side of the road.

Stuart stopped. This was bloody stupid. There wasn't anyone there. *This is what comes of getting ideas for horror films,* he thought. He continued to walk, the lonely sound of his footsteps on the road somehow challenging the darkness. But he still couldn't lose the feeling that something was moving over there.

Must be a cow.

Another five minutes or so passed as he walked. For an instant, he thought he saw something slinking past a gap in the hedgerow. Again, he stopped and stared at the hedge. There wasn't anybody there, surely? Funny thing, though, standing there in the moonlight staring at the hedgerow as he was, Stuart had to admit that by a trick of the light it *did* look as if something was just visible on the other side. Something that crouched and watched.

Stuart laughed and kept on walking. He conjured up pictures of Cary Grant in a similar situation. Alighting from a bus in the film "North by Northwest", he had found himself out in the open. Isolated and vulnerable. And then he'd been attacked by a crop-dusting aeroplane.

But that was in the daytime. No homicidal plane pilot in sight. Just a rustling in the hedgerow which seemed to be keeping pace with him as he walked.

Unconsciously, he found himself walking slightly into the road; away from the gravel at the roadside which had been crunching under-foot. Was he afraid of giving away his position? Could that be his own shadow somehow reflecting in the shubbery? No... his own shadow was right there on the road. The foolishness of the situation stopped him from crossing the road and peering over the hedge.

A scudding cloud covered the moon like a giant veil, and the countryside was plunged into an even greater darkness.

Stuart had read the clichés about fear jolting a person's nervous system like an electric shock. He had heard how a person's blood could "turn to ice" and of how his heart could "leap into his mouth". But he was totally unprepared for it to happen to him.

As if waiting for the moon to disappear, something large crashed through the hedge and was bounding across the road. What happened next seemed to be a series of impressions... of "frozen frames" in a film. Everything happened so quickly. Something came dashing at him through the dark. Something which panted heavily and loudly as it approached. Stuart was frozen in his tracks. In an instant, there was the horrific impression that something wanted to catch him very desperately. Something altogether bestial, hungry and decidedly unpleasant. A glint in the dark from what seemed to be an eye or a tooth made him realise that his assailant was almost on top of him. Almost at his ear there came an animal-like snarl as he ducked down instinctively onto his haunches. A brush of hair on his cheek. A savage glancing blow on his back. The ripping of cloth. The crash of undergrowth as his attacker burst through the other hedge behind him.

Stuart wheeled around to face the hedge just as the moon reappeared, throwing out everything around him in crystal clear vision. A gaping hole had been torn into the hedge, the inner fringes of which still twisted and writhed from the passage of... whatever it had been.

Stuart could actually feel his heart pounding in his chest. His throat seemed dry and constricted. He was no longer drunk.

An impression remained in his mind of a man-like shape. But not a man.

"No..." Stuart muttered under his breath, his eyes flickering the length of the hedgerow. "...not a werewolf either. More like some stupid bugger dressed in a ridiculous werewolf costume from a very bad horror B-feature."

It all seemed perfectly clear. Somebody was dressed up and trying to scare the hell out of him. Well... he'd done a pretty good job so far. If Stuart hadn't left Steve on the bus, he would have sworn that this would be the sort of thing *he* would pull after their conversation on film plots.

Stuart started to run, still scanning the bushes at his left, not sure whether the sound of his own gasping was covering the horrific panting and growling of something keeping abreast with him on the other side of the hedge. Hardly even altering his speed, he stooped and grabbed half of a housebrick from the grass verge. Still running, he weighed the brick in his hand. The very fact that it was a housebrick and not just some rock was a comfort. A brick made by a builder for a house. For people. Out in the wild, it was a comfort to know that his grab for a weapon had given him something which was man-made. Now, even the lonely stretch of road didn't seem quite so cut off from civilisation as before, and the feeling that there was nothing more supernatural than a lunatic in a Halloween costume following him, made Stuart's fear re-channel itself into something approaching rage. Just one more glimpse of the bastard, and he'd have to contend with a skull fracture.

Stuart's anger reached a peak. Veering in towards a gap in the hedge where anyone on the other side would have to pass, he suddenly halted, whirled, and raised the brick ready to throw.

Just show yourself for one second...

Sucking in lungfuls of air, he tensed... waiting for his assailant. His own heartbeats thudded like the footsteps of an approaching giant.

Nothing.

Clouds of breath streamed around his face.

Nothing.

The branches of a nearby tree shook and rattled in the wind.

Nothing.

Slowly, Stuart began to move along the road again, still with the brick half raised in his hand, ever watchful for any sign of movement. A flicker of light between the trees suddenly caught his eyes.

A farm! Crowfast Farm!

He realised that he'd run almost two miles. Normally, running for a bus would have completely winded him. But the circumstances here were entirely different. If the farm had a telephone—which it surely must have—he could phone for a taxi and be on his way home in no time at all. On instinct, Stuart turned quickly as he ran. About twenty-five yards behind him something suddenly dashed across the road from right to left and vanished into a copse of trees. Something which crouched as it ran, but with extremely broad shoulders and long arms. And... pointed ears?

Stuart began to run even faster than before. The road twisted to the right, and, just at the turn, he saw on the left-hand side a twisted, roughly hewn gate bearing a hand-etched inscription... "Crowfast Farm".

Deep in the trees he could see the glow which had first caught his eyes. Reaching the gate, Stuart took a running leap by bracing one hand on the topmost bar of the gate. Years of sitting behind a desk and insufficient exercise suddenly caught up with him as his foot caught against the bar and sent him cartwheeling into the deep grass on the other side of the gate. Spitting out soil, he pulled himself to his feet. His leg felt about six inches longer than the other one. The thought of being hemmed in by trees was suddenly unnerving. At least in the open road he could almost see if anyone was lurking nearby. But with all of those trees...

Crashing into the copse, Stuart dodged in and out around the tree trunks with his eyes fixed steadfastly on the glowing light up ahead. No less than ten yards into the trees he heard something blundering into the gate behind him.

Bastard!

Spinning around, Stuart swung his arm back to throw the brick and for the first time really saw his pursuer, crouched at the gate and with the moonlight shining full on its face.

As a child, Stuart had once dreamed that someone was standing in the shadows at the foot of the bed. Frozen by some strange force, he had watched as the figure silently moved around the bed and approached him. It was only when the figure had suddenly thrust itself forward into the moonlight that he had been able to scream and pull the bedclothes over his head. The same immobility now came over him as he saw the slavering jaws, the balefully glowing red eyes, and the hideously pointed wolf's ears. This was no lunatic in a Halloween costume...

The stooped figure paused at the broken gate and swung its head backwards and forwards, looking for him; the clawed arms swinging restlessly like some horrific ape. The figure suddenly became rigid and Stuart realised that it had seen him. As the horror, with terrible strength, loped over the gate and lunged into the trees towards him, the spell broke and Stuart heaved the brick with more strength than he thought he had. At once, he knew that he had thrown wide of the mark. He watched as the projectile twisted through the air, as if in slow motion. The man-beast thrashed between the trees, and it seemed as if the missile would hit one of the tree boles. Unaware of the projectile, the beast stepped straight into its path.

The brick struck the animal full on the temple with an audible crunch of bone, and sent it reeling into the undergrowth. Turning, Stuart dashed through the trees and was suddenly aware of the most chilling howl of rage and pain from behind him. He had never heard a wolf howl before. Only on film. Never in real life. Again, the thought came back to him that he had been caught in the fantasy world of a B-film character.

But for no more than an instant. This nightmare was real. The iced air tore at his lungs as he charged through the undergrowth. The tangled grass and weeds seemed to deliberately clutch at his legs, slowing him down.

The farmhouse *must* be up ahead somewhere. The light flashed clearly only twenty yards away. From somewhere behind him came the sound of crashing vegetation. Only ten yards to go. A thicket obscured the light. Thrusting through the shrubbery, Stuart came into a small clearing and saw the source of the light.

"What the bloody hell...?"

A lantern hung from the low limb of an ash tree, throwing out the surrounding trees in bright relief. A lantern, but no farm house.

Jesus! There had to be a farmhouse somewhere. Realising that he'd run into the copse only to find that there was no sanctuary and that the thing behind him was still approaching rapidly made panic clutch at his throat. There *must* be a farmhouse nearby. Who had put the light there? And why? Stuart dashed around the clearing frantically searching for some sign of human habitation.

The farmhouse was up ahead, surrounded on all sides by thick undergrowth and twisted trees. Stuart had a flitting glimpse of dilapidated buildings, a crumbling wall and rusting farm equipment as he launched himself towards the main thatched building. A dull light shone through one of its windows. The solid oak door seemed to swing towards him at a crazy angle as he pounded into a small paved yard, leapt over the rusting plough and crashed against the panelling. Grasping the large gargoyle doorknocker, he pounded on the door.

"Let me in!"

Looking over his shoulder as he hammered on the solid oak, he saw a dark shadow lurching through the trees just beyond the glow of the lantern in the clearing.

"Let me in!"

As he pounded, he realised that the creature could easily find him by the noise he was making. A crash from somewhere behind, and the yellow glow of the lantern was extinguished.

"LET ME IN!"

Suddenly, there came the judder and rattle of a large bolt being thrown on the other side of the door, and Stuart practically fell inside as the heavy door swung inwards. A had grasped his arm to steady him as he staggered across a musty room and into a chair. The door slammed shut and he heard the bolt being pushed back into position. Gasping for breath, Stuart looked up and saw a small and very wrinkled old man with an extremely benign face and faded-blue eyes standing at the door holding a small lantern above his stooped head. Its guttering light made shadows loom and sway throughout the room.

The old man smiled.

"Happy Birthday, son. We've been expecting you."

Stuart pointed at the window, unable to speak, as he sucked in lungfuls of stale air. The old man slowly followed his pointing finger, smiled again, and crossed to the far side of the room to a battered door. In the gloom, Stuart could just make out the ancient furniture in the room. A gigantic cobweb stretched from an old spinning wheel in the corner to a dust-covered sideboard.

The old man opened the door and without taking his eyes from his visitor, called to someone beyond.

"Violet. He's come."

Stuart stood up, chest heaving, and moved to the fly-stained window. The faint light from within the room cast a faint reflection out into the yard but the blackness beyond hid anything that might... that *was* lurking outside.

"Listen," Stuart said and turned again to the old man, who had shut the door and moved to the table in the centre of the room, "Have you got a phone?"

The old man smiled.

"A phone? Have you got a phone?" Stuart demanded angrily. "There's a dangerous animal out there. Somebody's got to phone the police!"

"You know we haven't got a phone, Matthew," said the old man.

The door behind him opened with a slight creak, and an old woman appeared, stooped and shambling. Stuart could see that her face held the same indulgent smile as that of the old man. Her eyes lit up as she looked at Stuart from under a furrowed brow.

"Matthew," she said, "We knew that you'd come back to us. Happy Birthday, son."

Stuart braced himself and looked at the couple, anger beginning to swell inside.

"I'm not Matthew, whoever he is. And if we don't do something..."

Another figure entered the room. A younger man with a checked shirt and a notably extravagant expression of grim determination. However, the most noticeable thing about him was the 12-bore shotgun which he held pointed at Stuart's chest.

The old man placed a hand on Stuart's shoulder.

"Sit down, my boy."

As he sat, the younger man shut the door with his foot and hissed at the old woman: "Is it him?"

The old lady smiled, nodded, and pulled up a chair at the table across from Stuart and the old man.

This is crazy! thought Stuart.

"Ten years to the day, Matthew," croaked the old man, "And here you are, just as you said you would be. You were always true to your word. Punctuality. Punct-u-ality."

Stuart began to stand again. The younger man waved the shotgun in a gesture which made Stuart realise that not only was there great danger outside, but also a very real danger *inside.*

"Would you mind telling me just what's going on?" he asked.

"You *know,* Matthew. It's been a long time now since we last saw you. And I suppose we really should explain a few things. You have every right to be angry with us for what we did, but it was all for the best. All for the best." Stuart sat down again and the old man crossed his arms on the table, before continuing. "If you hadn't been such a wild rover in the first place, Matthew, nothing would have come of it. But... well, when you returned to your mother and I after all those years abroad we *were* glad to see you again." The old man pointed at the younger man with the gun. "Arnold always missed his brother, didn't you Arnold? And as for all that money you brought back with you... It's still here, you know. We've never touched a bit of it. Locked up in the cellar for ten years. 'Matthew's money'—that's what your mother calls it. We've been keeping it for you."

Stuart shifted uncomfortably in his seat and glanced at the window.

The old man continued: "So we've never stolen anything, son. You've got to understand that we didn't kill you for your money."

Stuart looked at the old man again. He *must* be mad.

"We really didn't want to kill you in the first place. But you know how it was when you came back to us. You were changed. And when the killings started, we did shelter you, didn't we? We would never have given you away, would we, mother? We suffered for a long time, Matthew. The old gypsy lady told us what was happening and what we should do. When the little boy was killed, we had no alternative..."

The old lady leaned forward, "We were never cruel parents, Matthew. Were we, father?"

"No, of course we weren't." The old man shook his head slowly and earnestly, "But anyway... you're here now, just like you said you would be. And you're not angry with us anymore for what we did."

Stuart turned to the younger man. "Listen, mate. There's an animal out there. It looks like a... well, it's... You've got to get a message to the police or something. Have you got a car?"

The young man remained impassive, shotgun still pointed at him.

"We can't have a birthday without a birthday party, can we, Violet?" said the old man.

Smiling like a small child who has just thought of a new game to play, the old woman scurried past the shotgun-wielding Arnold and into the darkness beyond.

"I'm not your son," protested Stuart, "You should know that. My name's..."

"Of course you are, Matthew," replied the old man indulgently.

"Look, I don't even... Have you got a picture? A picture of your son?"

Arnold stood slightly to one side and motioned with the shotgun at a picture hanging over the spinning wheel.

"I can't see it clearly."

Stretching across, Arnold took down the picture and gingerly placed it in front of Stuart, the barrels of the shotgun coming uncomfortably close to his face. Wiping the dust from the glass frame, Stuart saw that the face was of a very ordinary looking young man in his mid twenties. Glassy eyes. Dark hair. The likeness to the threatening young man with the gun was unmistakeable.

"Brother?" Stuart asked.

For the first time, Arnold spoke. In a voice that quivered with fear.

"Yes."

"Listen, old man," said Stuart. "This picture doesn't even remotely look like me."

The old man wagged a reproachful finger at Stuart. "The gypsy lady said that you would be changed when you came back. Being able to change was always one of your tricks, you know."

The woman returned from her mission carrying a wooden tray. On the tray rested a cake. A huge birthday cake covered in candles, many of which were cracked and broken. A wickedly sharp cake knife lay alongside it. Stuart could see that the cake itself was old. Very old.

Cobwebs fluttered on its surface. Through the mould, he could just make out that the cake had been once decorated with the legend, "Happy Birthday Matthew."

The old man gestured to Arnold to sit down with them at the table. As he sat, the woman handed him a paper party hat and then, reaching across the table, gave another to Stuart and the old man. The old man smoothed it onto his balding pate. A green hat with long spikes that rustled in the still air like a strange crown.

"Come on Matthew. Join in the fun."

Stuart again rose to his feet, pushing the chair back as he did so.

"If you think…"

Arnold leapt to his feet and swung the shotgun up.

"Sit down, Matthew."

The old man gripped Stuart by the coatsleeve.

"Sit… *down* and join in the fun," he hissed vehemently through clenched teeth, the air of gentility completely gone from his voice. Stuart sat, slowly and reluctantly, putting the orange paper hat on his head. The old lady had begun to light the candles on the cake.

"It has to be done this way," hissed the old man, "The old lady said so. When you promised to come back to us, Matt… as you were dying… you were very angry. You would have killed us. The old lady said you would come back on your birthday. Today. And that if we didn't arrange things properly, there wouldn't be… wouldn't be any stopping you. You do see that don't you son?" The tone of the old man's voice had changed again. Now he was imploring Stuart, explaining something and trying to make him understand. "'You've got to have a special cake ready for him when he returns.' That's what the old lady said. 'A special cake. And you've got to make him welcome. That's important. You must always keep a special lantern burning out there in the clearing where the deed was done.' And you can see, can't you son? We *have* made you welcome. You'll always be our boy. Nothing can change that.

Stuart banged his fist down hard on the table in anger, making the guttering candles on the cake shake, creating new shadows which leapt threateningly from the corners of the room. The old woman cried out in alarm, and the old man seized him by the wrist.

"Matthew! We've done everything that gypsy woman said. But I should warn you. Arnold has put pieces of silver into his shotgun. Violet! Cut the cake!"

This is absolutely bloody crazy! thought Stuart. And then the nightmare and its logic fitted together perfectly. The whole insane sequence began to make sense.

Quietly, Stuart leaned across to the old man.

"I'm not Matthew. But he *is* out there—somewhere in the dark. I know he's a werewolf. He attacked me out there on the road and followed me up to the farm. He's come back alright and he's out there prowling around the house. I don't know whether this... this... ritual is supposed to placate him or something. But *believe* me... you've got the wrong person."

The old woman shoved a plate across the table with a wedge of cake on it. It came to rest with a rattle, right in front of Stuart. Two warped candles flickered madly from the concrete-hard icing.

"Eat!"

"What?" gasped Stuart incredulously, You must be joking..." A grey worm, cut in half by the cake knife, writhed and squirmed its way free from the cake mixture onto the plate.

"Eat!"

A gossamer thread of cobweb was caught in the flame of one of the candles and it hissed as it dissolved. With stomach heaving, Stuart picked up the piece of cake and looked at the trio sitting around the table. Sitting there, in their paper hats, the shadows from the candles creeping and fluttering on their faces. For all the world it looked as if they were engaged in some weird grimacing competition.

"Eat!"

The room vibrated to the ululating howl of a savage wolf.

Stuart dropped the cake and leapt backwards in his chair from sheer fright—which probably saved his life. As he fell to the floor, there was an ear-shattering roar as the shotgun spat bright yellow flame and sparks across the table and huge slivers of wood were ripped from the wall where Stuart had been sitting. The recoil sent Arnold hurtling backwards.

Hell had suddenly erupted in the cottage.

The fly-blown window beside the oak door suddenly exploded into a thousand glittering fragments, and as Stuart rolled on the floor he had the impression that a long clawed arm had come thrusting through the window.

The old woman screamed again as a howling wind blasted through the gaping aperture and blew out all the candles on the cake. The lantern crashed to the floor and fizzled out. Above the noise of the howling wind, and the reverberating echo of the shotgun blast, Stuart could make out the old man's voice sobbing in the darkness.

"Matthew! Matthew! We *did* love you."

The large oak door shuddered violently under the massive weight of something outside. Hammering. Scratching. Ripping. The bolt of the door rattled and clattered noisily. With the rending noise of a tree being felled, the hinges on the door screeched in protest as the oak burst inwards. Lying on the floor, Stuart tried to avoid the oak panelling as it crashed to the floor. But a length of wood struck him on the shoulder as he tried to rise, and knocked him to the ground yet again. For an instant, the doorframe was blackened by something entering. And then Stuart could see the moon shining brightly in the sky as the figure passed.

Something had come into the room.

But as it passed, Stuart heard a voice. Not a human voice. More like a human snarling from behind a mask. Muzzled. Spoken through lips that were never meant to speak.

Stuart kicked the oak panelling to one side and leapt through the shattered doorway. Trees swam at him crazily as he waited for the nightmare padding sound of clawed feet and inhuman panting which would mean that the thing was pursuing him again. Out into the main road again, he never looked back for fear of seeing that abominable shape crashing through the bushes after him.

Of his flight back to civilisation, he could never really remember very much—and would never have thought it possible that he could run twelve miles back into the town. But he did.

In the months to come the fact that Crowfast Farm didn't appear on any map didn't really surprise him. And when, three years later, he passed that bend in the road again where he had crashed over the gate, he wasn't at all surprised to find that there was no gate in evidence. He didn't even bother to look for the signpost which indicated that Crowfast Farm was two miles up the road. He knew it wouldn't be there.

He would have doubted his own sanity if it hadn't been for one thing.

The warped birthday candle which he found in his pocket.

The whole sequence of events would never be very clear again. But the voice which Stuart had heard in the doorway would stay with him for ever. Inhuman it may have been. And spoken in a horribly distorted voice. But the words were clear enough.

Matthew had returned home to even the score.

"Many Happy Returns!"

gordy's a-okay

HE'S NINE YEARS OLD, BUT LOOKS YOUNGER.

A band of freckles darkens the bridge of his nose and dots his cheeks. His eyes are a kind of faded blue; almost the same colour as the sky above him as he wheels in a crazy arc on the rough wooden swing in the garden. His name is Gordy and his mouth is opened wide in a silent, exhilarated shout of happiness as he embraces the clouds. It's a familiar expression which seems to say: *It's great to be alive.*

Which is crazy, of course.

He leans back in the small wooden seat as the swing reaches the apex of its new ascent and then hurtles backwards again. He adjusts his position and frog-kicks his legs for greater impetus and height on the next return. His jeans have ridden up almost to his knees, revealing scabbed shins. They're the same jeans he was wearing on the day when... but I cancel that thought as he swings even higher and makes me afraid that he might go too far and fall. I move forward in alarm, but check myself before I can do anything. After all, how could he hurt himself even if he fell? He can't be hurt now.

Which is also crazy, of course.

Gordy's feet scrape the ground as he swings back again, the impact rattling the tightly clutched seat chains. He throws his head back and laughs his silent laugh again.

I turn from the garden, where I've been watching him now for fifteen minutes and walk slowly back across the patio, noticing from the corner of my eye the slight twitching of a curtain in the living room of our ever-watchful neighbour Mrs. Grant, who lives alone in the large white house beyond the fence. Maybe she's been watching Gordy.

But that's even crazier, of course.

I reach the French windows and enter the house, gathering the kids' plates up from the kitchen table and dunking them in the sink. I pause to look up through the kitchen window as Gordy continues his silent assault on the sky (*Or is it surrender?* I ask, not really understanding why that thought should come to me.)

"Why is it always during the school holidays, Gordy?" I ask myself quietly as I begin the washing up.

Dennis has taken the kids to the pictures, after failing to live up to three previous promises. But it's not such a chore, since he enjoys the kids' movies just as much as the kids do themselves. Barry is the same age as Gordy and about the same size; but he's heavier and has fair hair like his Dad. He has a brace on his teeth, likes fast bikes and comics; and is a secret founder member of the gang which smokes sly cigarettes in a the small quadrangle, screened from the rest of the schoolyard. It's a precarious occupation for him, I think, because his sister—my daughter Jane—goes to the same school and hounds him continually with threats of "telling on him" and horror tales about the dreaded weed. She's seven, doesn't like dolls, but loves cartoons, Cherry Surprise chocolates and Mark Pagett from No 7 Burlington Terrace. (I've seen the unposted love letters lying on sofas, chairs and even one day in the fridge, of all places. Cold hands, warm heart? I don't know.) Anyway, she's beautiful now and she'll be even more beautiful when she's older, which makes me wonder if Mark Pagett of Number 7 Burlington Terrace will regret his rejection of Jane's advances after he's reached the age where such things aren't regarded as "soft" anymore.

The swing-chain rattles again, and I look up to see Gordy twist out of his seat in mid-air and land agilely in the garden, deliberately rolling over and over on the ground. He begins to practice handstands. I stand and watch for a while and then return to swabbing the dishes.

I married Dennis, the oldest brother in the Baxter family, ten years ago. We get along just fine. There was a rough patch five years ago when we seemed to just get on each other's nerves all the time, but that's all resolved now—every marriage has its share of problems—and we're really happy. Well, let's put it this way: the relationship is happy, we love each other and the kids. Everything on that side of things is fine.

But I'm not really happy in myself, if you know what I mean. And it has to do with that nine-year-old freckled kid out there who is walking on his hands and who now leaps back to his feet and begins to climb the tree at the bottom of the garden. There's a Frisbee snared in the upper branches which we've been trying to retrieve for the past six weeks with thrown stones and a clothes prop. Climbing is out of the question, of course—it's much too high and dangerous. Gordy scrambles upwards, and I know that he's going to try and reach it. Again, I check the impulse not to bang on the window glass and tell him to come down before he hurts himself. But, of course, I'm being stupid again. He won't fall out of the tree, and even if he does, it won't matter.

I love Gordy. I always will. And, perhaps, that's the reason why things are the way they are. Perhaps that's why he comes. This makes me wonder whether my love is like a chain which holds him here and it can't be right if I'm keeping him here against his will.

Then I look at his face again and I think: *No, that's not really it. He wouldn't be here if he didn't want to be. Just look at his face. He's smiling, always smiling.*

Of course, I start to cry, which is the worst thing I can possibly do. Every time I cry, every time I try to speak to him and ask him what it's all about, he goes away.

I try to stop myself. I choke it back, but as I look up I see that Gordy, who never ever looks at me or recognises my presence, has heard or sensed me. He freezes in the tree, a small hand clutching up for the Frisbee, fingers only inches away. He makes a half turn of his head in my direction (but not *at* me, you understand) then pulls his hand back.

I realise now that it's too late and that this will be the end of his visit today.

He goes away.

The tears really flow now while I busily dry the dishes on the draining board, as if wiping them dry can dry the tears themselves. It doesn't work, of course.

"Why, Gordy? Why?" I ask again as if he was still here to answer me.

When I feel a little better I move into the living room, wondering if Gordy will be back again tomorrow—there never seems to be a set pattern for his visits. I find my magazine and slump onto the sofa. A box of chocolates lies open on the coffee table with the Cherry Surprise missing from its tray while the television has been playing to a lost audience. But the quiz-show host, who beams at me from the screen, doesn't seem too bothered. I begin to read my magazine and it's only when I've read the same paragraph six times without taking anything in that I realise my mind is too absorbed in other things to allow for light reading. Nevertheless, I do my best not to think about Gordy and flip through the pages of the magazine.

"...the latest design from La Froliere is perhaps a little too outrageous for even the most extroverted, but sales of this new line have indicated..."

Why, Gordy? Why?

"Dear Jane, I am writing to you because of my mother-in-law. Ever since I married my husband, John, three years ago, I have been increasingly concerned..."

And why only during the School holidays? Is it because the kids are around the house more often during the day? Is that it?

"...the film is an adaptation of the best seller by Joseph Wambaugh and is the first starring role for Brooke Matthews, whose previous minor roles in..."

Why can't I even speak to you, Gordy? Why do you always go away when I try?

-⊕⊕⊕-

The next day is Saturday and both of the kids are re-enacting the key scenes from the movie they saw with Dennis; up and down the stairs, over the furniture and under my feet. Dennis can sense that I've had a bad night (sleep did not come easily) and that I'm on edge this morning. He takes charge of the chores and bundles the kids out into the garden without having to ask how I'm feeling.

We talk small talk for a while. We're going out with friends this evening and Dennis has just telephoned to fix the final details of where we're meeting and who's catching up with us later on at the restaurant. I'm talking about what to wear and he's telling me that the "kid-sitting" arrangements are fine now.

We're saying all of these things to each other, but what we're really saying between the lines is:

Are you okay, Anne?

Fine.

You're not feeling good today. I can tell.

I'm going to be fine, Dennis. Just give me a little time.

You're feeling strained again, I know. What can I do to help?

Nothing. Really. Just a little time is all I need.

Dennis has got some work to do about the house this morning while I've arranged to meet Geraldine for shopping. We'll have coffee and she'll tell me all about her problems at home. But I probably won't be able to concentrate on Geraldine's problems today.

There is a rattle and clatter from the garden and I look up quickly, heart pumping, expecting to see Gordy on the swing, swooping backwards and forwards with that beautiful smile on his face. But it isn't Gordy, it's Barry, and the disappointment I feel makes me terribly ashamed. It's as if I'd rather see Gordy than my own son out there.

Dennis encircles my waist from behind and presses his chin down onto my shoulder. The bad feeling disappears for a while. I smile and kiss him, then gather up my shopping bag and coat.

-⊕⊕⊕-

When I get home and begin unpacking the shopping onto the kitchen bench, I look out of that window again, and this time I do see Gordy.

He's standing by the fence, arms hooked through the tines and lifting his feet up to his chest—one-two, one-two. Barry and Janet are squabbling over the lost Frisbee up in the tree again. It's Barry's Frisbee and they had been taking turns throwing it. When it had been Janet's turn, a freak gust of air had carried it away from Barry and into the uppermost branches. They both move to the base of the tree, only ten feet or so from Gordy, who is still preoccupied with his one-two one-two, but don't see him. And Gordy, apparently, doesn't see them.

The kids' argument is becoming too heated. I bang on the window and they look around. Gordy must know that the knocking is for the kids' benefit, so he doesn't freeze and then go away. Dennis leaves the pine bench on which he's been working and goes out into the garden to see if he can settle them down. He joins them at the foot of the tree, hands on hips, looking up and trying to decide on a new course of action to retrieve the Frisbee.

Gordy begins to cartwheel over the grass and comes within inches of Dennis, but he never sees him.

Then I get to thinking about that day again, and this time the memory is too strong to be resisted or denied.

He was nine years old when it happened, wearing the same clothes he's wearing today; the same jeans, the same sandshoes.

The first thing I saw when I pushed through the crowd on the pavement were the fish and chips he'd just bought for supper from the shop on the other side of the road. For some reason, it's the memory of that supper and the scattered newspaper in which it was wrapped, trodden underfoot by a gawping crowd of passersby, which is the most unbearable. Gordy himself seemed untouched—as if he'd just decided to go to sleep in the middle of the road, face resting lightly on the tarmac and with the same expression I'd seen on his face a hundred times before when I'd tiptoed into his bedroom. Innocent, open-mouthed and face down on his pillow, lost in the land of Nod. That's the way he looked then, as if he were at home in bed.

I was twelve. And it was my fault for what happened, because I'd sent him to the fish and chip shop that night while I stopped to talk to my friend on the street corner. Gordy, you see—Gordon, that is—was my little brother.

He started to come again just after I married Dennis. That would be... let's see... when I was nineteen. I'm twenty-nine now. I probably don't have to tell you what I thought when he first started to appear, you can no doubt guess. But Gordy's real, of course. Real in the sense that he comes to me during the school holidays even though no one else can see him. Not Dennis—not Janet—not Barry—not even nosy Mrs. Grant.

I've also learned that I can't approach him or speak to him, because he always disappears if I do that. And when I cry, of course, this is worst of all.

"Why do you come, Gordy?" I mumble under my breath, for fear of being heard. "What are you trying to tell me?"

Yes, I'm sure that he's trying to tell me something. He knows I'm here, even though he never looks directly at me. It's as if a direct confrontation or recognition might somehow sever the strange laws which enable Gordy to be here so long after that terrible accident. Sometimes, though, I can tell that he's watching out of the corner of his eye, as if entreating me to acknowledge and realise... something. I still don't know what.

Of course, Dennis and the kids know nothing about this. No one knows. How could they possibly understand?

Dennis has persuaded the kids that the Frisbee is a lost cause and bundles them indoors and upstairs to tidy up their bedrooms, leaving me alone. The shopping's unpacked, so I wander out into the garden.

Gordy's gone again. This isn't surprising, but I feel sad that I haven't had a chance to watch him playing for as long as I'd like. I walk over to the swing and sit on it, holding the chains and swaying slightly back and forth listening to the hollow screech of the chains on the metal poles. I'm thinking of that mysterious something which I know is the reason for Gordy's appearances, just as I've thought about it these long years gone by. Today is like any other day; there's no real reason to suppose I'm ever going to find out what he wants me to know, but somehow I've got this *feeling* that I might just be closer to the truth on this Saturday than I've ever been before. If only Gordy had stayed a little longer and given me a chance to watch him and think...

I rise from the swing and walk towards the tree, arms folded before me and wondering when he'll next appear. Someone is whistling somewhere. The kind of high-pitched, shrill whistle that can only be made by using two fingers in your mouth.

I look back at the house to see who's making the sound, but there's no sign of Dennis or the kids. Again, the whistling, and I look over the fence onto the pathway but see no one. When the whistling comes yet again, I'm starting to feel irritated. It is very shrill, making my eardrums vibrate, and it seems very close. But there is no one to be seen.

I look up.

Gordy is sitting in the top branches of the tree, one hand held to his mouth. Again, I resist the urge to yell at him to come down before he falls and breaks his neck. Because as I've said before, this would be a crazy thing to do. Instead, I let my pleasure in knowing that he hasn't gone away yet take over.

Then, it hits me. Gordy is the whistler. Yet in ten years he's never made a sound before.

My heart is really hammering now as I strain to look up at him in the tree. Is it just a trick of the light, or is he really looking *directly at me* with that great big, beaming smile? I take a couple of steps back, shading my eyes with my hand and now I'm sure, yes I'm sure. There's a feeling of joy inside me, the kind of joy that hurts your throat, to know that finally, after all these years, Gordy is actually looking at me and recognising me.

"Gordy! Gordy! Gordy!" I shout. And that's all I can find to shout as he takes his hand from his mouth and waves at me. I wave back furiously, not ever wanting him to go away again. But as we wave and our eyes drink each other in, something happens. Don't ask me how it happens, but it does. I suddenly realise things that I've never realised before. It's as if Gordy is telling me things, true things that can't be denied. He's not speaking to me, though, he's just looking at me, smiling. And I listen and understand; although even *listen* isn't the right word. I just know.

I know now that I can't blame myself for what happened. An accident can happen anytime, anywhere, and just because I'd sent Gordy for supper that night, it didn't make me responsible for what happened. There's been a shadow on my life all these years. It's never allowed me to be really happy.

Gordy says, although *says* isn't the right word, that I've spent too long being unhappy and it's time to stop. He says that it would have been better if I'd come to these realisations myself. But I've been incapable of it; that's why he's been coming, although he wasn't allowed to acknowledge my presence or speak to me.

And why in the school holidays? Well, of course, that's when the accident happened. That's when I feel really bad and need Gordy the most.

Gordy is telling me that the simple things are the best things. Love is a simple thing. The simplest and best thing. Gordy tells me that grief is normal and necessary, but it shouldn't last for so long.

It's time to let go, says Gordy. Time to stop feeling pain. Keep our love because death can't end it. He raises his hand and I can see that he's holding something in it.

It's the Frisbee.

He smiles again and then makes the sign with his other hand, a sign which he used to make all the time when he was alive and which, until now, I'd forgotten about. He pinches his thumb and forefinger together in a circle and holds it in a salute to me. He doesn't speak, but I can still hear the familiar phrase in that silly pseudo-American accent, which used to make the whole family fall about laughing whenever he used it.

"Gordy's A-Okay!"

He smiles again and throws the Frisbee, which sails gracefully down from the tree towards me. Suddenly, it becomes terribly important that I catch the Frisbee and don't drop it. But I don't really have to try, because the Frisbee dips down towards the ground and then floats up on an updraught of air right into my hands.

I look up again. Gordy smiles.

And then he's gone.

Only this time, I know he won't be back. That knowledge doesn't make me sad because now I know that everything's okay.

Dennis and the kids come running out of the house because they heard me shouting earlier. Their look of concern changes when they see the Frisbee in my hands. Dennis asks me how I did it and I tell him that the wind blew it out of the tree. But I know by the look on his face that he can sense that something else happened. Something important. He kisses me, but doesn't ask, and we both feel good.

I give the Frisbee to the kids, but somehow that piece of ordinary, round blue plastic now seems to be much, much more than just a Frisbee. And my giving it to the kids seems important, though I don't know why.

The kids run away, squabbling over it. A warm wind caresses the upper branches of the tree as if something has flown away. I look up and feel for the first time that I can live my life without an awful shadow hanging over it.

Gordy's A-Okay.

And that's fine by me.

the secret

Do you want to know a secret?

Are you sure? If I told you that knowing this secret would place your life in jeopardy—perhaps your very soul—would you still want to know? You would? Then read on...

It began on a Thursday night in September. A dreary, sopping wet Thursday night at Ryan's Place. Sitting at the bar on a high stool, with a whisky and American Ginger in front of me and the occasional car hissing through the drizzling rain outside the bar's bay windows. I wasn't in the mood for company.

It was late and the place was fairly empty. The very reason, in fact, that I had chosen this bar to do some heavy drinking and to feel sorry for myself. Ryan, whoever he was, obviously didn't care to spend money on making his bar more attractive to prospective customers. A dozen beer-stained tables occupied the floor; most of the seats were worn bare or torn, revealing yellow foam rubber beneath. The floor was littered in dog-ends and liberally splattered with the bronchial phlegm of previous customers.

Across the room, sitting on an alcove beside the bay windows, was an aged hag coated in gaudy make up. Occasionally, she would give vent to a raucous laugh, occasioned by the amorous suggestion of a young Pakistani boy who sat next to her with his arm around her shoulders. I turned away as the boy's hand began to creep over the crone's knee and looked across at the only other occupant of the bar. An old, drunken man with a flat cap: propped up in a corner of the room and looking as if he'd just been thrown there like some battered rag doll. Most of the beer in his wavering glass seemed to be splashing into his lap as he attempted to manoeuvre it into his mouth.

My eyes wandered to the bay windows and to the rain which occasionally streaked the panes. Even from where I sat, I could hear the gurgling rain-water in the drains; the sodden footsteps of a passerby wending his way homeward. A large red neon sign from a Chinese restaurant across the street threw down a strange, almost hellish mosaic across the rainwashed pavement outside the window.

Just the right kind of setting to be miserable.

Tonight, my office colleagues would be "on the town": a weekly pub-crawl to relieve the frustrations of a nine to five existence in a great, grey monolith in the city centre. Lots of alcohol once a week to help the days go by. A visit to all the best pubs in town, which, by definition, excluded Ryan's place. This would be the last place to visit, and that was another reason why I had chosen the bar. Out of the way. Knowing I wouldn't be in good company, I'd deliberately chosen this hole to be alone, do some thinking, feel sorry for myself. And get very drunk.

And why not? The bitch had done it after all, hadn't she? Linda had left me for good.

My eyes wandered back to the bar and the obese, half-drunken bartender with the broken cigarette dangling from this thick, rubbery lips. Ryan? Maybe. God, what an ugly specimen, I thought.

My thoughts turned back to Linda and the final storming argument which had led her to leaving. And then I thought of the arguments that had preceded that: a seemingly endless succession of bitten invective. Hurtful insults and frustration occasionally placated by hurried, almost desperate love-making. Who had been wrong? Neither of us, I suppose. Or both of us, perhaps. I don't know. Like a cassette being played and rewound, these thoughts were whirling around in my head: going nowhere in particular.

I began to trace out patterns in the spilt beer on the bar before me. If only I hadn't hit her or maybe if... sod it! I felt a strange *blank* feeling creep over me. An emotional blackness which also felt curiously comforting. A total, complete, Godforsaken, emotional blank. I emptied my glass, ordered another drink and watched as the barman poured another measure. He obviously didn't want to engage in conversation, and that's the way I preferred it.

Somewhere off to my right the hissing, swishing noise of rain and traffic was louder for an instant as the bar door opened and someone came in.

"Shut the door, for crying out loud!" slurred the drunk in the corner. The door thudded shut and after a few seconds, I became aware of shuffling feet and a presence at my right hand shoulder.

"Mind if I sit here?"

I lifted the glass to my lips and sipped at the burning liquid: at the same time moving my eyes only slightly, to take in the small, soaked figure in the dirty grey overcoat. I looked away again without answering as he sat down on a bar stool beside me. Under normal circumstances, I might have told him to get lost. Obviously a drunk on the scrounge for the next free drink. But the blank feeling inside me negated the impulse. Let him sit where he wanted. It was a free world.

As he ordered himself a pint of Best, I took in his battered appearance. God knows how long he'd been wearing that mac. His sparse, mousey hair lay plastered in strands across his balding head, and his fidgeting hands began to tear strips from a wet barmat lying on the bar. He looked about forty or forty-five years of age, but could have been older. I was always a bad judge of age. But the most interesting thing about him were his eyes. Frightened eyes which darted nervously around the bar in general and at the outside door in particular. The eyes of a field mouse expecting death at any moment from the claws of a circling barn owl.

The fat barman pulled a pint of beer and banged it down unceremoniously in front of The Mouse; white froth spilling onto the already drenched counter. I watched as The Mouse paid in small change, and then was surprised to note that he took only one small sip from his glass. Surprised because, assuming his fidgeting demeanour to be the result of alcoholism, I had expected him to down his drink in one swallow. Turning suddenly, he gave his full attention to me.

"Do you want to know a secret?"

I turned away from him again, and after a short while I heard him sigh deeply.

"I don't blame you. What's the point of having secrets these days? People aren't able to keep them. That's the way of life. People betraying trusts." He paused for a while and then continued: "But there are secrets and *secrets*."

I noted the peculiar emphasis he placed on the last word but my mind was beginning to wander back to Linda again. I couldn't be bothered to tell this fool to push off.

"Little secrets," The Mouse continued, "And big secrets. I suppose people have been killed because of secrets, haven't they? After all, it's a big business, isn't it? International espionage, and all that."

Despite my general apathy and wandering thoughts, I could still sense that there was something about this peculiar character which didn't quite scan. In spite of his generally tatty appearance, unshaven face, and down-and-out manner, his speech was decidedly Oxbridge and there was a certain nervous activity behind his eyes which I didn't care for very much. It disturbed me for reasons I couldn't explain. I decided to move my seat.

Swinging around on the bar stool away from him, I made for a nearby table and sat down, noting with distaste that The Mouse was following me. He pulled up another chair and sat down opposite me.

"You think I'm a nut case, don't you?" said The Mouse, matter-of-factly, shuffling his chair closer to the table and taking another small sip of beer. For a second I just looked at him. Then, nodding my agreement, I returned to my whisky and my private thoughts. To Linda. And the mad fortnight crammed with laughter, sex and exhilaration which had led to our marriage. A mistake, apparently, that everyone but ourselves could see. Some time passed before my consciousness returned to my empty glass. The Mouse seemed to have been talking for some time, taking my silence as an invitation to give me his life story.

"...but truth to tell, I never did enjoy being a lawyer. I think that I was reasonably good at it. Hell, I was a very good lawyer. But I couldn't help feeling afterwards that I shouldn't have been so independently minded; that I should have taken up my father's offer and gone into the family business. Still, no use crying over spilt milk. Of course, my greatest regret in becoming a lawyer with Lewis and Bradshaw was that I found myself invited to that terrible party thrown by a client. If I had gone into the family business, I would never even have heard of Lewis and Bradshaw. And someone else would be in my present... situation."

I began to rise from my seat with the intention of moving back to the bar for a refill. Suddenly galvanised into action, The Mouse jumped from his seat, snatching my glass for the table.

"Whisky, isn't it?"

A sardonic smile crept around the edges of my mouth. Sighing, I slumped back into my seat, feeling the effect of the alcohol. Let the poor idiot spend his money on me if he wanted. The thought suddenly struck me that he might be gay and on the look-out of a pick-up.

"You're not trying to pick me up, are you? I'm straight."

The Mouse was suddenly defensive: "Oh no! not at all! I'm married... was married. But you want to hear my secret, don't you?"

I waved my hand apathetically and watched as The Mouse scurried back to the bar and ordered another drink. Eagerly, he made his way back to my table and continued where he had left off. Had he really been a lawyer? Some poor little rich kid propped up by daddy's money? A success story fallen on hard time? Or was he just a nut-case? Why was I considering it at all? I had my own problems.

"As I said," he continued, "The party. We had just won a very successful court action against... but I won't bore you with the details. These social affairs are all the same really. A chance to get yourself talked about, get yourself noticed by the influential. Anyway, I was quite drunk by about 2:00 a.m. and had been trying to talk a very attractive young lady into my bed..."

I permitted myself a small, choked laugh at the thought of this character attempting to chat up a blonde from the cover of "Mayfair". Encouraged by my apparently jocular interest in his tale, The Mouse continued eagerly.

"I wasn't successful. Don't get me wrong. I wasn't dressed like this." He indicated his battered raincoat with a sweep of his hand. "Nothing but the best for me in those days. Clothes, wine, food... and especially women." The Mouse gave a small, bitter laugh. "A lot can happen in six months..."

I took a deep swallow from my drink. Was he kidding? Let him ramble.

"She went home there-and-then. I suppose I was too drunk. I may have said something out of order. You know what it's like sometimes when you're drunk and spouting a load of rubbish. I began to console myself with a vodka bottle. Practically everyone else had gone home or fallen asleep. Then I saw him. A curious fellow, really. About my age and a little... well, shabby for that kind of party, I couldn't help thinking. I'd never seen him before, but he seemed to be keen to talk to me. Since he appeared to be the only one left conscious, I made a bee-line for him. As it turned out—*he* had made the bee-line for *me*. So, we talked. And that's when I found out The Secret. The greatest Secret in the world. Shortly afterwards, he disappeared. I tried to find out who he was, where he'd gone and who'd invited him to the party. But no one seemed to know who I was talking about. A real mystery-man..."

Suddenly parched by his speech, The Mouse took a deep draught from his glass and then continued: "And the thing with this Secret, do you see, is that it can only be known by one person at a time. Because after it's been passed on, the teller will forget. And the person who then becomes the Keeper of the Secret must pass it on again before... Anyway, don't ask me how it works. I don't know. I don't like to think about it. Of course, there are consequences for the knowledge..."

The same look of fear which had been in The Mouse's eyes upon his arrival had suddenly re-appeared with all its former intensity.

"After all, it is *the* most important Secret in the world... in the universe, I suppose. So... if you want to know the secret, I have to ask you something first."

The Mouse paused and took another drink: "If knowing this Secret was to place your life... your very soul... in jeopardy; would you still want to know? Would you? That's the only way it'll work, do you see? You must *want* to know The Secret, knowing that this danger is involved. Once I've told you... passed it on... I'll forget. And then it won't be after me anymore."

It? After him? Maybe he had a persecution mania. Poor sod.

"So do you want to know my Secret? In spite of everything I've told you?"

Why not? Keep the miserable little wretch happy. I nodded my head gently.

"You do? You do?" The mouse sat bolt upright. "Are you sure? You must say 'yes.'"

With all the drunken seriousness I could muster, I said: "I do."

The Mouse seemed visibly to shrink back into his seat like a collapsing balloon, a look of incredible relief on his face. He wiped a grimy had across his forehead and for a second I thought he was going to weep.

"The Secret...," he sat forward again. "The Secret. But first, let's have another..."

The sound of a car swishing past in the rain seemed to draw his attention urgently to the bay windows. "Did you hear it?" he said. "That noise?"

"A car," I replied, "in the rain."

"No," replied The Mouse in a hushed tone. "Not that. The other noise..."

"I didn't hear anything." I said, sipping again at my drink.

"It knows I'm here. It's been following me." The Mouse turned to face me once more; leaning across the table, his voice almost a whisper. "I can't waste any more time. The Secret is..." The Mouse leaned forward even further and whispered confidentially in my ear: "We're all in Hell."

"You can say that again," I mumbled.

"Don't laugh!" The Mouse's tone was decidedly serious. "We are. We're all in Hell. Every single one of us is damned." The Mouse paused, his eyes glinting with that strange nervous energy. I smiled ruefully and shook my head.

"Listen... humankind thinks that it's so bloody perfect. But it's not. Quite the reverse, in fact. You and I, and everyone else in the world are all human in the strictly *physical* sense. But there is another ethereal existence where the true essence of mankind exists. It exists in another plane, in another form; a state of near-perfection. Heaven, I suppose. But subject to the same kind of evil influences we all know about here on Earth. Life there is totally different to our existence. But everyone knows that organisms can't exist, can't develop, in a vacuum. The only way for the human 'essence' to achieve perfection is to resist the evil side. Those who do become perfect. Those who don't are imperfect and must keep on trying.

"But those who taste the evil side, and succumb to it too easily—and that means you and I and every other Godforsaken soul on this planet—well, those others are punished. They're damned. And banished. Banished from their ethereal existence and placed on a boulder of rock spinning in space in another existence.

"A *physical* existence, with all former memories wiped away. Stripped of everyspiritual attainment and faced with the task of coping with a physical body; a body which must continuously absorb protein and oxygen to live. Subject to all the fears, desires, stresses, pain, suffering, aggression and cruelty of this life.

"Don't you see how hideous that must be to the others who live in that other sphere? It *is* Hell to them. Everything here is Hell! A decent... moral, if you like... life may be given another chance at the end of their life span to return to that other existence. God only knows how short we all fall of that target. Those who can't, or won't, are condemned forever. And on we go, bringing others into this world through the physical mechanics of sex. Providing the means for damnation. The greatest saint on Earth would still be a savage compared to his former self in his former existence."

The Mouse paused for breath. He looked exhausted.

"That's what the man at the party told me, and although I was drunk, I reacted exactly the same way that I think you must be reacting now. I thought he was insane."

I finally had The Mouse sussed. He was a religious maniac.

"As soon as he told me the tale, he left. But not before telling me about the danger. And that's what I must tell you now. You see, The Secret is not supposed to be known. How it came to be known, I've no way of guessing. But the very fact that it *has* become known means that the balance and order of reality is in danger. The carrier of The Secret poses a threat. Don't ask me how! I've been through it in my head for these past six months. I know what you're thinking: if only one person can know at a time, how can it be a threat? I don't know. But nevertheless, it *is* a threat. And some... thing... is hunting the one who knows."

The Mouse tried to suppress a convulsive shudder.

"I don't know what it is. But I think I know where it comes from. There is a nether region somewhere in our minds, deep in the darkest part of our souls. Another Hell. I don't know how it exists, or why it exists. The man didn't tell me. But it is a dark, hideous, most evil place. The evil side. It reveals itself in man's darker nature. The mythological Hell. I don't think that humans can normally end up there within the normal scheme of things. But..."

The Mouse's voice began to trail away, but was suddenly brought alert by another swishing of the rain outside.

"But I know that something is walking the streets searching for the Keeper of The Secret. Something that has been sent from that other Hell. It can... sniff The Secret out, I suppose. I've never seen it properly. But I've heard it. I know it's not human, and that it's been following me these past six months. Every time I move to another town it always manages to find me again. It seems that I can only ever keep ahead of it by a couple of weeks. Then I sense that it's arrived. And that it's out there, looking for me. "

Despite my whisky befuddled brain, there was something about the way The Mouse told the story that made me shudder. Perhaps it was the conviction in his voice.

"So now that I know The Secret," I said, "The Devil is going to come and get me?" I smiled sourly, downing my whisky.

"The Devil?" The Mouse looked thoughtful for a second. "Yes, I suppose it may be. Whatever it is—it'll certainly come to take you. Down to that other terrible place where The Secret will remain secret forever. A man could go mad just thinking about it." The Mouse suddenly looked puzzled, as if he was trying to remember something else he'd had in mind to tell me. "I think you'll have a year before it finally gets to you. But you must always keep on the move. Never stay in any one place for more than two weeks. Always keep moving. Don't worry. You'll find someone who'll take the burden for you. Someone willing to become the Keeper of The Secret."

The Mouse stood up, and leaning across the table, he took my hands in a firm double-handshake. When he spoke again, his voice was quivering with emotion. "Thank you. You'll find someone. Don't worry. But now... you'd better go. It knows you're here and you don't have much time." As he opened his mouth to speak again, puzzlement etched itself into his face. For a second, he looked around the bar, as if not realising where he was. Then he looked down to where he held my hands, dropping them hastily, as if *I* was the tattered tramp who had taken his hands so earnestly. When he looked at me again, it was as if for the first time.

"Have you forgotten, then?" I smirked. Pulling myself to my feet, I headed for the bar and ordered myself another two drinks—a pint for the nutcase and a whisky for myself. My alcohol intake seemed to have softened the ugly lines of the man behind the bar.

"You Ryan?" I slurred.

"Ryan's dead," replied the bartender.

I stumbled back to my seat. The Mouse had gone. Outside, the rain was sheeting up against the window.

"Last orders, please," cried the bartender. An unnecessary yell, bearing in mind that I was now the sole occupant of the bar. I gave a snort of laughter and looked drunkenly back at the pint of beer and the whisky standing on the table. All the more for me. I began to drain the pint as the barman began banging glasses and making noises that indicated he wanted to be out of the place as soon as possible. I thought of The Mouse out there in the rain somewhere, soaked to the skin, probably headed for the nearest Salvation Army hostel for a cup of soup and somewhere dry to sleep. Maybe it was the drink, but I really felt sorry for that pathetic little man, telling his strange, warped story to anyone who would listen. A strange little man, convinced that he was being stalked by demons. It seemed to momentarily place a new perspective on my own problems. But for some reason, the old quotation, "Wine is a mocker," seemed to spring to my mind and I realised that once I was sober again, the reality of my own situation would come flooding back and I wouldn't have time to worry about other people's devils. I had my own to contend with. I finished the pint, downed the whisky and began to fasten up my coat in preparation to brave the elements.

"Charming little place you have here." I said to the barman. "Quite charming."

"Bugger off," he replied. Not such a charming host, however.

-⊕⊕⊕-

Outside the wind had built itself up into a gale. The rain slashed at my face and I could feel the freezing wind biting at my ears, even through the alcoholic blur. Almost by instinct, and through my drunken stupor, my body was making its way home. My mind seemed curiously detached; as if I was a passenger in a coach. The feeling appealed to me. I giggled.

"Home, legs. And don't spare the trousers."

Reaching the end of the decrepit block of which Ryan's Place was a part, I turned sharp left and began to make my way towards the city centre over a patch of waste ground. Unheeding of the mud and dirt which splashed over my shoes, I blundered ahead through the darkness. Fifty yards or so ahead of me I could make out a streetlamp which cast a long orange-blue oily streak in the pools on the ground. During demolition, the lamp post had obviously been bumped by a tractor or lorry, resulting in a crazy tilt which splashed the light unequally over the ground and across a ruined wall. It was a curiously angular image of light and shadow which reminded me of that old film starring Conrad Veidt: "The Cabinet of Dr. Caligari". I giggled again as I thought of myself as the Doctor's somnambulist/zombie, staggering through the night.

Avoiding a pile of rubble hidden in the darkness, I steadied my hand on a rusted bed frame and continued on my way towards the patch of light.

I'll never forget that moment. Because something happened just as I touched the frame that dragged my mind out of its stupor and made me totally sober again.

At first, I thought that the weight of my body on the bed frame as I passed had made the old mattress springs creak in protest. But, then I realised that the noise had come from somewhere else. Over on the other side of the waste ground perhaps. Somewhere in the darkened, drenched back yard at the rear of Ryan's Place. And not a creak, exactly. More of a groan. A sigh which, in its tone, seemed to say: *There you are.*

I hurried on. I can't really explain the pronounced effect that the sound had on me. You see, there was something... something not quite *right* about it. I just had to get away. And above all else, I had the unnerving feeling that someone was moving over there in the dark and, having heard my footsteps, was now making his way as quickly as possible towards me. Don't be stupid, I told myself. That idiot in the pub has put the wind up you. Just get out of here and into the light as quickly as you can.

A little further on, my fears were realised. Someone *was* following me. There was no doubt in my mind. I could hear him.

I concentrated on the streetlamp up ahead as I hurried onwards. Somehow, I had the feeling that if I could get to the light, I would be safe. From behind, I heard the sound of something brushing against the old bedstand as it passed and realised that my pursuer was almost on top of me. In panic, I broke into a run, my fear bubbling up in my throat as my pursuer hastened his pace to match my own. The lamp post swung at me crazily from the broken pavement and I just managed to catch it with the crook of my arm, swinging around to face whoever was behind me.

Of the countless times I've been over the series of events on that terrible night, that moment will remain indelibly printed on my mind forever. Because that was when I felt true *terror*.

At once, I was aware of my own heartbeat, aware of the reality that out there in the dark before me was something whose very being was anathema to human existence. Even now, although I can vividly recall my own overwhelming terror, I can never fully explain what it was that I saw. All that remains is a fleeting series of images: images so terrible that I can't dwell on them for long.

I remember a dark shape at the periphery of the circle of light cast by the streetlamp. Something of vaguely human proportions which moved like a large, black bear. A curious, shambling shape that still somehow gave the impression of being capable of tremendous agility and speed. For a second, it stood silently in shadow, weaving slightly back and forth, as if contemplating what move to make. I remained frozen to the lamp post, every sense in my being telling me that I was in the presence of something unspeakably evil. And then, to my unutterable horror, it began to move around the circle of light. Groping, feeling, shambling. As if looking for a weakness in the streetlamp's beam.

Please God, I thought. *Keep the light burning. Keep the light burning...*

I tried to move to the other side of the lamp as the thing began to veer towards me, but found myself frozen to the spot. Only a supreme effort enabled me to step slowly around to the other side of the lamp post.

I watched as the shape circled around me. Like a big, black sheet flapping on a washing line. I continued to move, keeping the lamp between myself and the thing; seeing that it was moving towards an area where the light was cast closer to the lamp post. As the shape advanced, I tried to close my eyes. But I couldn't. Fumbling and rustling towards me, it drew closer. And as it did so I realised that, whatever it was, the creature was *blind*. And what I had at first thought to be a rustling noise, was the sound of the thing *sniffing*. Like some unearthly bloodhound, kept at bay only by the light. Not more than six feet away, yet still strangely indistinct, the shape stopped in its tracks. I knew that it had found me.

Still wreathed in the darkness of night, and with rivulets of rain running on its horrible blackness like oilcloth, the thing took a step forward towards me. It cocked its head to one side, listening. And although that terrible, terrible head was also still hidden by the night, I got the impression that not only was the thing eyeless... it was also, somehow, faceless.

One more step and I would be sure.

My lungs were bursting. How long could I hold my breath? I felt like screaming. *I don't want to know The Secret! I won't tell. I'll give it to somebody else. But for God's sake, don't... don't...*

The thing cocked its head to the other side. I saw a glint of something, somewhere within its blackness: a glint of sharp metal... or of claws. I heard something that sounded like a bestial and hideous snigger as it took another step towards me.

No! No! No! Not me... NOT ME!!

Somewhere behind, in the back lane behind Ryan's Place, a dustbin lid clattered to the cobbles and a man cursed.

The horribly indistinct black mass whirled away from me towards the sound, and I heard it sniffing eagerly again as the rain washed over it. I began to let my breath out slowly and quietly as its head swayed from side to side.

The dustbin lid clattered again and now, through the slashing rain, I could see a dingy orange light from the backyard where the guy who ran Ryan's Place kept his empty crates. I could see his blurred silhouette now as he shoved more bar room rubbish into the dustbin, eager to be done and on his way home.

The dark shape turned its head slowly back in my direction. I held my breath again.

And then the man cursed again and shoved an empty crate across the yard to the wall. The thing turned away from me, stooped down on its haunches... and then began to lope away across the wasteground, towards the source of this new sound. I watched it swoop away from me like some hideously huge bat with broken wings, or like one of those night-black manta rays skimming like a smothering black sheet over a ragged seabed.

That's when I began to run.

I heard the screaming from Ryan's backyard, of course. And I never want to hear anything like it again.

I ran... and ran... and ran.

I don't think I've ever moved as fast as that in my life. I remember that I was alternately weeping and praying as I ran, never daring to look back in case I saw that intensely horrible black mass skimming across the street after me.

It took me an hour to get home. And I suppose I must have collapsed when I got there, because when I awoke the next morning in bed I was fully clothed and splattered with mud.

I prayed that it had been a dream; prayed that I'd had too much to drink and that the whole damned thing had been a fantasy born from alcohol.

But then I read the headlines in the morning papers about the murder of Joseph Hines, the man who ran Ryan's Bar. I don't have to tell you about what state they found the body in. You may have read about it; you're bound to know that the police are still looking for the maniac or maniacs responsible. Reading the headline brought the horror back to me, and that nightmare has remained; refusing to be rationalised.

A new *sense* was born inside me, you see. A sense which told me without any doubt that the terrible thing which I had encountered on that night was still out there somewhere, waiting for darkness, intent on sniffing me out, hunting me down...

Unless I could keep ahead of it.

And that's precisely what I've done. I've left everything behind. My job, my family, even Linda. All of them left behind. The irony of the situation is that she wanted to start again with me; give it another try. Only this time, I knew that it was no good. I had to keep moving. I had a substantial amount of money in a savings account which I drew out and used to rent another flat, in another town, miles away. Hoping beyond hope that I could find myself another job and keep myself hidden away in a new place, begin all over again… where it couldn't find me.

But it did.

And it always does.

Just like The Mouse said, it usually takes a couple of weeks before it arrives, giving me a couple of days to move on again. And so it's been for the past year. Trudging the streets, money running out, getting shabbier, trying to shake off the ever present fear. And always trying to get someone to listen to my Secret.

A year. That's how long it's supposed to take before it finally catches up with me. At least, that's what The Mouse said. And I know now that he was telling the truth.

But there's one chance for me.

And I can only hope and pray that it'll work. I suppose I'll know for sure, sooner or later. It was a desperate gamble, but it might pay off.

What did I do?

Well, first of all, I managed to rent this pokey little hole of a flat with its crumbling walls, its damp and its rats, and then I managed to steal a typewriter. And, having done that, I committed my story to paper and sent it off for publication.

It's so nice to share one's secrets.

Because after all, now *you* know the Secret.

Don't you?

pot luck

"Look," said Eddie indulgently, "We've all got to eat, haven't we?"

The crab scuttled across the top of the kitchen bench and clattered against an empty Domestos bottle.

"That's true," clicked the crab in the dry, brittle voice which had so astounded Eddie when he had lifted it out of the bucket. "But what I fail to understand is why you should take such a particular interest in me when you've got a cupboard full of food over there."

Eddie put his hands on his hips and sighed, wearily shaking his head.

"I *happen* to feel like a nice boiled crab, actually."

The crab waved its pincers defensively and began to edge along the sink towards the metallic dripping of the taps at the other side, never taking its antennaed gaze from Eddie's body for one moment.

"Do yourself a favour," said the crab. "Open a can of beans."

"Beans are OK, I suppose," Eddie retorted, manoeuvring himself into a position where he could grasp the crab by the back of its carapace, thus avoiding the sharp pincers. "But when I get my mind fixed on a certain delicacy, I refuse to be budged."

Eddie was really getting tired of the whole affair. Coping with a live crab and trying to entice it into a pot of boiling water was bad enough. But to find out that by some strange freak of nature and/or mutation, you had come upon a crab that was able to telepathically draw on your own language patterns, and speak back to you in an Oxbridge accent, was extremely tiresome. Anyway, he'd never been to Oxford *or* Cambridge... so where did it get off using an accent like that?

"I'm not sure whether I like being referred to as a delicacy," clicked the crab, "It presumes a certain amount of inferiority on my part..."

"Given the present circumstances," said Eddie, "I am definitely in the superior position. So cut the crap and get in the pot, will you?"

The crab scuttled sideways around the perimeter of the sink and managed to scrabble behind a bread-bin.

"Bloody hell!" exclaimed Eddie, "I bet I wouldn't have had this trouble with a lobster."

"Lobsters," retorted the crab, "Are not nice crustaceans to know. They occupy a sort of second-class citizen status where I come from. In retrospect, I should pop out and buy one if I was you."

"If you don't come out from behind that bread-bin, I'm going to bloody *brain* you..."

Eddie was becoming annoyed. He was getting hungry.

"Has it ever occurred to you," said the crab, "That a telepathic crab could make your fortune? You could be to crabs what Uri Geller is to ruined cutlery."

"I think you're trying to talk your way out of this," said Eddie wearily.

"I find the fact that you consider me only to be worthy of satisfying your culinary requirements extremely tedious and not a little insulting."

The crab emerged and headed for the far side of the kitchen bench. Eddie swooped with both hands and caught the animal by its shell.

"Gotcha!"

"I wouldn't do it if I was you," said the crab, with a measured warning in its voice. "I have other talents at my disposal..."

"Talk, talk, talk! That's all I hear," replied Eddie, dropping the encrusted creature into the boiling water.

"Told you so," said the crab, which now occupied Eddie's body. It turned went to make itself a cup of coffee, maybe watch some television. "Boiling things alive is a barbaric habit."

From within the pot, Eddie could only agree.

bleeding dry

A FLASH OF ELECTRIC BLUE LIGHTNING SPLIT THE ENSHROUDING DARKNESS, THROWING OUT THE JAGGED RUINS OF CASTLE FRANKENSTEIN IN CLEAR RELIEF AGAINST THE OMINOUS, BROODING MOUNTAIN PEAKS BEHIND.

The dense, tangled forest which surrounded the castle writhed like some living animal in the grip of the thunderous electric storm, and rain-drenched branches seemed to claw at the battlements like hosts of skeletal fingers clutching upwards from the pit of Hades at the ankles of their awesome Overlord above. A shrieking banshee wind howled maniacally like a thing at the Gates of Hell.

In the jagged, angular laboratory at the top of the castle's tallest grim turret, its walls blackened and scarred and bearing testimony to the fact that this devil's workshop had once been ravaged by fire in times long gone—something evil was taking place. Baron Otto Von Frankenstein, great-grandson of the infamous creator of monsters, was scouring through the yellowed pages of his great-grandfather's notebook.

"Of course, of course," he muttered with dawning realisation, looking up sharply as Ygor lurched into the room with a large glass bottle under his arm.

"I have the brain, Baron," chuckled the evil little man.

"Do you have a happy cat? You don't? Well, maybe he isn't getting the right sort of food. Have you tried Friskybites? Friskybites contain…"

Julian Fortnam rose from his armchair, jumped over the pile of comic books lying at his feet and made his way into the kitchen for a glass of milk and a sandwich. Outside, through the bay windows, he could see that a storm was building, and he hoped that it would be a real thunderer, just like the one he'd seen on television. It was funny. You never seemed to get a storm like that in real life. Julian Fortnam was ten years old and spent a lot of time on his own. Some said that the child was far too solitary and old tongues had wagged frequently in the neighbourhood. "Poor little tyke! Locked away in that house with just his sister and older brother. It's not healthy, I tell you! He never seems to mix at school, does he? My Joey tells me that no one in the class likes him. I mean, it's nice to have all that money—but what good does it do if you stay locked away in that… that… castle, all your life?"

People had often wondered about Julian. His younger sister, Phillipa, seemed quite normal by comparison, except, perhaps, for her strange obsession with knots. Loop knots, hitch knots, double-cross-overs, granny knots—she knew them all, and had even invented one or two of her own. Phillipa would tie knots in anything and was very adept at the skill for an eight-year-old. And as for the older brother, James, who had effectively inherited the Fortnam fortune when their parents had been killed in a car smash… well, he was so ill, poor dear, that he rarely had a chance to go out.

Was Julian maladjusted? Didn't he like people? The fact of the matter was that Julian liked to be alone. Not that he shunned company, in particular. But he never sought it out. Julian liked horror films.

Julian dashed back to his seat and discovered that Frankenstein had finished work on another monster. Ranting and raving, the mad creator was stalking back and forth across the laboratory, wringing his hands and propounding on how, like God, he had created a creature in his own image. Julian couldn't help but think, looking at the ghastly countenance of the Baron's creation, that Frankenstein couldn't really have such a terribly high opinion of himself. Settling back with his glass of milk and his sandwich, Julian shivered in a sort of gleefully nervous way, in anticipation of the horrors to come. The story unwound. The monster was born, escaped, and accidentally killed a couple of incredibly stupid villagers. The village was in an understandable uproar. The "Curse" had begun again! Hadn't everyone seen the flashes of unearthly light coming from the ruined castle at night? Castle Frankenstein had been burned once before. Let's finish the job!

The castle was burned yet again, the monster killed its creator and perished in the flames after throwing Ygor from the highest battlements. The end. All very sad really. Even Julian's young mind could discern that the people were the monsters really and that Frankenstein' childlike creation was more human than any of them.

As his widened, incredulous eyes returned to their normal size, Julian ran a small, chubby hand through his fine blonde hair and struggled from his seat to switch channels. If he was quick enough, he just might catch the beginning of "Curse of the Faceless Thing" on channel 4.

James entered the darkened room and crossed to the bay window, looking at the approaching storm. His tall figure was too thin. The face was a shade too gaunt. "Aren't you going to bed, then?" he asked quietly, smiling at the little figure in the crumpled jeans and teeshirt. James' lungs were aching badly tonight. The doctor had told him that it might get worse and that all he could do was to take the treatment prescribed and do nothing strenuous. His twenty-five-year-old face was not unhandsome, but bore the quiet, peaceful look of someone who has known a lot of pain and somehow come to terms with it.

"Just got to see this film, and then I'm straight off to bed, James. Honest."

"Homework all done?"

"Yep!"

"Chores all finished?"

"Yep!"

Mrs. Doughtery had served as Fortnam housekeeper for as long as James could remember and seemed as much a part of the Fortnam House as the antique furniture. Life without the plump, elderly woman and her permanently sniffling colds would have seemed intolerable. In fact, he had come to regard her as a semi-permanent fixture who left every night at eight-thirty promptly and returned punctually every morning at nine to begin once more her neverending toil. A ceaseless, systematic labour backwards and forwards through the musty house. She reminded James of the painter of some huge girder bridge who finished work after several months only to find that the paint on the other side of the river is old and peeled. So the whole thing would have to be started again.

James smiled again, drew the curtains and crossed the room to where Julian sat.

"Looks like a storm. It'll set the scene for your horror films."

James ran his hand playfully through Julian's tousled hair. Tomorrow, he decided that he must go out for a breath of fresh air. For five weeks he had been indoors; too weak to really do anything, and he had decided that tomorrow he would take up Mr. Devenish's offer of attending the charity concert. He paused at the door, toying with the idea of suggesting that perhaps Julian should accompany him—and then changed his mind. Maybe it was his fault that he didn't encourage his younger brother to go out more often and mix with the other kids. He really would have to do something about that. But perhaps charity concerts weren't the in-thing for ten-tear-olds. Particularly for Julian, who was so bored with *ordinary* occupations.

"Don't be late to bed, Julian."

"Goodnight, James."

James crossed the landing of the massive Fortnam Home and ascended the staircase which led to his room. The place was really big. Too big, perhaps, for just the three of them. James had considered selling up and moving somewhere more "compact." But there was something about the house. Perhaps the fact that there had been so many good times here in the past, or that generations of Fortnams had lived there. The house had a comfortable, secure feeling. James' gaunt shadow spilled angular shadows in the orange light of his bedroom doorway. They were abruptly snuffed out as the door snicked shut behind him.

Downstairs the Faceless Thing had captured the heroine and was heading for the crypt.

-⊕⊕⊕-

The concert hall buzzed with the anticipation of its youthful audience. On stage, the various speakers and electronic paraphernalia which accompanied every performance of "The Pukerzoids" had been positioned and connected to a complex generator backstage which hummed quietly to itself with invisible power. It was the very generator, in fact, which had successfully electrocuted the group's former bass player six months earlier. The resultant publicity had boosted the group's popularity far beyond anything that their musical ability or agent had been available to achieve. *"Who will it happen to next?"* screamed the trade papers as the terrible trio wrenched their three-chord combinations from super-charged equipment and thrashed themselves to a frenzy amidst screaming blue lights, electronic thunderclaps and sulphurous yellow fumes.

Waylon Devenish clapped James on the shoulder, beaming at the crowded concert hall and the fact that all the tickets for tonight's performance had sold out the first day of sale. American by birth and upbringing, now British by residence, Waylon Devenish was a fat man. So fat, in fact, that he appeared to have been poured into the thick upholstered chair which overlooked the auditorium below, and had congealed there. James wondered what would happen if Waylon suddenly decided to stand up. Would the chair remain fixed around his enormous hips? James covered his slight smile with a long, slender finger across the lips and looked out over the audience.

"Well, what do you think, Jimmy? I've done pretty good, getting these boys over here, haven't I?" Waylon beamed from the shrouds of lard around his face. A deep chuckle bubbled up from somewhere within the fat man's bulk, like porridge simmering on a stove. His close-set eyes glimmered happily from a small face; a face that seemed to have accumulated layers of pudge in much the same way that a small snowball rolling down a winter slope increases its bulk before it cracks. Wherever Waylon went, and whatever else he happened to be wearing, he always sported an enormous, fully buttoned purple waistcoat, and today was no exception. James was waiting for the day when the waistcoat exploded under the strain, and the essence that was Waylon Devenish escaped into the atmosphere like a burst balloon, leaving behind sixteen stones of pink plasticine where he had been sitting.

"They certainly seem to have a lot of devoted fans, don't they?" mused James.

"They sure do, boy! Tthey sure do!" enthused Waylon. "The box office receipts are fantastic!"

"The Benevolent Fund will be glad of that."

"They sure will," said Waylon. *You stupid jerk,* he added mentally. *The Benevolent Fund will be glad of 70% of it—but I'll be happy enough with the rest.*

Cheating was a way of life for Waylon Devenish. In his ceaseless efforts to maximise his own huge bulk and lifestyle, Waylon had succeeded in taking almost everyone he had ever known for a ride. James Fortnam was the latest object of his attention: a keen charity supporter and, unconsciously, a Waylon Devenish supporter.

"I've got someone here I'd like you to meet, Jimmy," said Waylon at last, eyes glinting mischievously. He was setting the trap.

A young woman suddenly materialised on the balcony beside them. James was slightly taken aback by her abrupt, noiseless appearance but, in a glance, had taken in the woman's voluptuous body which appeared to have a low cut dress painted on it.

"This is Syrena DeMere," said Waylon slowly, his beady eyes fixed on James' face for any sign of a reaction. Syrena, with her large green eyes and sensuous smile was an exceptionally beautiful woman. James rose to his feet and offered her a seat, heart hammering, throat dry, and Waylon felt like chortling with glee. The trap was sprung. Everything he had squeezed out of Fortnam in the past would be chicken feed compared to what he was about to extract. Now, it was all up to Syrena.

"Hello, James," said Syrena, flashing her perfectly even, sparkling teeth at the now enraptured inheritor of the Fortnam millions.

Syrena DeMere, actually Agnes Hogg by birth, was probably the most beautiful woman in the world. But underneath her attractive wrapping was a soft centre of pure poison. Waylon Devenish could have taken lessons from Agnes (Syrena that is) when it came to bleeding people dry. An endless procession of broken men and marriages lay in her wake, and her ability to use people had even astonished Waylon, making him realise that here was the person who could *really* get her clutches into the naïve James Fortnam. With a slight prompting from himself, of course.

Unwittingly, and in the tradition of all great poetic justice, Waylon had fallen into the very trap which he had himself so often set for others. Knowing Syrena as he did, he was still unable to realise that any show of affection towards him on her part could only be a ruse; particularly when one considered his obese, frankly unattractive body, and equally unattractive personality. But Waylon had been snared in Syrena's web and as he watched her begin the first phase of her plan to inveigle herself into James' heart, he believed in some curiously twisted way that she was doing it for *him*.

Her sparkling eyes bore testimony to the effectiveness of her extremely expensive, tinted contact lenses, gained at the expense of an affair with an optician; her sparkling teeth to the free dental treatment which she had received after finding out about a dentist with the habit of taking unprofessional advantage of his female patients under anaesthetic. He had been only too pleased to cap every one of her teeth at absolutely no charge at all—if only she would destroy the photographs which, needless to say, remained hidden in a safe place should they ever need to be used again.

"The Pukerzoids" suddenly appeared on stage to a rousing cheer and thunderous applause from their eager audience. James was too far away from the stage to notice that the lead guitarist was looking across at him, a broad sly grin appearing on his face...

-⊕⊕⊕-

Theresa sat in front of the huge decorative mirrors of her bedroom, combing her hair and dreaming of the handsome young nobleman who had stood alone on the windswept hill just below the gallows; watching the arrival of the coach which had carried her across the mysterious mountains and valleys of Carpathia to the home of her uncle, Professor Vandorf. Standing straight and erect, the young man had silently watched the coach trundling down the muddy dirt track on its way to the village of Karlstein.

"Driver," Theresa had called from the open coach window to the huddled form above her, "Who is that man?"

"I don't see anyone, Miss," growled the driver, lashing at the already exhausted horses. They were only barely controllable due to the presence of something which they could sense was unnatural and entirely evil. The coachman's eyes remained fixed on the road ahead. Over the clatter of the wheels and the pounding of the hooves on the rough ground, Theresa seemed to hear the coachman exclaim grimly: "It'll be dawn soon!"

Theresa looked back to the spot where she had seen the young man, but found to her astonishment that he had vanished from sight.

Now, in her uncle's house, she remembered how strangely her uncle had reacted when she had mentioned the young man to him. She remembered how he had questioned her so intently about every physical appearance of this young man. How had she known that he was a nobleman? Well, surely he *must* be a nobleman.

"I mean... he *looked* like a nobleman. Do you know, Uncle... I have no idea why I presumed so. It was as if a quiet voice in my head told me."

Theresa remembered how grim her uncle had become, his mouth set in a firm, straight line. A vein was pulsing in his temple as he took a silver crucifix from the drawer of his desk and gave it to her.

"Why Uncle, it's lovely..."

"Theresa my dear, you must promise me that you will wear this crucifix always. And on no account must you ever remove it."

"Well, of course, Uncle, but why...?"

"I must leave now, my dear. There is a job to be done. *He* has returned."

So saying, the Professor was gone, leaving Theresa to ponder over his strange behaviour. There had been something extremely attractive about the young man on the hill with his black cloak blowing so romantically in the wind. Behind Theresa, the French windows were open, leading out onto the balcony which overlooked the courtyard below. Carried by a sudden gust of wind, autumn leaves rustled and fluttered into the room. Theresa rose and crossed to the windows, looking out across the moonlit streets and up to the brooding, silent castle swathed in silently bustling grey clouds.

A sudden chill made her draw her shawl up around her shoulder as she closed the windows gently. As she returned to the mirror, the quiet soothing voice which she seemed to have heard before was creeping stealthily back into her mind. It was calling her name gently, like the crooning whisper made by the wind. For some reason she could not understand, Theresa's hand was moving towards her throat, to the clasp which held the crucifix around her neck. And now she had removed the glittering cross and dropped it unceremoniously onto the dressing table.

"I'd put that back on if I were you," said Julian.

Theresa turned very slowly once again to face the French windows which were even now, slowly opening as if by some invisible hand.

"Run away!" shouted Julian.

In one swift, slithering motion, the vampire seized the helpless young girl, plunged its sharp fangs into her white, yielding throat and began to drink its fill.

"Just wait until the Professor finds out about this..." said Julian indignantly.

-⊕⊕⊕-

From the very beginning, Syrena knew that she was going to have trouble with Julian. The little creep was always watching television for crying out loud, especially horror films. Syrena's charm and ability to deceive had worked perfectly on James and Phillipa. But little Julian remained unimpressed and that made Syrena suspect that his attitude was an expansion of distrust; not realising that Julian acted that way with *everybody*. She decided that the main danger to her plan lay not with the other occupants of the house—even Mrs. Doughtery had been taken in my Master James' Girlfriend with a capital G—but with the little freak.

After two dates in one week, James had finally asked Syrena back to the Fortnam House, an event which she had relished with true anticipation and also a little impatience due to the fact that Waylon had been overly attentive towards her since the plan had been out into operation. With stylish professionalism, Syrena had managed to keep away from Waylon's pudgy grasp before anything untoward happened.

The plan was relatively simple. Syrena would gain James' confidence gradually, and then, after suitable groundwork had been laid, suggest that James invest in her great uncle's business (actually a Waylon Derevish enterprise) which could accomplish *so* much if only there was a large cash injection to get things moving along. At least, that was Waylon's idea. But unknown to him, Syrena's ideas were far more grandiose—and decidedly murderous.

On the first night back at the Fortnam House, Syrena had contrived to get James alone in the vast lounge which occupied most of the ground floor. Mrs. Doughtery had long since gone home. Phillipa had been tying knots all night and had fallen asleep exhausted in her room. Julian was upstairs fully engrossed in "Fangs of Doom".

Syrena stretched out on the huge sofa, one slender arm caressing the expensive leather bound cushions in as suggestive way as she could muster, her long fingernails plucking at the buttons. James had never felt better than he did now, indeed anyone not aware of his condition might have been tempted to say that he was positively glowing with health. He sat almost formally, with both arms crossed, smiling at the gorgeous creature in the slinky black dress who seemed so totally engrossed in him. Syrena had been dropping large hints all night about how they should spend the rest of the evening but James, frankly naïve and very innocent, had never once listened between the lines. A more direct approach was now necessary. Sliding across the sofa, Syrena rested one arm lightly on James' shoulder and began playing with his shirt buttons.

"Aren't you hot, James?" she asked in a sultry tone.

"I can arrange to have the heating turned down, Syrena..."

"No!" she said impatiently and then, realising that her tone might betray her, "No dear. What I mean to say is... have you... have you ever had a woman before, James?"

"Had a woman for what?"

This was going to be much harder work than she could ever have imagined. Men usually had to be fought off when she applied her charms, and for one horrible moment the thought crossed her mind that perhaps James didn't like *women*...

An even more direct approach was necessary.

Syrena slid right up alongside James, her left hand moving smoothly around his waist, the other caressing his neck. She began to nibble gently at his ear. Her fears had been unfounded. James was responding immediately. Following a pre-determined, mechanical pattern, Syrena's kisses became even more urgent, her soft pink tongue probing into his ear. James began to shudder and moan, and Syrena increased the pace of her mechanical lovemaking to keep pace with his mounting desire. Soon, her full red mouth had nibbled its way to James' lips and, as they both slowly fell back into a prone position on the sofa, she had unbuttoned her blouse and was guiding his hand down silicone valley.

If it had not been for the fact that "Fangs of Doom" had broken down in transmission and been replaced by the usual "There is a Fault: Please Do Not Adjust Your Set" card, Julian would at that moment have been watching the Claw Murderer hunting down his victims in the Old Dark House. However, Julian had chosen to take advantage of the intermission to descend from his room to look for a horror magazine. His search brought him to the lounge...

James and Syrena obviously did not hear Julian's entry as he pushed the large oak door open slowly. For an instant, Julian stood frozen in mid-step, his mouth wide and eyes staring at the wrestling match on the sofa. As Syrena crushed her mouth down onto James' lips, she suddenly caught sight of him standing in the doorway. Their eyes met in a long silent stare but Syrena made no attempt to move or stop what she was doing. Not even recognising his presence, Syrena buried her face into James' neck, smiling wickedly at the look on the small boy's face. James was too preoccupied to notice his younger brother. When Syrena looked up again, Julian had gone.

-⊕⊕⊕-

"I just don't get it," said Sheriff Andrews, standing up from his examination of the mutilated corpse which lay sprawled and broken under the bleaching desert sun. He looked out across the shattered remnants of the Whitby farmhouse; one complete side of which had been torn out. As a result, the roof had caved in. Clouds of plaster dust swirled and eddied with each gust of the warm sirocco wind. Broken furniture and household implements had been dragged and scattered over a large area as, indeed, had the Whitbys themselves. A caravan lay twisted on its side, a gaping hole torn in the roof and a nearby Chevrolet looked as if some gigantic, spoilt child had grown weary of his toy and stamped down hard on its roof.

"I just don't get it, Thorpe," said Sheriff Andrews, "What could have done all this?"

"Giant spiders," said Julian.

Thorpe just looked at the Sheriff and shook his head.

-⊕⊕⊕-

Mrs. Doughtery was attacking the household chores with the vigorous determination of a priest exorcising demons and had gradually worked her way on a whirlwind of dust into the hall. James had often asked Mrs. Doughtery to move into Fortnam House permanently. After all, she had no family and was alone in the world, so she may as well stay full-time in one of the twenty-seven palatial rooms. But for some reason unknown to all but herself, the industrious Mrs. Doughtery had always declined the offer. She was much given to saying: "My heart aches for you, Master James," as she flurried through the house. James often wondered with amusement whether she meant it in a sympathetic way or because of some longing for romantic attachment. Considering her age and her roly-poly appearance, James hoped that it was the former.

"Mrs. Doughtery!" cried Phillipa, her eyes brimming with tears as she ran up the cellar steps and into the large hallway slanted with shafts of dusty light from the overhead skylight. "Make Julian stop it!"

Mrs. Doughtery stood at the foot of the staircase, a long feather duster in her hand, duelling with a large cobweb on the top of one of the banisters.

"Whatever's the matter, Phillipa?"

Phillipa flung herself into the matronly folds of Mrs. Doughtery's apron.

"Julian's downstairs in the cellar hunting for spiders again..."

Mrs. Doughtery bustled past Phillipa. She had told him about playing down there. It was dark and dangerous. Why, only last week he had grazed his knee on one of the stone steps in the darkness. Besides, all that dirt...

"He's hunting for spiders," sobbed Phillipa, "And burning them in their webs with lighter fuel."

"Lighter fuel?" Mrs. Doughtery was outraged. "Where on Earth did he get that from? He knows he shouldn't play with matches and the like!"

From the depths of the cellar, Julian's distant but echoing voice seemed to reach her ears. "This one's for the Whitbys!"

Swinging the cellar door wide like an avenging angel, Mrs. Doughtery stepped into the darkness, missed her footing and crashed down the cold granite steps to her death.

-⊕⊕⊕-

Syrena couldn't believe her luck. Everything had been working so well so far. And now, the old reliable Mrs. Doughtery had taken a fatal tumble; which meant that the Fortnam trio—and especially James—were now completely alone in the world, and so much more vulnerable to her wiles.

In the days that followed, Syrena had spent much more time at the Fortnam house. Every evening, in fact. And despite the fact that James was becoming more and more entranced yet remained unaware of her cunning plan, Julian seemed to become even more remote, which in turn was making her more and more uneasy. The one flaw in her scheme seemed to be the little brat in front of the television set. Always watching those damn horror movies! Julian seemed to represent the one loose end in the fabric of her plans which, if plucked at often enough, would unravel her whole scheme. Something was going to have to be done about Julian Fortnam.

Syrena secretly prided herself that she had introduced sex to James Fortnam and in the weeks that followed, James was a very happy man. After all, Syrena was the answer to every lonely man's dreams and James was glad to have her around; especially as his attacks seemed to have become more prolonged and painful than they had ever been in the past. Perhaps if he had taken time to think about it, James might have noticed that the attacks were always worse after Syrena had paid a visit to his bedroom. But James was a trusting young man, and would never have believed his new love capable of gradually introducing new drugs into his medicine which would ultimately result in an untimely death. And he certainly would not have believed that she had obtained these drugs from "Spook", the lead guitarist of "The Pukerzoids", who had thrilled countless tone deaf fans throughout the country; nor that she was having an affair with him to get to the group's agent, to get to the Recording Manager, to get to his boss, to get to the Big Time...

Julian had just finished watching the Double Terror Feature on BBC2 and had bounced up and down on his bed in sheer excitement when the Lizard Man had finally met his doom at the hands of the Rat Man. Tonight's horror helping had been more than taxing on his energy reserves and when he found that his own refrigerator was relatively bare, he decided to venture downstairs for a midnight snack. As he crossed the landing, Julian suddenly heard James' door at the top of the flight click open gently, spilling a wide beam of light down the stairs and making his own shadow rear and loom behind him like the very monster he had been watching on TV moments ago. Crouching low, Julian slipped back into the shadows just as Syrena appeared in the doorway, her long satin nightgown fluttering gently, the outlines of her body revealed by the light shining from behind.

Noiselessly, the door closed and Syrena flowed down the stairs past Julian and into the darkness below. Julian had been holding his breath as she passed and he exhaled slowly now, in case he was heard. Waiting until he was sure that she had vanished back to her own room, Julian crept up the stairs to James' room and opened the door.

The sight that met his eyes was not pretty. James looked terrible. Lying in bed at the far side of the room, his breath seemed to be more tortured than it had ever been. His white face seemed taut, the air hissing between the grim, set lines of his bloodless lips. Julian crept to his brother's side, pulled up a chair and sat listening to his rusty wheezing until the first light of dawn crept through the window.

-⊕⊕⊕-

Waylon Devenish was a very unhappy fat man. Stepping out into the fresh morning air, he slammed the front door of his well-furbished, tastefully decorated home behind him and wobbled down the stairs with all the aggression of someone who has spent a night without sleep and is looking for someone to blame. His red-rimmed eyes were like gobstoppers that had been sucked and sucked until the colour had run.

Agnes wasn't playing ball. He realised now how distant she had become in recent weeks; how she had avoided any contact with him since her introduction to James Fortnam. Well, the conniving bitch had better come around to his way of thinking or she would be the worse for it. He'd dealt with broads like that before and he wasn't going to let this one get away with it. All sorts of revenge were brimming and bubbling inside Waylon's pudgy head as he manoeuvred himself into his Chevrolet and slammed the door hard against his side, packing him in like dough in a baking tin.

As the car pulled away, he deliberately aimed at a pigeon which had been strutting across the road. Disappearing past the windscreen in a flurry of feathers, the bird deposited a certain substance directly in his line of vision, an action which Waylon took as a direct personal insult. Venting his anger on the accelerator, Waylon suddenly found that whereas he could easily increase his speed he could not, in fact, slow down. His foot stamped uselessly on the brakes as the Chevrolet screamed through a red light at the end of the street and into the stream of city-bound traffic on the main highway.

Waylon wrenched and twisted at the wheel, stamping his foot down hard on the brake as his car flashed between a bright orange sales van and a transporter. Waylon realised that he had crossed the highway without a mishap and as a large tract of waste ground veered towards him, his frozen white face twitched with a flicker of hope. Perhaps the rough ground, the old bed frame and the rubbish tip would sufficiently impede the car's progress and tangle the wheels as to stop it altogether.

Unfortunately, Gustav Richter, after wrestling with the problem all night, had decided that he *would* meet his next-door-neighbour's wife on the rubbish tip out of sight of prying eyes, as she had suggested. Even more unfortunately, he had parked his petrol tanker right smack dab in the middle of it.

The Chevrolet slammed under the tanker and for a split-second was wedged there, squashed flat, the back wheels still roaring. And then the tanker erupted like a second Hiroshima, belching orange flame over a wide area, resulting in a multiple pile-up on the highway and coitus interruptus for Mr. Richter.

A mile away, on the main street, "Spook" smiled quietly to himself as passersby glanced up on hearing the echoing boom which filled the sky like the slamming of a distant vault door, turning up their collars in anticipation of a storm. Slipping a screwdriver into his back pocket, he flicked back his long, tattered hair and jauntily made his way home, whistling his latest composition.

Clouds of oily smoke billowed and curled over the waste ground carrying the unmistakeable odour of roast pork. Draped over the back of a ragged and abandoned armchair, a large, unmarked and still fully buttoned purple waistcoat fluttered in the wind.

-⊕⊕⊕-

"I'm afraid, my dear," said Doctor Whickett, "That James' condition will only deteriorate over the next few months." The doctor placed a reassuring hand on Syrena's quivering shoulders. Her face was buried in a silk handkerchief to hide the floods of crocodile tears which had so suddenly appeared. James had taken a turn for the worse during the night and the doctor had been called in once more to ease his pain.

"I really think that James should be admitted for a little while. Or at least have a..."

"No, doctor," sobbed Syrena, "This is the way that James wants it to be. He wants to stay close to Phillipa and Julian after everything that's happened."

"Yes, yes... of course. I do sympathise with you. For a while you know, it seemed as if he was improving remarkably well..." Doctor Whickett was an extremely professional man and, as such, had dealt with many similar tragic circumstances; displaying the calm and sympathetic manner expected of someone in his line of work. But the multiple tragedies surrounding the Fortnam family, whom he had known for many years, had saddened him personally more than he would have cared to admit. His words of comfort to Syrena as she escorted him downstairs into the hall, seemed to have a hollow ring.

After the doctor had gone, Syrena made her way smiling to James' room again and paused briefly at the door to regain her look of bitter sorrow, before gliding back to his bedside. Propped up on two enormous pillows like giant marshmallows, James' bloodless face remained totally impassive but his eyes seemed to glint with renewed joy at her appearance.

"How are you feeling now, James?"

"Terrible!" James gave a hollow laugh. Syrena sat gently on the edge of the bed and took one of his hands into her own, pressing the palm gently against her cheek as if to convey some of her own vibrant warmth and vitality into James' rapidly failing body. "You've made me very happy, Syrena. I only wish that..." A coughing spasm racked his frail body. "I only wish that we could have met a little sooner. If it hadn't been for Mr. Devenish's charity concert, you wouldn't even be here now." James paused. "There's something I'd like you to do for me," he continued at last.

In your state? thought Syrena.

"Tomorrow is Phillipa's birthday as you know. All her friends are coming over for her party. You know how much she's been looking forward to it. She was hoping that..."

"Mrs. Doughtery is gone—and you want me to help out. Is that it?" Syrena squeezed his hand. "Of course, darling. I've already put a lot of work into making sure that she enjoys herself. The children should start arriving at 3 o'clock. Everything's ready and she's already *decided* that she's going to have a good time.

"There's something else, Syrena."

"What is it?"

"Will you marry me?"

AT LAST! screamed Syrena inwardly, howling with glee. *I've done it! I've finally done it!* "Yes darling," said Syrena quietly, passionately, kissing his brow.

Slipping from the bedroom when James had finally gone to sleep, Syrena found great difficulty in keeping the broad grin from her face as she skipped downstairs into the lounge and directly to the drinks in the cabinet. It had been long, hard work but at last she had achieved what she had set out to do. Performing a small dance in front of the cabinet, she poured herself a large brandy and flopped into one of the enormous armchairs.

Julian had been watching.

He entered the room loudly, deliberately bringing his feel down heavily on the plush carpet so that Syrena would hear his entrance. Syrena gulped the brandy down quickly and hid the glass by the side of her chair as he came around to face her?

"How is James?" asked Julian.

For the first time, Syrena realised that the little creep was *afraid* of her.

"He's resting now, dear," she replied.

"What did the doctor say?"

"He's going to be just fine."

"Oh," said Julian, turning to leave. And then, "Would you like some coffee?"

"Why yes, Julian. Thank you. That would be very nice."

Julian rose from the room, leaving Syrena to ponder this change of character. Perhaps her plan was working better than she imagined. As James' health deteriorated perhaps Julian was realising that, apart from his little snot of a sister, Syrena was the only person in the world to whom he could turn. A feeling of intense satisfaction swept over her, made even more complete by the warmth of the brandy inside. Phillipa suddenly appeared from one of the side rooms, carrying a doll which was almost as large as she was. From where Syrena sat, it looked as if the doll was carrying her instead of the other way around. Phillipa blundered across to her chair.

"What have you been doing, Phillipa?" asked Syrena sweetly. *You little shit.*

"Tying knots," chortled Phillipa. "Look!" she proffered the doll's head to Syrena, revealing that its pigtails had been knotted tightly into a rather professional hairstyle.

"It's very nice. What's the doll's name?"

"I've called it after you. Syrena!" said Phillipa, flinging the doll to one side. As it pirouetted across the carpet, she leapt up onto Syrena's lap, knocking all the breath from her body. "Do you like it here?" asked Phillipa at last, putting one grubby hand around the back of Syrena's neck. "I wish you could stay here with us. I'm the only girl. And I think that James likes you a lot..."

"Well I like you *all*. Perhaps one of these days I might come and stay all the time, instead of just visiting you in the evenings."

"That would be nice," said Phillipa, "I wish you could stay forever."

Julian re-entered the room, carrying a large ornate tray with a cup of steaming coffee on it. "One sugar, Syrena?"

"Well, thank you," said Syrena, smiling sweetly at her new conquest, taking the coffee from the tray. Phillipa jumped down from Syrena's knee and went to retrieve her doll as Syrena lifted the cup to her lips, not noticing that Julian had taken a few hurried steps back as she did so. Syrena drank. And then gagged, jumping to her feet, spilling the contents of the cup onto the carpet.

"You little bastard! You've put garlic in the coffee!"

Julian fled from the room and thundered up the staircase as fast as he could move.

"Julian, you're a beast!" screamed Phillipa.

Regaining her composure, Syrena straightened her dress and walked briskly and calmly out of the room after him. "Phillipa, angel. Would you get a cloth and clean up the mess, please?"

"Alright," replied Phillipa, sharing Syrena's outrage. "I *hate* Julian sometimes."

Syrena began to ascend the staircase as Phillipa trotted off towards the kitchen. Pausing for a second, Phillipa turned and called after Syrena. "What's a bastard?"

"It's someone who puts garlic in your coffee," said Syrena calmly as she continued her ascent.

Julian was not in his room. In fact, Julian was nowhere to be found. Syrena stood in the centre of the little den contemplating her revenge. And then, with an evil smile, her eyes came to rest on the television set. Walking briskly into the small kitchenette, she rummaged through a drawer until she had found a small pair of pliers. Returning to the television, she snipped the plug from the wire, returned the pliers to the drawer and left the room, weighing the plug in her hand as if contemplating where to throw it. Joining Phillipa in the kitchen downstairs, Syrena dropped it in the wastebin.

That night, Syrena joined James in his bed and lay listening to the sound of his sibilant breathing, wishing that he would shut up for just a little while so that she could get some sleep. She wondered what "Spook" was doing. "Spook", in fact, was in a large plastic bag in the municipal mortuary. "The Pukerzoids" had delivered the goods yet again. During a performance of their most famous number, "Burning up with Love", the earth on his guitar had somehow become disconnected and he had jerked and lunged across the stage in a frenzy of noise and singeing flesh for a full three minutes before anyone realised that is was not a part of the act.

Upstairs, in Julian's darkened room, the television set sat silently like a blinded cyclops. But a dim, blue light issued from under the sheets in the middle of Julian's bed, and small tinny voices whispered in the air.

"You must understand. When the full moon rises, I turn into a wolf. I kill people. Please can't you do something to help me?"

"The old gypsy woman is probably your best bet," said Julian.

-⊕⊕⊕-

On the dawn of Phillipa's eighth birthday, Syrena arose early and set about arranging party decorations with all the joy of a bride-to-be. Phillipa seemed overjoyed with the raffia set which Syrena had given to her as a present. She had guessed right in assuming that anything to do with knots or weaving would go down well with her future sister-in-law. When Syrena caught her tying knots in the streamers which fluttered from the lounge walls and ceiling, Syrena had suggested that perhaps she should start laying out the kitchen table instead of helping with the decorations.

Syrena had just finished attaching the last paper chain to the hall when Julian appeared at the top of the staircase reading a comic book, completely oblivious to her presence. She stepped down from the chair and waited, hands on hips, as he descended slowly, his attention completely taken with the strip cartoons.

"So you've finally decided to make an appearance, have you?"

Julian seemed to miss his footing and crumpled down into a sitting position, the comic book fluttering from his hands and scattering its pages over the stairs. His eyes were wide in alarm and, at first, Syrena thought that the sudden fright of hearing her voice when he had been so wrapped up in his reading, was the reason for his reaction. But when the look on his face persisted, that same look of fear she had seen yesterday—but this time so much more intense—she realised that Julian really was dreadfully afraid of her.

"I hope that you've learned your lesson," she continued. "The reason that you didn't see any television last night was that I threw the plug away. What's more, you won't be seeing any more television for some time, until you learn that it's wicked to play practical jokes."

Julian began to slowly collect the scattered pages from the stairs, his wide eyes remaining fixed on Syrena.

"You may as well know, Julian, that very soon I'll be living here with you. So the sooner you come to accept that the better..."

Julian dashed to the bottom of the stairs and headed for the library, kicking the door open. Intrigued by his strange behaviour, Syrena tiptoed after him, and looked in, pushing the door quietly open. One complete wall of the library was shelved, and Julian had pulled out the small stepladders which were used for reaching books on the uppermost shelves, clambering to the top step. For a second, he paused there, searching for a particular volume. He glanced back over his shoulder, but Syrena managed to dodge out of sight before he could see her. When she looked back, he had found the book and was now hastily flicking through the pages as he descended. Climbing down, Julian slumped into an armchair and became engrossed in its pages.

The little creep.

Syrena returned to her work in the lounge, blowing up a huge red balloon. Directly above her, James was lying in his bed. As her eyes surveyed the ceiling on the spot where she presumed his bed might be, her fingers tightened unconsciously on the huge red balloon. Her sharp red nails punctured it. The balloon exploded and withered. She imagined that Waylon Devenish must have exploded and withered in much the same way.

Julian remained in the library all day reading the same book, and only when Syrena entered to tell him that lunch was ready did he reluctantly set the book to one side, slipping past her as if expecting a blow at any moment. As he joined Phillipa at the table which had been prepared in the lounge, Syrena started to close the library door behind her but caught sight of the book lying face-down on the armchair. Looking back to make sure that Julian was at the table, she crept into the room and picked it up.

"I might have known!" she sneered.

The book was *"Dracula"* by Bram Stoker, and Julian had pressed the pages back hard against the spine so that it fell open at a certain page. He had underlined a passage in pencil and Syrena started to read it. Something to do with Count Dracula having been seen in the daylight at a railway station. Giving it up with a snort of disgust, she snapped the volume shut, threw it back onto the chair and returned to the lounge.

-⊕⊕⊕-

The children arrived *en masse* for the party at 3 o'clock. As they trouped through the front door and were greeted one by one by Phillipa, Syrena wondered how many of their parents had instructed their offspring to be as nice as possible to those stinking rich Fortnams.

"Hello John. Hello Barbara. Hello Jackie… I thought I told you *not* to come, Eric. Hello Peter…"

Very soon, the house was filled with the sound of screeching laughter and small legs pounding up and down stairs on their way to and from the toilet.

"Please be quiet if you have to go upstairs, children," said Syrena. "Mr. Fortnam is not feeling very well." Really, she didn't care one way or the other, but Phillipa was listening. Syrena was not cut out for kid's parties, and very soon the whole thing began to wear her down. Phillipa had begun to act with all the irritability of a miniature prima donna when it became obvious that she was to be the centre of attention. "Where's Julian?" asked Syrena at length.

"I don't know where he is," replied Phillipa. "I should think that he's probably watching television. He's got another set, you know."

Syrena continued to round up the rampaging youngsters into the lounge, but was considerably hampered by a small creature who insisted on tugging at her dress.

"I want some jelly *now!*" the midget demanded, and Syrena quelled the urge to ram the whole plateful down the little brat's neck.

"What a good idea," she said in a somewhat brittle voice. "Let's all eat." Seated at the table, Syrena felt rather like Snow White at a party being held by the Seven Dwarves for their friends.

"I feel sick," said a ginger-haired boy after a while, the enormous green paper hat which he was wearing continually slipping down over his eyes.

So do I, thought Syrena. "Oh dear. Show him where to go, please, Phillipa."

Once the food had been consumed, Phillipa decided that the games must be resumed as soon as possible, much to Syrena's irritation. She had hoped that they would be so full of cream cakes and trifle that they would be able to do little else but fall asleep or go home. While Syrena's games organisation consisted basically of Pass-The-Parcel and Musical Chairs, it soon became apparent that this was not enough.

"I know!" shouted Phillipa. "Let's play Hide and Seek!"

"Who's going to be *it*?" squealed a girl with a knot in one pigtail who had been sitting next to Phillipa.

Phillipa's eyes scanned across the room passing over each one of her guests in turn, eventually coming to rest on Syrena sitting the corner, looking a little the worse for wear. "Syrena!"

"I'm sure that one of your friends would rather play instead," said Syrena wearily, rising to her feet and slipping off her shoes.

"But I want *you* to play!" said Phillipa huffily.

"Yes, come on, Syrena!" the other children cried as one.

"No, I don't think so."

"We'll *make* you play!" shouted Phillipa, rushing towards her, shrieking with childish laughter. Her friends took up the call and before she could resist, Syrena was suddenly overwhelmed by a mass of small bodies tugging at her arms.

Cut it out, you little bastards! "Children, children. Please!" cried Syrena. Caught off-balance, with one foot raised in the air, Syrena felt herself toppling over and was suddenly lying on the carpet.

"You've got to count to one hundred," said one of the children. "And then you can come look for us."

Syrena felt something being hastily wrapped around her wrists and cried out in pain as something bit into her ankles a moment later. "What are you doing? Let me up! This game has gone too far!" shouted Syrena, failing this time to remove the iciness from her voice. Suddenly, the surrounding crowd had leapt to their feet and were scurrying for the door.

"Remember, Syrena," called Phillipa. "You've got to count to one hundred. And just to make sure that you don't cheat, I've tied your hands and legs..."

Syrena tried to rise from the carpet, but was unable to do so. Using lengths of the thick string used in the Pass-The-Parcel game, Phillipa had tied one of Syrena's wrists to the leg of the table and the other to the arm of a heavy chair in a complex tangle of knots. Sitting up as far as she could, Syrena tugged at her bonds but could not break free. Looking down, she saw that her legs had been tied first together and then to a fender in the large ornate fireplace at the far side of the room.

"Phillipa! How can I play if I can't get free! Phillipa!"

But Syrena's cries failed to reach the children's ears. They had all taken it on themselves to hide outside in the spacious gardens of the Fortnam House.

"*Julian!*" Syrena's suppressed nastiness was seething to the surface. "I'll kill them! *Julian!*"

The lounge door swung open and Julian entered, staring at her uncomprehendingly as she struggled on the floor. "What are you doing down there?" he asked at last.

"Julian! Your silly sister's done this to me. Go and get something to cut me free." Syrena tugged again with her left wrist and winced at the pain. Julian just stood and stared at her. "Well, go on then!" Julian remained unmoved and seemed to be thinking something over. "Cut me free you little swine!"

Turning on his heels, Julian dashed from sight. Syrena heard his footsteps clattering down to the kitchen stairs and the slamming of the kitchen door as he rushed out into the back gardens.

"Where are you going?" shouted Syrena. She lay quietly listening for the sounds of his return until it became apparent that Julian was not coming back.

"James! Phillipa! Cut this string at once!"

Finally, Syrena decided that her shouting was obviously going to remain unheard or ignored and concentrated instead on how to get out of her present predicament. When she did get free, the first thing she intended to do was to set a date for the marriage, get rid of James, and parcel the other two off to an orphanage or something. Syrena tried to rub her ankles together but succeeded only in laddering her tights. Looking around the room, her eyes came to rest on the table, to which her right wrist had been tied. If she could just reach the tablecloth, she could pull it off and perhaps get her hands on a knife...

Straining hard over to her right, Syrena's fingers groped for the tasselled tablecloth like a drowning man grasping at the proverbial straw. The material fluttered almost mockingly at her very fingertips, but she could not reach it. Letting out a great sob of anger and frustration, Syrena slumped back into a prone position and contemplated her next move.

As she lay, the rasping sound of a grindstone seemed to drift down to her hears from the garden shed out back. The sound drifted down the corridor, buzzing and droning intermittently like a distant aeroplane. Syrena realised that Julian must be doing something out there.

"Julian! This is no time to be playing at handicrafts! Come back here!"

After a while, the sound of the shed door slamming shut made Syrena cease her struggle, and when she heard Julian's footsteps returning along the corridor towards the lounge, Syrena delivered her ultimatum

"Julian. James won't be here forever, you know. And then who will you have to look after you? If you don't get a knife or something this instant, I'll put you in a home."

Julian reappeared around the door and walked slowly into the lounge, both hands behind his back. Easing the door shut with his heel, never taking his eyes from Syrena for one moment and keeping his back away from her, Julian edged around her prone body and out of sight. Syrena strained her head backwards and upside down, saw Julian's feet retreating to the sideboard. There was a *clumping* sound as he placed something heavy on the sideboard shelf.

"This is your last chance, Julian," said Syrena in a measured tone. Julian's feet were returning and Syrena sat up as far as she could as he approached her from behind. Suddenly a length of cloth had been looped around her head and between her teeth, gagging her completely. She struggled and twisted her head as Julian knotted the gag behind her head.

"You're not getting a chance to bite *me!*" said Julian ruthlessly.

Syrena writhed and squirmed furiously, shaking the table so that the bone china tea service rattled in protest.

Julian returned to the sideboard and collected whatever it was that he had placed there before stepping cautiously around to face Syrena. Her eyes blazed in undiluted hate. Julian began to approach her, again with his hands held behind his back; step by careful step, as if fearing that she would suddenly break her bonds and leap up on him.

"I won't let you do it," said Julian. "I'm not going to let you have James."

Syrena suddenly realised that he had been aware of her plan from the very beginning. The cunning little devil had figured her out.

"I don't really want to do this. But it's the only way..."

Julian brought his hands around in front of him and Syrena saw for the first time what it was that he had been hiding from her. In his left hand was a short, heavy sledgehammer covered in rust after years of neglect lying in the garden shed. In the other, Julian held a length of wood about a foot long, one end of which had been sharpened on the grindstone into a wicked looking point.

Syrena was totally baffled. What on Earth was he playing at? She struggled to sit up once more, but Julian had rushed in upon her and placed a knee on her left shoulder, pinioning her body to the floor. Frantically, she struggled to dislodge him, still uncomprehending. Only when Julian had placed the point of the stake directly over her heart, dimpling the silicone, did Syrena fully understand what was about to happen. But at the back of her mind, something told her that it wasn't really happening. She would wake up in James' bed, and then she would have to set about arranging Phillipa's birthday party.

As Julian swung the sledgehammer up as high as could be permitted by its leaden weight, a long bubbling moan issued from her gagged lips. And when the hammer came down for the first blow, Syrena was suddenly caught in a crimson wave of screaming hell which splashed in her face until she was drowning in it. Somewhere, a million miles away perhaps, she could hear a heavy, regular thumping sound like a giant heartbeat or piledriver. The sound seemed to be propelling her very being into another world. A world that had ways of dealing with people like Syrena.

-⊕⊕⊕-

"Where's Syrena?" asked Phillipa. "We were going to play Hide and Seek. But when she didn't come we went to play down by the lily pond."

Julian was washing his hands in the sink. "She's gone," he said quietly. "And she won't be coming back."

"Oh," said Phillipa. "Isn't she? Well, I suppose I'd better get everybody ready to be collected by their parents, then." Phillipa jumped up the kitchen steps and rejoined her friends in the garden out front.

Julian reflected on how Syrena had not shrivelled away into dust as she was supposed to do when he had stopped hammering at the stake. After the first blow, it had been a lot easier than he'd expected. The most difficult part was when he had to saw off her head. The hacksaw kept snagging as it wobbled from side to side. In the end he couldn't bring himself to look. He had forced the cloves of garlic into her mouth and clicked the jaw shut when he had finished. Cutting the strings which held her body, he had wrapped the blood-soaked carpet around the remains and dragged them hurriedly out back before anyone could see him. After all, if Phillipa had found out what had happened, she wouldn't really understand.

Pushing the carpet and its contents into the hole in the garden which he had hastily unearthed, Julian had shovelled the soil back as quickly as he could and covered it with a fresh layer of turf, so that the green of the spacious garden was as unbroken as it had been previously.

Unhallowed ground.

Drying his hands on the patterned towel on the bench, Julian hurried upstairs to look in on James to see how he was feeling. Now that he had finished what had to be done, he knew that James would recover. If he was quick enough, he might just catch "Return of the Lizard Man" on Channel 4…

THE NIGHTMARE BEGAN ON A SULTRY AUGUST AFTERNOON.

McLaren had been standing outside his ramshackle "office", leaning against the rusting hulk of a Ford Cortina, his belly full of beer after a boozing session at the pub around the corner. For half an hour he had stood there, smoking one of the cheap cigars his brother-in-law brought him back from Spain regularly. The cheap aroma seemed to radiate from him continuously; in his clothes, his hair, his breath.

From his vantage point, he had a clear view of the entire junk yard from which he made his living. He watched as Tony Bastable manoeuvred the jib of the crane, bringing the huge mechanical claw down heavily onto a battered Austin Allegro, crushing the roof like tissue paper. It gave McLaren a curious sense of satisfaction to see the car crushed like that. Only the week before, some fat cat had been sitting behind the wheel of that car, probably on his way to a big-shot business meeting. Looking forward to champagne and caviar; not realising that the articulated truck just ahead of him was about to jack-knife on a patch of oil on the motorway and that his nice new Allegro was going to slam, bang right into the back of it, leaving lots of little pieces of fat cat all over the road.

The Allegro was hoisted into the air and swung across the yard to The Crusher. In a few minutes, all that would remain would be a solid cube of metal.

McLaren took the cigar from between his teeth and crumpled it in his hand in much the same way that the mechanical claw had just crushed the Allegro.

"You are, no doubt, the proprietor of this establishment?"

The voice which sounded from behind McLaren made him jump forward a couple of feet, shoulders hunched up into his bull neck as if expecting attack. But it was not a loud voice. Silky soft and with a thick accent.

"What the hell do you want to creep up on me like that for?" boomed McLaren, taking in the tall, angular figure which appeared to have materialised from nowhere. The stranger was tall, impeccably dressed and wore a homberg hat.

"My apologies. I assume that you were engrossed in your thoughts," said The Stranger. His pale face had an expression of vulpine amusement. When he smiled, McLarne could see two rows of perfectly even teeth. Striking eyes sparkled with amusement beneath the dark, heavy brows.

"Never mind. What do you want?" McLaren thought: *Only Jews wear hombergs. But he doesn't look Jewish. That accent sounds... I dunno... Hungarian or something.* The Stranger had his hands clasped at chest level, as if he were about to pray. Big white pulpy fingers writhed like a handful of worms.

"I am looking for certain... bits and pieces."

"Well, bits and pieces are what you see scattered all over the yard, mister. What are you looking for in particular?"

"May I browse for a while?"

"This isn't a bloody library, mister. Why don't you just tell me what you want?"

"Ah, a businessman," said The Stranger, in a way that McLaren didn't like one bit. Like he was being humoured or something. "You have it in mind to make an immediate transaction. Very well. I require a transmission from a 1963 Ford Cortina."

McLaren opened his fingers and let the crumpled cigar fall to the ground before dusting off his hands. "Pretty specific. But we don't have one in working order."

The Stranger smiled as if to humour him. The afternoon sun seemed to be playing with his eyes and teeth, which seemed to capture and reflect the light. McLaren noted in particular the curious effect the sun played on his eyes. It was like the photograph that he'd taken at his nephew's wedding last Spring. The flash cube had turned everyone's iris a deep reflective red. And now The Stranger stood before him, like some forgotten and uninvited intruder at that wedding, grinning into the camera.

"The transmission need not be in working order."

From the other side of the yard, McLaren heard The Crusher begin to growl, followed by the squealing shriek of metal as the Allegro began its first crushing compression.

"Indeed, the condition of the transmission is not, within limits, of outstanding importance."

Again, the silky voice. The eyes with their stolen embers of sun. The scream of tortured metal.

"However, I do require that the equipment in question be taken from a 1963 Ford Cortina... *any* 1963 Ford Cortina... But the automobile must have ended its days as the result of a crash. And at least one passenger in the car must have been killed instantaneously."

"Get out of my junk yard, mister. Before I set my dog on you. I've got a business to run. I suggest that you save however much you were going to pay me and use it on a shrink. Now, get out." McLaren turned away from the Stranger to lean on the wreck behind him. "Atlas!" he shouted. On the other side of the yard was a shed which Jackie Shannon, the night watchman, laughingly called the "office". The shed was surrounded by a mesh fence and McLaren's Alsation dog prowled restlessly back and forth like a caged wild animal... which, in effect, it was. On hearing its name called, the dog leapt up against the mesh with a sharp ringing clatter. McLaren smiled and turned back to The Stranger to see if he had taken the point.

The Stranger now stood less than three feet away from him. Silently, he appeared to have glided right up close to McLaren while his back was turned. The Stranger's grin was wider but there was no trace of humour on his face. The eyes burned with amber fire now—a fire which came not from the sun, but from within. McLaren involuntarily pressed himself back against the wreck.

The Stranger's thumbs began to intertwine back and forth, back and forth in the white nest of his fingers. The squealing of metal against metal seemed to be reaching a new crescendo as The Stranger spoke again; his soft, satin voice still clear over the cacophony.

"At least one fatality, Mr. McLaren."

How does he know my name? thought McLaren with something like panic beginning to take hold. *Because your name's on the sign over the gate, that's why, you idiot!* But the answer failed to stem the fear which crept over him. His uneasiness in The Stranger's company had now turned to an unreasoning terror. Sweat trickled between his shoulderblades and moulded his shirt to his back. It ran down his face and dripped from the tip of his bulbous nose.

"Age or sex is immaterial. But I expect you to provide me with my requirements by tomorrow evening at the same time. Do I make myself clear?"

McLaren could not find his voice. It lay shrivelled and fearful in the pit of his stomach.

"Do I make myself clear?" said the vulpine face again as it began to move terribly and hypnotically closer.

"Yes!" McLaren's fear had found the mislaid response. The face halted inches from his own and McLaren could see now without any question that the flames of Hell burned hungrily in The Stranger's eyes. A white hand like the dried, shrivelled husk of a dead spider moved to McLaren's chest and he felt something being pushed into his top jerkin pocket.

"Tomorrow, Mr. McLaren."

McLaren wanted to look away from that horrible face but was afraid that if he did, those frightfully sharp teeth would dart quickly forward for his throat.

And then The Stranger was gone, turning sharply on his heels and striding purposefully towards the junkyard gates. The screeching sound had dwindled to a dull churning and crunching. Atlas gave vent to a long, low, pitiful howl. McLaren turned to see the dog slinking back from the mesh fence towards the shed. When he looked back to watch the departing figure, there was no one in sight. This was crazy! It was a good three minute walk to the gates.

But The Stranger was gone.

Tomorrow.

McLaren wiped the sweat from his face. His hand was trembling violently. Now able to move at last, he pushed himself away from the wreck and began to pick his way nervously amidst the junk towards the shed, casting anxious glances back over his shoulder.

Tony was still concentrating on The Crusher. "Hi, Frank!" he called as McLaren stumbled quickly to the mesh gate and let himself in without once looking his way. "Up yours then, you bastard!" he growled under his breath as a four foot metal cube of Austin Allegro trundled past on a conveyor belt.

McLaren moved quickly to the shed. Atlas rounded the corner, glanced sheepishly at his master and then, as if sensing the fear which still lingered around McLaren like an invisible cloud of his rancid cigar smoke, slunk away out of sight again. McLaren clattered across the shed to a small safe, twisted the dials to the right combination and pulled out a bottle of MacInlays and a glass. Sitting at a cluttered table in the centre of the room, McLaren poured a glassful and downed it in one shot, staring out through the grease-stained window which overlooked the spot where he had encountered the Stranger. He drank another and then remembered the something that The Stranger had stuffed into his top pocket. Fingers still trembling, he pulled out twenty ten-pound notes.

Two hundred quid! For a lousy transmission that doesn't have to work.

A 1963 Ford Cortina which has been involved in an accident, a voice seemed to echo somewhere. *And at least one person must have been killed instantaneously in the wreck.*

McLaren drank again and watched as Tony climbed into the crane, swung the jib over The Crusher, plucked the metal cube from the conveyor belt and swung it across the yard; the late afternoon sun glinting on the wrinkled metal.

-⊕⊕⊕-

McLaren spent four of the crisp new ten-pound notes on booze in the "Crane and Lever" pub that night. And as the alcohol seeped into his corpulent bulk, the unreasoning fear which had overcome him in the presence of The Stranger began gradually to dissolve. By closing time, he had rationalised the situation completely. The man was an eccentric, a queer, a pervert. He got his kicks from weird mementos. Hadn't he once read somewhere that the pieces from the car wreck which had killed James Dean in the '50's were treasured souvenirs? So what if this fella was sick? He had paid two hundred smackers, cash in advance, and the stuff he wanted didn't even have to be in working order. And, anyway, he knew for a fact that there was a battered Cortina just behind the compound with its transmission intact. It was useless of course; strictly junk value. Two kids on a bender had been cut out of the car on the Coast Road. One of them had been dead on arrival at the County Hospital. McLaren had always been interested in how his cars came to the junkyard. Now it looked as if his interest was going to pay off.

On the following day, when the effects of the alcohol had worn off, McLaren's reasoning did not seem as watertight as it had previously. He suffered from butterflies in the stomach from the moment he climbed out of bed, and they stayed with him as he supervised the extraction of the transmission from the Cortina. His nervousness also angered him so that when Tony asked him why the hell he was bothering with this piece of junk, McLaren had told him to get the hell on with it and earn his living.

As the afternoon crept on towards the appointed time, McLaren's apprehension and temper grew. By 4:00 p.m. the bottle of whisky in his safe was empty. Atlas had sensed his master's discomfort and was keeping well out of the way under the table in the "office". At 4:31 p.m. the dog looked up, sniffed the air, snarled and then slunk quickly out.

McLaren knew before looking out of the window that The Stranger would be standing in the same place as yesterday, hands held clasped in front of him, staring at the "office".

McLaren made his way over to the silent figure, trying to avoid looking at the face with the ivory glint of teeth and the twin orbs of copper-fire. There was a twelve foot gap between them when McLaren stopped. The transmission rested against the rusted hulk of machinery which McLaren now leant against, waiting for The Stranger to break the silence.

"This is the transmission I requested?"

"Yeah..."

"Capital, capital. I think that this will suit my purpose admirably."

Bloody creep.

"I trust that you can store this equipment for me in a secure place here in your yard?" The silky smooth voice purred like a contented cat gloating over a recently slaughtered mouse.

"Well..."

"For a suitable fee, of course." The stranger's thumbs were intertwining again as he surveyed the battered transmission.

"How long do you want me to keep it for you?" ventured McLaren, wiping the sweat from his brow and averting his gaze from The Stranger to scan the junkyard behind him unnecessarily.

"Not for long. I have numerous other requirements which I trust you will also be able to provide."

Look, mister. Why don't you take your junk and just clear off. Leave me alone. Take your eyes and your teeth to someone else.

"Like what?"

"A rear axle from a 1971 Morris Marina. Undamaged. And the driver must have suffered leg injuries in the crash. Fatal or otherwise, but the leg injuries are the important factor."

Jesus!

Thirty seconds and thirty pounds later, McLaren was walking back to the office, feeling his hands shaking again and not wanting to turn around in case he really did see The Stranger suddenly vanish in a puff of smoke. Tomorrow. Same time, same place. That evening, there were two new whisky bottles in the safe and another on the "office" table.

And so the days began to blur into each other.

McLaren fought his fear with the whisky bottle and decided, at the height of his drunkenness, on various means of dealing with The Stranger. How about the threat of physical violence? Setting the dog on him and telling him never to come back? (If, that is, Atlas could be persuaded to stop crawling on his belly.) Hiring a couple of heavies from the "Crane and Lever" to lean on him? Calling the police to complain about his nuisance?

But every evening at the allotted time, McLaren found himself standing trembling beside the twisted hulk with The Stranger as he showed him the latest acquisition. McLaren was becoming a very rich man. But for the first time in his life, the money meant nothing to him. He hoped fervently that each latest piece of junk would be the last. But it never was.

The rear seat from an Anglia: the back-seat passenger must have been killed, preferably decapitated.

The front wheels from a Volkswagen: condition irrelevant. But two bystanders must have been injured in the crash. At least one fatality required. Leg injuries essential.

An unruptured petrol tank from a Datsun Cherry: One child fatality required.

And for reasons McLaren could not explain, he found himself obeying The Stranger's strictly specific requirements to the letter even though they were becoming more and more bizarre, more and more difficult to find. Panic often threatened to overtake him on his quest, which now took him to other junkyard owners: men who had once called him friend but now only took his money, noted his whisky-tainted breath and, shaking their heads sadly, directed him to the required junk. Somehow McLaren succeeded in meeting The Stranger's requirements every time.

Until, that is, The Stranger made his request for the *unmarked windscreen from a hit-and-run car. No particular model of car necessary. But the victim must have suffered damage to the eyes.*

McLaren knew immediately that, this time, he would never be able to meet The Stranger's requirements. It was impossible. How the hell could he provide something like that?

On The Stranger's next visit, he said so.

And then wished that he hadn't as The Stranger turned his doll-like visage on him and the ember-filled eyes sparkled displeasure. When The Stranger smiled, it was with the face of something that had been dead for a long time. McLaren burbled that he would have the windscreen ready for him at the same time tomorrow night.

When The Stranger had gone, McLaren stood looking miserably at the pile of junk which lay cluttered in the middle of his junkyard. The recently acquired two-hundred-and-fifty pounds fluttered loosely in one dangling hand. The pile made no sense at all. He could make no sense of this ill-assorted heap of scrap metal. It was useless. Rubbish.

Junk. When McLaren moved towards the "office" at last, he failed to notice that The Stranger's ten-pound-notes had fallen from his loose grasp and now lay fluttering on the muddy ground.

-⊕⊕⊕-

The following day passed agonisingly slowly for McLaren in a whisky-sodden haze. He had tried everywhere for the windscreen, knowing that the request was impossible. How the hell would anyone know if any of his own cars or any of the wrecks in the other junkyards he visited were hit-and-run? Only the police were apt to have that kind of information. And in one of the junkyards he'd visited that day the owner had threatened to give him a good working-over after he had made his sick request.

At three o'clock that afternoon, McLaren sat in his "office" trying to drown the fear in his guts once more with alcohol. After a while, it seemed to be working. But McLaren knew that he must keep himself sufficiently "topped-up" to carry out the plan which he had finally prepared. He was faced with no other alternative. And if his fear of The Stranger was allowed to surface, he would never be able to do it.

First of all, he made a none too steady tour of the junkyard and found an intact windscreen from a Citroen. Then he called Tony over and instructed him to take it out carefully... *very carefully*... ignoring the look of disgust on his employee's face. What the hell? He was drunk and he knew it, and only by staying drunk was he going to solve this problem.

By the time that Tony had propped the windscreen up against the pile of junk which had been accumulated by The Stranger, the sun was beginning to sink in the late afternoon sky.

"Mind if I ask a question?" said Tony, lighting a cigarette as he cast a glance at the peculiar debris.

McLaren grunted. It could have meant "yes" or "no".

"What the hell's all this stuff for?"

"You get paid to do a job, Tony. And that's all. Just do it and don't stick your nose in." McLaren finished his statement with a rattling belch.

"You always were a pig, McLaren." Tony blew a stream of smoke in his direction. "And until now, I've just put up with it because I needed the work. Now I don't. So you can stuff your job as of now."

McLaren stepped forward.

"Try it and I'll lay you out," said Tony easily. McLaren stopped, swaying slightly. "But before I do go I think I should give you a piece of advice. See a shrink. You're acting pretty weird, McLaren. I think the whisky bottle has addled your brains."

Casting a last, derisory glance at The Stranger's junk, Tony walked past McLaren towards the gates.

Oh, yeah? thought McLaren. *Big man! If you'd been through what I've been through, you wouldn't be so loudmouthed. If you'd had to look into those bloody eyes, just what state would* your *nerves be in?* He wanted to say all of those things to Tony. But only one word would come out.

"Bastard!"

Tony ignored him. Funnily enough, McLaren's passing remark was entirely factual.

Back in the "office", McLaren replenished himself, cooing gratefully to the bottle, carressing its neck like some strange glass pet. Underneath the table, Atlas began to make low, grumbling sounds in his throat. It was time.

The stranger stood in the usual spot, his own angular shadow joining with the sharp, ragged shadows of the surrounding junk as the sun finally began to creep past the horizon. McLaren's hands were no longer trembling as he stood up purposefully, the chair clattering backwards to the floor. The dog whined and began to crawl across the floor on its stomach until it had reached the far corner.

Walking stiff-legged, eyes staring, McLaren moved to the bench, found what he was looking for and tucked it tightly into his belt behind him, feeling its hard coldness in the small of his back. The walk across the junkyard to The Stranger seemed to take place in a dream-like slow-motion. He seemed to be walking on a moving treadmill and never actually getting any closer.

The Stranger was smiling or grimacing... McLaren couldn't decide which... but he hoped above everything else that he could not read his mind and see his intention. The Stranger's mouth opened, lips writhing back from glistening teeth, as McLaren arrived.

"You have obtained the necessary?"

"Yes... it's over there behind you." *All this whisky and I'm still so Goddamned frightened. Can he hear it? Can he hear how frightened I am?*

"Good. Let me see it."

McLaren gestured for him to move forward and The Stranger turned to look at his pile of junk. The Windscreen was propped against the transmission. It dimly reflected The Stranger's angular shape as he leaned down to touch it. McLaren had moved up behind him as The Stranger crouched down and stroked the glass.

And then McLaren heard the sharp intake of breath that sounded more like the warning of a rattlesnake about to strike. The Stranger was turning from his crouched position, mouth twisting in a cruel grimace. One eye was swivelling back to look at him like some hideous chameleon.

"This is *not*..." began The Stranger as McLaren stepped swiftly forward, fumbling at the small of his back. In the next instant, the spanner had cracked open The Stranger's skull like a ripe melon. The mouth grinned, eyes rolled up to white and The Stranger jerked over backwards with the spanner still imbedded in his brain, arms and legs writhing in a dance of death. Then he was still.

McLaren stood frozen in position, one arm held out before him in the act of the fatal blow. Stunned, he stared at The Stranger. It had been so easy. So damned easy. One blow. And he was dead.

Lurching away, McLaren vomited a stream of pure alcohol onto the ground, his stomach heaving and straining until there was nothing left to come.

The Stranger lay twisted and angular like some hideous praying mantis, the whites of his eyes still reflecting the dying light as McLaren finally moved towards him again. He purposefully avoided those eyes as he leaned behind the twisted car wreck against which The Stranger's junk was propped, trembling fingers finding the oil-smeared tarpaulin he had placed there earlier. McLaren felt so terribly cold, so bloodless, as he threw the tarpaulin on the ground beside the corpse. Wiping one trembling hand across his mouth, he kicked the body over onto the tarpaulin, unable to bring himself to touch The Stranger with his hands. The body rustled easily over onto the sheet. The spanner squelched from its resting place.

Controlling his stomach, McLaren drew the canvas up around the body and rolled it over; once, twice, three times... until The Stranger's corpse was firmly wrapped in a cocoon of tarpaulin. McLaren threw an anxious glance back at the "office". Jackie Shannon, the nightwatchman, would be arriving at any moment. There wasn't much time. McLaren grabbed the tarpaulin around The Stranger's feet and began to drag his package across the junkyard. The sun had finally slipped past the horizon as McLaren reached the rusted hulk of the Ford Cortina; the jagged piled silhouettes of rusted cars and twisted metal painted with the blue-black of night. It was like some bizarre, elephant's graveyard.

Hinges screeched as he pulled open the driver's door and McLaren heard Atlas give vent to a long solitary howl from the "office". Now McLaren would have to use his hands and felt disgust as he roughly bundled the corpse across the driver's seat, still glancing fearfully behind him for any sign of Shannon. Finally, the bundle was stuffed into the car and McLaren slammed the door shut with unnecessary force, feeling the cold sweat on his face, the dull ache in his gut.

Within seconds, he was in the driving cab of the crane. As he had so rightly guessed, Tony had left the keys in the dash. The engine roared into life and the grab swung across the yard to hover like some mythical roc's claw above the wreck and its grisly occupant. The engine gasped and the claw suddenly descended under its own weight, crumpling the roof of the car. The claw tightened, punching in the windows, splintering and cracking the bodywork. In silhouette, it seemed as if some stalking Tyrannosaurus Rex had caught its prey and was in the process of taking the corpse to its lair.

The black, rectangular maw of The Crusher yawned wide to receive the car as the crane gently lowered the wreck. For five agonisingly long seconds, the prey refused to be parted from the hunter, before finally crashing down into the machine. Five minutes later, McLaren stood at The Crusher's control; still furtively looking over his shoulder, eyes darting, fingers twitching, beads of sweat marbling his face.

He set The Crusher in motion.

The squealing and rending of metal was almost too much for him. He turned his back on The Crusher, hands clasped to his ears to deafen the insane cacophony of tortured metal. McLaren tried to shut out the recurring mental image of what must be happening to the tarpaulin-wrapped body in the car. It would all be over soon. But now, as the car began to reach the first stage of its compression before the hydraulic ram could start on the inexorable forward movement which would finally reduce the car to a solid cube of metal, the squealing had taken on a new and decidedly more horrific tone.

It seemed to sound like someone screaming.

No, that can't be! thought McLaren, squeezing his hands tightly over his ears. *He was dead. I know he was dead. I crushed his skull...*

The squealing and crunching abruptly subsided to a lower, rumbling noise under the unstoppable grumbling of The Crusher. The conveyor belt began to move.

McLaren moved away from The Crusher controls and around to one side, straining nervously forward to catch sight of the car's remains.

A cube of compressed metal, four feet square, trundled out of The Crusher's maw.

McLaren walked around it. There was no blood. No tell-tale shoe poking out of the side. No hideous, clutching hands. He turned back to the crane and climbed into the cabin.

The claw descended. The cube was hoisted across the junkyard. McLaren swung the cube up high over the impenetrable tangle of steel and iron in the middle of his yard, until it dangled over the most inaccessible depths of his junk pile. The claw opened.

The cube plunged into the junk pile with a screeching crash and the pile seemed to shift uncomfortably, adjusting its bulk to take account of this unwelcome intruder. It groaned, murmured, protested. And then, with a final squeal of protest, the cube began to slip. Slowly at first, and then faster and faster the cube slid into the widening, yawning fissure of a junk earthquake.

Perfect! thought McLaren, licking dry lips. *Bloody perfect!*

The cube vanished from sight under an avalanche of metal, a twisted wreath of wiring and steel frame crashing down and effectively burying it from sight for good. The junk heap rumbled once and was still.

Perfect!

"Working late, Mr. McLaren?"

The voice just outside the cab door sent a bolt of electric blue lightning racing through McLaren's heart, bottlenecking in his throat with a convulsive heave. Shannon had climbed up to the cab and watched as McLaren had manoeuvred the cube into the junk heap.

"Just... it was..." McLaren heard himself say. "Bloody stuff was no good! Just in the way all the time." And then, hastily and defensively: "Wouldn't have had to do it myself if it hadn't been for Bastable. I had to sack him this afternoon!"

"Tony? Really?" Shannon began to climb down as McLaren switched off and began to follow him, legs like jelly. "Ah, well. I could see it coming. His heart was never in it."

Back at the office, McLaren could hear that Atlas was barking fit to burst again. But this time, it seemed that his dog's barking seemed healthier, less fearful. McLaren began to feel a great pressure lifting from him.

"Fancy a glass of whisky?" he asked Shannon.

Shannon's jaw dropped. That kind of offer from McLaren was unknown. "Don't mind if I do," he replied after he had regained his composure, adding mentally: *Sacking people must agree with you. I'd better watch my step.*

McLaren smiled heartily and clapped Shannon's back so heavily that the old man's dentures nearly popped out.

"Celebrating, Mr. McLaren?"

"Let's just say I've got a pressing problem off my mind."

-⊕⊕⊕-

The nightmare began again a week later.

McLaren had found himself unable to go anywhere near the pile of junk which he had accumulated for The Stranger. Every time he passed it, he promised himself that he would have it gathered up and slung out later. Later. Always later. And then, a week to the day that he had rid himself of that *thing*, he noticed that the junk was gone.

His first reaction was one of relief. He had given no order to any of his men to get rid of the stuff and normally he would have flown into a vindictive rage because of that fact. But not this time. He asked his workmen in as casual and appreciative a manner as possible, who had done it... George, Ray and Barney hill. Even Jackie Shannon. And something like unease began to creep over McLaren as each worker in turn denied having touched any of the stuff. He fought it down. *Somebody* must have moved the bloody stuff. But whatever that person's reason for keeping quiet bout it, McLaren decided to be thankful for this not-so-small mercy and ask no more questions. The junk was gone. That was the important thing.

On Thursday morning, McLaren let himself in through the main compound gate for another working day and as he approached the "office" could see immediately that something was wrong. Shannon was standing in the doorway hopping from foot to foot, obviously waiting anxiously for him. Atlas was pacing back and forwards behind the mesh.

"What's up, Jackie?"

"Prowlers, Mr. McLaren. Early this morning; about three o'clock."

"Catch anybody?" asked McLaren, pushing past him into the "office" and making straight for the freshly boiled kettle.

"Never saw a soul. Heard them, though. I reckon Atlas put the wind up them."

"Where?"

"Over on the other side of the compound. They couldn't have been professionals, Mr. McLaren. They made one hell of a racket. Crashing and banging, pulling the bloody junk about. I let Atlas go and then followed him. I reckon when they heard him barking, they took off. They must have been fast, though... I didn't see a soul. Not even with those lights blazing away."

"Probably kids," said McLaren. *Then why the hell do I feel scared all of a sudden? What the hell's the matter with me?*

"Did you check the fence?"

"No breaks. They must have come over the top. Must have been keen if they wanted to risk losing a bollock on that barbed wire. Shall I report it?"

"Naw," said McLaren, gulping hot, strong tea. "Not worth it. Just keep your eyes open tonight." *Tomorrow night. In the junkyard. In the dark. And I'll be home, drinking whisky. Far away from this place. Far away and safe.*

Why did the junkyard at night suddenly seem such an unpleasant prospect?

McLaren gulped his tea and started a long, unsuccessful day of trying to rid himself of a bloody awful creepy feeling that he thought had vanished with the passing of The Stranger.

-⊕⊕⊕-

It had been a long, arduous day. McLaren, still feeling clammy, had spent two hours in the "Crane and Lever" that evening until the whisky had numbed him to it. Returning home, he had finished off a six-pack from the fridge and fallen asleep in front of the television. His dreams were vague and troubled. The images were confused and disturbing. The junkyard at night. The Crane. The Crusher. A tall, angular shadow standing up against the compound fence, fingers hooked through the mesh, face obscured apart from two hideously shining red eyes looking straight at him with hungry intent. The squealing and shrieking of rending metal. The shrieking of steel turning to the shrieking of a human voice. Closer and closer. Closer... louder... *Close... closer... here... Now!*

McLaren woke with a scream clenched tightly in his teeth; his heart was hammering, and he half-expected to find himself standing alone in the junkyard listening to the sounds of shambling footsteps behind him. The familiarity of his living room made him slump backwards with a deep sigh. The television buzzed angrily at him, the speckled snowstorm on the screen the sole light in the room.

But why could he still hear the shrieking?

He panicked again. But no, it wasn't The Crusher, or the car, or The Stranger. It was the telephone.

Groaning again, McLaren struggled to his feet, accidentally kicking over an empty beer can with a reverberating clank. He wiped his face, yawned, and then answered the telephone.

It was Shannon.

"I'm sorry to bother you so late, Mr. McLaren. But I think you'd better come down here straightaway."

McLaren looked at his watch. It was one-thirty. "What the hell's wrong?"

"It's Atlas. He's been hurt pretty bad."

"How? No... wait! I'll be right down!"

-⊕⊕⊕-

As always, the junkyard was brilliantly floodlit, but the harsh black shadows that filled the ragged gaps and crevices of the junkpile brought the crawling taste of fear back to McLaren. The booze had worn off. He felt dry and hollow; and the hollowness was filling up rapidly with that creepy sick feeling again. The gates were open... Shannon had obviously seen to that... and McLaren's car roared though, kicking up dust. The car screeched to a halt and McLaren flung himself out past the nightwatchman and into the "office", unaware of Shannon's agitated burblings, and realising for the first time (*truly* for the first time) how much he loved that dog and didn't want to lose it. He knew that it was going to be bad.

But not as bad as this.

Atlas lay on a blanket beside the table, making low, hopeless gurling sounds in the back of his throat. He whimpered when it saw him. McLaren moved forward and saw the blood. The dog's body was covered in deep lacerations, its foreleg almost severed at the knee. Shannon had tied a makeshift tourniquet above the knee with masking tape.

"Oh God, Atlas..." was all that McLaren could say as he knelt beside his dying dog, knowing that he had lost too much blood to be saved. The dog licked his hand. McLaren choked back tears.

"What the hell happened here?"

"That's what I've been trying to tell you, Mr. McLaren. There's something weird going on. I don't think I want to work here no more..."

"What have you done to my dog?"

"We've been hearing noises all night, Mr. McLaren!" Shannon's voice struggled to retain control. "Somebody's out there in the junk, moving stuff around. And everytime we got near to where we thought the noise is coming from, it stopped and then started again somewhere else. Atlas was sniffing around at the foot of that big pile of junk in the middle of the yard... just like he'd found something in there. Then he started squealing. When I got to him I saw that he'd got his leg caught in some wiring. I couldn't get him loose, Mr. McLaren! He just kept getting more tangled in the junk. He bit me while I was trying to help him. Look!"

Shannon showed him the crescent-shaped mark on his forearm but McLaren was looking beyond him, through the open door and into the junkyard. "Show me, Jackie. Show me where it happened." McLaren's voice was quavering. Instinctively, he knew where it had happened. But he still had to see. "Show me."

"The dog...?"

"He's as good as dead. Show me."

McLaren followed Shannon outside."

"I'm sorry, Mr. McLaren. Really I am. But we just couldn't find whatever was making the noise. It stopped after Atlas was hurt..."

"Show me."

They walked through the starkly lit, deeply shadowed automobile graveyard; passing ruined metal carcasses heaped one upon the other. The Crane stood its silent dinosaur vigil, dagger-toothed head stooped and waiting. As McLaren had guessed, Shannon headed straight for the centre pile where The Stranger's remains lay buried in a four foot square, cubed coffin. McLaren became aware of a buzzing in his head and tried to shake it off, finally realising at last that the sound was coming from the arc lights overhead. The first of their multiple shadows reached the pile before them. Shannon pointed at the foot of the pile.

"There. That's where it happened."

A pool of Atlas' blood glistened darkly like machine oil.

What am I going to do? thought McLaren desperately.

"Maybe we should get the police..." began Shannon.

"No!" snapped McLaren. "No police!" *God knows what they might find if they start snooping around.*

And then the lights started to go out.

During their walk the buzzing sound had grown steadily louder before ending abruptly. At that moment, one of the arc lights beside the "office" had suddenly gone out. Both men turned to look as another light went out on the far side of the compound. They turned again. Another light went out. And then another. Section by section, the junkyard was being plunged into utter darkness.

"What the...?"

Only one light now remained in operation: the light which towered above the centre pile at which they were standing. McLaren and Shannon stool vulnerably in the droning spotlight.

"Power failure?" said Shannon in hopeless dismay.

The last light went out.

McLaren almost gave into his first instinctive reaction. To run screaming from the junkyard. Fighting to control himself, knowing that he was not going to wake up this time in the safety of his own armchair, McLaren fumbled through the dark to touch Shannon's arm. Shannon jerked in shock at the touch.

"Use the flashlight."

Shannon unfastened the torch from his belt and switched on the beam, sweeping over the twisted wreckage of the junkpile.

"We'll walk back to the 'office' slowly. No point in breaking our necks on a pile of junk."

Something shifted in the junkpile behind them.

Shannon swung around and the torch beam danced over the pile again.

"Keep walking!" said McLaren, pulling Shannon's arm.

"There's something in there," said Shannon tightly.

"I can see... sparks... or something."

"Come on!"

"No, wait. Look there." Shannon switched off the torch. The darkness swamped them again. McLaren could feel his heart racing. Despite himself, he turned to look.

Deep inside the junkpile, obscured by tangled machinery and wiring, McLaren could see a brief sputtering of light. Sparks danced and hissed somewhere in the very heart of the junkpile as if someone was at work in there with an oxy-acetylene torch.

"We've got to get out, Jackie!"

The junk shifted again. The sparks crackled and jumped.

"No... wait a minute, Mr. McLaren... I can see something... I can see..." Shannon had moved forward, pulling away from McLaren's grip.

"Jackie, I'm going for the police. Come on. It's kids or something." McLaren kept backing away as Shannon put one hand on the pile of junk and strained forward to peer inside. He raised the torch and pointed it through a ragged gap.

"Come on, Jackie!"

"No... wait a minute, Mr. McLaren... I can see something... I can see..." Shannon switched on the torch, pushing forward head-first into a gap in the junkpile.

At first, McLaren thought that he was back on that terrible day again and that he had just switched on The Crusher. The horrifying screech of metal had turned into the screaming of a human voice. The screaming had started again—loud, desperate, and horrifying.

A screeching and crunching noise that froze McLaren in his tracks. But of course, it was not The Crusher. It was Shannon.

And McLaren could only stand and watch in horror as something unseen began to drag Shannon into the junkpile by his head. The torch clattered down into the pile, providing an angled cross-lit framework of the tangled junk as Shannon thrashed, screamed and kicked. The junk shifted. Shannon slipped further inside, his shrieking now hoarse and mortally desperate. His legs kicked spasmodically, the junk shifted again, and Shannon disappeared quivering and silent into the pile. The hissing and sputtering sparks danced again.

At last, McLaren screamed. He turned and ran blindly into the dark, away from the junkpile. Too late, he became aware of something directly before him. Something slammed into his forehead, sparks danced in his brain, and he was aware now that he was lying on his back. He groaned, wiped his hand across his head and felt blood. He looked up. A length of girder was protruding from the open window of a Ford Estate car. McLaren had run straight into it. And he knew that the girder had not been there before.

Frantically, he clambered to his feet and began moaning in terror as the pile began to slither and crash behind him like a living thing. McLaren blundered away again, trying to orientate himself and find the direction which would lead him to the "office".

But as he ran, he felt like a stranger in someone else's junkyard. The terrain was unknown to him. The landscape of piled junk, the jagged peaks and valleys of wrecked cars and ruined machinery were completely alien.

It's as if something's been moving the junk around so that I would get lost! McLaren heard himself thinking, blind terror now taking hold. He continued to run, screaming and scrabbling through the junk like an animal as the centre pile crashed and heaved in the darkness. *Something's breaking out! That's what it is... he's breaking out!* Jagged steel edges lacerated his hands and shredded his sleeves as he plunged blindly ahead. Something screeched rustily in the darkness behind him.

Please God, let me get out! I'll be a good boy... I promise... Just let me out!

McLaren's foot tangled in a broken radio set and he crashed heavily to the ground again, knocking the breath out of his lungs. Sobbing painfully, he scrabbled into the shadows of a rusted car hulk, squeezing himself partially beneath it.

The noises from the pile ceased.

McLaren struggled to control his wheezing, now the only sound in the darkness. The centre pile was obscured by other mazed mounds of twisted junk. There was no sound; no movement of any kind. McLaren tried to assess his exact whereabouts in the junkyard, scanning the darkness and the black silhouettes of metal carcasses. None of the junk was familiar. He closed his eyes, hands clasped to heaving chest, and concentrated. He thought quickly back to his first approach towards the centre pile with Shannon, gauged how far his desperate flight had taken him, and then looked around again. If he headed *over there...*

And then McLaren heard the first sound off to his right. A hollow, shivering clank from somewhere in the centre of the darkness. It didn't come from the centre pile, of that much he was certain. Perhaps, he thought, with rising hope, it was Ray, or George, or...

Something moved across the open patch of ground on McLaren's right. Something that was long, twisted and indistinct. It seemed to hop, skip, and then turn end over end as it moved quickly across the ragged ground, rattling and clanking. McLaren refused to believe that it was a car exhaust, moving of its own volition and headed in the direction of the centre pile. Junk did not move by itself. Tyres did not suddenly squeeze themselves out of the junk and roll sedately away into the darkness. Headlights, axles and car seats did not emerge from the night, scuttling and bouncing on their unknown destination. Even when a rear-view mirror whistled past his face, slitting his ear and drawing blood, McLaren did not believe. Things like that only happened in nightmares. And if this was a nightmare, he would be waking up soon. A wild, living tangle of valves and wiring whispered past his arm, like some insane man-made tumbleweed.

The screeching, hammering and grinding from the centre pile began again. McLaren squeezed further under the car wreck, face smeared with blood and rust. This had to be a dream.

For two hours, McLaren lay in that position, listening to the crashing and rending of metal; the hiss and sputtering of something that made sparks. And for two hours, he firmly believed that he would awake at any second in his armchair at home. When he did, he would make straight for the fridge and break open another six-pack. After a while, the procession of ambulatory junk had stopped. Now, there was only the noise.

When the noise stopped, McLaren screwed his eyes shut, willing himself to wake up. *It's time to wake up now! This is it! The nightmare's finished. Come on...*

Something large and decidedly ferocious coughed once in the darkness and then began to roar throatily. The sound was filled with threat and rage. It was hungry. It wanted somebody. It wanted him.

It began to move in his direction.

McLaren scrabbled out from under the car, sobbing desperately. The roaring sound filled the night air, reverberating and echoing from the mounds of junk. He raced in the direction he had identified earlier.

I want to get out!

McLaren rounded a corner, tottering on one foot, trying to find the "office". It was useless. Everything looked so bloody different. Behind him, something large and monstrous ploughed through a mound of junk with explosive force.

He ran. And ran. And ran.

The junkyard was a maze. McLaren was lost. And behind him, getting ever closer as it followed his scent, came a bellowing, Minotaur. McLaren leapt over an old tractor engine with an agility borne out of mortal terror and slipped into another unfamiliar alley. The bellowing behind him changed tone to a gasping, hydraulic hiss. It was as if some great animal was angrily drawing in breath and scanning the junk for any sign of its quarry. McLaren pressed tightly and silently into the darkness, holding his breath. The gasping noise began to move away. McLaren listened until the noise had receded into the distance and when it had vanished, he exhaled desperately, heaving air into his lungs. When he had recovered sufficiently, he began to creep forward through the junk, scanning the twisted wreckage for movement; searching desperately for the "office". On his left, the dim outline of an arc light reared up against the night sky. Using it as a guide, he searched for the others. One, two, three... and *there* was the light with the broken girder.

That means the "office" is over there!

Quietly, fearfully, McLaren picked his way through the junk to the arc light; slipping between rusted car wrecks, squeezing through gaps and crevices. The night swamped everything. Fighting down claustrophobia,

McLaren pushed through yet another tangle of metal. As he pushed at a ruined lawn mower, the junk shifted with a grinding clatter. McLaren froze, expecting the bellowing, hissing unseen thing in the dark to round a corner and roar down upon him. But there was no noise.

McLaren eased through the junk, hope and relief flooding his soul as he saw the dim outline of his "office" and the compound fence. His car was parked beyond and waiting. Beyond it, the gates were wide open. In one minute flat, he would be roaring away from this nightmare forever.

He ran quickly forward, crouching low and darting anxious glances in the darkness as he made for his car. Something metallic snared his shin in the pitch blackness. He cursed under his breath at the pain. Finally, he reached the dim outline of his car, knowing that the keys were still in the dash. The doors were not locked. He would be gone in seconds.

Quicker than thought, he wrenched open the door and dived into the driver's seat. He slammed the door and reached for the keys. They were gone. He fumbled in the darkness for them. They had not fallen on the floor, as far as he could see. Muttering a short prayer, McLaren reached up for the light switch above the windscreen, which did not seem to be where it should be. His fingers found an unfamiliar switch. He pressed it and a blue light came on overhead.

Now he knew he was not in his car.

McLaren was sitting in a nightmare tangle of wiring and twisted metal; a bizarre creation of freshly welded junk. Rusted piping throbbed with hideous life. A twisted radiator grille, soldered to the exhaust which McLaren remembered procuring for The Stranger, hissed angry steam. With mounting terror, McLaren recognised the other items of The Stranger's junk, all hideously welded into some nightmarish, contorted and utterly alien design.

He was sitting inside some monstrous machine that only barely resembled a car. He knew now what had chased him in the junkyard. McLaren didn't want to look, but he did.

Shannon's severed head gazed up at McLaren, the eye sockets pierced by living wires. But it wasn't the head that made McLaren scream. It was the object on which Shannon's head rested and into which the wiring from his eye sockets had been soldered.

It was the hideous cube of metal which McLaren had buried in the junkpile. The cube which contained the mangled remains of The Stranger.

The eye socket wiring sputtered, Shannon's jaw twitched and McLaren saw the machine's headlights flare on beyond the rusted frame of the shattered windscreen. Now, it could see. McLaren scrabbled at the door but could not find a handle.

"Let me out! For God's sake let me…!"

A band of corrugated steel flashed from the darkness around his waist, pinning McLaren to the seat like some insane seatbelt. Frantically clawing at the unyielding metal, McLaren failed to see the dashboard open slowly up before him. Steam hissed angrily. The interior blue light flickered as the monstrous engine coughed into rumbling life.

"No no no no! No! No!…"

A rusted pipe, slick with oil, stabbed outwards from the dashboard. McLaren watched it plunge into his chest in a crimson implosion with a look of mild surprise on his face. The pipe tore into his heart, sucking greedily. Beneath McLaren's spasming legs, the tangled cube of metal began to vibrate. Now refueled, the Doomsday Machine roared out of the yard, scattering junk.

The noise of its coughing, roaring engine was soon swallowed by the beckoning night.

notes on the writing of the stories

He Who Laughs

This story was commissioned by Steve Jones for the relaunched Pan Book of Horror Stories - under the new title 'Dark Voices'. As a kid, I'd collected all of the original anthologies edited by Herbert Van Thal - had at least one paperback copy confiscated by a teacher when I was caught reading it in the back row of class instead of concentrating on the lesson. It was a special buzz for me then to be approached by Steve as new joint editor of the reborn anthology series to contribute a story. One of those lifetime-ambition things. It's difficult to put my finger on where the theme came from; other than I've always been interested in the philosophy of comedy, and of those who profess to be the life and soul of the party but have a very predatory undercurrent to their reasons for wanting to make people laugh. As a character in the story says, "Each laugh is like a little death". If I have one enduring memory of the numerous strands that went into the story, it's of a visit to a television studio (as an audience member) to watch the recording of a then popular series called *Jokers Wild*. Two teams of comedians would compete to tell the best joke on a given topic. One of the comics - who I'll be kind in refraining from naming - was ebullient and full of fun while the camera was rolling, but between takes he not only 'switched off' to his peers and the audience, but was also an arrogant, bad mannered and nasty piece of business. When the cameras rolled again, he was all smiling-face and cracking jokes - but with an undercurrent of resentment that came from the fact that the audience now knew what he was really like, and they just weren't prepared to respond to him. Consequently, his determination to get a laugh and his rising resentment at not being able to do so made for an escalating performance of paranoia that I'll never forget. Like I say, only one element, among many others that went into the creation of the story.

Black Cab

I've had a long association with cab drivers. Some of them friendly, some less so. And whether it's the Yellow Cabs of the States or the Black Cabs of England, their reputation for strongly held opinions and their need to let you have the benefit of their knowledge during a journey - wanted or unwanted - seems to be the same. Personally, I've always been entertained by the huge variety of personal experience they're likely to divulge during a journey. Hack cabs - that is, the ones that pick you up from the street, rather than private hire vehicles - tend to have a richer variety of experience to recount. Principally, I suppose, because they're most likely to pick up total strangers (unlike private hire, who get to know the faces of their regular customers). Over the years, I've been happy to listen to their woes and joys. As someone with a total genetic disinterest in sport and no knowledge at all of football (my loss, I know). I pride myself on an ability to discuss any game - past, present or game to come - with any cab driver for the duration of a fifteen minute ride and come out of it convincing him (or her) that I'm just as big a fan as the next guy - simply by bouncing off the cab driver's opinions. And I've conducted my own personal poll among them, too. For instance, did you know that male hackney cab drivers face more aggression and open violence on a day-by-day basis from women passengers than from male?(Well, that holds true for England - I can't speak for the American situation) That most 'runners' (that is, people who make a dash for it at the end of their journey without paying), are female?

I guess that *Black Cab* is an accumulation of those chats with cab drivers, the fact that most people wouldn't dream of picking up a total stranger in their car on the off-chance that he or she'd be a psycho on the prowl - but taxi drivers have to do it for a living. (Does *anyone* still hitchhike?) And also a real-life case many years ago, where a young woman hailed a taxi at Newcastle railway station - except that it wasn't a taxi - and that was the last time she was seen alive. All of the locations in this story are real, and the Ouseburn area down by Newcastle's quayside - where a certain nastiness takes place - is where I used to play as a kid, and was a principal real-life location for my second novel, *Spectre*.

Man Beast

This was a story I wrote many years ago, while I was trying to find my voice. It's unusual in the sense that it has a slightly mystical, fantastical 'otherworld' setting - which is an area I don't write in. I sincerely hope that you didn't see the punchline coming, but I won't be offended if you did. When the editors of *Peeping Tom* magazine asked me if I had anything they could use, the story came to mind. I reworked and rewrote it, hopefully taking away a lot of its naieve prose. Of all the stories in this collection, I don't think you'll find my real 'voice' in here. The characters aren't really flesh and blood, with everything aimed at the denouement. Looking back on it now, I detect a Rod Serling/O. Henry influence where the twist-in-the-tail becomes the *raison d'etre*. I subsequently found that the 'real' and the 'here and now' were much more exciting and interesting places for explorations into, and skirmishes with, the supernatural.

The Song My Sister Sang

The abandoned open-air swimming pool which is the centrepiece of this story really did exist. The central character's description of the place is completely factual. His memories of playing there, the sights and the sounds - they're all mine. The history of the pool is also true.

It remained derelict for many years, just as described in the story. The place always haunted me, and I knew that one day - when I had the right story - it would feature in my work in some form or other. When I was writing my novel *Somewhere South of Midnight* a friend of mine who works for the local authority responsible for the site, managed to get permission for me to get through the padlocked gate with a video camera. I spent a half-day exploring the pool, the sluices and the derelict changing rooms with their rusted curtain rails and disintegrating tile floors. It was perfect for what I had in mind - the setting for a confrontation between the novel's main character and a professional hit-man.

Then the fates moved against me. I'd just finished the sequence for *Midnight* when my friend telephoned me to tell me that the local Council had just held a meeting about the derelict building - and had decided to demolish it! (This had already happened to me before. The Imperial Cinema in Byker, which was a real-life location for my second novel *Spectre,* was demolished just weeks before the book was published. It seems that my writing about these haunted places dooms them to instant oblivion.) I knew then that I would have to rewrite the sequence, setting it in a different location - subsequently a fictitious deserted health spa up on Whitley Bay promenade. You might ask me why I felt the need to make the change? Well, I guess I could have left it as it was - but all of the other locations were real, and still in existence. So it seemed to me - rightly or wrongly (and there are friends who think I should have left it in) - that including the swimming-pool in the narrative when it would be demolished by the time the book came out, would have instantly 'dated' the novel. So - the sequence was rewritten, and my pad of notes about the place were shoved into a drawer next to about twenty minutes of camcorder footage taken as I crept around that deserted, eerie place.

But this strangely haunting location just wouldn't leave me alone. I knew that there was a story there somewhere, waiting to happen. Eventually, it did - when Steve Saville asked me for a contribution to his anthology *Red Brick Edens* and its theme of urban disintegration and decay. I knew then that the location had found not only its story but its home. Even as I wrote the story, the site was being razed and transformed into what the Council calls an 'open air sea-life feature' (that is, it had been demolished and the foundations transformed into boulders and rocks that would form natural pools for sea-life with the coming and going of the tide. Isn't that what was there *before* the swimming pool was built? Go figure).

It took many years for the story to 'get there', but something about its final incarnation just seemed right. And it gave me great pleasure when, like *The Crawl*, it was subsequently chosen to appear in *'The Year's Best Fantasy and Horror'*

YESTERDAY I FLEW WITH THE BIRDS

One of the big personal breakthroughs for me came courtesy of the Sunday Sun newspaper. A play that I'd co-written with a friend had been considered sufficiently competent by a Script Adviser at the BBC for them to take an interest in us, and there had been several trips to television centre in London, and a couple of would-be writers' seminars. We'd been deeply affected by a series of television plays in the sixties and seventies entitled *Play for Today* and *Armchair Theatre*, and by the work of television writers Galton and Simpson and, particularly, Dick Clement and Ian Le Frenais. Given that the latter two's work was often set right on our doorstep, I guess that we were modelling ourselves on them. Our courtship with the BBC was tortuos. Lots of meetings and discarded scripts. Finally, we'd written one that they really, *really* liked - *Home on the Range* (the story of a Glaswegian bus driver who lives and behaves like a cowboy from the Old West.) After a year of to-ing and fro-ing, the screenplay was subsequently turned down, not on artistic merit, but on grounds of cost. As it was put to us at the time, The Board were unprepared to risk a big slab of the drama budget (much of it was 'outside broadcast') on two unknown writers. The effect was devastating on the writing partenrship , which ended - although we remain very close friends. However, in a fit of depressive rage, I decided to write something for myself in a genre that was close to my heart. After all, we'd spent a year rewriting the screenplay to suit everybody else at the BBC. That's when I saw that the Sunday Sun were organising a short story competition. I wrote three stories, all in the 'fantasy' genre. And I guess that something important must have happened then. Perhaps for the first time I truly found my own individual 'writing voice'. Because the stories won first, second and third prizes. I could hardly believe it. (I try to ignore the little voice that whispers in my ear: *Don't fool yourself, Laws. Maybe they only got three entries in total.*) The prize was an electric typewriter, and the shot of confidence was enormous. On that typewriter, I wrote *Yesterday I Flew With The Birds* - something else that came out of my heart. I submitted it to a Joint BBC/Rediffusion Short Story Competion on Radio Newcastle - and it won the prize, subsequently being broadcast. Although you won't find the three newspaper stories in this collection - I just felt that despite their importance in my career they're a little too parochial and haven't really stood the test of time - I'm pleased to include *Yesterday*. Not least because my late father once told me that of everything I'd written there was something in this one that had really spoken to him and had really affected him. Certainly, if not for his love and inspiration - and for his own passion and enthusiasm for stories, which lit my own fuse - I probably wouldn't have picked up the story-writing pen in the first place. AsWordsworth says in *My Heart Leaps Up* - 'The Child is the father of the man'. The success of *Yesterday,* so soon on the heels of the newspaper stories, prompted me to write something major, again in the genre that I love. That labour of love was my first novel, *Ghost Train.*

The Fractured Man

Aren't there times when you wish you could just go back and do things differently? Don't you wish that you had been able to prepare a better excuse when the boss caught you out that morning? Don't you wish that you'd found a better way of handling the situation when the school bully cornered you in the schoolyard? Or some other way to have found a really cool line for that person you'd always wanted to ask out on a date - instead of totally screwing the situation up and walking away with a red face? I bet you've played similar scenes back to yourself; envisaged all the different ways you could have handled the situation and emerged with so much more dignity and self respect. So - what if a psychopath had nursed similar ineptitudes and grievances all his life? What if, twenty or thirty years later, the weight of those grievances finally made him snap and he returned to put things straight and right all those perceived wrongs? After all that time, wouldn't those vengeful atrocities be the perfect crimes? How could the police find motives for real and imagined slights that happened twenty or thirty years ago? Actually, The Fractured Man has a happy ending - for him.

The Crawl

"Where do you get your ideas from?"

I never thought that I'd ever get the opportunity to give a straight answer to this most often-asked question of a writer. It usually gets weary eyebrows raised whenever it's asked during Panel discussions, as if there's a magic bag you can buy somewhere, full of ideas that are just waiting to be developed into a short story, a novel or a screenplay. At the 'Welcome to My Nightmare' Festival in Swansea, I actually bought a kids 'Horror Bag' in the town centre's indoor market and when the question arose during a talk being given by Jonathan Carroll and myself, I produced it from my ocket. "Let's see what's in here ... a giant white shark terrorises beachside community. Nope. Girl possessed by evil spirit can spin her head 360 degrees. Nah. Rubic's Cube opens doorway to Hell and sado-masochistic fulfilment. No, can't do a thing with that either." But for the first time, I can give a pretty straightforward answer to where one story idea - *The Crawl* - came from. In the words of the story's narrator: " ... the whole thing began on the A1 just a half-mile from Boroughbridge."

It's the first time that an image has leapt into my mind, apparently from nowhere. Just like the couple in the story, my wife and I were driving home after an Easter stay with her parents. Unlike the fictional couple, we weren't having an argument at the time. Byt just as we passed the roadway sign: Boroughbridge- Half Mile, I had the most alarming and intense image that a scarecrow figure was going to step out from the hard-shoulder and lay a hand-scythe across the windscreen, shattering the glass. Now, don't get me wrong. I don't live in a state of perpetual anxiety, waiting for things like this to happen. And I hadn't been thinking of anything beforehand that might lend itself to such a violent and disturbing fantasy. But there it was - one moment, daydreaming (my wife was driving); the next - the motorway sign. And then, *bam!* It was such a powerful and disturbing image that I grabbed up my briefcase from the back seat, found my scribbling pad and jotted it down, together with the exact location.

"Are you alright?" asked Melanie, not understanding my sudden energetic acticity, and my apparent discomfort.

"Yeah," I said in a puzzled sort of way. "I think so."

I didn't get round to the story straightaway. But when I did, some months later, the power of the image hadn't gone away. And when I began to wroite, it was as if the story already existed and was just waiting to be discovered. I finished it in a high fever, suffering one of the worst bouts of influenza I've ever experienced. When it was done, I remember thinking: "Now where the hell did *that* come from?"

Deep Blue

One of the reasons that my first short story collection has been so long in appearing is simply down to the fact that there haven't been enough stories to justify it. Since my first novel appeared, I haven't really written short stories 'on spec'. Not because I've become precious about it, simply that my work schedule for the longer work is so intense, it doesn't leave a lot of time for the smaller work. For me, writing a good short story takes a great deal of time - I can't just knock 'em off. So they would usually only appear when I was specifically asked for a contribution by an editor. A few years ago, Kim Newman asked me for a contribution to a collection of short stories about rock music. He knows my passion for film music, so perhaps he thought he'd get something related to the field. Instead, I found myself creating something around the death of Buddy Holly. However, the work schedule for the then novel-in-progress became so intense that the story remained half-developed when the deadline for the anthology came and went. In the two years since that time, I found myself looking at the story occasionally - and wishing that I had time to finish it. Then, along came an old mate - Graeme Hurry - looking for something from me for his writers' group magazine *Kimota*. I had just delivered a new manuscript to my publisher, my next research trip wasn't due for a couple of weeks. The perfect chance to finish *Deep Blue*, which made its debut in Graeme's magazine, and subsequently in Andrew Haig's *Scaremongers*.

Guilty Party

For some reason, this is the most widely anthologised of my short stories, recently making an appearance in a French edition of werewolf stories. It was also my first big sale to a professional magazine, *Fear* - for which I subsequently went on to become a columnist. Again, there's an aspect of real life to the story. As a local government officer, working nine-to-five in a city centre office block, I'd occasionally be pressed into service as social secretary. Once a year, we'd hire a mini-bus to drive out of the city to a country pub in Stamfordham (in Northumberland) for some heavy-duty partying. The drunken conversation at the beginning of the story is true - the rest of the story was created at one of the office typewriters after everyone had gone home.

Gordy's A-Okay

In a way, this is a companion piece to *Yesterday I Flew With The Birds*. It's most definitely cut from the same emotional cloth, but its genesis still remains mysterious to me. There are times, in the middle of writing a novel, when I'm ploughing ahead and the whole enterprise seems to take on a life of its own. I know roughly where I'm heading, but suddenly everything comes together - the characters, the plot, the direction - all of it seems to shape itself, engendering its own vitality. With energy flooding the story, and with everything firing on all cylinders - suddenly, in a quite literal rush - it all comes together in a way that I'd not quite envisaged. I've heard other writers describe this feeling and, without getting too mystical and pretentious about it, it almost feels like a state of grace. This happened to me with *Gordy's A-Okay*. It was written in one sitting, and it quite literally poured out of me. I hadn't planned anything about it. It just came in a flood of emotion. Reading it out loud to a friend on the following day during a long car journey, I was surprised to find how emotionally I was Reacting in magazine format and then in Pete Crowther's anthology, *Heaven Sent*. But just where to it. Like *Yesterday,* the story brought me a very positive and touching fan response when it appeared the story came from, I've no idea. Other than from the heart.

The Secret

My novel *Ghost Train* contains - like many first novels - a great many of the inspirations and influences that shaped me as a writer. You'll find, perhaps, trace echoes of Richard Matheson, Nigel Kneale, Stephen King and even Hammer Films in that first book. Not, I hasten to add, that I was ripping any of them off. Like most first novelists, all of the books and movies I had devoured, all the life experiences, muses and 'what ifs' went through that special inner matrix. Hopefully, what came out of the other end of that sieve was an undiluted essence of Stephen Laws. One such early influence was H.P. Lovecraft. You'll find it in the creation of the mind-demon Azimuth from that novel, although I'm not and never have been a 'Mythos' writer. In truth, it was an early influence which was well and truly exorcised from my writing after my third novel - *The Wyrm* - was published. Which brings me to *The Secret*, one of my early stories and which contains a suggestion of Lovecraft in the story. In fact, I guess what I've done here is to create a hybrid of Lovecraft's real and cosmic terrors with the shadowy anxieties of M.R. James - particularly, in the latter case, his story *Casting the Runes* and its wonderful screen incarnation *Night of the Demon*. On a more personal note, I was once crossing an abandoned building site at night with my brother, Ray. I guess I was about ten years old, Ray would be seven. A piece of black tarpaulin, or plastic sheeting, had been caught in telephone wires over that site, which was lit by only one crooked streetlamp. The sheet was hanging silent and invisible as we crossed that site. Just as we reached it, a sudden gust of wind caused that sheet to flap and rear in mid-air just like some gigantic bat. Ray and I fled in terror. This, more than anything else, is where *The Secret* Came from.

Pot Luck

Of the abandoned manuscripts and dozens of short stories I produced way back in the early days, only one or two are in any way readable. *Pot Luck* was written while I was trying to find my voice and at a time when Roald Dahl's *Tales of the Unexpected* was very popular. That possible influence aside, I have no idea where this story came from. Pen was applied to paper, ink flowed - and this was the result.

Bleeding Dry

Pete Crowther is one of the really good guys in the genre. An anthologist and short story writer of great success, his labour-of-love novel *Escardy Gap* (co-written with James Lovegrove) is fnally getting the success that it so richly deserves. *Bleeding Dry* was written on request for his collection *Narrow Houses*, using 'superstitions' as its theme. The story gave me the chance to indulge in my passion for old horror movies and also deal with the odd reference in Stoker's *Dracula* to the fact that the Count is seen out and about on the streets during daytime, something which I'd been trying to rationalise ever since my first magical reading of the novel as a kid. There's also a touch of gruesomeness and black humour left over from my readings of the Gaines horror magazines and the Herbert Van Thal horror anthologies.

Junk

"I've read Stephen Laws' *Junk*," said Brian Lumley when he was introducing me as Guest of Honour at the British Fantasy Society Convention. "And it's great stuff." By the twinkle in Brian's eye, and the laughter of the audience, I've a feeling that I might have been set up. Brian was a contributor - along with many top authors - to the Scare Care iniative. This idea for an anthology, all proceeds of which would be contributed to various child protection charities in England and America, came courtesy of Graham Masterton who - like Brian - needs no introduction to fans of the horror genre. Looking back on the story, I can see where some of the seeds for my novel *The Frighteners* had been planted. Man into machine and vice versa.

stephen laws curriculum vitae

Stephen Laws is a full-time novelist, born in Newcastle upon Tyne in 1952. Married, with three children, he still lives and works in his birthplace. Educated at Manor Park Technical School, he left to take up a career in local government. During this time, his short stories appeared on radio and appeared in various anthologies, winning him a number of awards. Concentrating on a genre which is close to his heart - supernatural horror thrillers - his first novel , GHOST TRAIN was published in 1985 and gained excellent reviews, together with a degree of notoriety when subsequently published in paperback: posters of the novel, bearing the logo 'A journey into innermost terror' were removed by British Rail from each of their mainline stations due to fears that 'passengers might confuse this with our own advertising and become alarmed ...' A £30,000 publicity campaign went down the tubes as a result.

Laws' second novel - SPECTRE - followed in 1986 and is set in his birthplace, Byker.

(A horror from the past stalks a group of childhood friends) The novel consolidated his position as a forerunner in the field of supernatural horror. THE WYRM followed in 1987 (with its locale based on Hexham and Elsdon) and THE FRIGHTENERS in 1989 (an Underworld novel in both senses of the term; in which a gangland war is fought using supernatural 'hit-men'),

In 1992, Laws' police-procedural/horror-thriller, DARKFALL, was published to great critical acclaim - dealing with an electrical storm descending on an office block, resulting in the disappearance of everyone inside it. (Chariot Film Productions have optioned the movie rights after a bidding-war with a Los Angeles film company and Laws has recently delivered the screenplay. Pre-production begins shortly.)

This was followed in 1993, by GIDEON - a 'vampire' novel with a difference which won the Best Novel Award that year from The Dracula Society.

MACABRE was published in 1994 and concerns the activities of a Cult operating on the streets of a Big City in England. Ostensibly handing out free meals and offering places to sleep for vagrants, itinerants and runaways, the Latter Day Church of the Sabbarite is actually kidnapping people from the streets for their own purposes. Laws almost drowned during research for this novel, when a scuba-dive in a Stockport Canal went horribly wrong.

In 1995, Laws' novel DAEMONIC was described as 'the novel that Stephen Laws was born to write.' With a dedication to film guru Roger Corman, it revisits the B-Movie frighteners of yesteryear and has been described as a 'high-octane thriller of the first order'.

SOMEWHERE SOUTH OF MIDNIGHT was published in 1996, Once again set in his native North-East, it deals with a motorway pile-up in Northumberland shortly after midnight during a heat-wave, when the traffic collides with an unidentified 'white light'. The survivors emerged 'changed', with apparently supernatural powers of healing or the ability to kill with a touch. Their struggle in coming to terms with what has happened to them also raises questions about what they collided with on that fateful night, leading to an edge-of-the-seat climax.

Lat year saw the publication of Laws' magnum opus: CHASM. A supernatural-horror-disaster-thriller in the tradition of Stephen King's THE STAND. An epic in the true sense of the word, this 546 page blockbuster is something that, in Laws' own words, is: "Something I've been building towards ever since I began writing. I always knew that somewhere down the line, I was going to end up writing this book - a mammoth undertaking. It took two years, and carved a chunk out of my soul. Everything I'd done beforehand was a signpost to this book, and I invested an enormous amount of emotional energy into the narrative. I'm proud of it in the sense that the real 'me' emanates from its pages - surely what any writer of any worth must aspire to. I opened veins in my arm, dipped in the pen and wrote the story in blood. Love it or hate it - but don't be indifferent to it. At two inches thick in hardback, it would make one hell of an impression if I hit you over the head with it."

To date, Stephen Laws' novels have been published in America, Canada, Germany, France, Spain, Japan, Norway, Denmark, the Netherlands, and Italy. His short stories have appeared on local radio and in various newspapers, winning awards on BBC Radio and in the 'Sunday Sun'. Other short stories have appeared in NARROW HOUSES, DARK VOICES 3: THE PAN BOOK OF HORROR STORIES, FEAR, SCARE CARE, THE ANTHOLOGY OF HORROR STORIES, ANGELS, DARK HORIZONS, THE MAMMOTH BOOK OF TERROR, PEEPING TOM , DARK ASYLUM, BEYOND, KIMOTA, DARK ASYLUM, SCAREMONGERS, DARK OF THE NIGHT and the 'Byker Phoenix'. A collection of his stories was published in America, jointly with Mark Morris, entitled VOYAGES INTO DARKNESS. NORTHERN CHILLS also featured Laws' work, along with Horror Godfather Ramsay Campbell and Stephen Gallagher. His first solo collection of short stories - THE MIDNIGHT MAN - is to be published by Darkside Press later this year. Laws was also an irregular columnist for the late-lamented 'Fear' magazine, and his critical appraisals of films and fiction can be found in HORROR:BEST 100 BOOKS, JAMES HERBERT:BY HORROR HAUNTED, THE BFI COMPANION TO HORROR and Million magazine.

Laws also lectures on horror to various institutions and is a regular guest interviewer at the Manchester Festival of Fantastic Films. He was Assistant Director on the BBC Documentary on Hammer Films 'Flesh and Blood', shown on BBC in August 1994.

He became a full time writer in 1992 and cites his primary influences as Richard Matheson, Nigel Kneale and (of course) Stephen King.

Notwithstanding his local government career, Laws has been a number of other things in his time: a parachutist with a fear of heights, an accounts clerk who can't add up, a skindiver with claustrophobia and asthma, an actor with stage fright, a pianist with a slightly dodgey left hand whose compositions have been given the full syymphonic treatment on pre-Civil War Yugoslav television and a pseudononymous cartoonist in a national magazine whose identity, if known, could lead to charges of libel.

The Midnight Man

has been published in an edition of 860 copies of
which 850 have been offered
for sale as follows:

50 Deluxe Numbered 1-50

300 Limited Numbered 1-300

500 Trade Unnumbered

This is copy: